HERMAN MELVILLE was born in New York City in 1819, a descendant of English and Dutch colonial families. His father died bankrupt in 1832, leaving his family in penury. Melville left school at 15 and sailed on a trading ship to Liverpool in 1839. In 1840 he joined the whaling ship *Acushnet*, bound for the South Seas, abandoning it with a companion in the Marquesas Islands. After a period in Honolulu, he returned to the USA in 1843-4 aboard the frigate *United States*. With no visible prospects, Melville turned to literature, dramatizing his South Seas adventures in the novels *Typee* (1846) and *Omoo* (1847). In *Mardi* (1849) he developed from a genial traveloguer into a philosophical symbolist. *Redburn* (1849) and *White-Jacket* (1850) followed, founded on his sailor experience. His greatest work, *Moby-Dick* (1851), was dedicated to Nathaniel Hawthorne, who became his close friend and neighbour when Melville and his family moved to a farm in Pittsfield, Massachusetts in 1850. Reviews of *Moby-Dick* were mixed, and in *Pierre* (1852) Melville turned upon his audience, with disastrous results. His career as a novelist now in shambles, he began to cultivate and excel in a new form, the magazine tale. After a final novel, *The Confidence-Man* (1857), he abandoned fiction for nearly thirty years. In 1866 he assumed the position of Inspector of Customs at the Port of New York and his volume of Civil War poetry, *Battle-Pieces and Aspects of the War*, was published, to scant critical notice. Still less successful was his long narrative and philosophical poem, *Clarel* (1876). After retirement in 1885, Melville privately published two additional collections of poetry, *John Marr and Other Sailors* (1888) and *Timoleon* (1891). He died in obscurity in 1891, leaving behind two unfinished manuscripts, *Weeds and Wildings* (poetry), and *Billy Budd, Sailor*.

ROBERT MILDER, Professor of English at Washington University in St Louis, Missouri, has published widely on Melville and other mid-nineteenth-century American writers. He is editor of *Critical Essays on Melville's 'Billy Budd, Sailor'* and author of *Reimagining Thoreau*.

OXFORD WORLD'S CLASSICS

HERMAN MELVILLE

Billy Budd, Sailor
and Selected Tales

Edited with an Introduction and Notes by
ROBERT MILDER

OXFORD
UNIVERSITY PRESS

OXFORD

UNIVERSITY PRESS

Great Clarendon Street, Oxford OX2 6DP

Oxford University Press is a department of the University of Oxford.
It furthers the University's objective of excellence in research, scholarship,
and education by publishing worldwide in

Oxford New York

Athens Auckland Bangkok Bogotá Buenos Aires Cape Town
Chennai Dar es Salaam Delhi Florence Hong Kong Istanbul Karachi
Kolkata Kuala Lumpur Madrid Melbourne Mexico City Mumbai Nairobi
Paris São Paulo Shanghai Singapore Taipei Tokyo Toronto Warsaw

with associated companies in Berlin Ibadan

Oxford is a registered trade mark of Oxford University Press
in the UK and in certain other countries

Published in the United States
by Oxford University Press Inc., New York

First published as a World's Classics paperback 1997
Reissued as an Oxford World's Classics paperback 1998
Reissued 2009

British Library Cataloguing in Publication Data

Data available

Library of Congress Cataloging in Publication Data
Melville, Herman, 1819–1891.
Billy Budd, sailor and selected tales / Herman Melville; edited
with an introduction and notes by Robert Milder.
(Oxford world's classics)
Includes bibliographical references (p.   ).
Contents: Bartleby, the scrivener—Cock-a-doodle-doo!—The
fiddler—The paradise of bachelors and the tartarus of maids—
The lightning-rod man—The Encantadas, or, Enchanted Isles—
Benito Cereno—I and my chimney—Billy Budd, sailor.
1. Adventure stories, American. 2. Sea stories, American.
I. Milder, Robert. II. Title. III. Series.
PS2382.M55 1997 813'.3—dc21 97–8211

ISBN 978-0-19-953891-1

13

Printed in Great Britain by
Clays Ltd, Elcograf S.p.A.

CONTENTS

ACKNOWLEDGEMENTS

I would like to thank Stephanie J. Gannon for her meticulous research and assistance in helping me prepare the Explanatory Notes to this volume. I would also like to thank the Graduate School at Washington University for a Summer Research Grant that helped support this project.

INTRODUCTION

BY inclination and talent, Melville was not a writer of short stories, like Hawthorne and Poe, or of novellas, like Henry James. Aside from 'The Town-Ho's Story', excerpted from *Moby-Dick* and published in *Harper's New Monthly Magazine* as a promotion for the forthcoming book, Melville had never seriously attempted short fiction before 1853, nor did he find it congenial. His imagination required a larger canvas, his style a broader discursiveness, and his themes a more thoughtful audience than that of the popular magazines, the usual outlet for short stories. Financial necessity and nervous exhaustion, together with the appearance of two quality periodicals in the early 1850s, *Harper's* and *Putnam's Monthly Magazine*, combined to make a story-writer of Melville—and, in doing so, to reshape his relationship to his craft. If Melville is no longer an exuberant writer after 1852, he is a greatly more disciplined one, a master of irony and point of view whose fables ripple outward in concentric circles of meaning rather than overwhelm the reader with rhetorical force. Several of the tales —'Bartleby, the Scrivener', 'Benito Cereno', 'The Encantadas', 'The Paradise of Bachelors and the Tartarus of Maids', even the extravagant 'Cock-A-Doodle-Doo!' and 'I and My Chimney'—are acknowledged masterpieces, and nearly all command attention. The experimentation of the magazine pieces contributed formatively to the rhetorical control of *The Confidence-Man*, Melville's last published novel, and to the brooding intensity of *Billy Budd, Sailor* (1886–91; pub. 1924), his most widely read and variously interpreted work after *Moby-Dick*.

Had Melville not published in the magazines from 1853 to 1856, it is doubtful whether he would have continued to publish at all. By 1852, the career that had begun so auspiciously a half-dozen years earlier with *Typee*, Melville's fictionalized account of his benign captivity among the Marquesan islanders, had foundered amid charges that he had lost his literary senses, if not altogether his mind. Received with mixed reviews, *Moby-Dick* (1851) had sold disappointingly, and in his next work, *Pierre* (1852), Melville had turned against himself, his audience, and, it would seem, life itself to produce a work of moral and metaphysical nihilism that catastrophically estranged him from his readership. Pressed financially on all sides and with a growing family to support—a third child would be born to the Melvilles in 1853, a fourth in 1855; Melville's mother and three unmarried sisters also shared his Pittsfield, Massachusetts, farmhouse—Melville found himself without a novelistic career. In the winter and spring of 1852–3 he apparently wrote and attempted to place a narrative entitled *The Isle of the Cross*, but for unknown reasons the project fell through.[1] Meanwhile, concern over his 'health' —a family euphemism for problems as much psychological as physical—led relatives to mount a letter-writing campaign aimed at securing him a foreign consulship from newly elected President Franklin Pierce. This effort also failed, and by the late spring or early summer of 1853 Melville turned to the magazines as the most promising literary outlet available to him and the only immediate source of income.

Founded in 1850 largely as a vehicle for republishing the popular British writers of the day (commonly without payment), *Harper's New Monthly Magazine* soon began accepting quality American work and was by far the most successful magazine in the United States. More nativist in character, *Putnam's Monthly Magazine*, begun early in 1853, was even more distinguished—'much the best Mag. in the world', Thackeray is said to have called it.[2] Both journals valued Melville highly as a contributor and paid him at their top rate of $5 per page; published in two instalments, 'Bartleby, the Scrivener', for example, earned him $85. On his side, Melville not only consented to the practice of anonymous publication (authorship of magazine pieces was generally an

---

[1] See Hershel Parker, 'Herman Melville's *The Isle of the Cross*: A Survey and a Chronology', *American Literature*, 62 (1990), 1–16.

[2] Quoted in Historical Note to *The Piazza Tales and Other Prose Pieces* (Evanston and Chicago: Northwestern Univ. Press and The Newberry Library, 1987), 513.

open secret in New York literary circles) but tacitly agreed
to abide by genteel prohibitions of content, attitude, and
tone. 'I engage that the story shall contain nothing of any
sort to shock the fastidious', he assured publisher G. P.
Putnam about his serialized novel, *Israel Potter* (1854–5), adding, 'There will be very little reflective writing in it; nothing weighty.'[3] *Putnam's* did in fact reject one Melville piece,
'The Two Temples', that trod on the sensibilities of wealthy
church-goers, but for the most part Melville found he could
broadly have his say if he said things obliquely enough, assigned them to a genial or crotchety narrator, or clothed them
in symbolism. A few years earlier he had praised Hawthorne
as a practitioner of 'the great Art of Telling the Truth' whose
pleasant surfaces overlaid 'a blackness, ten times black'.[4] In
the magazine pieces—all but universally applauded for their
engaging charm—Melville came to master such a double-
faced art himself, whether for purposes of social criticism or
in pursuit of those existential questions he had explored in
Moby-Dick and *Pierre*.[5]

Altogether, the fourteen stories and sketches Melville published between 1853 and 1856 ('The Two Temples' remained
unprinted at his death) earned him something more than
$1,330, hardly a sufficient income but enough to ease his
situation and confirm the fact that whatever his novelistic
fortunes he was still a working writer. The magazine pieces
rescued Melville from what might have become a premature silence, but their deeper service during this period was
to rescue him from misanthropy and despair. Physically ailing (with rheumatism and sciatica) and exhausted from the
effort of publishing seven books in seven years, Melville at

[3] Melville, *Correspondence*, ed. Lynn Horth (Evanston and Chicago: Northwestern Univ. Press and The Newberry Library, 1993), 265.
[4] Melville, 'Hawthorne and His Mosses', in *The Piazza Tales*, 244, 243.
[5] As William Charvat noted, Melville 'masks his rejections of public values and
slogans so skilfully that, although twelve out of fifteen of his magazine pieces deal
essentially and unsentimentally with some kind of loss, poverty, loneliness, or
defeat, some of the blackest of these were praised as "quaint," "fanciful," "life-
like," "genial," and "thoroughly magazinish."' (Charvat, 'Melville and the Common Reader', in Matthew J. Bruccoli (ed.), *The Profession of Authorship in America:
The Papers of William Charvat* (Columbus: Ohio State Univ. Press, 1968), 279.

the age of 33 felt himself on the downward slope toward
dissolution and death. No doubt writing *Moby-Dick* had
'permanently aged him',[6] yet even as he was finishing the
book and working at the height of his powers, he likened
his growth to the organic cycle of a plant and confided to
Hawthorne a strange premonition of decay: 'But I feel that
I am now come to the inmost leaf of the bulb, and that
shortly the flower must fall to the mould.'[7] *Pierre* was the
fulfilment of this terrible prophecy—a book about intellectual disintegration whose lesson was that nothing could
be known, least of all the knower himself. Compounding
Melville's scepticism was his bitterness toward his philistine
audience and, with the departure of Hawthorne from nearby Lenox in the fall of 1851, his spiritual isolation. On all
sides—intellectual, emotional, social, economic, physiological
—the walls seemed to be closing in upon him; only the size
of his family was on the rise.

It is fitting, perhaps, that the narrators in several of these
tales should be elderly or otherwise disillusioned men, but to
speak of Melville's identification with these figures is to sim-
plify the process through which he comedically projected himself into extravagant personae and came to terms with his
situation through an art by turns humorous, satiric, ironic,
tragicomic, and grotesque but never self-pitying. Merely to
write of his frustrations in displaced form was to divert his
attention from them to the formal challenges of a new genre.
The stories were not simply 'therapy' in the usual sense of
cathartically venting an unbearable pain; still less were they
resolutions of problems Melville knew were stubbornly insol-
uble. Thematically, their common (but by no means exclusive)
subject is how to conduct oneself in the face of suffering
—personal, social, or cosmic. 'May one be gay upon the
Encantadas?' Melville asks of the Galapagos Islands, a physically blighted world emblematic of our larger, more variously blighted one. Melville has no unequivocal answer to

[6] Dan McCall, *The Silence of Bartleby* (Ithaca, NY: Cornell Univ. Press, 1989),
34.
[7] Melville, *Correspondence*, 193.

this question save as the virtuosity of his art is itself a form
of gaiety. Brooding on his hurt and anger, Melville came to
distance himself from them, moving steadily from *Pierre*'s
pained intimacy toward the magisterial irony and detachment of *The Confidence-Man*.

Not surprisingly, the first stories Melville composed—'The
Fiddler', 'Cock-A-Doodle-Doo!', 'Bartleby, the Scrivener',
and a lesser piece titled 'The Happy Failure', all from the
spring or summer of 1853[8]—are among the most autobio-
graphical in theme, if never in actual situation. All deal with
frustration and defeat. In 'The Fiddler' a poetaster named
Helmstone chafing at critical scorn and popular neglect
finds a model in the example of Hautboy, a former child
prodigy who has tasted fame, voluntarily renounced it, and
now expresses his genius by fiddling away 'right merrily
at Yankee Doodle and other off-handed, dashing, and disdainfully care-free airs'. Genius is self-sufficient and self-
pleasing, the tale seems to imply, and its wisest effort lies
in cultivating the art of life with a mixture of keen perception, appreciative good humour, and philosophical balance:
'It was plain that Hautboy saw the world pretty much as it
was, yet he did not theoretically espouse its bright side nor
its dark side. Rejecting all solutions, he but acknowledged
facts. What was sad in the world he did not superficially
gainsay; what was glad in it he did not cynically slur; and
all which was to him personally enjoyable, he gratefully took
to his heart.'

Melville's stories will reverberate with the opposition between 'bright' and 'dark' views of life, as will *The Confidence-
Man*. Did he hit upon the norm with Hautboy right at the
start? The tale's third character, Standard (aptly or ironically named?), appears to think so, along with a number of
Meville's critics. But there are ambiguities in the story that
make its attitude virtually indeterminable. Hautboy may be
anomalous, an ideal but not an imitable pattern (' "There's

---

[8] For a discussion of the chronology of the short fiction, see Merton M. Sealts's
Historical Note to the Northwestern–Newberry edition of *The Piazza Tales and
Other Prose Pieces 1839–1860*, ed. Harrison Hayford *et al.* (Evanston and Chicago:
Northwestern University Press and The Newberry Library, 1987), 492–3, 496.

only one Hautboy in the world"', Standard tells the narrator). Further, Hautboy (also aptly named?) seems ultimately an overgrown boy or at least an apostate from the spiritual aspiration that would always be consecrating for Melville. Is it a virtue to acknowledge nothing but facts? to gainsay sadness only 'superficially'? to deny the full scope of one's powers as if virtuosity of style exercised on trivialities could atone for a want of substance? ' "*With* genius and *without* fame"', Hautboy ' "is happier than a king"', Standard says. Yet can genius realize itself apart from those risks the artist takes in renouncing the commonplace? And is happiness, after all, the highest measure of life's success? Through Hautboy Melville seems to have been exploring a stance that was available and in some ways attractive to him, a philosophy of accommodation that would allow him to fiddle cheerfully at his own Yankee Doodles for *Putnam's* and *Harper's* while abjuring fame and the strenuousness of a deeply philosophical art. The inconclusiveness of the tale reflects Melville's own ambivalences, but in crafting it he has comically externalized his situation and transformed it from a private torment into a small labyrinth of moral possibilities.

The dramatic form of 'The Fiddler'—an encounter between the narrator and an 'extraordinary other'—recurs in several of the stories as Melville divides himself philosophically, projects his moods into obsessive, almost caricatured figures, and cultivates (as never before) the ironic potentials of unreliable narration. One party in these encounters typically holds a bright view of life, the other a dark; one (always the narrator) is realistically drawn, if somewhat eccentric, and invites a psychological reading, while the other—mysterious and fragmentary, a legate from a different order of literary reality—resonates symbolically to give the tale an ambiguous or multi-layered meaning.[9]

In 'Cock-A-Doodle-Doo!' the 'extraordinary other' is an exuberant rooster, Trumpet, along with its owner, an impoverished wood-sawyer named Merrymusk; in 'Bartleby, the

---

[9] See William B. Dillingham, *Melville's Short Fiction 1853–1856* (Athens: Univ. of Georgia Press, 1977), 5.

Scrivener' it is a pallid law-copyist of no determinable antecedents. Written in mid-1853 and published more or less
concurrently ('Bartleby' in *Putnam's*, 'Cock-A-Doodle-Doo!'
in *Harper's*), the stories are reversed images of one another
in a way that anticipates formally bipartite sketches like 'The
Paradise of Bachelors and the Tartarus of Maids' and 'The
Two Temples'. In 'Bartleby' a constitutionally genial, com-
placent narrator is brought to a sense of tragedy through
the agency of his scrivener; in 'Cock-A-Doodle-Doo!' a
splenetic narrator is equivocally 'redeemed' through the life-
affirming crow of a marvellous cock. Both stories have strong
biographical affinities, not simply as they evoke Melville's
state of mind ('Cock-A-Doodle-Doo!') or his literary situation
('Bartleby'), but as they extend themes and motifs from his
earlier writings that were central to his own orientation to life.

The opening paragraphs of 'Cock-A-Doodle-Doo!' read
like a downsized pastoral version of *Moby-Dick*, with Ishmael
and Ahab collapsed into a single comic-obsessive figure. A
narrator afflicted with the 'hypoes' (melancholy or depression) sets out on a journey—a country walk in lieu of
Ishmael's whaling voyage. Disillusioned with all creation,
he 'spitefully thrust[s]' his walking-stick into the 'oozy sod',
much as the *Pequod* 'thrust her vindictive bows into the cold
malicious waves'; he even reflects in Ahabian fashion on
the cruel indifference of the heavens to human tragedies—
indeed, of the heavens' ultimate responsibility for them, 'else
they could not happen'.[10] Setting his tale in a familiar rural
world and speaking serio-comically through his country proprietor, Melville could safely address the theme of cosmic
(mis)governance that readers found offensive in the grandi-
loquent, openly blasphemous Ahab; he could even join the
metaphysical to the mundane and jovially thumb his nose
at creditors and duns. Indeed, the story seems so affirmat-
ive—' "Glory to God in the highest!" ' Trumpet seems to
crow, and the narrator with him—that its ironies are often
overlooked. The narrator is an enthusiast, as extreme in his

[10] Joel Porte discusses Ahabian echoes in 'Cock-A-Doodle-Doo!' in *In Respect
to Egotism* (Cambridge Univ. Press, 1991), 189–212.

new-found optimism as he had earlier been in his spleen, and insensible to the grotesqueness of an ' "All well" ' spoken or crowed amid a devastating scene of carnage. Beneath its nominal celebration of the triumph of spirit over flesh, the story turns upon two quite different responses to evil: on one side, a 'calm, good-natured rapture of defiance' reminiscent of Ishmael's 'genial, desperado philosophy' and founded similarly on an absurdist affirmation of self within a meaningless universe; on the other side, a quasi-transcendental assertion of faith mounted *against* the demonstrable nature of experience and bizarrely self-parodic in the light of it. The narrator may well be confused in his metaphysics; not so Melville himself, who would exploit this same ambiguity in 'The Lightning-Rod Man', ostensibly praising God's absolute sovereignty while covertly arraigning it.

As a journey into darkness rather than into purported light, 'Bartleby' inverts the movement of 'Cock-A-Doodle-Doo!' and is at once Melville's most comic, most pathetic, and most symbolically fertile story. Leo Marx long ago noted the relationship between Bartleby's profession as writer and Melville's own,[11] though the fact that he could compose a 'Bartleby' is proof that Melville himself did not retreat into proud, catatonic silence. The root temptation that Bartleby succumbs to and Melville resists is the temptation to despair: the negativist insistence that the dead-wall in its manifold significance is the all-defining reality. Bartleby's 'I would prefer not to' may be a scaled-down version of Ahabian defiance—a morbid brooding upon the omnipresence of the wall rather than a furious effort to thrust through it—but the forlorn dignity of Bartleby is sufficient only to make him an image of human suffering on all its fronts (psychological, social, economic, metaphysical), never a diminutive model of heroic resistance.

As a figure in himself—'character' would be too representational a term—Bartleby has been taken to signify a host of symbolic possibilities, but the emphasis of criticism has long

---

[11] Leo Marx, 'Melville's Parable of the Walls', *Sewanee Review*, 61 (1953), 602–27.

been upon his influence on the lawyer-narrator, whom he impels (with much resistance) toward a recognition of human pathos. 'An eminently *safe* man', the narrator, though kind and reflective after his fashion, is one of those 'bachelors' Melville had been sketching since *Mardi* (1849) and would make a central feature of his stories—comfortable, sanguine men who are 'not only free of family responsibilities', as Merlin Bowen observed, but who 'have ascended no higher than the first degree of knowledge and perceive as yet only the surface of truth'.[12] Those who regard the narrator as a selfish hypocrite underestimate the complex humour of the story, much of which is the narrator's own, but there is no question that the 'overpowering stinging melancholy' the narrator feels on discovering Bartleby's terrible isolation amounts to a kind of conversion experience, impressing on him 'the bond of common humanity' and awakening a generous but ineffectual solicitude he would have preferred to avoid. Is Bartleby, then, a guardian angel mysteriously 'billeted' upon the narrator by 'an all-wise Providence'? is he a Christ figure? a representative of Freud's 'uncanny'? No precise identification seems adequate or even wholly to the point: Bartleby is a given whose role is to disrupt the narrator's social and philosophical world and uncover for him an elemental 'wrongness' so close to the heart of life as to seem virtually ineradicable.

The achievement of 'Bartleby'—and of stories like 'Benito Cereno' and 'The Paradise of Bachelors and the Tartarus of Maids'—is to establish this 'wrongness' on a multitude of interpretative planes, not least a socio-historical one. Whatever else it may signify, the subtitle of the tale, 'A Story of Wall-Street', is an indication that Melville is shaping his fable with *laissez-faire* capitalism in mind. The lawyer-narrator is not a cruelly exploitative employer—if anything, his copyists rather control *him*—but he is a man who looks upon human relationships contractually, as if his responsibility to his scriveners began and ended with their performance as functionaries. It is precisely the *normalcy* of this attitude that

[12] Merlin Bowen, *The Long Encounter* (Univ. of Chicago Press, 1960), 67.

Melville implicitly measures against the Christian ideal of fraternity—'Christianity' in this sense referring not to the supernatural or salvific but to the morality embodied for Melville in the Sermon on the Mount. So far as Bartleby's withdrawal can be ascribed to the demeaning employments available to him, his story is a reflection, like so many of Dickens's novels, on the demoralizing effects of modern commercial life. But it is reductive to emphasize the historical level of meaning to the exclusion of the existential; it is difficult even to disentangle them. Like his contemporaries Emerson and Hawthorne, Melville saw history as having a logic of its own, whether immanent or Providential, so that the societal order in place, however callous, had a provisional necessity to it, or at least a stultifying inertia. Emerson and Hawthorne persuaded themselves of an ultimate teleological benevolence; Melville did not. Why, if God existed, were human affairs allowed to proceed in their brutal way? And if God did not exist, what hope was there, in view of the monumental forces at work, for the collective will to forge an ameliorative entry into history? Melville was not a tragic thinker *rather than* a historical one; his sense of tragedy was nourished by his sensitivity to social injustice, which his bent toward cosmic questions led him to transpose to the plane of metaphysics. If the oppressions of class and power were largely economic in origin, the facts of economic life were themselves symptoms of a deeper, perhaps incurable natural ill, as if the scheme of experience were poisoned at its very root.

'The Paradise of Bachelors and the Tartarus of Maids' is an excellent example of how contexts of meaning blend almost indivisibly in Melville's tales. On the most explicit level, the Devil's Dungeon paper-mill visited by the seedsman-narrator is a representation *in extremis* of countless New England factories scattered throughout the stream-fed landscape. The initial hope of such enterprises, as proclaimed in the late 1820s by the founders of the Merrimack mills in Lowell, Massachusetts, was to avoid the Stygian filth and misery of the English manufacturing cities by locating factories in the countryside, employing a transient work-force of farm girls, and supervising the girls with a paternalistic attention to their moral and religious health as well as a sharp eye to their productivity. At stake was the issue raised by Thomas Jefferson in the 1780s of whether a republic could morally afford a system of manufactures. For a decade or more, before Irish immigration, hard times, and increased competition changed the nature of the operation, Lowell was a showcase of American industry and a 'celestial countertype to infernal Manchester'. As John Kasson observes, 'the dramatic natural setting along the banks of the Merrimack, nestled in the hills, with views reputedly as far as the White Mountains, no less than the crisp, clean aspect of the town itself, gave Lowell an air of "rural freshness" which dazzled foreign guests'.[13]

In 'The Paradise of Bachelors and the Tartarus of Maids' an American alternative to hell is depicted as hell itself. The Merrimack River becomes the Blood River; the nestling hills, Woedolor Mountain; the crisp, clean town, a 'whited sepulchre'; the air of freshness, a bone-chilling frigidity; and the mill-girls themselves, pallid, blue-lipped 'operatives'. Drawing partly upon his own trip to a nearby paper-mill (with geographical touches from the rugged White Mountains), Melville is responding to the terrible paradox of the industrial revolution: that 'machinery—the vaunted slave of humanity'—has instead become its enslaver. On one level, the mill-girls are representatives of the working class generally; on another, they are specifically female victims sacrificed on the male altar of capitalist productivity—victims not only of the 'dark-complexioned' man who oversees the operation but of the merry bachelors in the opening section of the tale (paper-consumers all) whose comfortable lives rest on a comparable substructure of dehumanized labour.

Alongside this social theme, and complexly interwoven with it, is a biological one, as Melville leads his narrator through a terrain minutely suggestive of the female anatomy and through a papermaking operation symbolic of human insemination,

---

[13] John F. Kasson, *Civilizing the Machine* (1976; repr. New York: Penguin, 1977), 82–3. For a history of the Lowell experiment, see Kasson, pp. 55–106.

gestation, and birth. With his own family growing apace, childbirth was much on Melville's mind, as perhaps were the remembered delights of bachelorhood. Biology was nature's trap. For men it entailed an economic burden and a loss of monastic peace; for women, socially dependent and lured by romance—the maids at the paper-mill are kept at (and perhaps figuratively drawn to) their labours by a smiling, dimpled youth named Cupid—it imposed a servitude more elemental and consuming. Today we would call women's situation 'socially constructed', but in mid-nineteenth-century rural households like the Melvilles' (or like Emily Dickinson's in nearby Amherst) the realities of birth, child-rearing, sickness, and death were presided over by women with an inevitability that seemed to make them the con-stituted servants of biological process. As 'The Tartarus of Maids' develops, the iron machinery of the paper-mill thus expands symbolically into the organic machinery of nature, the maids signifying all women caught in the round of repro-duction whether as mothers themselves or, like Melville's three unmarried sisters, as virginal attendants. To what end is this driving fecundity? Nature itself hardly seems to know, turning out human beings—most of them the equivalent of cheap, disposable foolscap—with the stolid regularity of a factory. By comparing the blank sheets of paper produced at the mill to Locke's theory of 'the human mind at birth', Melville carries the reference of the tale still further, mak-ing it an allegory of the countless human generations as well as of generation itself. These various levels of mean-ings are not discretely stratified but belong ultimately to a single vision expressed, as in 'Bartleby', by the narrator's closing apostrophe: 'Oh! Paradise of Bachelors! and oh! Tartarus of Maids!' Melville's full subject is the pathos of the human condition, whose natural horrors are aggravated by the horrors society invents, and whose pleasures are con-tinuously available only to those who turn their bachelor eyes from 'the thing called pain, the bugbear styled trouble'.

A subordinate but prophetic theme in 'The Paradise of Bachelors and the Tartarus of Maids' is Melville's compli-cated attitude toward the past, which included America's

INTRODUCTION xix

English heritage. As much as he belonged to his nation and times and possessed what he called 'a correspondent coloring', Melville was drawn to earlier centuries partly for the vitality of their literature and partly from a sense, not unlike Hawthorne's, that however superstitious and intolerant his remote ancestors might have been, they at least had the virtue of taking life seriously. Echoes of Charles Lamb and Samuel Johnson make the journey to the Temple a literary as well as a hedonistic pilgrimage, as it manifestly had been for Melville himself during his winter 1849–50 visit to London. Melville's delight and immersion in English literature, so evident in *Moby-Dick*, give his stories an allusive resonance crucial in a genre requiring economy and subtle disguise. Melville used literature to *make* literature, not simply as an ornament, a source, or an adjunct to local meaning, but as a backdrop against which life assumed distinctive shape and as a standard for measuring the grandeur or diminutiveness of the present. The lawyers who gather to feast in the Temple are set mock-heroically against their medieval predecessors, the Knights Templars, 'the long two-handed sword' giving way to 'a one-handed quill', 'the vowed opener and clearer of all highways leading to the Holy Sepulchre, now [having] it in particular charge to check, to clog, to hinder, and embarrass all the courts and avenues of Law'. Melville is writing ironically with no deep affection for feudal appurtenances save as they testify to a strenuousness of thought and feeling he finds sadly relaxed. There is no greater condemnation of the modern-day Templar than that his 'fall' from old ways 'has but made him all the finer fellow'—not that geniality didn't rank high on Melville's scale of virtues, but that it needed to be tempered by an earnestness in confronting social and metaphysical evil.

Coexisting, then, with Melville's indignation at slavery, class injustice, and the manifold abuses of power in contemporary America was a strain of conservatism that led him to honour the moral sobriety of the past even if he could not abide its social and political institutions. The other side of this feeling was an impatience with all types of shallow or specious newfangledness. Among its many meanings, 'The

Lightning-Rod Man' is a protest against the desacralizing of experience, even (or especially) the divine terror of experience, by meddling, pretentious science.[14] 'I and My Chimney' develops a similar theme in its opposition between the stodgy, reverential narrator and his positivistic up-to-the-minute wife. Though still in his middle thirties, Melville was beginning to feel himself socially in the rear of his age, if only (as he would say years later) 'as a counterpoise to the exorbitant hopefulness, juvenile and shallow, that makes such a bluster in these days'. By the end of the Civil War and onward through *Billy Budd* this conservatism would draw heavily upon another emotion—nostalgia. In the stories of 1853–6, however, Melville was a traditionalist largely in defiance of a rootless, diminished age, and a pessimist chiefly, as he said, to remind his contemporaries that darkness was half, or more than half, of life's reality.

'The Encantadas' is Melville's most dramatic evocation of darkness, cast safely in the travelogue form contemporary readers so much admired in his work. The Spenserian epigraphs to the sketches subtly deepen and moralize Melville's account of the Galapagos, as does the persistent imagery of Plutonian blight. Even so, 'The Encantadas' has seemed, in Lea Newman's words, 'a piece whose structure is suspect and whose meaning is enigmatic',[15] and indeed it may be best not to insist on too elaborate a coherence. The overall movement of the sketches seems to run from the descriptively and symbolically geographical to the metaphysical to the moral—that is, from a picture of the island world to a cosmic speculation upon it to a history of how various human beings have shaped their lives within it. The volcanic barrenness of the islands makes them almost unique in Creation, but their 'emphatic uninhabitableness' links them to other desolate or hostile Melvillean settings—ocean (*Moby-Dick*), mountaintop (*Pierre*), desert (*Clarel*), and prairie (the late poem 'John Marr')—images of the blank face of God

---

[14] See Allan Moore Emery, 'Melville on Science: "The Lightning-Rod Man"', *New England Quarterly*, 56 (1983), 555–68.
[15] Lea Bertani Vozar Newman, *A Reader's Guide to the Short Stories of Herman Melville* (Boston: G. K. Hall, 1986), 192.

in nature. 'In no world but a fallen one could such lands exist', Melville comments, alluding not so much to the fall of man as to the fall of nature itself into a blasted quasi-malevolence reminiscent of Salvator Rosa's seventeenth-century landscapes ('The Encantadas' was first published under the pseudonym Salvator R. Tarnmoor). Precisely because they showed Creation at its stark extremity, oceans and deserts were most revealing for Melville of the terrifying substructure of reality normally hidden beneath its benign surface. What sort of deity would make such a world, 'The Encantadas' tacitly asks of its emblematic setting, and how are we to conduct ourselves once we have fronted its core of inhospitable truth? 'For whoever once hath fastened | His foot thereon may never it recure | But wandreth ever-more uncertaine and unsure': so Melville prefaces the tale with an epigraph from *The Faerie Queene*, and so his narrator testifies at the end of Sketch First when he describes being recalled from 'scenes of social merriment' by the image of a Galapagos tortoise 'heavily crawling along the floor . . . with "Memento ****" burning in live letters upon his back'.

With Sketch Sixth 'The Encantadas' divides in half as Melville turns from the nature of the island world to the range of human beings who have inhabited it. Here Melville shows himself what Warner Berthoff has aptly termed him: 'a recorder of life-histories . . . concerned to demonstrate what capacities may be called forth in the creature, man, by the fatalities and accidents of his existence'.[16] From the buccaneers of Barrington Isle to the Dog-King of Charles's Isle and the depraved hermit Oberlus, Melville traces not only human types but microcosmic social and political communities, each representative of some possibility in the larger world. But the moral weight of 'The Encantadas' is upon the marooned Indian woman, Hunilla, who watches helplessly as her husband and brother drown, then ekes out a solitary living in the harshest of worlds. Betrayed by man—first by a whaling captain who breaks his 'blithesome promise' to return

---

[16] Warner Berthoff, *The Example of Melville* (Princeton Univ. Press, 1962), 92.

her to the mainland, then by a boat's crew who rape her—
Hunilla is also 'dall[ied] with' by 'feline Fate'. The example
she presents is not one of religious faith or Crusoe-like
ingenuity but, as with so many of Faulkner's women, of a
numbed but indomitable endurance in the face of unending tragedy. 'Humanity, thou strong thing,' Melville writes,
'I worship thee, not in the laurelled victor, but in this
vanquished one.' Though by no means a symbol of Christ,
Hunilla is Christlike both in her patience beneath suffering
and in the redemptive generosity she evokes in the sailors who
rescue her. Evidence suggests that the theme of patience had
dominated the manuscript novel *The Isle of the Cross* which
Melville tried to place in the spring of 1853. It was a theme
he arrived at late in his fictive career and partly by chance,
having been struck by the story of a local woman during an
1852 visit to Nantucket, but it was one that came to assume
additional meaning as he, too, struggled with what he considered the betrayals of man and the indifference of God.
Hunilla the 'vanquished one' is his symbol for all life's casualties, who might yet in defeat bear themselves with dignity
and calm.

For all that the stories of 1853–6 show Melville subtilizing
his craft and moved by a more intimate sympathy with suffering, they also display a curious intellectual fixity. 'Bright'
and 'dark' are the categories in which his mind has come
to operate, and though he clearly saw that some resolution
of these antitheses was necessary—'Enjoy the bright, keep
it turned up perpetually if you can, but be honest and don't
deny the black', he advised in 'The Encantadas'—the tales
themselves are polar rather than synthesizing in vision, their
characters holding either to an untenable optimism or to a
debilitating pessimism.

'Benito Cereno' carries this opposition to an extreme in
the contrast between the good-natured and 'singularly undistrustful' American captain, Amasa Delano, and his gloom-
ridden Spanish counterpart, Benito Cereno. Drawing its
plot situation from the actual Delano's *Narrative of Voyages
and Travels, in the Northern and Southern Hemispheres* (1817),
Melville's account of a slave rebellion aboard a Spanish ship

is a brooding, intricately woven tale whose ambiguities of circumstance are clarified toward the end only to leave a deeper ambiguity of subject and meaning. Delivered from his captors, Benito Cereno remains spiritually oppressed. ' "You are saved; what has cast such a shadow upon you?" ' Delano asks. ' "The negro." '

On these words, interpretation of the story divides itself between those who read it as a parable about the discovery of evil and those who regard its subject as slavery or race. No American author writing of a slave rebellion in the mid-1850s could have done so *without* an immediate political reference; the question is where Melville's emphasis lies. In adapting Delano's unadorned but riveting narrative, Melville made several important alterations, three of which seem especially suggestive of his purposes: he changed the name of Delano's ship from the *Perseverance* to the *Bachelor's Delight*; he rechristened Benito Cereno's ship the *San Dominick*; and he intensified the violence of the events in some places while muting it in others. The bachelor Delano, sunny by nature and sharing his culture's stereotypes about black docility, is ill prepared to unravel the mystery of appearances on the *San Dominick*, but neither is Delano an utter fool. First-time readers follow and to some degree share his oscillations between trust and misgiving, sceptical of Delano's reasonings and sensible of the motifs of knots, locks and keys, and riddles, but in no position to see beyond him to the truth of the situation. The opening description of the scene—a grey sky with 'flights of troubled gray fowl' and 'troubled gray vapors'; 'Shadows present foreshadowing deeper shadows to come'—establishes a mood of ominousness and ambiguity that implicates reality itself in the play of equivocal surfaces. While hardly an everyman, Delano is caught in a life-and-death epistemological drama whose resolution might elude far subtler minds than his. In this respect 'Benito Cereno', as Berthoff remarked, might 'fairly be seen as composing a paradigm of the secret ambiguity of appearances —an old theme with Melville—and, more particularly, a paradigm of the inward life of ordinary consciousness, with all its mysterious shifts, penetrations, and side-slippings, in a world in which this ambiguity of appearances is the baffling norm'.[17]

The renaming of Cereno's ship, on the other hand, was a gesture not toward the broadly philosophical but toward the specifically political. Santo Domingo, the island where Columbus first landed and promptly subjugated the natives, had been the scene of a successful black-led revolution in the 1790s. Santo Domingo was thus the Americas in miniature, both in its sin of slavery and in its prophecy of racial insurrection. So Melville suggests when he has the rebels substitute the skeleton of slave-holder Aranda for the ship's 'proper figure-head—the image of Christopher Colon, the discoverer of the New World'. The order of the Dominicans, known in England as the Black Friars and alluded to as such in the text, was also instrumental in the establishment and perpetuation of New World slavery.

Melville's attitude toward slavery had always been severely critical, though his scepticism made him wary of abolitionist remedies. The *Amistad* case decided by the United States Supreme Court in 1841 had established the right of Africans aboard ship to revolt against their enslavers, so there was historical and legal precedent for Melville to treat the rebels heroically if such had been his intent. In fact, however, Melville 'heightened the barbarity'[18] of Babo and the other slaves—the Negro women, for example—while suppressing narrative details about the vengeance of the Spanish sailors, including an attempt by the original Benito Cereno to stab a shackled slave.[19] Melville's handling of his source has been troublesome to critics wishing to read the story polemically as (in Robert S. Levine's words) 'a scornful attack on Delano's blinding innocence, a damning indictment of the evils of chattel slavery, and a rousing celebration of black

---

[17] Berthoff, *The Example of Melville*, 153.

[18] Allan Moore Emery, 'The Topicality of Depravity in "Benito Cereno"', *American Literature*, 55 (1983), 319.

[19] Amasa Delano's account of the incident is reprinted in the Appendix to this edition; depositions and other documents relating to it can be found in the Northwestern–Newberry edition of *The Piazza Tales and Other Prose Pieces*, 827–47.

rebellion'.[20] Anti-slavery readings are viable, of course, indeed are common, but they are persuasive to the degree that they confront this complicating evidence and use it to transpose the question of Melville's purposes to a higher conceptual level.

The split between philosophical and political approaches to 'Benito Cereno' is an extreme case of the critical division on nearly all the stories. Is Melville a tragic writer or a historical one? Allan Moore Emery tries to resolve this apparent opposition by arguing that ' "Benito Cereno" treats human depravity . . . for specific historical reasons', the contemporary debate over the nature of the Negro having revived for Melville the question of human nature generally. 'In "Benito Cereno," "the negro" stands for all mankind', Emery concludes,[21] absolving Melville of racism by convicting him of even-handed misanthropy. Yet 'depravity' in 'Benito Cereno' is not exclusively a human quality, nor was it ever such for Melville, who, unlike Hawthorne (as F. O. Matthiessen long ago observed), was 'not so concerned with individual sin as with titanic uncontrollable forces which seem to dwarf man altogether'.[22] Though brutally indifferent to human needs, Creation for Melville was not actively malignant; it could, however, seem *acquiescently* so whenever he relinquished his naturalism and viewed the world as a divinely constructed order in which Someone should have been, but manifestly was not, superintending events. An 'interregnum in Providence', Ishmael called this chronic suspension of divine vigilance. The sanguine Delano entertains and dismisses the same idea when he asks whether he, 'Amasa Delano, Jack of the Beach, as they called me when a lad', will be allowed 'to be murdered here at the ends of the earth . . . by a horrible Spaniard'. 'Too nonsensical to think of! . . . There is

[20] Robert S. Levine, *Conspiracy and Romance* (Cambridge Univ. Press, 1989), 166. Levine is not advancing his own reading here but describing 'the new critical consensus' that emerged 'from a flurry of activity during the 1960s and 1970s' (166).

[21] 'The Topicality of Depravity', 317, 331.

[22] F. O. Matthiessen, *American Renaissance* (New York: Oxford Univ. Press, 1941), 441.

some one above', he blithely reassures himself, as he will again after later misgivings when the sight of 'benign' nature 'taking her innocent repose in the evening' shames him for having momentarily yielded to 'an almost atheist doubt of the ever-watchful Providence above'. To reinforce his theme and extend it beyond Delano, Melville fabricates the detail (absent from his source) that one of the Spaniards mistakenly killed by Delano's men on boarding the ship was carrying a jewel 'meant for the shrine of our Lady of Mercy in Lima' as a 'votive offering' for his safe journey.

Though a metaphysical reading of 'Benito Cereno' should not be allowed to displace a political one, it can help explain Melville's refusal to heroicize the rebellious slaves. There is no simple good and evil in this sombre tale of grey. Appearances are deceptive; social systems are oppressive and cruel, but so are the insurrections against them; one race is as capable of brutality as another. 'Benito Cereno' is unsatisfying as an attack on slavery not because Melville was lukewarm in his detestation of it but because his literary purposes were centred elsewhere. In the brief but powerful coda—entirely Melville's invention; the historical Benito Cereno proved an ingrate and a scoundrel—Delano expresses surprise that the Spanish captain should not recover his spirits: ' "But the past is passed; why moralize upon it? Forget it. See, yon bright sun has forgotten it all, and the blue sea, and the blue sky; these have turned over new leaves." ' ' "Because they have no memory," ' Cereno answers, ' "because they are not human." ' By this measure, Delano himself is scarcely human, like Melville's other bachelors who cannot or will not recognize that darkness pervades the very warp of things.

The coda suggests that Melville is using the horror of slavery as an occasion to reflect more universally on the character of experience. It is important to add, however, that Melville's sense of the 'universal' did not arise in a historical vacuum. It was precisely a question like slavery—an evil without a visible remedy—that inclined him to regard the scheme of life as inherently flawed. *Laissez-faire* capitalism was another such enormity; Western colonialism, whose predations he witnessed in the Pacific, was a third. In

The Burden of Southern History historian C. Vann Woodward ascribed the tragic vision of modern Southern writers to the region's experience of defeat and frustration, which 'did not dispose [it] very favorably toward such popular American ideas as the doctrine of human perfectibility, the belief that every evil has a cure, and the notion that every human problem has a solution'.[23] The Melville of mid-century was an egalitarian progressive, not a hierarchical conservative, but his social idealism only aggravated his feeling of the disparity between what ought to be and what was. Even in democratic America, history stumbled along according to its own cruel and wasteful logic, fed by the partisanship of the best-intentioned persons as well as by the callousness and greed of the worst, and visibly unaffected by anything resembling a divine plan. Melville was a tragedian not because he ignored his age or 'transcended' it but because he responded so deeply to its conflicts and, despairing of their foreseeable solution, came to view them *sub specie aeternitatis* as testimony to the enduring nature of the human condition. Benito Cereno's last words, ' "the negro" ', are a shorthand for the 'great power of blackness' Melville found in Hawthorne and all 'deeply thinking' minds, sensitive as they inescapably were to 'the uneven balance' of evil and good in the world.[24] To his own mind, Melville was a metaphysical writer more than a specifically social one, but his metaphysics were themselves shaped by the impasses of his historical situation, whether or not he understood them as such.

What kept Melville from the despondency of a Benito Cereno were his zest for life (even in the troubled mid-1850s), his resilience, and his writing. As he explored the various accommodations open to human beings, the antithesis of 'bright' and 'dark' gradually redefined itself as a question of 'trust' versus 'distrust'—in humanity, in nature, in God, and in the self. This would be his focus in *The Confidence-Man*, which rings dizzying changes on the paradoxes of

---

[23] C. Vann Woodward, *The Burden of Southern History* (1960; repr. New York: New American Library, 1969), 28.

[24] Melville, 'Hawthorne and His Mosses', in *The Piazza Tales and Other Prose Pieces*, 243.

belief, central among them the fact that while '"the too-sober view [of life] is, doubtless, nearer true than the too-drunken"',[25] it may also be desiccating. How was one to combine an allegiance to truth with a saving delight in experience and a feeling for its grandeur? In 'The Lightning-Rod Man' the salesman who peddles insurance against divine wrath is a sower of cosmic distrust rightly scorned by 'a lover of the majestic' like the narrator. In his own view of the heavens ('the Deity will not, of purpose, make war on man's earth') the narrator is naïvely sanguine, but his at least is a generous belief—a mountain-dweller's eagerness to front the divine—while the lightning-rod man's—a creaturely terror that lacks the profundity of tragic knowledge—is demeaning.

The fact that narrator and character in 'The Lightning-Rod Man' are both unreliable is typical of the distancing techniques that allowed Melville to externalize the issues preying upon him and exploit their ironic possibilities. The artistry he developed here was undoubtedly therapeutic, yet, conducive as it was to endless comic experiments, it also postponed the kind of reckoning that might have resolved the matter of 'trust' or at least freed him from its labyrinthine passages. The challenge he faced in 1853–6 was to unite his vision of darkness with a life-affirming sense of self-worth and, if possible, a provisional belief that darkness was not final. Nearly all his stories address this question, either directly or indirectly; none approaches a solution. A verse Melville marked in Job, probably in the early 1850s, may come closest to his private ideal: 'Though he slay me, yet will I trust in him: but I will maintain mine own ways before him' (Job 13: 15; Melville's underlining).

By 1856 Melville had not found a way to believe in God, but he had, through his writing, come more firmly to believe in himself. Not everyone thought this a happy development. Three years earlier his family had apparently arranged to have him examined for mental illness, and nothing in his

---

[25] Melville, *The Confidence-Man*, ed. Harrison Hayford *et al.* (Evanston and Chicago: Northwestern University Press and The Newberry Library, 1984), 134.

emotional bearing since that time is likely to have assuaged their fears. The family's solution, characteristically, was to remove him from his writing-desk, which his father-in-law, Judge Lemuel Shaw, eventually did late in 1856 by generously underwriting a journey to Europe and the Holy Land. Meanwhile, ensconced in a household of five adult females and four children, Melville must have felt himself domestically besieged. 'I and My Chimney' has been read biographically as Melville's symbolic rendering of his mental examination, with the narrator's chimney representing his inviolable core of self.[26] The tenacity with which the narrator defends the chimney against his 'enterprising wife' and daughters, who would remodel it away, may also reflect Melville's determination to preserve his identity as a writer against continuing pleas in the name of his 'health'. ' "No, no, wife," ' the narrator protests, ' "I can't abolish my backbone." ' Others have interpreted the story differently—as a political allegory of the divided Union, for example, or a debate between reformism and conservatism. There is no reason why such readings may not coexist. Although critical discourse is by nature divisive, Melville himself was an artist, not a logician, and his stories, while nearly always on some level personal in reference, resonate outward toward other meanings if only because his response to experience— historical, philosophical, and psychological—was organically whole. The remarkable thing about 'I and My Chimney', at any rate, is how wonderfully comic it is, how little it is given to bitterness, self-pity, or despair. One of the last of Melville's tales, it is also one of the most genial, the work of a man who has come to take a virtuoso's pleasure in his craft and thereby, without ever solving the problems that troubled him, slowly to find his way back to the living.

Five of the *Putnam's* stories—'Bartleby, the Scrivener', 'Benito Cereno', 'The Lightning-Rod Man', 'The Encantadas', and

---

[26] See Merton M. Sealts, Jr., 'Herman Melville's "I and My Chimney"', *American Literature*, 13 (1941), 142–54; repr. in Sealts, *Pursuing Melville 1940–1980* (Madison: Univ. of Wisconsin Press, 1982), 11–22. In the same volume, see also 'Melville's Chimney, Reexamined', 171–92.

'The Bell-Tower', along with a preface, 'The Piazza'—were
published in 1856 by Dix and Edwards, the new owner of
Putnam's, as *The Piazza Tales*. The volume was a commer-
cial venture with little aesthetic rationale; 'Cock-A-Doodle-
Doo!' and 'The Paradise of Bachelors and the Tartarus of
Maids' were excluded because they were *Harper's* stories,
while 'I and My Chimney' and another *Putnam's* tale, 'The
Apple-Tree Table', were submitted too late for inclusion.
Although favourably reviewed, *The Piazza Tales* sold poorly
and Melville received no royalties for the volume. *The
Confidence-Man*, a tour de force of verbal and situational
irony, was not even well received. By the time Melville sailed
for Europe in the autumn of 1856, his fictive career, as he
must have known, was effectively over.

Studies of Melville's writing commonly bridge the thirty-
five years between *The Confidence-Man* and *Billy Budd, Sailor*
with a vague remark about 'the long silence'. In truth,
Melville was not silent at all, except in prose. His 1856–7
journey to the Holy Land concluded one phase of his career
only to begin another. His medium now was poetry, and his
frame of reference, even when he wrote of America, was
increasingly transatlantic and macrohistorical. His first published volume of poems, *Battle-Pieces and Aspects of the War*
(1866), is arguably the most ambitious and profound contemporary treatment of the American Civil War, far more
so than Whitman's better-known *Drum-Taps*. But it is *Clarel*
(1876), his long dramatic and philosophical poem about a
modern-day pilgrimage to the Holy Land, that establishes
Melville as a major nineteenth-century poet and a chronicler
of the Victorian crisis of belief to be set alongside Arnold,
Tennyson, and Browning. A decade later, Melville the poet
turned to the sea in *John Marr and Other Sailors* (1888), a
striking, heterogeneous volume that experiments with a
variety of verse-forms, among them three Browningesque
dramatic monologues assigned to common sailors.

Begun in or around 1886, *Billy Budd, Sailor* developed
from the prose headnote to an early version of the poem
'Billy in the Darbies', a monologue apparently intended
for *John Marr* and now the conclusion to *Billy Budd*. The

original Billy was an older man and would-be mutineer awaiting execution, but at some point during the writing his character sprang to imaginative life, and by November 1888 Melville
had transformed his ballad into what he then considered
a complete narrative of more than 150 manuscript leaves
(well under half the final number) in which Billy, recast as
the Adamic figure of later versions, is sentenced to hang for
striking and killing his false accuser, Master-at-arms John
Claggart. During the last three years of his life Melville took
up the manuscript yet again, elaborating the portrait of
Captain Vere and adding the chapters between Claggart's
death and Billy's that have long claimed the bulk of critical
attention. Melville was still revising the story when he died
in September 1891, leaving behind a chronologically complete
manuscript in such physical disarray that an authoritative
text of *Billy Budd* would not appear until the Hayford–Sealts
edition of 1962, here reprinted.[27]

Ever since its initial publication in 1924, more than three
decades after Melville's death, *Billy Budd* has impressed
readers as a 'testament' of one sort or another, but a testament of what? To Raymond Weaver, its first editor, the story
was Melville's effort to 'justify the ways of God to man', but
for other readers, including British critic E. L. Grant Watson
who coined the phrase 'testament of acceptance', *Billy Budd*
was an affirmation of *human* ways amid the absence or indifference of God. When Watson argued that Melville was 'no
longer a rebel', he meant that Melville had got beyond his
social and metaphysical anger and his bitterness at critical
neglect, not that he had settled down to political conservatism and religious orthodoxy.[28] Unfortunately, the notion of
a 'testament of acceptance' became widely identified with
both these things to the exclusion of the story's resonant
allusiveness and ambiguity. In the 1950s a revisionist criticism
challenged the old consensus and pronounced *Billy Budd*

---

[27] For a full discussion of the composition of *Billy Budd*, see Harrison Hayford
and Merton M. Sealts, Jr., Editors' Introduction to *Billy Budd, Sailor (An Inside
Narrative)* (Univ. of Chicago Press, 1962), 1–24.

[28] See E. L. Grant Watson, 'Melville's Testament of Acceptance', *New England
Quarterly*, 6 (1933), 319–27.

ironic in mode, democratic or anti-authoritarian in theme, and indignant in spirit—a protest against militarism, naval and social tyranny, hidebound traditionalism, and/or patriarchal repression. The adequacy of Captain Vere's character and behaviour became the centre of critical debate, as it has remained, with significant exceptions, ever since.[29] 'Given the situation in the British fleet at the time of the Great Mutiny of 1797, with an engagement with the French always imminent,' as Merton M. Sealts, Jr., describes the issues at stake, 'did Vere act responsibly or precipitously in immediately trying Billy aboard the *Bellipotent*? Was the trial conducted fairly, and were the verdict and the sentence properly arrived at—in terms not only of military necessity but also of law, of justice, and of morality? And where does Melville himself stand with respect to these questions and to their larger ethical and philosophical implications?'[30]

Through the rise and fall of interpretative fashions—humanistic, New Critical, psychoanalytic, Marxist, feminist, deconstructionist, New Historical—these questions have been raised, addressed, and raised again for more than forty years, sometimes with illuminating results, but often with a repetition of old arguments in new or not-so-new vocabularies. The issue has also been joined by commentators outside traditional literary studies, among them psychologists, judges, and professors of philosophy, law, and political science, who bring their special contexts to bear upon the tale. The question of Vere's culpability in Melville's eyes is finally irresolvable, not only because *Billy Budd* is a structural and linguistic hall of mirrors but because the matters it deals with are of vital importance in the extra-textual world, inviting readers to interpret the evidence according to their own philosophical and political commitments. As a result, *Billy Budd* criticism has been unusually passionate and divisive, and since few interpreters make an effort to master the late

[29] For the development of *Billy Budd* criticism, see Robert Milder, *Critical Essays on Melville's 'Billy Budd, Sailor'* (Boston: G. K. Hall, 1989), 1–21.

[30] Merton M. Sealts, Jr., 'Innocence and Infamy: "Billy Budd, Sailor"', in John Bryant (ed.), *A Companion to Melville Studies* (Westport, Conn.: Greenwood, 1986), 409–10.

Melvillean context that might help resolve their disputes, it has frequently been unscholarly and sometimes downright uninformed.

Compounding the difficulties of interpretation is the fact that *Billy Budd*, as an 'unfinished' text, has more than its share of apparent inconsistencies, especially in its presentation of Captain Vere. These may be deliberate—'Truth uncompromisingly told will always have its ragged edges', Melville reminds us—but they may also derive from changes in conception or emphasis that reflect the story's long period of gestation and that render it, as one critic has argued, so internally problematic as to frustrate all efforts at coherent interpretation.[31] The point is a good one, but it neglects Melville's practice in his longer works of passing freely from theme to theme, focus to focus, as his subject opened up to him or as his mood or interests changed. There is no evidence for assuming that, had he lived, Melville would have brought *Billy Budd* to a more conventional aesthetic unity; on the contrary, his late pencil revisions betray an impulse toward greater complication and a more pervasive irony. The absence of thematic unity in the traditional sense, however, does not mean that the unfolding of the narrative is without an internal logic of its own; it simply directs attention to the larger context of Melville's development during the five years of *Billy Budd*'s composition, a development replicated by and large in the sequential thematic emphases of the published text.

In its initial conception and, for the most part, in its published form up to the death of Claggart, *Billy Budd* was and is Melville's retelling of the story of the Fall, with Billy an 'upright barbarian, much such perhaps as Adam presumably might have been ere the urbane Serpent wriggled himself into his company', Claggart a shipboard Satan, and Vere a disciplining God. The parable functions on other levels as well. Psychologically, Billy 'falls' from innocence to experience, simplicity to complexity, childhood to adulthood;

---

[31] Hershel Parker, *Reading 'Billy Budd'* (Evanston, Ill.: Northwestern Univ. Press, 1990), 174.

historically, from primitivism to modern civilization; and sexually, from androgyny—a happy balance of masculine strength and feminine sweetness and beauty—to a more severe maleness consonant with the repressions of patriarchal society. Like Hawthorne's *The Marble Faun*, *Billy Budd* thus reenacts the life history of the socialized individual as well as the history of Western civilization itself—and, since Billy is also reminiscent of Melville's Polynesians, of the imposition of that civilization upon the spontaneous peoples of the non-Western world.

None the less, the controlling context of the early chapters, particularly with the introduction of Claggart, is theological. Though akin to Shakespeare's Iago in his gratuitous malice, Claggart is less a character of human envies and ambitions than a ' "mystery of iniquity" ' explicable (if explicable at all) only through a metaphorical appeal to 'Holy Writ'. Milton's Satan is the chief model for Claggart, who, 'apprehending the good, but powerless to be it', looks upon Billy with the same commingled 'disdain of innocence' and desire for innocence with which Satan looks upon Adam and Eve. Milton spends most of Book III in *Paradise Lost* exonerating his omniscient, omnipotent God from responsibility for Satan's malignity and the impending Fall; Melville, having chafed for more than forty years against the problem of evil, openly lays accountability where he feels it belongs. 'Like the scorpion for which the Creator alone is responsible', he writes, a nature such as Claggart's has no 'recourse . . . but to recoil upon itself' and 'act out to the end the part allotted it'. Good may eventually come from the immediate triumph of evil, traditional apologetics assure us, but no such implication governed the 1888 *Billy Budd*, which, lacking the rhetorically charged execution scene that some readers have interpreted as Melville's Christian acceptance, seems rather an anti-*Paradise Lost* designed to impugn the ways of God to man.

Though never an atheist and certainly not a scoffer, Melville had moved by the 1880s toward a largely naturalistic sense of life, so his theological idiom in *Billy Budd* must be understood as a cultivated indulgence. Melville is not literally arraigning God so much as he is personifying and rhetorically pitting himself against an indifferent and otherwise faceless universe. His seeming blasphemy is the imaginative protest of a religious sensibility against the prospect of cosmic meaninglessness and the indignity of passive endurance. More satisfying to go mad like Ahab and rail against the heavens than to allow that the 'heavens' are merely atmospheric gases and condensations of vapour. If nothing else, to indict God for not being godly enough in ruling Creation was to preserve at least the aura of religion and record one's own indignation at evil whether or not there was anyone above to acknowledge the protest.

Melville never erased the anti-Christian emphasis of the early *Billy Budd*; he simply outlived it. As had happened years earlier with *Moby-Dick*, the very act of registering his anger may have freed him from its emotional grip. Yet catharsis alone cannot explain the new direction his narrative took. Two magazine articles on the *Somers* incident of 1842, the first appearing in the spring of 1888, may have kindled Melville's memories of his cousin Guert Gansevoort, a first lieutenant on the US training brig *Somers* when an acting midshipman and two sailors were hanged for conspiracy,[32] and prompted Melville to brood on questions of justice and authority. Whatever the reason, Melville returned to his manuscript and began to address the thinly drawn figure of Vere, carrying the action forward beyond Claggart's death while leaving the focus of existing chapters substantially untouched. Claggart with his violet eyes and Billy with his welkin-blue had been less—or more—than roundly human characters, but with Claggart's death the fall and its attendant interests became a given and the story descended to the naturalistic universe of grey-eyed Vere in which moral and political questions needed to be resolved in post-lapsarian terms against 'the monotonous blank of the twilight sea'.

[32] For a discussion of the *Somers* incidents, see the note to p. 345 in the Explanatory Notes to *Billy Budd*.

It was the tragedy of governance—a new subject for him—
that absorbed Melville now and drew him outward beyond
his quarrel with the universe, first toward the political world,
then toward the psyche, with a humaneness and breadth of
comprehension approached only in *Clarel*. The long trial scene
in Chapter 21 is a masterpiece of studied ambiguity, with
Vere from one perspective an anguished but duty-bound
representative of the political state, from another a myopic
conservative whose narrow and exacting application of a
wartime code tyrannical in itself is a double indictment of a
martial society that sacrifices justice to expediency and de-
humanizes even its most conscientious men. That both readings are not merely justified but demanded by the text is
a sign that Melville is requiring of his audience something
more than an ideological choosing of sides or a painless
literary tolerance of alternatives. Convinced of the need for
social bulwarks against nature's chaos—Vere's 'forms, measured forms'—Melville knew that any particular forms were
likely to be flawed in theory, formulaic in their institutional
embodiment, and imperfect (sometimes brutally so) in their
application. He also knew that forms had to be administered
by human beings enmeshed in events and compromised
both by the preoccupations of their age and by their private
tendencies, limitations, passions, and interests. It is difficult
enough holding in mind and crediting two opposing sides of
a question; in *Billy Budd* Melville presents a circumstanced
'case' with more perspectives on it—and attitudes toward
it—than a mortal consciousness can easily bear, and he challenges us to rise to it as a representation of tragic experience in its irreducible and overwhelming truth.

Manuscript evidence suggests that Melville composed a
good part of the trial and execution scenes before he inter-
polated the character analysis of Chapters 6 and 7 that establishes Vere as a Burkean conservative of a peculiarly inward
sort—bookish, prone to dreamy gazing 'at the blank sea' (as
Bartleby gazes at blank walls), and touched with ' "a queer
streak of the pedantic" '. Melville's political themes were in
place, that is to say, before he shifted his narrative from
an abstract consideration of justice and law to a study of

fallible men living and acting in time. Just as Melville's parable of the Fall led him to questions of governance in the fallen world, so his exploration of public judgement shaded naturally into a concern with its psychosocial roots in the character of the judges. The contrast between Vere—a man of 'sterling qualities' but 'without any brilliant ones'—and the magnanimous Admiral Nelson, who could transcend the statute book and rule a crew 'by force of his mere presence and heroic personality', raises the possibility that the death of Billy might have resulted as much from the idiosyncrasies of Vere's nature as from the supposed necessity of the situation. Even more suggestive is the testimony of the ship's surgeon, who not only feels that the case should be referred to the fleet admiral but privately surmises that Vere may be mad. In his late revisions of the manuscript Melville enlarged the role of the surgeon, undercutting the authority of Vere's judgement and subtly redirecting the interest of the story from politics to character, or to politics as they are *shaped* by character.

After an initial movement upward from dramatic monologue to theological myth, *Billy Budd*, during its years of composition, travelled progressively downward toward the particularized world of human action, which it addressed with a combined pathos and irony that few of its commentators have managed to keep equally in sight. Novelists commonly speak of their characters escaping the roles imagined for them and leading their creators onward; in *Billy Budd* Melville seems genuinely to be responding to the latent possibilities of his story and, toward the end, to the forward pull of Vere and Billy themselves. Thus, with the conclusion of Billy's trial the focus of the narrative shifts again as issues of justice and political morality give way to the purely human spectacle of two men confronting tragedy with generosity and strength. The Vere who had argued for coolness during the trial scene is 'melt[ed] back into what remains primeval in our formalized humanity' and softened by the weight of a judgement made conscientiously and with full awareness of tragic sacrifice, disastrously wrong as it may be. Billy's role—to feel Vere's pain more than his own—is

greater still, but his growth is made visible only at the
last when, 'spiritualized now through late experiences so
poignantly profound', he becomes, not a symbol of Christ,
but an example of humanity's Christlike capacity for self-
transfiguration.

Has Melville in his last years reconciled himself to God
and society? We cannot finally know. The answer depends
partly on how one takes the Christian symbolism of the
hanging scene and responds to Billy's last words, 'God bless
Captain Vere!' Are we meant to feel a visceral rage at the
miscarriage of justice or a faith that the wrongs of tem-
poral experience will be more than sufficiently redressed in
eternity? The 'soft glory' that 'chanced' to illuminate 'the
vapory fleece hanging low in the East' may or may not be
the sign of some ultimate Providential watchfulness, and
therefore of Melville's near-deathbed affirmation of belief.
What is clear, in any case, is that the Divine (if it exists)
does not interpose itself in the sublunary world of affairs,
as Billy's 'pinioned figure' sways lifelessly in the 'slow roll' of
a 'great ship ponderously cannoned'. Although consecrated
with the metaphor of 'ascension', Billy's triumph is essentially personal—a glory he achieves in his lifetime through
moral growth and generosity of spirit rather than a gift
bestowed on him posthumously by a merciful God.

In the end, *Billy Budd* does not seem a justification of
God's ways or the ways of the state, but neither is it the
embittered protest some have taken it to be. As a mood of
hushed contemplation descends upon the scene of Billy's
death, we are made to marvel at the timeless heroism of
human beings trapped by circumstances and swayed by the
imperatives of their nature yet capable toward the last of
extraordinary gestures of magnanimity. It hardly matters that
self-serving officialdom will garble Billy's story or the crew
superstitiously fashion a cult of Billy-as-Christ from a nobility it is theirs to imitate. Such will always be the world's
judgements, Melville implies. The value of 'an inside narrative' is that it presents a truth beyond crude appearances,
and though that 'truth' may only be one of the author's creation, it is for precisely that reason a testament to his own

moral nature and his feeling for the possibilities of life. The most an angry, wounded Melville could imagine in the mid-1850s was the pathos of his lawyer-narrator's 'Ah, Bartleby! Ah, humanity!' Like Shakespeare's late romances, *Billy Budd* looks beyond pathos—and beyond tragedy itself—to the redemption human beings may win for themselves. Without accommodating himself to God or society, Melville has come to feel that the spiritual is no less exalted for being located entirely within the human soul and going unrecognized by the world. In this respect, *Billy Budd* is Melville's epitaph for his 45-year career, an outward failure if judged by sales or critical reputation but a record of continuous striving. Melville has not, in *Billy Budd*, relaxed his quarrels with the universe and human institutions, but he does seem to have arrived at an assurance of self-worth and, thereby, at a qualified peace.

NOTE ON THE TEXTS

THE text of the eight short stories included in this volume is the critical text established by Harrison Hayford, Alma A. MacDougall, G. Thomas Tanselle, and others, the editors of *The Piazza Tales and Other Prose Pieces 1839–1860* (Evanston and Chicago: Northwestern Univ. Press and The Newberry Library, 1987). Four of the stories originally appeared in *Harper's New Monthly Magazine*, four in *Putnam's Monthly Magazine*. In the absence of extant manuscripts and later printings supervised by Melville, the *Harper's* texts are authoritative aside from occasional minor errors corrected by the Northwestern–Newberry editors. With the exception of 'I and My Chimney', however, the *Putnam's* stories were revised by Melville for publication in *The Piazza Tales* (1856), with significant additions, deletions, and alterations; in-house editors at Melville's publisher, Dix and Edwards, also made changes of punctuation that Melville is on record as opposing. The Northwestern–Newberry critical text tries to distinguish Melville's alterations from those of his publisher and thus to produce a text closer to the author's final intentions than any actual printed text. All scholarly writing on Melville uses the Northwestern–Newberry text as a matter of course.

Unpublished at Melville's death, *Billy Budd, Sailor* was edited by Raymond Weaver in 1924 for the Constable Edition of Melville's *Complete Works* and again by Weaver, with variations, for *The Shorter Novels of Herman Melville* (New York: Horace Liveright) in 1928. Drawing upon Weaver's second edition but interpreting its materials in a different fashion, F. Barron Freeman produced a third version, *Melville's Billy Budd* (Cambridge, Mass.: Harvard Univ. Press) in 1948. In 1962 Harrison Hayford and Merton M. Sealts, Jr., carefully re-examined the manuscript evidence and published what has since become the standard text of *Billy Budd, Sailor: An Inside Narrative* (University of Chicago Press),

reprinted in this volume. The forthcoming Northwestern–
Newberry edition of *Billy Budd* is expected to follow the
Hayford–Sealts text on substantive matters while adopting
a somewhat more conservative policy toward regularizing
Melville's spelling and punctuation.

SELECT BIBLIOGRAPHY

THE definitive biography of Melville up to the publication of *Moby-Dick* is Hershel Parker's *Herman Melville: A Biography, Volume I, 1819–1851* (volume II is in progress), which includes vast quantities of information not available to earlier biographers Leon Howard (*Herman Melville*, Berkeley: Univ. of California Press, 1951) and Edwin Haviland Miller (*Melville*, New York: George Braziller, 1975). Also useful, though by no means as exhaustive or scrupulously accurate as Parker's book, is Laurie Robertson-Lorant's *Melville* (New York: Clarkson Potter, 1996). Jay Leyda's documentary *Melville Log*, due to be updated, is a convenient sourcebook for some of the major events of Melville's life. Other valuable resources include the Northwestern–Newberry edition of Melville's *Correspondence* (ed. Lynn Horth, 1993) and Merton M. Sealts, Jr.'s *Melville's Reading* (Columbia: Univ. of South Carolina Press, rev. edn. 1988).

Criticism of Melville abounds, but the most insightful general study of Melville the writer—and the best overview of his career—is Warner Berthoff's *The Example of Melville* (Princeton Univ. Press, 1962). Scholarship and criticism of the short stories should begin with Sealts's Historical Note to the Northwestern–Newberry edition of *The Piazza Tales and Other Prose Pieces 1839–1860* (1987). Until the publication of the Northwestern–Newberry edition of *Billy Budd, Sailor*, the starting-point for interpretation of the story is the Introduction and the Notes and Commentary to the Chicago text edited by Harrison Hayford and Sealts (University of Chicago Press, 1962), which also includes an extensive bibliography up to early 1962. For more recent criticism of *Billy Budd* and the stories, readers should consult the Melville chapter in *American Literary Scholarship: An Annual* (1963–), a descriptive review of the year's work.

Short Stories

Bergmann, Johannes D., 'Melville's Tales', in John Bryant (ed.), *A Companion to Melville Studies* (Westport, Conn.: Greenwood, 1986), 241–78.

Burkholder, Robert E., *Critical Essays on Melville's 'Benito Cereno'* (Boston: G. K. Hall, 1992).

Dillingham, William B., *Melville's Short Fiction 1853–1856* (Athens: Univ. of Georgia Press, 1977).

Emery, Allan Moore, 'The Cocks of Melville's "Cock-A-Doodle-Doo!"', *ESQ: A Journal of the American Renaissance*, 28 (1982), 89–111.
—— 'The Political Significance of Melville's Chimney', *New England Quarterly*, 55 (1982), 201–28.
—— 'Melville on Science: "The Lightning-Rod Man"', *New England Quarterly*, 56 (1983), 555–68.
—— 'The Topicality of Depravity in "Benito Cereno"', *American Literature*, 55 (1983), 316–31.
Fisher, Marvin, *Going Under: Melville's Short Fiction and the American 1850s* (Baton Rouge: Louisiana State Univ. Press, 1977).
Fogle, Richard Harter, *Melville's Shorter Tales* (Norman: Univ. of Oklahoma Press, 1960).
Inge, M. Thomas (ed.), *Bartleby the Inscrutable: A Collection of Commentary on Herman Melville's Tale 'Bartleby the Scrivener'* (Hamden, Conn.: Archon, 1979).
Karcher, Carolyn L., *Shadow over the Promised Land: Slavery, Race, and Violence in Melville's America* (Baton Rouge: Louisiana State Univ. Press, 1980).
Leavis, Q. D., 'Melville: The 1853–56 Phase', in Faith Pullin (ed.), *New Perspectives on Melville* (Kent, Ohio and Edinburgh: Kent State Univ. Press and Edinburgh Univ. Press, 1978).
Levine, Robert S., *Conspiracy and Romance* (Cambridge Univ. Press, 1989) (on 'Benito Cereno').
McCall, Dan, *The Silence of Bartleby* (Ithaca, NY: Cornell Univ. Press, 1989).
Marx, Leo, 'Melville's Parable of the Walls', *Sewanee Review*, 61 (1953), 602–27.
Newman, Lea Bertani Vozar, *A Reader's Guide to the Short Stories of Herman Melville* (Boston: G. K. Hall, 1986).
Parker, Hershel, *Herman Melville: A Biography*, 2 vols.; i: *1819–1851* (Baltimore: Johns Hopkins Univ. Press, 1996). Volume ii forthcoming.
Sattelmeyer, Robert, and Barbour, James, 'The Sources and Genesis of Melville's Norfolk Isle and the Chola Widow', *American Literature*, 50 (1978), 398–417.
Sealts, Merton M., Jr., 'Herman Melville's "I and My Chimney"', in *Pursuing Melville 1940–1980* (Madison: Univ. of Wisconsin Press, 1982), 11–22.
—— 'Historical Note' to Melville, *The Piazza Tales and Other Prose Pieces 1839–1860*, ed. Harrison Hayford *et al.* (Evanston and Chicago: Northwestern Univ. Press and The Newberry Library, 1987), 476–514.

Stern, Milton R., 'Towards "Bartleby the Scrivener"', in Duane
    MacMillan (ed.), *The Stoic Strain in American Literature* (Univ.
    of Toronto Press, 1979), 19–41.
Sundquist, Eric J., *To Wake the Nations* (Cambridge, Mass.:
    Harvard Univ. Press, 1993), 135–221 (on 'Benito Cereno').

Billy Budd

Adler, Joyce Sparer, *War in Melville's Imagination* (New York Univ.
    Press, 1981).
Milder, Robert (ed.), *Critical Essays on Melville's 'Billy Budd, Sailor'*
    (Boston: G. K. Hall, 1989) (reprints essays by Fogle, Berthoff,
    Brodtkorb, Stern, Adler, Johnson, Thomas, and others).
Parker, Hershel, *Reading 'Billy Budd'* (Evanston, Ill.: Northwestern
    Univ. Press, 1990).
Rogin, Michael Paul, *Subversive Genealogy: The Politics and Art of
    Herman Melville* (New York: Knopf, 1983).
Scorza, Thomas J., *In the Time Before Steamships* (DeKalb, Ill.:
    Northern Illinois Univ. Press, 1979).
Sealts, Merton M., Jr., 'Innocence and Infamy: "Billy Budd,
    Sailor"', in John Bryant (ed.), *A Companion to Melville Studies*
    (Westport, Conn.: Greenwood, 1986), 407–30.
Stern, Milton R., Introduction to *Billy Budd, Sailor* (Indianapolis:
    Bobbs-Merrill, 1975), pp. vii–xliv.

A CHRONOLOGY OF
HERMAN MELVILLE

1819   Born 1 August in New York City, third child of Allan
        Melvill (*sic*), a well-to-do importer, and Maria Gansevoort
        Melvill, each descended from prominent Revolutionary
        War forebears.

1830   Allan Melvill goes bankrupt, moves his family to Albany,
        New York, establishes a fur business.

1831   Allan Melvill dies (January).

1830–8 Melville attends Albany Academy, Albany Classical School,
        and Lansingburgh Academy but is periodically withdrawn
        from school to help support the family.

1839   Sails to Liverpool and back on the merchant ship *St
        Lawrence*.

1841   Unable to find employment ashore, leaves for the Pacific
        on the New England whaler *Acushnet*; visits the Galapagos
        Islands.

1842   Melville and a companion desert ship on the island of
        Nukahiva in the Marquesas; they find their way across
        the mountain into an interior valley and spend nearly
        four weeks among the tribe of Typees; Melville leaves or
        escapes on the whale-ship *Lucy Ann*.

1842–4 Serves aboard the whalers *Lucy Ann* and *Charles and Henry*;
        works at various jobs in Honolulu; signs on as an ordin-
        ary seaman on the naval frigate *United States*; discharged
        from the US Navy October 1844 and returns to the fam-
        ily home in Lansingburgh, near Albany, New York.

1845   Writes *Typee*, a fictionalized account of his residence in
        the Marquesas; successfully places the manuscript with
        British publisher John Murray.

1846   *Typee* published in London as *A Narrative of a Four
        Months' Residence among the Natives of a Valley of the
        Marquesas Islands* and in New York as *Typee; A Peep at
        Polynesian Life*. Book is favourably received and becomes
        a popular success, though criticism of its treatment of mis-
        sionaries causes Melville to offer a revised edition later in
        the year.

1847   Publishes *Omoo*, based on his experiences in the Society Islands. Marries Elizabeth Shaw, daughter of Lemuel Shaw, Chief Justice of the Supreme Court of Massachusetts and a Melvill family friend; resides with his wife and newly married brother, Allan, in New York City; enters into the literary life of New York, especially the Young America circle of editor/critic Evert Duyckinck.

1849   Publishes *Mardi*, a philosophical romance set in a mythical Polynesian archipelago; book is poorly received but essential to his growth as a writer. Birth of his first son, Malcolm. Writes and publishes *Redburn*, based on his 1839 voyage to Liverpool; completes *White-Jacket*, an account of life aboard a man-of-war. Sets sail for England (October) to negotiate for the British publication of the book; also visits the Continent; sails home to New York (December).

1850   Publishes *White-Jacket*. During a summer visit to the Berkshire Mountains in western Massachusetts, meets Nathaniel Hawthorne, reads Hawthorne's *Mosses from an Old Manse*, and writes his review-essay 'Hawthorne and His Mosses'. With help from his father-in-law, purchases a farm (Arrowhead) in Pittsfield, Mass., a few miles distant from Hawthorne's residence in Lenox; friendship with Hawthorne flourishes until Hawthorne leaves the Berkshires in the autumn of 1851.

1851   Publishes *Moby-Dick* to mixed reviews and disappointing sales. Second son, Stanwix, is born.

1852   Publishes *Pierre*; book is scathingly reviewed, seriously impairing his career as a novelist. Visits Nantucket Island with Judge Shaw; hears the story of islander Agatha Hatch Robertson; suggests to Hawthorne that he (Hawthorne) fictionalize the Agatha material. Presumably writes the Agatha story himself under the title *The Isle of the Cross*; work is not accepted by Harper's; no manuscript survives.

1853   Unsuccessfully pursues a consular appointment under newly elected President Franklin Pierce. Daughter Elizabeth born. Submits first stories to *Harper's* and *Putnam's* magazines.

1854   Continues to publish stories in *Harper's* and *Putnam's*; *Israel Potter*, a historical novel, begins its serialization in *Putnam's*.

1855   *Israel Potter* published in book form. Daughter Frances born.

1856   Publishes *The Piazza Tales*, which includes five of the *Putnam's* stories, along with a preface, 'The Piazza'. Writes his last completed novel, *The Confidence-Man*. Departs for Europe and the Holy Land on a journey funded by Judge Shaw; visits Hawthorne in Liverpool.

1857   Sails for America in May after seeing Hawthorne once again. Publishes *The Confidence-Man*, which receives little notice and brings in no royalties.

1857–60   Lectures with very modest success, primarily in the Midwest; begins to write poetry.

1863   Moves from Pittsfield to New York City, where he will reside for the remainder of his life.

1866   Publishes *Battle-Pieces and Aspects of the War*, a volume of poems chronicling events from the hanging of abolitionist John Brown in 1859 to the end of the Civil War and the assassination of President Lincoln in 1865. Assumes duties as Inspector of Customs at the Port of New York, a position he will hold until 1885.

1867   Son Malcolm, 18 years old, dies of a self-inflicted pistol wound.

1876   Publishes *Clarel*, a long narrative and philosophical poem about a group of contemporary pilgrims in the Holy Land.

1885   Resigns his post in the New York Customs House.

1886(?)   Begins *Billy Budd*.

1888   Privately publishes *John Marr and Other Sailors* (poems).

1891   Privately publishes *Timoleon* (poems). Dies 28 September, leaving two manuscripts in a nearly completed state, *Billy Budd* and *Weeds and Wildings* (poems).

1924   *Billy Budd* edited and published by Raymond Weaver.

1962   *Billy Budd, Sailor (An Inside Narrative)* assembled afresh from the manuscript leaves by Harrison Hayford and Merton M. Sealts, Jr., and published by the University of Chicago.

BILLY BUDD, SAILOR

AND

SELECTED TALES

BARTLEBY, THE SCRIVENER
A Story of Wall-Street*

I AM a rather elderly man. The nature of my avocations
for the last thirty years has brought me into more than ordinary contact with what would seem an interesting and somewhat singular set of men, of whom as yet nothing that I
know of has ever been written:—I mean the law-copyists or
scriveners. I have known very many of them, professionally
and privately, and if I pleased, could relate divers histories,
at which good-natured gentlemen might smile, and sentimental souls might weep. But I waive the biographies of all
other scriveners for a few passages in the life of Bartleby,
who was a scrivener the strangest I ever saw or heard of.
While of other law-copyists I might write the complete life,
of Bartleby nothing of that sort can be done. I believe that
no materials exist for a full and satisfactory biography of this
man. It is an irreparable loss to literature. Bartleby was one
of those beings of whom nothing is ascertainable, except from
the original sources, and in his case those are very small.
What my own astonished eyes saw of Bartleby, *that* is all I
know of him, except, indeed, one vague report which will
appear in the sequel.

Ere introducing the scrivener, as he first appeared to me,
it is fit I make some mention of myself, my *employés*, my
business, my chambers, and general surroundings; because
some such description is indispensable to an adequate understanding of the chief character about to be presented.

Imprimis: I am a man who, from his youth upwards, has
been filled with a profound conviction that the easiest way
of life is the best. Hence, though I belong to a profession
proverbially energetic and nervous, even to turbulence, at
times, yet nothing of that sort have I ever suffered to invade
my peace. I am one of those unambitious lawyers who never
addresses a jury, or in any way draws down public applause;
but in the cool tranquillity of a snug retreat, do a snug

business among rich men's bonds and mortgages and title-deeds. All who know me, consider me an eminently *safe* man. The late John Jacob Astor,* a personage little given to poetic enthusiasm, had no hesitation in pronouncing my first grand point to be prudence; my next, method. I do not speak it in vanity, but simply record the fact, that I was not unemployed in my profession by the late John Jacob Astor; a name which, I admit, I love to repeat, for it hath a rounded and orbicular sound to it, and rings like unto bullion. I will freely add, that I was not insensible to the late John Jacob Astor's good opinion.

Some time prior to the period at which this little history begins, my avocations had been largely increased. The good old office, now extinct in the State of New-York, of a Master in Chancery,* had been conferred upon me. It was not a very arduous office, but very pleasantly remunerative. I seldom lose my temper; much more seldom indulge in dangerous indignation at wrongs and outrages; but I must be permitted to be rash here and declare, that I consider the sudden and violent abrogation of the office of Master in Chancery, by the new Constitution, as a — premature act; inasmuch as I had counted upon a life-lease of the profits, whereas I only received those of a few short years. But this is by the way.

My chambers were up stairs at No. — Wall-street. At one end they looked upon the white wall of the interior of a spacious sky-light shaft, penetrating the building from top to bottom. This view might have been considered rather tame than otherwise, deficient in what landscape painters call "life." But if so, the view from the other end of my chambers offered, at least, a contrast, if nothing more. In that direction my windows commanded an unobstructed view of a lofty brick wall, black by age and everlasting shade; which wall required no spy-glass to bring out its lurking beauties, but for the benefit of all near-sighted spectators, was pushed up to within ten feet of my window panes. Owing to the great height of the surrounding buildings, and my chambers being on the second floor, the interval between this wall and mine not a little resembled a huge square cistern.

At the period just preceding the advent of Bartleby, I had two persons as copyists in my employment, and a promising lad as an office-boy. First, Turkey; second, Nippers; third, Ginger Nut.* These may seem names, the like of which are not usually found in the Directory. In truth they were nicknames, mutually conferred upon each other by my three clerks, and were deemed expressive of their respective persons or characters. Turkey was a short, pursy Englishman of about my own age, that is, somewhere not far from sixty. In the morning, one might say, his face was of a fine florid hue, but after twelve o'clock, meridian—his dinner hour—it blazed like a grate full of Christmas coals; and continued blazing—but, as it were, with a gradual wane—till 6 o'clock, P.M. or thereabouts, after which I saw no more of the proprietor of the face, which gaining its meridian with the sun, seemed to set with it, to rise, culminate, and decline the following day, with the like regularity and undiminished glory. There are many singular coincidences I have known in the course of my life, not the least among which was the fact, that exactly when Turkey displayed his fullest beams from his red and radiant countenance, just then, too, at that critical moment, began the daily period when I considered his business capacities as seriously disturbed for the remainder of the twenty-four hours. Not that he was absolutely idle, or averse to business then; far from it. The difficulty was, he was apt to be altogether too energetic. There was a strange, inflamed, flurried, flighty recklessness of activity about him. He would be incautious in dipping his pen into his inkstand. All his blots upon my documents, were dropped there after twelve o'clock, meridian. Indeed, not only would he be reckless and sadly given to making blots in the afternoon, but some days he went further, and was rather noisy. At such times, too, his face flamed with augmented blazonry, as if cannel coal had been heaped on anthracite. He made an unpleasant racket with his chair; spilled his sand-box; in mending his pens, impatiently split them all to pieces, and threw them on the floor in a sudden passion; stood up and leaned over his table, boxing his papers about in a most indecorous manner, very sad to behold in an elderly man like him. Nevertheless, as he was in many ways a most valuable person to me, and all the time before twelve o'clock, meridian, was the quickest, steadiest creature too, accomplishing a great deal of work in a style not easy to be matched—for these reasons, I was willing to overlook his eccentricities, though indeed, occasionally, I remonstrated with him. I did this very gently, however, because, though the civilest, nay, the blandest and most reverential of men in the morning, yet in the afternoon he was disposed, upon provocation, to be slightly rash with his tongue, in fact, insolent. Now, valuing his morning services as I did, and resolved not to lose them; yet, at the same time made uncomfortable by his inflamed ways after twelve o'clock; and being a man of peace, unwilling by my admonitions to call forth unseemly retorts from him; I took upon me, one Saturday noon (he was always worse on Saturdays), to hint to him, very kindly, that perhaps now that he was growing old, it might be well to abridge his labors; in short, he need not come to my chambers after twelve o'clock, but, dinner over, had best go home to his lodgings and rest himself till tea-time. But no; he insisted upon his afternoon devotions. His countenance became intolerably fervid, as he oratorically assured me—gesticulating with a long ruler at the other end of the room—that if his services in the morning were useful, how indispensable, then, in the afternoon?

"With submission, sir," said Turkey on this occasion, "I consider myself your right-hand man. In the morning I but marshal and deploy my columns; but in the afternoon I put myself at their head, and gallantly charge the foe, thus!"— and he made a violent thrust with the ruler.

"But the blots, Turkey," intimated I.

"True,—but, with submission, sir, behold these hairs! I am getting old. Surely, sir, a blot or two of a warm afternoon is not to be severely urged against gray hairs. Old age —even if it blot the page—is honorable. With submission, sir, we *both* are getting old."

This appeal to my fellow-feeling was hardly to be resisted. At all events, I saw that go he would not. So I made up my mind to let him stay, resolving, nevertheless, to see to it, that during the afternoon he had to do with my less important papers.

Nippers, the second on my list, was a whiskered, sallow, and, upon the whole, rather piratical-looking young man of about five and twenty. I always deemed him the victim of two evil powers—ambition and indigestion. The ambition was evinced by a certain impatience of the duties of a mere copyist, an unwarrantable usurpation of strictly professional affairs, such as the original drawing up of legal documents. The indigestion seemed betokened in an occasional nervous testiness and grinning irritability, causing the teeth to audibly grind together over mistakes committed in copying; unnecessary maledictions, hissed, rather than spoken, in the heat of business; and especially by a continual discontent with the height of the table where he worked. Though of a very ingenious mechanical turn, Nippers could never get this table to suit him. He put chips under it, blocks of various sorts, bits of pasteboard, and at last went so far as to attempt an exquisite adjustment by final pieces of folded blotting-paper. But no invention would answer. If, for the sake of easing his back, he brought the table lid at a sharp angle well up towards his chin, and wrote there like a man using the steep roof of a Dutch house for his desk:—then he declared that it stopped the circulation in his arms. If now he lowered the table to his waistbands, and stooped over it in writing, then there was a sore aching in his back. In short, the truth of the matter was, Nippers knew not what he wanted. Or, if he wanted any thing, it was to be rid of a scrivener's table altogether. Among the manifestations of his diseased ambition was a fondness he had for receiving visits from certain ambiguous-looking fellows in seedy coats, whom he called his clients. Indeed I was aware that not only was he, at times, considerable of a ward-politician, but he occasionally did a little business at the Justices' courts, and was not unknown on the steps of the Tombs.* I have good reason to believe, however, that one individual who called upon him at my chambers, and who, with a grand air, he insisted was his client, was no other than a dun, and the alleged title-deed, a bill. But with all his failings, and the annoyances he caused me, Nippers, like his compatriot Turkey, was a very useful man to me; wrote a neat, swift hand; and, when he chose, was not deficient in a gentlemanly sort of deportment. Added to this, he always dressed in a gentlemanly sort of way; and so, incidentally, reflected credit upon my chambers. Whereas with respect to Turkey, I had much ado to keep him from being a reproach to me. His clothes were apt to look oily and smell of eating-houses. He wore his pantaloons very loose and baggy in summer. His coats were execrable; his hat not to be handled. But while the hat was a thing of indifference to me, inasmuch as his natural civility and deference, as a dependent Englishman, always led him to doff it the moment he entered the room, yet his coat was another matter. Concerning his coats, I reasoned with him; but with no effect. The truth was, I suppose, that a man with so small an income, could not afford to sport such a lustrous face and a lustrous coat at one and the same time. As Nippers once observed, Turkey's money went chiefly for red ink.* One winter day I presented Turkey with a highly-respectable looking coat of my own, a padded gray coat, of a most comfortable warmth, and which buttoned straight up from the knee to the neck. I thought Turkey would appreciate the favor, and abate his rashness and obstreperousness of afternoons. But no. I verily believe that buttoning himself up in so downy and blanket-like a coat had a pernicious effect upon him; upon the same principle that too much oats are bad for horses. In fact, precisely as a rash, restive horse is said to feel his oats, so Turkey felt his coat. It made him insolent. He was a man whom prosperity harmed.

Though concerning the self-indulgent habits of Turkey I had my own private surmises, yet touching Nippers I was well persuaded that whatever might be his faults in other respects, he was, at least, a temperate young man. But indeed, nature herself seemed to have been his vintner, and at his birth charged him so thoroughly with an irritable, brandy-like disposition, that all subsequent potations were needless. When I consider how, amid the stillness of my chambers, Nippers would sometimes impatiently rise from his seat, and stooping over his table, spread his arms wide apart, seize the whole desk, and move it, and jerk it, with a grim, grinding motion on the floor, as if the table were a perverse voluntary agent, intent on thwarting and vexing him; I plainly perceive that for Nippers, brandy and water were altogether superfluous.

It was fortunate for me that, owing to its peculiar cause— indigestion—the irritability and consequent nervousness of Nippers, were mainly observable in the morning, while in the afternoon he was comparatively mild. So that Turkey's paroxysms only coming on about twelve o'clock, I never had to do with their eccentricities at one time. Their fits relieved each other like guards. When Nippers' was on, Turkey's was off; and *vice versa*. This was a good natural arrangement under the circumstances.

Ginger Nut, the third on my list, was a lad some twelve years old. His father was a carman, ambitious of seeing his son on the bench instead of a cart, before he died. So he sent him to my office as student at law, errand boy, and cleaner and sweeper, at the rate of one dollar a week. He had a little desk to himself, but he did not use it much. Upon inspection, the drawer exhibited a great array of the shells of various sorts of nuts. Indeed, to this quick-witted youth the whole noble science of the law was contained in a nut-shell. Not the least among the employments of Ginger Nut, as well as one which he discharged with the most alac- rity, was his duty as cake and apple purveyor for Turkey and Nippers. Copying law papers being proverbially a dry, husky sort of business, my two scriveners were fain to moisten their mouths very often with Spitzenbergs* to be had at the numerous stalls nigh the Custom House and Post Office. Also, they sent Ginger Nut very frequently for that peculiar cake—small, flat, round, and very spicy—after which he had been named by them. Of a cold morning when business was but dull, Turkey would gobble up scores of these cakes, as if they were mere wafers—indeed they sell them at the rate of six or eight for a penny—the scrape of his pen blending with the crunching of the crisp particles in his mouth. Of all the fiery afternoon blunders and flurried rashnesses of

Turkey, was his once moistening a ginger-cake between his lips, and clapping it on to a mortgage for a seal. I came within an ace of dismissing him then. But he mollified me by making an oriental bow, and saying—"With submission, sir, it was generous of me to find you in stationery on my own account."

Now my original business—that of a conveyancer and title hunter, and drawer-up of recondite documents of all sorts— was considerably increased by receiving the master's office. There was now great work for scriveners. Not only must I push the clerks already with me, but I must have additional help. In answer to my advertisement, a motionless young man one morning, stood upon my office threshold, the door being open, for it was summer. I can see that figure now— pallidly neat, pitiably respectable, incurably forlorn! It was Bartleby.*

After a few words touching his qualifications, I engaged him, glad to have among my corps of copyists a man of so singularly sedate an aspect, which I thought might operate beneficially upon the flighty temper of Turkey, and the fiery one of Nippers.

I should have stated before that ground glass folding-doors divided my premises into two parts, one of which was occupied by my scriveners, the other by myself. According to my humor I threw open these doors, or closed them. I resolved to assign Bartleby a corner by the folding-doors, but on my side of them, so as to have this quiet man within easy call, in case any trifling thing was to be done. I placed his desk close up to a small side-window in that part of the room, a window which originally had afforded a lateral view of certain grimy back-yards and bricks, but which, owing to subsequent erections, commanded at present no view at all, though it gave some light. Within three feet of the panes was a wall, and the light came down from far above, between two lofty buildings, as from a very small opening in a dome. Still further to a satisfactory arrangement, I procured a high green folding screen, which might entirely isolate Bartleby from my sight, though not remove him from my voice. And thus, in a manner, privacy and society were conjoined.

At first Bartleby did an extraordinary quantity of writing. As if long famishing for something to copy, he seemed to gorge himself on my documents. There was no pause for digestion. He ran a day and night line, copying by sun-light and by candle-light. I should have been quite delighted with his application, had he been cheerfully industrious. But he wrote on silently, palely, mechanically.

It is, of course, an indispensable part of a scrivener's business to verify the accuracy of his copy, word by word. Where there are two or more scriveners in an office, they assist each other in this examination, one reading from the copy, the other holding the original. It is a very dull, wearisome, and lethargic affair. I can readily imagine that to some sanguine temperaments* it would be altogether intolerable. For example, I cannot credit that the mettlesome poet Byron* would have contentedly sat down with Bartleby to examine a law document of, say five hundred pages, closely written in a crimpy hand.

Now and then, in the haste of business, it had been my habit to assist in comparing some brief document myself, calling Turkey or Nippers for this purpose. One object I had in placing Bartleby so handy to me behind the screen, was to avail myself of his services on such trivial occasions. It was on the third day, I think, of his being with me, and before any necessity had arisen for having his own writing examined, that, being much hurried to complete a small affair I had in hand, I abruptly called to Bartleby. In my haste and natural expectancy of instant compliance, I sat with my head bent over the original on my desk, and my right hand sideways, and somewhat nervously extended with the copy, so that immediately upon emerging from his retreat, Bartleby might snatch it and proceed to business without the least delay.

In this very attitude did I sit when I called to him, rapidly stating what it was I wanted him to do—namely, to examine a small paper with me. Imagine my surprise, nay, my consternation, when without moving from his privacy, Bartleby in a singularly mild, firm voice, replied, "I would prefer not to."

I sat awhile in perfect silence, rallying my stunned faculties. Immediately it occurred to me that my ears had deceived me, or Bartleby had entirely misunderstood my meaning. I repeated my request in the clearest tone I could assume. But in quite as clear a one came the previous reply, "I would prefer not to."

"Prefer not to," echoed I, rising in high excitement, and crossing the room with a stride. "What do you mean? Are you moon-struck? I want you to help me compare this sheet here—take it," and I thrust it towards him.

"I would prefer not to," said he.

I looked at him steadfastly. His face was leanly composed; his gray eye dimly calm. Not a wrinkle of agitation rippled him. Had there been the least uneasiness, anger, impatience or impertinence in his manner; in other words, had there been any thing ordinarily human about him, doubtless I should have violently dismissed him from the premises. But as it was, I should have as soon thought of turning my pale plaster-of-paris bust of Cicero* out of doors. I stood gazing at him awhile, as he went on with his own writing, and then reseated myself at my desk. This is very strange, thought I. What had one best do? But my business hurried me. I concluded to forget the matter for the present, reserving it for my future leisure. So calling Nippers from the other room, the paper was speedily examined.

A few days after this, Bartleby concluded four lengthy documents, being quadruplicates of a week's testimony taken before me in my High Court of Chancery. It became necessary to examine them. It was an important suit, and great accuracy was imperative. Having all things arranged I called Turkey, Nippers and Ginger Nut from the next room, meaning to place the four copies in the hands of my four clerks, while I should read from the original. Accordingly Turkey, Nippers and Ginger Nut had taken their seats in a row, each with his document in hand, when I called to Bartleby to join this interesting group.

"Bartleby! quick, I am waiting."

I heard a slow scrape of his chair legs on the uncarpeted floor, and soon he appeared standing at the entrance of his hermitage.

"What is wanted?" said he mildly.

"The copies, the copies," said I hurriedly. "We are going to examine them. There"—and I held towards him the fourth quadruplicate.

"I would prefer not to," he said, and gently disappeared behind the screen.

For a few moments I was turned into a pillar of salt,* standing at the head of my seated column of clerks. Recovering myself, I advanced towards the screen, and demanded the reason for such extraordinary conduct.

"*Why* do you refuse?"

"I would prefer not to."

With any other man I should have flown outright into a dreadful passion, scorned all further words, and thrust him ignominiously from my presence. But there was something about Bartleby that not only strangely disarmed me, but in a wonderful manner touched and disconcerted me. I began to reason with him.

"These are your own copies we are about to examine. It is labor saving to you, because one examination will answer for your four papers. It is common usage. Every copyist is bound to help examine his copy. Is it not so? Will you not speak? Answer!"

"I prefer not to," he replied in a flute-like tone. It seemed to me that while I had been addressing him, he carefully revolved every statement that I made; fully comprehended the meaning; could not gainsay the irresistible conclusion; but, at the same time, some paramount consideration prevailed with him to reply as he did.

"You are decided, then, not to comply with my request—a request made according to common usage and common sense?"

He briefly gave me to understand that on that point my judgment was sound. Yes: his decision was irreversible.

It is not seldom the case that when a man is browbeaten in some unprecedented and violently unreasonable way, he begins to stagger in his own plainest faith. He begins, as it were, vaguely to surmise that, wonderful as it may be, all the justice and all the reason is on the other side. Accordingly, if any disinterested persons are present, he turns to them for some reinforcement for his own faltering mind.

"Turkey," said I, "what do you think of this? Am I not right?"

"With submission, sir," said Turkey, with his blandest tone, "I think that you are."

"Nippers," said I, "what do *you* think of it?"

"I think I should kick him out of the office."

(The reader of nice perceptions will here perceive that, it being morning, Turkey's answer is couched in polite and tranquil terms, but Nippers replies in ill-tempered ones. Or, to repeat a previous sentence, Nippers's ugly mood was on duty, and Turkey's off.)

"Ginger Nut," said I, willing to enlist the smallest suffrage in my behalf, "what do *you* think of it?"

"I think, sir, he's a little *luny*," replied Ginger Nut, with a grin.

"You hear what they say," said I, turning towards the screen, "come forth and do your duty."

But he vouchsafed no reply. I pondered a moment in sore perplexity. But once more business hurried me. I determined again to postpone the consideration of this dilemma to my future leisure. With a little trouble we made out to examine the papers without Bartleby, though at every page or two, Turkey deferentially dropped his opinion that this proceeding was quite out of the common; while Nippers, twitching in his chair with a dyspeptic nervousness, ground out between his set teeth occasional hissing maledictions against the stubborn oaf behind the screen. And for his (Nippers's) part, this was the first and the last time he would do another man's business without pay.

Meanwhile Bartleby sat in his hermitage, oblivious to every thing but his own peculiar business there.

Some days passed, the scrivener being employed upon another lengthy work. His late remarkable conduct led me to regard his ways narrowly. I observed that he never went to dinner; indeed that he never went any where. As yet I had never of my personal knowledge known him to be outside of my office. He was a perpetual sentry in the corner. At about eleven o'clock though, in the morning, I noticed that Ginger Nut would advance toward the opening in

Bartleby's screen, as if silently beckoned thither by a gesture invisible to me where I sat. The boy would then leave the office jingling a few pence, and reappear with a handful of ginger-nuts which he delivered in the hermitage, receiving two of the cakes for his trouble.

He lives, then, on ginger-nuts, thought I; never eats a dinner, properly speaking; he must be a vegetarian then; but no; he never eats even vegetables, he eats nothing but ginger-nuts. My mind then ran on in reveries concerning the probable effects upon the human constitution of living entirely on ginger-nuts. Ginger-nuts are so called because they contain ginger as one of their peculiar constituents, and the final flavoring one. Now what was ginger? A hot, spicy thing. Was Bartleby hot and spicy? Not at all. Ginger, then, had no effect upon Bartleby. Probably he preferred it should have none.

Nothing so aggravates an earnest person as a passive resistance. If the individual so resisted be of a not inhumane temper, and the resisting one perfectly harmless in his passivity; then, in the better moods of the former, he will endeavor charitably to construe to his imagination what proves impossible to be solved by his judgment. Even so, for the most part, I regarded Bartleby and his ways. Poor fellow! thought I, he means no mischief; it is plain he intends no insolence; his aspect sufficiently evinces that his eccentricities are involuntary. He is useful to me. I can get along with him. If I turn him away, the chances are he will fall in with some less indulgent employer, and then he will be rudely treated, and perhaps driven forth miserably to starve. Yes. Here I can cheaply purchase a delicious self-approval. To befriend Bartleby; to humor him in his strange wilfulness, will cost me little or nothing, while I lay up in my soul what will eventually prove a sweet morsel for my conscience. But this mood was not invariable with me. The passiveness of Bartleby sometimes irritated me. I felt strangely goaded on to encounter him in new opposition, to elicit some angry spark from him answerable to my own. But indeed I might as well have essayed to strike fire with my knuckles against a bit of Windsor soap. But one afternoon the evil impulse in me mastered me, and the following little scene ensued:

"Bartleby," said I, "when those papers are all copied, I will compare them with you."

"I would prefer not to."

"How? Surely you do not mean to persist in that mulish vagary?"

No answer.

I threw open the folding-doors near by, and turning upon Turkey and Nippers, exclaimed:

"Bartleby a second time says, he won't examine his papers. What do you think of it, Turkey?"

It was afternoon, be it remembered. Turkey sat glowing like a brass boiler, his bald head steaming, his hands reeling among his blotted papers.

"Think of it?" roared Turkey; "I think I'll just step behind his screen, and black his eyes for him!"

So saying, Turkey rose to his feet and threw his arms into a pugilistic position. He was hurrying away to make good his promise, when I detained him, alarmed at the effect of incautiously rousing Turkey's combativeness after dinner.

"Sit down, Turkey," said I, "and hear what Nippers has to say. What do you think of it, Nippers? Would I not be justified in immediately dismissing Bartleby?"

"Excuse me, that is for you to decide, sir. I think his conduct quite unusual, and indeed unjust, as regards Turkey and myself. But it may only be a passing whim."

"Ah," exclaimed I, "you have strangely changed your mind then—you speak very gently of him now."

"All beer," cried Turkey; "gentleness is effects of beer—Nippers and I dined together to-day. You see how gentle *I* am, sir. Shall I go and black his eyes?"

"You refer to Bartleby, I suppose. No, not to-day, Turkey," I replied; "pray, put up your fists."

I closed the doors, and again advanced towards Bartleby. I felt additional incentives tempting me to my fate. I burned to be rebelled against again. I remembered that Bartleby never left the office.

"Bartleby," said I, "Ginger Nut is away; just step round to the Post Office, won't you? (it was but a three minutes walk,) and see if there is any thing for me."

"I would prefer not to."

"You *will* not?"

"I *prefer* not."

I staggered to my desk, and sat there in a deep study. My blind inveteracy returned. Was there any other thing in which I could procure myself to be ignominiously repulsed by this lean, penniless wight?—my hired clerk? What added thing is there, perfectly reasonable, that he will be sure to refuse to do?

"Bartleby!"

No answer.

"Bartleby," in a louder tone.

No answer.

"Bartleby," I roared.

Like a very ghost, agreeably to the laws of magical invocation, at the third summons, he appeared at the entrance of his hermitage.

"Go to the next room, and tell Nippers to come to me."

"I prefer not to," he respectfully and slowly said, and mildly disappeared.

"Very good, Bartleby," said I, in a quiet sort of serenely severe self-possessed tone, intimating the unalterable purpose of some terrible retribution very close at hand. At the moment I half intended something of the kind. But upon the whole, as it was drawing towards my dinner-hour, I thought it best to put on my hat and walk home for the day, suffering much from perplexity and distress of mind.

Shall I acknowledge it? The conclusion of this whole business was, that it soon became a fixed fact of my chambers, that a pale young scrivener, by the name of Bartleby, had a desk there; that he copied for me at the usual rate of four cents a folio (one hundred words); but he was permanently exempt from examining the work done by him, that duty being transferred to Turkey and Nippers, out of compliment doubtless to their superior acuteness; moreover, said

Bartleby was never on any account to be dispatched on the most trivial errand of any sort; and that even if entreated to take upon him such a matter, it was generally understood that he would prefer not to—in other words, that he would refuse point-blank.

As days passed on, I became considerably reconciled to Bartleby. His steadiness, his freedom from all dissipation, his incessant industry (except when he chose to throw himself into a standing revery behind his screen), his great stillness, his unalterableness of demeanor under all circumstances, made him a valuable acquisition. One prime thing was this,—*he was always there*;—first in the morning, continually through the day, and the last at night. I had a singular confidence in his honesty. I felt my most precious papers perfectly safe in his hands. Sometimes to be sure I could not, for the very soul of me, avoid falling into sudden spasmodic passions with him. For it was exceeding difficult to bear in mind all the time those strange peculiarities, privileges, and unheard of exemptions, forming the tacit stipulations on Bartleby's part under which he remained in my office. Now and then, in the eagerness of dispatching pressing business, I would inadvertently summon Bartleby, in a short, rapid tone, to put his finger, say, on the incipient tie of a bit of red tape with which I was about compressing some papers. Of course, from behind the screen the usual answer, "I prefer not to," was sure to come; and then, how could a human creature with the common infirmities of our nature, refrain from bitterly exclaiming upon such perverseness —such unreasonableness. However, every added repulse of this sort which I received only tended to lessen the probability of my repeating the inadvertence.

Here it must be said, that according to the custom of most legal gentlemen occupying chambers in densely-populated law buildings, there were several keys to my door. One was kept by a woman residing in the attic, which person weekly scrubbed and daily swept and dusted my apartments. Another was kept by Turkey for convenience sake. The third I sometimes carried in my own pocket. The fourth I knew not who had.

Now, one Sunday morning I happened to go to Trinity Church,* to hear a celebrated preacher, and finding myself rather early on the ground, I thought I would walk round to my chambers for a while. Luckily I had my key with me; but upon applying it to the lock, I found it resisted by something inserted from the inside. Quite surprised, I called out; when to my consternation a key was turned from within; and thrusting his lean visage at me, and holding the door ajar, the apparition of Bartleby appeared, in his shirt sleeves, and otherwise in a strangely tattered dishabille, saying quietly that he was sorry, but he was deeply engaged just then, and— preferred not admitting me at present. In a brief word or two, he moreover added, that perhaps I had better walk round the block two or three times, and by that time he would probably have concluded his affairs.

Now, the utterly unsurmised appearance of Bartleby, tenanting my law-chambers of a Sunday morning, with his cadaverously gentlemanly *nonchalance*, yet withal firm and self-possessed, had such a strange effect upon me, that incontinently I slunk away from my own door, and did as desired. But not without sundry twinges of impotent rebellion against the mild effrontery of this unaccountable scrivener. Indeed, it was his wonderful mildness chiefly, which not only disarmed me, but unmanned me, as it were. For I consider that one, for the time, is a sort of unmanned when he tranquilly permits his hired clerk to dictate to him, and order him away from his own premises. Furthermore, I was full of uneasiness as to what Bartleby could possibly be doing in my office in his shirt sleeves, and in an otherwise dismantled condition of a Sunday morning. Was any thing amiss going on? Nay, that was out of the question. It was not to be thought of for a moment that Bartleby was an immoral person. But what could he be doing there?—copying? Nay again, whatever might be his eccentricities, Bartleby was an eminently decorous person. He would be the last man to sit down to his desk in any state approaching to nudity. Besides, it was Sunday; and there was something about Bartleby that forbade the supposition that he would by any secular occupation violate the proprieties of the day.

Nevertheless, my mind was not pacified; and full of a restless curiosity, at last I returned to the door. Without hindrance I inserted my key, opened it, and entered. Bartleby was not to be seen. I looked round anxiously, peeped behind his screen; but it was very plain that he was gone. Upon more closely examining the place, I surmised that for an indefinite period Bartleby must have ate, dressed, and slept in my office, and that too without plate, mirror, or bed. The cushioned seat of a ricketty old sofa in one corner bore the faint impress of a lean, reclining form. Rolled away under his desk, I found a blanket; under the empty grate, a blacking box and brush; on a chair, a tin basin, with soap and a ragged towel; in a newspaper a few crumbs of ginger-nuts and a morsel of cheese. Yes, thought I, it is evident enough that Bartleby has been making his home here, keeping bachelor's hall all by himself. Immediately then the thought came sweeping across me, What miserable friendlessness and loneliness are here revealed! His poverty is great; but his solitude, how horrible! Think of it. Of a Sunday, Wall-street is deserted as Petra;* and every night of every day it is an emptiness. This building too, which of week-days hums with industry and life, at nightfall echoes with sheer vacancy, and all through Sunday is forlorn. And here Bartleby makes his home; sole spectator of a solitude which he has seen all populous—a sort of innocent and transformed Marius brooding among the ruins of Carthage!*

For the first time in my life a feeling of overpowering stinging melancholy seized me. Before, I had never experienced aught but a not-unpleasing sadness. The bond of a common humanity now drew me irresistibly to gloom. A fraternal melancholy! For both I and Bartleby were sons of Adam. I remembered the bright silks and sparkling faces I had seen that day, in gala trim, swan-like sailing down the Mississippi of Broadway; and I contrasted them with the pallid copyist, and thought to myself, Ah, happiness courts the light, so we deem the world is gay; but misery hides aloof, so we deem that misery there is none. These sad fancyings—chimeras, doubtless, of a sick and silly brain—led on to other and more special thoughts, concerning the eccentricities of Bartleby. Presentiments of strange discoveries hovered round me. The scrivener's pale form appeared to me laid out, among uncaring strangers, in its shivering winding sheet.

Suddenly I was attracted by Bartleby's closed desk, the key in open sight left in the lock.

I mean no mischief, seek the gratification of no heartless curiosity, thought I; besides, the desk is mine, and its contents too, so I will make bold to look within. Every thing was methodically arranged, the papers smoothly placed. The pigeon holes were deep, and removing the files of documents, I groped into their recesses. Presently I felt something there, and dragged it out. It was an old bandanna handkerchief, heavy and knotted. I opened it, and saw it was a savings' bank.

I now recalled all the quiet mysteries which I had noted in the man. I remembered that he never spoke but to answer; that though at intervals he had considerable time to himself, yet I had never seen him reading—no, not even a newspaper; that for long periods he would stand looking out, at his pale window behind the screen, upon the dead brick wall; I was quite sure he never visited any refectory or eating house; while his pale face clearly indicated that he never drank beer like Turkey, or tea and coffee even, like other men; that he never went any where in particular that I could learn; never went out for a walk, unless indeed that was the case at present; that he had declined telling who he was, or whence he came, or whether he had any relatives in the world; that though so thin and pale, he never complained of ill health. And more than all, I remembered a certain unconscious air of pallid—how shall I call it?—of pallid haughtiness, say, or rather an austere reserve about him, which had positively awed me into my tame compliance with his eccentricities, when I had feared to ask him to do the slightest incidental thing for me, even though I might know, from his long-continued motionlessness, that behind his screen he must be standing in one of those dead-wall reveries of his.

Revolving all these things, and coupling them with the recently discovered fact that he made my office his constant abiding place and home, and not forgetful of his morbid moodiness; revolving all these things, a prudential feeling began to steal over me. My first emotions had been those of pure melancholy and sincerest pity; but just in proportion as the forlornness of Bartleby grew and grew to my imagination, did that same melancholy merge into fear, that pity into repulsion. So true it is, and so terrible too, that up to a certain point the thought or sight of misery enlists our best affections; but, in certain special cases, beyond that point it does not. They err who would assert that invariably this is owing to the inherent selfishness of the human heart. It rather proceeds from a certain hopelessness of remedying excessive and organic ill. To a sensitive being, pity is not seldom pain. And when at last it is perceived that such pity cannot lead to effectual succor, common sense bids the soul be rid of it. What I saw that morning persuaded me that the scrivener was the victim of innate and incurable disorder. I might give alms to his body; but his body did not pain him; it was his soul that suffered, and his soul I could not reach.

I did not accomplish the purpose of going to Trinity Church that morning. Somehow, the things I had seen disqualified me for the time from church-going. I walked homeward, thinking what I would do with Bartleby. Finally, I resolved upon this;—I would put certain calm questions to him the next morning, touching his history, &c., and if he declined to answer them openly and unreservedly (and I supposed he would prefer not), then to give him a twenty dollar bill over and above whatever I might owe him, and tell him his services were no longer required; but that if in any other way I could assist him, I would be happy to do so, especially if he desired to return to his native place, wherever that might be, I would willingly help to defray the expenses. Moreover, if, after reaching home, he found himself at any time in want of aid, a letter from him would be sure of a reply.

The next morning came.

"Bartleby," said I, gently calling to him behind his screen. No reply.

"Bartleby," said I, in a still gentler tone, "come here; I am not going to ask you to do any thing you would prefer not to do—I simply wish to speak to you."

Upon this he noiselessly slid into view.

"Will you tell me, Bartleby, where you were born?"

"I would prefer not to."

"Will you tell me *any thing* about yourself?"

"I would prefer not to."

"But what reasonable objection can you have to speak to me? I feel friendly towards you."

He did not look at me while I spoke, but kept his glance fixed upon my bust of Cicero, which as I then sat, was directly behind me, some six inches above my head.

"What is your answer, Bartleby?" said I, after waiting a considerable time for a reply, during which his countenance remained immovable, only there was the faintest conceivable tremor of the white attenuated mouth.

"At present I prefer to give no answer," he said, and retired into his hermitage.

It was rather weak in me I confess, but his manner on this occasion nettled me. Not only did there seem to lurk in it a certain calm disdain, but his perverseness seemed ungrateful, considering the undeniable good usage and indulgence he had received from me.

Again I sat ruminating what I should do. Mortified as I was at his behavior, and resolved as I had been to dismiss him when I entered my office, nevertheless I strangely felt something superstitious knocking at my heart, and forbidding me to carry out my purpose, and denouncing me for a villain if I dared to breathe one bitter word against this forlornest of mankind. At last, familiarly drawing my chair behind his screen, I sat down and said: "Bartleby, never mind then about revealing your history; but let me entreat you, as a friend, to comply as far as may be with the usages of this office. Say now you will help to examine papers to-morrow or next day: in short, say now that in a day or two you will begin to be a little reasonable:—say so, Bartleby."

"At present I would prefer not to be a little reasonable," was his mildly cadaverous reply.

Just then the folding-doors opened, and Nippers approached. He seemed suffering from an unusually bad night's rest, induced by severer indigestion than common. He overheard those final words of Bartleby.

"*Prefer not*, eh?" gritted Nippers—"I'd *prefer* him, if I were you, sir," addressing me—"I'd *prefer* him; I'd give him preferences, the stubborn mule! What is it, sir, pray, that he *prefers* not to do now?"

Bartleby moved not a limb.

"Mr. Nippers," said I, "I'd prefer that you would withdraw for the present."

Somehow, of late I had got into the way of involuntarily using this word "prefer" upon all sorts of not exactly suitable occasions. And I trembled to think that my contact with the scrivener had already and seriously affected me in a mental way. And what further and deeper aberration might it not yet produce? This apprehension had not been without efficacy in determining me to summary measures.

As Nippers, looking very sour and sulky, was departing, Turkey blandly and deferentially approached.

"With submission, sir," said he, "yesterday I was thinking about Bartleby here, and I think that if he would but prefer to take a quart of good ale every day, it would do much towards mending him, and enabling him to assist in examining his papers."

"So you have got the word too," said I, slightly excited.

"With submission, what word, sir," asked Turkey, respectfully crowding himself into the contracted space behind the screen, and by so doing, making me jostle the scrivener. "What word, sir?"

"I would prefer to be left alone here," said Bartleby, as if offended at being mobbed in his privacy.

"*That's* the word, Turkey," said I—"*that's* it."

"Oh, *prefer*? oh yes—queer word. I never use it myself. But, sir, as I was saying, if he would but prefer—"

"Turkey," interrupted I, "you will please withdraw."

"Oh certainly, sir, if you prefer that I should."

As he opened the folding-doors to retire, Nippers at his desk caught a glimpse of me, and asked whether I would prefer to have a certain paper copied on blue paper or white. He did not in the least roguishly accent the word prefer. It was plain that it involuntarily rolled from his tongue. I thought to myself, surely I must get rid of a demented man, who already has in some degree turned the tongues, if not the heads of myself and clerks. But I thought it prudent not to break the dismission at once.

The next day I noticed that Bartleby did nothing but stand at his window in his dead-wall revery. Upon asking him why he did not write, he said that he had decided upon doing no more writing.

"Why, how now? what next?" exclaimed I, "do no more writing?"

"No more."

"And what is the reason?"

"Do you not see the reason for yourself," he indifferently replied.

I looked steadfastly at him, and perceived that his eyes looked dull and glazed. Instantly it occurred to me, that his unexampled diligence in copying by his dim window for the first few weeks of his stay with me might have temporarily impaired his vision.

I was touched. I said something in condolence with him. I hinted that of course he did wisely in abstaining from writing for a while; and urged him to embrace that opportunity of taking wholesome exercise in the open air. This, however, he did not do. A few days after this, my other clerks being absent, and being in a great hurry to dispatch certain letters by the mail, I thought that, having nothing else earthly to do, Bartleby would surely be less inflexible than usual, and carry these letters to the post-office. But he blankly declined. So, much to my inconvenience, I went myself.

Still added days went by. Whether Bartleby's eyes improved or not, I could not say. To all appearance, I thought they did. But when I asked him if they did, he vouchsafed no answer. At all events, he would do no copying. At last, in reply to my urgings, he informed me that he had permanently given up copying.

"What!" exclaimed I; "suppose your eyes should get entirely well—better than ever before—would you not copy then?"

"I have given up copying," he answered, and slid aside.

He remained as ever, a fixture in my chamber. Nay—if that were possible—he became still more of a fixture than before. What was to be done? He would do nothing in the office: why should he stay there? In plain fact, he had now become a millstone to me,* not only useless as a necklace, but afflictive to bear. Yet I was sorry for him. I speak less than truth when I say that, on his own account, he occasioned me uneasiness. If he would but have named a single relative or friend, I would instantly have written, and urged their taking the poor fellow away to some convenient retreat. But he seemed alone, absolutely alone in the universe. A bit of wreck in the mid Atlantic. At length, necessities connected with my business tyrannized over all other considerations. Decently as I could, I told Bartleby that in six days' time he must unconditionally leave the office. I warned him to take measures, in the interval, for procuring some other abode. I offered to assist him in this endeavor, if he himself would but take the first step towards a removal. "And when you finally quit me, Bartleby," added I, "I shall see that you go not away entirely unprovided. Six days from this hour, remember."

At the expiration of that period, I peeped behind the screen, and lo! Bartleby was there.

I buttoned up my coat, balanced myself; advanced slowly towards him, touched his shoulder, and said, "The time has come; you must quit this place; I am sorry for you; here is money; but you must go."

"I would prefer not," he replied, with his back still towards me.

"You *must*."

He remained silent.

Now I had an unbounded confidence in this man's common honesty. He had frequently restored to me sixpences and shillings carelessly dropped upon the floor, for I am apt to be very reckless in such shirt-button affairs. The proceeding then which followed will not be deemed extraordinary.

"Bartleby," said I, "I owe you twelve dollars on account; here are thirty-two; the odd twenty are yours.—Will you take it?" and I handed the bills towards him.

But he made no motion.

"I will leave them here then," putting them under a weight on the table. Then taking my hat and cane and going to the door I tranquilly turned and added—"After you have removed your things from these offices, Bartleby, you will of course lock the door—since every one is now gone for the day but you—and if you please, slip your key underneath the mat, so that I may have it in the morning. I shall not see you again; so good-bye to you. If hereafter in your new place of abode I can be of any service to you, do not fail to advise me by letter. Good-bye, Bartleby, and fare you well."

But he answered not a word; like the last column of some ruined temple, he remained standing mute and solitary in the middle of the otherwise deserted room.

As I walked home in a pensive mood, my vanity got the better of my pity. I could not but highly plume myself on my masterly management in getting rid of Bartleby. Masterly I call it, and such it must appear to any dispassionate thinker. The beauty of my procedure seemed to consist in its perfect quietness. There was no vulgar bullying, no bravado of any sort, no choleric hectoring, and striding to and fro across the apartment, jerking out vehement commands for Bartleby to bundle himself off with his beggarly traps. Nothing of the kind. Without loudly bidding Bartleby depart—as an inferior genius might have done—I *assumed* the ground that depart he must; and upon that assumption built all I had to say. The more I thought over my procedure, the more I was charmed with it. Nevertheless, next morning, upon awakening, I had my doubts,—I had somehow slept off the fumes of vanity. One of the coolest and wisest hours a man has, is just after he awakes in the morning. My procedure seemed as sagacious as ever,—but only in theory. How it would prove in practice—there was the rub. It was truly a beautiful thought to have assumed Bartleby's departure; but, after all, that assumption was simply my own, and none of Bartleby's. The great point was, not whether I had assumed that he would quit me, but whether he would prefer so to do. He was more a man of preferences than assumptions.

After breakfast, I walked down town, arguing the probabilities *pro* and *con*. One moment I thought it would prove a miserable failure, and Bartleby would be found all alive at my office as usual; the next moment it seemed certain that I should find his chair empty. And so I kept veering about. At the corner of Broadway and Canal-street, I saw quite an excited group of people standing in earnest conversation.

"I'll take odds he doesn't," said a voice as I passed.

"Doesn't go?—done!" said I, "put up your money."

I was instinctively putting my hand in my pocket to produce my own, when I remembered that this was an election day. The words I had overheard bore no reference to Bartleby, but to the success or non-success of some candidate for the mayoralty. In my intent frame of mind, I had, as it were, imagined that all Broadway shared in my excitement, and were debating the same question with me. I passed on, very thankful that the uproar of the street screened my momentary absent-mindedness.

As I had intended, I was earlier than usual at my office door. I stood listening for a moment. All was still. He must be gone. I tried the knob. The door was locked. Yes, my procedure had worked to a charm; he indeed must be vanished. Yet a certain melancholy mixed with this: I was almost sorry for my brilliant success. I was fumbling under the door mat for the key, which Bartleby was to have left there for me, when accidentally my knee knocked against a panel, producing a summoning sound, and in response a voice came to me from within—"Not yet; I am occupied."

It was Bartleby.

I was thunderstruck. For an instant I stood like the man who, pipe in mouth, was killed one cloudless afternoon long ago in Virginia, by summer lightning; at his own warm open window he was killed, and remained leaning out there upon the dreamy afternoon, till some one touched him, when he fell.

"Not gone!" I murmured at last. But again obeying that wondrous ascendancy which the inscrutable scrivener had over me, and from which ascendancy, for all my chafing, I could not completely escape, I slowly went down stairs and out into the street, and while walking round the block,

considered what I should next do in this unheard-of perplexity. Turn the man out by an actual thrusting I could
not; to drive him away by calling him hard names would
not do; calling in the police was an unpleasant idea; and
yet, permit him to enjoy his cadaverous triumph over me,—
this too I could not think of. What was to be done? or, if
nothing could be done, was there any thing further that I
could *assume* in the matter? Yes, as before I had prospect-
ively assumed that Bartleby would depart, so now I might
retrospectively assume that departed he was. In the legitimate carrying out of this assumption, I might enter my office
in a great hurry, and pretending not to see Bartleby at all,
walk straight against him as if he were air. Such a proceeding
would in a singular degree have the appearance of a home-
thrust. It was hardly possible that Bartleby could withstand
such an application of the doctrine of assumptions. But
upon second thoughts the success of the plan seemed rather
dubious. I resolved to argue the matter over with him again.

"Bartleby," said I, entering the office, with a quietly
severe expression, "I am seriously displeased. I am pained,
Bartleby. I had thought better of you. I had imagined you
of such a gentlemanly organization, that in any delicate dilemma a slight hint would suffice—in short, an assumption.
But it appears I am deceived. Why," I added, unaffectedly
starting, "you have not even touched that money yet," pointing to it, just where I had left it the evening previous.

He answered nothing.

"Will you, or will you not, quit me?" I now demanded
in a sudden passion, advancing close to him.

"I would prefer *not* to quit you," he replied, gently emphasizing the *not*.

"What earthly right have you to stay here? Do you pay
any rent? Do you pay my taxes? Or is this property yours?"

He answered nothing.

"Are you ready to go on and write now? Are your eyes
recovered? Could you copy a small paper for me this morning? or help examine a few lines? or step round to the post-
office? In a word, will you do any thing at all, to give a
coloring to your refusal to depart the premises?"

He silently retired into his hermitage.

I was now in such a state of nervous resentment that I thought it but prudent to check myself at present from further demonstrations. Bartleby and I were alone. I remembered the tragedy of the unfortunate Adams and the still more unfortunate Colt* in the solitary office of the latter; and how poor Colt, being dreadfully incensed by Adams, and imprudently permitting himself to get wildly excited, was at unawares hurried into his fatal act—an act which certainly no man could possibly deplore more than the actor himself. Often it had occurred to me in my ponderings upon the subject, that had that altercation taken place in the public street, or at a private residence, it would not have terminated as it did. It was the circumstance of being alone in a solitary office, up stairs, of a building entirely unhallowed by humanizing domestic associations—an uncarpeted office, doubtless, of a dusty, haggard sort of appearance;—this it must have been, which greatly helped to enhance the irritable desperation of the hapless Colt.

But when this old Adam of resentment rose in me and tempted me concerning Bartleby, I grappled him and threw him. How? Why, simply by recalling the divine injunction: "A new commandment give I unto you, that ye love one another."* Yes, this it was that saved me. Aside from higher considerations, charity often operates as a vastly wise and prudent principle—a great safeguard to its possessor. Men have committed murder for jealousy's sake, and anger's sake, and hatred's sake, and selfishness' sake, and spiritual pride's sake; but no man that ever I heard of, ever committed a diabolical murder for sweet charity's sake. Mere self-interest, then, if no better motive can be enlisted, should, especially with high-tempered men, prompt all beings to charity and philanthropy. At any rate, upon the occasion in question, I strove to drown my exasperated feelings towards the scrivener by benevolently construing his conduct. Poor fellow, poor fellow! thought I, he don't mean any thing; and besides, he has seen hard times, and ought to be indulged.

I endeavored also immediately to occupy myself, and at the same time to comfort my despondency. I tried to fancy that in the course of the morning, at such time as might prove agreeable to him, Bartleby, of his own free accord, would emerge from his hermitage, and take up some decided line of march in the direction of the door. But no. Half-past twelve o'clock came; Turkey began to glow in the face, overturn his inkstand, and become generally obstreperous; Nippers abated down into quietude and courtesy; Ginger Nut munched his noon apple; and Bartleby remained standing at his window in one of his profoundest dead-wall reveries. Will it be credited? Ought I to acknowledge it? That afternoon I left the office without saying one further word to him.

Some days now passed, during which, at leisure intervals I looked a little into "Edwards on the Will," and "Priestley on Necessity."* Under the circumstances, those books induced a salutary feeling. Gradually I slid into the persuasion that these troubles of mine touching the scrivener, had been all predestinated from eternity, and Bartleby was billeted upon me for some mysterious purpose of an all-wise Providence, which it was not for a mere mortal like me to fathom. Yes, Bartleby, stay there behind your screen, thought I; I shall persecute you no more; you are harmless and noiseless as any of these old chairs; in short, I never feel so private as when I know you are here. At last I see it, I feel it; I penetrate to the predestinated purpose of my life. I am content. Others may have loftier parts to enact; but my mission in this world, Bartleby, is to furnish you with office-room for such period as you may see fit to remain.

I believe that this wise and blessed frame of mind would have continued with me, had it not been for the unsolicited and uncharitable remarks obtruded upon me by my professional friends who visited the rooms. But thus it often is, that the constant friction of illiberal minds wears out at last the best resolves of the more generous. Though to be sure, when I reflected upon it, it was not strange that people entering my office should be struck by the peculiar aspect of the unaccountable Bartleby, and so be tempted to throw out some sinister observations concerning him. Sometimes an attorney having business with me, and calling at my office, and finding no one but the scrivener there, would undertake to obtain some sort of precise information from him touching my whereabouts; but without heeding his idle talk, Bartleby would remain standing immovable in the middle of the room. So after contemplating him in that position for a time, the attorney would depart, no wiser than he came.

Also, when a Reference was going on, and the room full of lawyers and witnesses and business was driving fast; some deeply occupied legal gentleman present, seeing Bartleby wholly unemployed, would request him to run round to his (the legal gentleman's) office and fetch some papers for him. Thereupon, Bartleby would tranquilly decline, and yet remain idle as before. Then the lawyer would give a great stare, and turn to me. And what could I say? At last I was made aware that all through the circle of my professional acquaintance, a whisper of wonder was running round, having reference to the strange creature I kept at my office. This worried me very much. And as the idea came upon me of his possibly turning out a long-lived man, and keep occupying my chambers, and denying my authority; and perplexing my visitors; and scandalizing my professional reputation; and casting a general gloom over the premises; keeping soul and body together to the last upon his savings (for doubtless he spent but half a dime a day), and in the end perhaps outlive me, and claim possession of my office by right of his perpetual occupancy: as all these dark anticipations crowded upon me more and more, and my friends continually intruded their relentless remarks upon the apparition in my room; a great change was wrought in me. I resolved to gather all my faculties together, and for ever rid me of this intolerable incubus.

Ere revolving any complicated project, however, adapted to this end, I first simply suggested to Bartleby the propriety of his permanent departure. In a calm and serious tone, I commended the idea to his careful and mature consideration. But having taken three days to meditate upon it, he apprised me that his original determination remained the same; in short, that he still preferred to abide with me.

What shall I do? I now said to myself, buttoning up my coat to the last button. What shall I do? what ought I to do? what does conscience say I *should* do with this man, or rather ghost? Rid myself of him, I must; go, he shall. But how? You will not thrust him, the poor, pale, passive mortal,—you will not thrust such a helpless creature out of your door? you will not dishonor yourself by such cruelty? No, I will not, I cannot do that. Rather would I let him live and die here, and then mason up his remains in the wall. What then will you do? For all your coaxing, he will not budge. Bribes he leaves under your own paper-weight on your table; in short, it is quite plain that he prefers to cling to you.

Then something severe, something unusual must be done. What! surely you will not have him collared by a constable, and commit his innocent pallor to the common jail? And upon what ground could you procure such a thing to be done?—a vagrant, is he? What! he a vagrant, a wanderer, who refuses to budge? It is because he will *not* be a vagrant, then, that you seek to count him *as* a vagrant. That is too absurd. No visible means of support: there I have him. Wrong again: for indubitably he *does* support himself, and that is the only unanswerable proof that any man can show of his possessing the means so to do. No more then. Since he will not quit me, I must quit him. I will change my offices; I will move elsewhere; and give him fair notice, that if I find him on my new premises I will then proceed against him as a common trespasser.

Acting accordingly, next day I thus addressed him: "I find these chambers too far from the City Hall; the air is unwholesome. In a word, I propose to remove my offices next week, and shall no longer require your services. I tell you this now, in order that you may seek another place."

He made no reply, and nothing more was said.

On the appointed day I engaged carts and men, proceeded to my chambers, and having but little furniture, every thing was removed in a few hours. Throughout, the scrivener remained standing behind the screen, which I directed to be removed the last thing. It was withdrawn; and being folded

up like a huge folio, left him the motionless occupant of a
naked room. I stood in the entry watching him a moment,
while something from within me upbraided me.

I re-entered, with my hand in my pocket—and—and my
heart in my mouth.

"Good-bye, Bartleby; I am going—good-bye, and God
some way bless you; and take that," slipping something in
his hand. But it dropped upon the floor, and then,—strange
to say—I tore myself from him whom I had so longed to
be rid of.

Established in my new quarters, for a day or two I kept
the door locked, and started at every footfall in the passages.
When I returned to my rooms after any little absence, I
would pause at the threshold for an instant, and attentively
listen, ere applying my key. But these fears were needless.
Bartleby never came nigh me.

I thought all was going well, when a perturbed looking
stranger visited me, inquiring whether I was the person who
had recently occupied rooms at No. — Wall-street.

Full of forebodings, I replied that I was.

"Then sir," said the stranger, who proved a lawyer, "you
are responsible for the man you left there. He refuses to do
any copying; he refuses to do any thing; he says he prefers
not to; and he refuses to quit the premises."

"I am very sorry, sir," said I, with assumed tranquillity,
but an inward tremor, "but, really, the man you allude to
is nothing to me*—he is no relation or apprentice of mine,
that you should hold me responsible for him."

"In mercy's name, who is he?"

"I certainly cannot inform you. I know nothing about him.
Formerly I employed him as a copyist; but he has done
nothing for me now for some time past."

"I shall settle him then,—good morning, sir."

Several days passed, and I heard nothing more; and
though I often felt a charitable prompting to call at the place
and see poor Bartleby, yet a certain squeamishness of I know
not what withheld me.

All is over with him, by this time, thought I at last, when
through another week no further intelligence reached me.

But coming to my room the day after, I found several persons waiting at my door in a high state of nervous excitement.

"That's the man—here he comes," cried the foremost one, whom I recognized as the lawyer who had previously called upon me alone.

"You must take him away, sir, at once," cried a portly person among them, advancing upon me, and whom I knew to be the landlord of No. — Wall-street. "These gentlemen, my tenants, cannot stand it any longer; Mr. B——" pointing to the lawyer, "has turned him out of his room, and he now persists in haunting the building generally, sitting upon the banisters of the stairs by day, and sleeping in the entry by night. Every body is concerned; clients are leaving the offices; some fears are entertained of a mob; something you must do, and that without delay."

Aghast at this torrent, I fell back before it, and would fain have locked myself in my new quarters. In vain I persisted that Bartleby was nothing to me—no more than to any one else. In vain:—I was the last person known to have any thing to do with him, and they held me to the terrible account. Fearful then of being exposed in the papers (as one person present obscurely threatened) I considered the matter, and at length said, that if the lawyer would give me a confidential interview with the scrivener, in his (the lawyer's) own room, I would that afternoon strive my best to rid them of the nuisance they complained of.

Going up stairs to my old haunt, there was Bartleby silently sitting upon the banister at the landing.

"What are you doing here, Bartleby?" said I.

"Sitting upon the banister," he mildly replied.

I motioned him into the lawyer's room, who then left us.

"Bartleby," said I, "are you aware that you are the cause of great tribulation to me, by persisting in occupying the entry after being dismissed from the office?"

No answer.

"Now one of two things must take place. Either you must do something, or something must be done to you. Now what sort of business would you like to engage in? Would you like to re-engage in copying for some one?"

"No; I would prefer not to make any change."

"Would you like a clerkship in a dry-goods store?"

"There is too much confinement about that. No, I would not like a clerkship; but I am not particular."

"Too much confinement," I cried, "why you keep yourself confined all the time!"

"I would prefer not to take a clerkship," he rejoined, as if to settle that little item at once.

"How would a bar-tender's business suit you? There is no trying of the eyesight in that."

"I would not like it at all; though, as I said before, I am not particular."

His unwonted wordiness inspirited me. I returned to the charge.

"Well then, would you like to travel through the country collecting bills for the merchants? That would improve your health."

"No, I would prefer to be doing something else."

"How then would going as a companion to Europe, to entertain some young gentleman with your conversation,— how would that suit you?"

"Not at all. It does not strike me that there is any thing definite about that. I like to be stationary. But I am not particular."

"Stationary you shall be then," I cried, now losing all patience, and for the first time in all my exasperating connection with him fairly flying into a passion. "If you do not go away from these premises before night, I shall feel bound —indeed I *am* bound—to—to—to quit the premises myself!" I rather absurdly concluded, knowing not with what possible threat to try to frighten his immobility into compliance. Despairing of all further efforts, I was precipitately leaving him, when a final thought occurred to me—one which had not been wholly unindulged before.

"Bartleby," said I, in the kindest tone I could assume under such exciting circumstances, "will you go home with me now—not to my office, but my dwelling—and remain there till we can conclude upon some convenient arrangement for you at our leisure? Come, let us start now, right away."

"No: at present I would prefer not to make any change at all."

I answered nothing; but effectually dodging every one by the suddenness and rapidity of my flight, rushed from the building, ran up Wall-street towards Broadway, and jumping into the first omnibus was soon removed from pursuit. As soon as tranquillity returned I distinctly perceived that I had now done all that I possibly could, both in respect to the demands of the landlord and his tenants, and with regard to my own desire and sense of duty, to benefit Bartleby, and shield him from rude persecution. I now strove to be entirely care-free and quiescent; and my conscience justified me in the attempt; though indeed it was not so successful as I could have wished. So fearful was I of being again hunted out by the incensed landlord and his exasperated tenants, that, surrendering my business to Nippers, for a few days I drove about the upper part of the town and through the suburbs, in my rockaway;* crossed over to Jersey City and Hoboken, and paid fugitive visits to Manhattanville and Astoria.* In fact I almost lived in my rockaway for the time.

When again I entered my office, lo, a note from the landlord lay upon the desk. I opened it with trembling hands. It informed me that the writer had sent to the police, and had Bartleby removed to the Tombs as a vagrant. Moreover, since I knew more about him than any one else, he wished me to appear at that place, and make a suitable statement of the facts. These tidings had a conflicting effect upon me. At first I was indignant; but at last almost approved. The landlord's energetic, summary disposition, had led him to adopt a procedure which I do not think I would have decided upon myself; and yet as a last resort, under such peculiar circumstances, it seemed the only plan.

As I afterwards learned, the poor scrivener, when told that he must be conducted to the Tombs, offered not the slightest obstacle, but in his pale unmoving way, silently acquiesced.

Some of the compassionate and curious bystanders joined the party; and headed by one of the constables arm in arm with Bartleby, the silent procession filed its way through all the noise, and heat, and joy of the roaring thoroughfares at noon.

The same day I received the note I went to the Tombs, or to speak more properly, the Halls of Justice. Seeking the right officer, I stated the purpose of my call, and was informed that the individual I described was indeed within. I then assured the functionary that Bartleby was a perfectly honest man, and greatly to be compassionated, however unaccountably eccentric. I narrated all I knew, and closed by suggesting the idea of letting him remain in as indulgent confinement as possible till something less harsh might be done—though indeed I hardly knew what. At all events, if nothing else could be decided upon, the alms-house must receive him. I then begged to have an interview.

Being under no disgraceful charge, and quite serene and harmless in all his ways, they had permitted him freely to wander about the prison, and especially in the inclosed grass-platted yards thereof. And so I found him there, standing all alone in the quietest of the yards, his face towards a high wall, while all around, from the narrow slits of the jail windows, I thought I saw peering out upon him the eyes of murderers and thieves.

"Bartleby!"

"I know you," he said, without looking round,—"and I want nothing to say to you."

"It was not I that brought you here, Bartleby," said I, keenly pained at his implied suspicion. "And to you, this should not be so vile a place. Nothing reproachful attaches to you by being here. And see, it is not so sad a place as one might think. Look, there is the sky, and here is the grass."

"I know where I am," he replied, but would say nothing more, and so I left him.

As I entered the corridor again, a broad meat-like man, in an apron, accosted me, and jerking his thumb over his shoulder said—"Is that your friend?"

"Yes."

"Does he want to starve? If he does, let him live on the prison fare, that's all."

"Who are you?" asked I, not knowing what to make of such an unofficially speaking person in such a place.

"I am the grub-man. Such gentlemen as have friends here, hire me to provide them with something good to eat."

"Is this so?" said I, turning to the turnkey.

He said it was.

"Well then," said I, slipping some silver into the grub-man's hands (for so they called him). "I want you to give particular attention to my friend there; let him have the best dinner you can get. And you must be as polite to him as possible."

"Introduce me, will you?" said the grub-man, looking at me with an expression which seemed to say he was all impatience for an opportunity to give a specimen of his breeding.

Thinking it would prove of benefit to the scrivener, I acquiesced; and asking the grub-man his name, went up with him to Bartleby.

"Bartleby, this is Mr. Cutlets; you will find him very useful to you."

"Your sarvant, sir, your sarvant," said the grub-man, making a low salutation behind his apron. "Hope you find it pleasant here, sir; nice grounds—cool apartments, sir—hope you'll stay with us some time—try to make it agreeable. May Mrs. Cutlets and I have the pleasure of your company to dinner, sir, in Mrs. Cutlets' private room?"

"I prefer not to dine to-day," said Bartleby, turning away. "It would disagree with me; I am unused to dinners." So saying he slowly moved to the other side of the inclosure, and took up a position fronting the dead-wall.

"How's this?" said the grub-man, addressing me with a stare of astonishment. "He's odd, aint he?"

"I think he is a little deranged," said I, sadly.

"Deranged? deranged is it? Well now, upon my word, I thought that friend of yourn was a gentleman forger; they are always pale and genteel-like, them forgers. I can't help pity 'em—can't help it, sir. Did you know Monroe Edwards?"* he added touchingly, and paused. Then, laying his hand pityingly on my shoulder, sighed, "he died of consumption at Sing-Sing. So you weren't acquainted with Monroe?"

"No, I was never socially acquainted with any forgers. But I cannot stop longer. Look to my friend yonder. You will not lose by it. I will see you again."

Some few days after this, I again obtained admission to the Tombs, and went through the corridors in quest of Bartleby; but without finding him.

"I saw him coming from his cell not long ago," said a turnkey, "may be he's gone to loiter in the yards."

So I went in that direction.

"Are you looking for the silent man?" said another turnkey passing me. "Yonder he lies—sleeping in the yard there. 'Tis not twenty minutes since I saw him lie down."

The yard was entirely quiet. It was not accessible to the common prisoners. The surrounding walls, of amazing thickness, kept off all sounds behind them. The Egyptian character of the masonry weighed upon me with its gloom. But a soft imprisoned turf grew under foot. The heart of the eternal pyramids, it seemed, wherein, by some strange magic, through the clefts, grass-seed, dropped by birds, had sprung.

Strangely huddled at the base of the wall, his knees drawn up, and lying on his side, his head touching the cold stones, I saw the wasted Bartleby. But nothing stirred. I paused; then went close up to him; stooped over, and saw that his dim eyes were open; otherwise he seemed profoundly sleeping. Something prompted me to touch him. I felt his hand, when a tingling shiver ran up my arm and down my spine to my feet.

The round face of the grub-man peered upon me now. "His dinner is ready. Won't he dine to-day, either? Or does he live without dining?"

"Lives without dining," said I, and closed the eyes.

"Eh!—He's asleep, aint he?"

"With kings and counsellors,"* murmured I.

*

There would seem little need for proceeding further in this history. Imagination will readily supply the meagre recital of poor Bartleby's interment. But ere parting with the reader, let me say, that if this little narrative has sufficiently interested him, to awaken curiosity as to who Bartleby was, and what manner of life he led prior to the present narrator's making his acquaintance, I can only reply, that in such curiosity I fully share, but am wholly unable to gratify it. Yet here I hardly know whether I should divulge one little item of rumor, which came to my ear a few months after the scrivener's decease. Upon what basis it rested, I could never ascertain; and hence, how true it is I cannot now tell. But inasmuch as this vague report has not been without a certain strange suggestive interest to me, however sad, it may prove the same with some others; and so I will briefly mention it. The report was this: that Bartleby had been a subordinate clerk in the Dead Letter Office at Washington,* from which he had been suddenly removed by a change in the administration. When I think over this rumor, hardly can I express the emotions which seize me. Dead letters! does it not sound like dead men? Conceive a man by nature and misfortune prone to a pallid hopelessness, can any business seem more fitted to heighten it than that of continually handling these dead letters, and assorting them for the flames? For by the cart-load they are annually burned. Sometimes from out the folded paper the pale clerk takes a ring:—the finger it was meant for, perhaps, moulders in the grave; a bank-note sent in swiftest charity:—he whom it would relieve, nor eats nor hungers any more; pardon for those who died despairing; hope for those who died unhoping; good tidings for those who died stifled by unrelieved calamities. On errands of life, these letters speed to death.

Ah Bartleby! Ah humanity!

COCK-A-DOODLE-DOO!
Or, The Crowing of the Noble Cock
Beneventano

IN all parts of the world many high-spirited revolts from
rascally despotisms* had of late been knocked on the head;
many dreadful casualties, by locomotive and steamer, had
likewise knocked hundreds of high-spirited travelers on the
head (I lost a dear friend in one of them); my own private
affairs were also full of despotisms, casualties, and knock-
ings on the head, when early one morning in Spring, being
too full of hypoes* to sleep, I sallied out to walk on my hill-
side pasture.

It was a cool and misty, damp, disagreeable air. The country looked underdone, its raw juices squirting out all round.
I buttoned out this squitchy air as well as I could with my
lean, double-breasted dress-coat—my over-coat being so long-
skirted I only used it in my wagon—and spitefully thrusting
my crab-stick into the oozy sod, bent my blue form to the
steep ascent of the hill. This toiling posture brought my head
pretty well earthward, as if I were in the act of butting it
against the world. I marked the fact, but only grinned at it
with a ghastly grin.

All round me were tokens of a divided empire. The old
grass and the new grass were striving together. In the low
wet swales the verdure peeped out in vivid green; beyond,
on the mountains, lay light patches of snow, strangely relieved against their russet sides; all the humped hills looked
like brindled kine in the shivers. The woods were strewn
with dry dead boughs, snapped off by the riotous winds of
March, while the young trees skirting the woods were just beginning to show the first yellowish tinge of the nascent spray.

I sat down for a moment on a great rotting log nigh the
top of the hill, my back to a heavy grove, my face presented
toward a wide sweeping circuit of mountains enclosing a rolling, diversified country. Along the base of one long range of

heights ran a lagging, fever-and-agueish river, over which was a duplicate stream of dripping mist, exactly corresponding in every meander with its parent water below. Low down, here and there, shreds of vapor listlessly wandered in the air, like abandoned or helmless nations or ships—or very soaky towels hung on criss-cross clothes-lines to dry. Afar, over a distant village lying in a bay of the plain formed by the mountains, there rested a great flat canopy of haze, like a pall. It was the condensed smoke of the chimneys, with the condensed, exhaled breath of the villagers, prevented from dispersion by the imprisoning hills. It was too heavy and lifeless to mount of itself; so there it lay, between the village and the sky, doubtless hiding many a man with the mumps, and many a queasy child.

My eye ranged over the capacious rolling country, and over the mountains, and over the village, and over a farm-house here and there, and over woods, groves, streams, rocks, fells—and I thought to myself, what a slight mark, after all, does man make on this huge great earth. Yet the earth makes a mark on him. What a horrid accident was that on the Ohio, where my good friend and thirty other good fellows were sloped into eternity at the bidding of a thick-headed engineer, who knew not a valve from a flue.* And that crash on the railroad just over yon mountains there, where two infatuate trains ran pell-mell into each other, and climbed and clawed each other's backs; and one locomotive was found fairly shelled, like a chick, inside of a passenger car in the antagonist train; and near a score of noble hearts, a bride and her groom, and an innocent little infant, were all disembarked into the grim hulk of Charon,* who ferried them over, all baggageless, to some clinkered iron-foundry country or other. Yet what's the use of complaining? What justice of the peace will right this matter? Yea, what's the use of bothering the very heavens about it? Don't the heavens themselves ordain these things*—else they could not happen?

A miserable world! Who would take the trouble to make a fortune in it, when he knows not how long he can keep it, for the thousand villains and asses who have the management

of railroads and steamboats, and innumerable other vital
things in the world. If they would make me Dictator in
North America a while, I'd string them up! and hang, draw,
and quarter; fry, roast, and boil; stew, grill, and devil them,
like so many turkey-legs—the rascally numskulls of stokers;
I'd set them to stokering in Tartarus*—I would.

Great improvements of the age!* What! to call the facil-
itation of death and murder an improvement! Who wants
to travel so fast? My grandfather did not, and he was no
fool. Hark! here comes that old dragon again—that gigantic
gad-fly of a Moloch*—snort! puff! scream!—here he comes
straight-bent through these vernal woods, like the Asiatic
cholera cantering on a camel. Stand aside! here he comes,
the chartered murderer! the death monopolizer! judge, jury,
and hangman all together, whose victims die always without
benefit of clergy. For two hundred and fifty miles that iron
fiend goes yelling through the land, crying "More! more!
more!" Would fifty conspiring mountains would fall atop of
him! And, while they were about it, would they would also
fall atop of that smaller dunning fiend,* my creditor, who
frightens the life out of me more than any locomotive—a
lantern-jawed rascal, who seems to run on a railroad track
too, and duns me even on Sunday, all the way to church
and back, and comes and sits in the same pew with me,
and pretending to be polite and hand me the prayer-book
opened at the proper place, pokes his pesky bill under my
nose in the very midst of my devotions, and so shoves himself between me and salvation; for how can one keep his
temper on such occasions?

I can't pay this horrid man; and yet they say money was
never so plentiful—a drug in the market; but blame me if I
can get any of the drug, though there never was a sick man
more in need of that particular sort of medicine. It's a lie;
money ain't plenty—feel of my pocket. Ha! here's a powder I was going to send to the sick baby in yonder hovel,
where the Irish ditcher lives. That baby has the scarlet fever.
They say the measles are rife in the country too, and the
varioloid, and the chicken-pox, and it's bad for teething children. And after all, I suppose many of the poor little ones,

after going through all this trouble, snap off short; and so they had the measles, mumps, croup, scarlet-fever, chicken-pox, cholera-morbus, summer-complaint, and all else, in vain! Ah! there's that twinge of the rheumatics in my right shoulder. I got it one night on the North River, when, in a crowded boat, I gave up my berth to a sick lady, and staid on deck till morning in drizzling weather. There's the thanks one gets for charity! Twinge! Shoot away, ye rheumatics! Ye couldn't lay on worse if I were some villain who had murdered the lady instead of befriending her. Dyspepsia too—I am troubled with that.

Hallo! here come the calves, the two-year-olds, just turned out of the barn into the pasture, after six months of cold victuals. What a miserable-looking set, to be sure! A breaking up of a hard winter, that's certain: sharp bones sticking out like elbows; all quilted with a strange stuff dried on their flanks like layers of pancakes. Hair worn quite off too, here and there; and where it ain't pancaked, or worn off, looks like the rubbed sides of mangy old hair-trunks. In fact, they are not six two-year-olds, but six abominable old hair-trunks wandering about here in this pasture.

Hark! By Jove, what's that? See! the very hair-trunks prick their ears at it, and stand and gaze away down into the rolling country yonder. Hark again! How clear! how musical! how prolonged! What a triumphant thanksgiving of a cock-crow! *"Glory be to God in the highest!"** It says those very words as plain as ever cock did in this world. Why, why, I begin to feel a little in sorts again. It ain't so very misty, after all. The sun yonder is beginning to show himself: I feel warmer.

Hark! There again! Did ever such a blessed cock-crow so ring out over the earth before! Clear, shrill, full of pluck, full of fire, full of fun, full of glee. It plainly says—*"Never say die!"* My friends, it is extraordinary is it not?

Unwittingly, I found that I had been addressing the two-year-olds—the calves—in my enthusiasm; which shows how one's true nature will betray itself at times in the most unconscious way. For what a very two-year-old, and calf, I had been to fall into the sulks, on a hill-top too, when a cock down in the lowlands there, without discourse of reason,* and quite penniless in the world, and with death hanging over him at any moment from his hungry master, sends up a cry like a very laureate celebrating the glorious victory of New Orleans.

Hark! there it goes again! My friends, that must be a Shanghai;* no domestic-born cock could crow in such prodigious exulting strains. Plainly, my friends, a Shanghai of the Emperor of China's breed.

But my friends the hair-trunks, fairly alarmed at last by such clamorously-victorious tones, were now scampering off, with their tails flirting in the air, and capering with their legs in clumsy enough sort of style, sufficiently evincing that they had not freely flourished them for the six months last past.

Hark! there again! Whose cock is that? Who in this region can afford to buy such an extraordinary Shanghai? Bless me —it makes my blood bound—I feel wild. What? jumping on this rotten old log here, to flap my elbows and crow too? And just now in the doleful dumps. And all this from the simple crow of a cock. Marvelous cock! But soft—this fellow now crows most lustily; but it's only morning; let's see how he'll crow about noon, and toward night-fall. Come to think of it, cocks crow mostly in the beginning of the day. Their pluck ain't lasting, after all. Yes, yes; even cocks have to succumb to the universal spell of tribulation: jubilant in the beginning, but down in the mouth at the end.

> . . . "Of fine mornings,
> We fine lusty cocks begin our crows in gladness;
> But when eve does come we don't crow quite so much,
> For then cometh despondency and madness."*

The poet had this very Shanghai in his mind when he wrote that. But stop. There he rings out again, ten times richer, fuller, longer, more obstreperously exulting than before! Why this is equal to hearing the great bell of St. Paul's* rung at a coronation! In fact, that bell ought to be taken down, and this Shanghai put in its place. Such a crow would jollify all London, from Mile-End (which is no end) to Primrose Hill* (where there ain't any primroses), and scatter the fog.

Well, I have an appetite for my breakfast this morning, if I have not had it for a week before. I meant to have only tea and toast; but I'll have coffee and eggs—no, brown-stout and a beef-steak. I want something hearty. Ah, here comes the down-train: white cars, flashing through the trees like a vein of silver. How cheerfully the steam-pipe chirps! Gay are the passengers. There waves a handkerchief—going down to the city to eat oysters, and see their friends, and drop in at the circus. Look at the mist yonder; what soft curls and undulations round the hills, and the sun weaving his rays among them. See the azure smoke of the village, like the azure tester over a bridal-bed. How bright the country looks there where the river overflowed the meadows. The old grass has to knock under to the new. Well, I feel the better for this walk. Home now, and walk into that steak and crack that bottle of brown-stout; and by the time that's drank— a quart of stout—by that time, I shall feel about as stout as Samson. Come to think of it, that dun may call, though. I'll just visit the woods and cut a club. I'll club him, by Jove, if he duns me this day.

Hark! there goes Shanghai again. Shanghai says, "Bravo!" Shanghai says, "Club him!"

Oh, brave cock!

I felt in rare spirits the whole morning. The dun called about eleven. I had the boy Jake send the dun up. I was reading Tristram Shandy,* and could not go down under the circumstances. The lean rascal (a lean farmer, too— think of that!) entered, and found me seated in an arm-chair, with my feet on the table, and the second bottle of brown-stout handy, and the book under eye.

"Sit down," said I; "I'll finish this chapter, and then attend to you. Fine morning. Ha! ha!—this is a fine joke about my Uncle Toby and the Widow Wadman! Ha! ha! ha! let me read this to you."

"I have no time; I've got my noon *chores* to do."

"To the deuce with your *chores!*" said I. "Don't drop your old tobacco about here, or I'll turn you out."

"Sir!"

"Let me read you this about the Widow Wadman. 'Said the Widow Wadman—'"

"There's my bill, sir."

"Very good. Just twist it up, will you;—it's about my smoking-time; and hand a coal, will you, from the hearth yonder!"

"My bill, sir!" said the rascal, turning pale with rage and amazement at my unwonted air (formerly I had always dodged him with a pale face), but too prudent as yet to betray the extremity of his astonishment. "My bill, sir!"— and he stiffly poked it at me.

"My friend," said I, "what a charming morning! How sweet the country looks! Pray, did you hear that extraordinary cock-crow this morning? Take a glass of my stout!"

"*Yours?* First pay your debts before you offer folks *your* stout!"

"You think, then, that, properly speaking, I have no *stout,*" said I, deliberately rising. "I'll undeceive you. I'll show you stout of a superior brand to Barclay and Perkins."

Without more ado, I seized that insolent dun by the slack of his coat—(and, being a lean, shad-bellied wretch, there was plenty of slack to it)—I seized him that way, tied him with a sailor-knot, and, thrusting his bill between his teeth, introduced him to the open country lying round about my place of abode.

"Jake," said I, "you'll find a sack of blue-nosed potatoes lying under the shed. Drag it here, and pelt this pauper away: he's been begging pence of me, and I know he can work, but he's lazy. Pelt him away, Jake!"

Bless my stars, what a crow! Shanghai sent up such a perfect pæan and *laudamus*—such a trumpet-blast of triumph, that my soul fairly snorted in me. Duns!—I could have fought an army of them! Plainly, Shanghai was of the opinion that duns only came into the world to be kicked, hanged, bruised, battered, choked, walloped, hammered, drowned, clubbed!

Returning in-doors, when the exultation of my victory over the dun had a little subsided, I fell to musing over the mysterious Shanghai. I had no idea I would hear him so nigh my house. I wondered from what rich gentleman's yard he crowed. Nor had he cut short his crows so easily as I had supposed he would. This Shanghai crowed till mid-day, at least. Would he keep a-crowing all day? I resolved to learn. Again I ascended the hill. The whole country was now bathed in a rejoicing sunlight. The warm verdure was bursting all round me. Teams were a-field. Birds, newly arrived from the South, were blithely singing in the air. Even the crows cawed with a certain unction, and seemed a shade or two less black than usual.

Hark! there goes the cock! How shall I describe the crow of the Shanghai at noon-tide? His sun-rise crow was a whisper to it. It was the loudest, longest, and most strangely-musical crow that ever amazed mortal man. I had heard plenty of cock-crows before, and many fine ones;—but this one! so smooth and flute-like in its very clamor—so self-possessed in its very rapture of exultation—so vast, mounting, swelling, soaring, as if spurted out from a golden throat, thrown far back. Nor did it sound like the foolish, vain-glorious crow of some young sophomorean cock, who knew not the world, and was beginning life in audacious gay spirits, because in wretched ignorance of what might be to come. It was the crow of a cock who crowed not without advice; the crow of a cock who knew a thing or two; the crow of a cock who had fought the world and got the better of it, and was now resolved to crow, though the earth should heave and the heavens should fall. It was a wise crow; an invincible crow; a philosophic crow; a crow of all crows.

I returned home once more full of reinvigorated spirits, with a dauntless sort of feeling. I thought over my debts and other troubles, and over the unlucky risings of the poor oppressed *peoples* abroad, and over the railroad and steam-boat accidents, and over even the loss of my dear friend, with a calm, good-natured rapture of defiance, which astounded myself. I felt as though I could meet Death, and invite him to dinner, and toast the Catacombs* with him, in pure overflow of self-reliance and a sense of universal security.

Toward evening I went up to the hill once more to find whether, indeed, the glorious cock would prove game even from the rising of the sun unto the going down thereof. Talk of Vespers or Curfew!—the evening crow of the cock

went out of his mighty throat all over the land and inhabited it, like Xerxes from the East with his double-winged
host. It was miraculous. Bless me, what a crow! The cock
went game to roost that night, depend upon it, victorious
over the entire day, and bequeathing the echoes of his thousand crows to night.

After an unwontedly sound, refreshing sleep I rose early,
feeling like a carriage-spring—light—elliptical—airy—buoyant
as sturgeon-nose—and, like a foot-ball, bounded up the hill.
Hark! Shanghai was up before me. The early bird that caught
the worm—crowing like a bugle worked by an engine—lusty,
loud, all jubilation. From the scattered farm-houses a multitude of other cocks were crowing, and replying to each other's
crows. But they were as flageolets to a trombone. Shanghai
would suddenly break in, and overwhelm all their crows with
his one domineering blast. He seemed to have nothing to do
with any other concern. He replied to no other crow, but
crowed solely by himself, on his own account, in solitary
scorn and independence.

Oh, brave cock!—oh, noble Shanghai!—oh, bird rightly
offered up by the invincible Socrates,* in testimony of his
final victory over life.

As I live, thought I, this blessed day will I go and seek
out the Shanghai, and buy him, if I have to clap another
mortgage on my land.

I listened attentively now, striving to mark from what
direction the crow came. But it so charged and replenished,
and made bountiful and overflowing all the air, that it was
impossible to say from what precise point the exultation
came. All that I could decide upon was this: the crow came
from out of the East, and not from out of the West. I then
considered with myself how far a cock-crow might be heard.
In this still country, shut in, too, by mountains, sounds were
audible at great distances. Besides, the undulations of the
land, the abuttings of the mountains into the rolling hill and
valley below, produced strange echoes, and reverberations,
and multiplications, and accumulations of resonance, very
remarkable to hear, and very puzzling to think of. Where
lurked this valiant Shanghai—this bird of cheerful Socrates

—the game-fowl Greek who died unappalled? Where lurked he? Oh, noble cock, where are you? Crow once more, my Bantam! my princely, my imperial Shanghai! my bird of the Emperor of China! Brother of the Sun! Cousin of great Jove! where are you?—one crow more, and tell me your master!

Hark! like a full orchestra of the cocks of all nations, forth burst the crow. But where from? There it is; but where? There was no telling, further than it came from out the East.

After breakfast I took my stick and sallied down the road. There were many gentlemen's seats dotting the neighboring country, and I made no doubt that some of these opulent gentlemen had invested a hundred dollar bill in some royal Shanghai recently imported in the ship Trade Wind, or the ship White Squall, or the ship Sovereign of the Seas; for it must needs have been a brave ship with a brave name which bore the fortunes of so brave a cock. I resolved to walk the entire country, and find this noble foreigner out; but thought it would not be amiss to inquire on the way at the humblest homesteads, whether, peradventure, they had heard of a lately-imported Shanghai belonging to any of the gentlemen settlers from the city; for it was plain that no poor farmer, no poor man of any sort, could own such an Oriental trophy—such a Great Bell of St. Paul's swung in a cock's throat.

I met an old man, plowing, in a field nigh the road-side fence.

"My friend, have you heard an extraordinary cock-crow of late?"

"Well, well," he drawled, "I don't know—the Widow Crowfoot has a cock—and Squire Squaretoes has a cock—and I have a cock, and they all crow. But I don't know of any on 'em with 'strordinary crows.'"

"Good-morning to you," said I, shortly; "it's plain that you have not heard the crow of the Emperor of China's chanticleer."*

Presently I met another old man mending a tumble-down old rail-fence. The rails were rotten, and at every move of the old man's hand they crumbled into yellow ochre. He had much better let the fence alone, or else get him new rails. And here I must say, that one cause of the sad fact why idiocy more prevails among farmers than any other class of people, is owing to their undertaking the mending of rotten rail-fences in warm, relaxing spring weather. The enterprise is a hopeless one. It is a laborious one; it is a bootless one. It is an enterprise to make the heart break. Vast pains squandered upon a vanity. For how can one make rotten rail-fences stand up on their rotten pins? By what magic put pith into sticks which have lain freezing and baking through sixty consecutive winters and summers? This it is, this wretched endeavor to mend rotten rail-fences with their own rotten rails, which drives many farmers into the asylum.

On the face of the old man in question incipient idiocy was plainly marked. For, about sixty rods before him extended one of the most unhappy and desponding broken-hearted Virginia rail-fences I ever saw in my life. While in a field behind, were a set of young steers, possessed as by devils, continually butting at this forlorn old fence, and breaking through it here and there, causing the old man to drop his work and chase them back within bounds. He would chase them with a piece of rail huge as Goliath's beam, but as light as cork. At the first flourish, it crumbled into powder.

"My friend," said I, addressing this woeful mortal, "have you heard an extraordinary cock-crow of late?"

I might as well have asked him if he had heard the death-tick. He stared at me with a long, bewildered, doleful, and unutterable stare, and without reply resumed his unhappy labors.

What a fool, thought I, to have asked such an uncheerful and uncheerable creature about a cheerful cock!

I walked on. I had now descended the high land where my house stood, and being in a low tract could not hear the crow of the Shanghai, which doubtless overshot me there. Besides, the Shanghai might be at lunch of corn and oats, or taking a nap, and so interrupted his jubilations for a while.

At length, I encountered riding along the road, a portly gentleman—nay, a *pursy* one—of great wealth, who had recently purchased him some noble acres, and built him a noble mansion, with a goodly fowl-house attached, the fame whereof spread through all that country. Thought I, Here now is the owner of the Shanghai.

"Sir," said I, "excuse me, but I am a countryman of yours, and would ask, if so be you own any Shanghais?"

"Oh, yes; I have ten Shanghais."

"Ten!" exclaimed I, in wonder; "and do they all crow?"

"Most lustily; every soul of them; I wouldn't own a cock that wouldn't crow."

"Will you turn back, and show me those Shanghais?"

"With pleasure: I am proud of them. They cost me, in the lump, six hundred dollars."

As I walked by the side of his horse, I was thinking to myself whether possibly I had not mistaken the harmoniously combined crowings of ten Shanghais in a squad, for the supernatural crow of a single Shanghai by himself.

"Sir," said I, "is there one of your Shanghais which far exceeds all the others in the lustiness, musicalness, and inspiring effects of his crow?"

"They crow pretty much alike, I believe," he courteously replied; "I really don't know that I could tell their crow apart."

I began to think that after all my noble chanticleer might not be in the possession of this wealthy gentleman. However, we went into his fowl-yard, and I saw his Shanghais. Let me say that hitherto I had never clapped eye on this species of imported fowl. I had heard what enormous prices were paid for them, and also that they were of an enormous size, and had somehow fancied they must be of a beauty and brilliancy proportioned both to size and price. What was my surprise, then, to see ten carrot-colored monsters, without the smallest pretension to effulgence of plumage. Immediately, I determined that my royal cock was neither among these, nor could possibly be a Shanghai at all; if these gigantic gallows-bird fowl were fair specimens of the true Shanghai.

I walked all day, dining and resting at a farm-house, inspecting various fowl-yards, interrogating various owners of fowls, hearkening to various crows, but discovered not the mysterious chanticleer. Indeed, I had wandered so far and deviously, that I could not hear his crow. I began to suspect that this cock was a mere visitor in the country, who had taken his departure by the eleven o'clock train for the South, and was now crowing and jubilating somewhere on the verdant banks of Long Island Sound.

But next morning, again I heard the inspiring blast, again felt my blood bound in me, again felt superior to all the ills of life, again felt like turning my dun out of doors. But displeased with the reception given him at his last visit, the dun staid away. Doubtless being in a huff; silly fellow that he was to take a harmless joke in earnest.

Several days passed, during which I made sundry excursions in the regions roundabout, but in vain sought the cock. Still, I heard him from the hill, and sometimes from the house, and sometimes in the stillness of the night. If at times I would relapse into my doleful dumps, straightway at the sound of the exultant and defiant crow, my soul, too, would turn chanticleer, and clap her wings, and throw back her throat, and breathe forth a cheerful challenge to all the world of woes.

At last, after some weeks I was necessitated to clap another mortgage on my estate, in order to pay certain debts, and among others the one I owed the dun, who of late had commenced a civil-process against me. The way the process was served was a most insulting one. In a private room I had been enjoying myself in the village-tavern over a bottle of Philadelphia porter, and some Herkimer cheese, and a roll, and having apprised the landlord, who was a friend of mine, that I would settle with him when I received my next remittances, stepped to the peg where I had hung my hat in the bar-room, to get a choice cigar I had left in the hall, when lo! I found the civil-process enveloping the cigar. When I unrolled the cigar, I unrolled the civil-process, and the constable standing by rolled out, with a thick tongue, "Take notice!" and added, in a whisper, "Put that in your pipe and smoke it!"

I turned short round upon the gentlemen then and there present in that bar-room. Said I, "Gentlemen, is this an honorable—nay, is this a lawful way of serving a civil-process? Behold!"

One and all they were of opinion, that it was a highly inelegant act in the constable to take advantage of a gentleman's lunching on cheese and porter, to be so uncivil as to slip a civil-process into his hat. It was ungenerous; it was cruel; for the sudden shock of the thing coming instanter upon the lunch, would impair the proper digestion of the cheese, which is proverbially not so easy of digestion as *blanc-mange*.

Arrived home, I read the process, and felt a twinge of melancholy. Hard world! hard world! Here I am, as good a fellow as ever lived—hospitable—open-hearted—generous to a fault: and the Fates forbid that I should possess the fortune to bless the country with my bounteousness. Nay, while many a stingy curmudgeon rolls in idle gold, I, heart of nobleness as I am, I have civil-processes served on me! I bowed my head, and felt forlorn—unjustly used—abused—unappreciated—in short, miserable.

Hark! like a clarion! yea, like a jolly bolt of thunder with bells to it—came the all-glorious and defiant crow! Ye gods, how it set me up again! Right on my pins! Yea, verily on stilts!

Oh, noble cock!

Plain as cock could speak, it said, "Let the world and all aboard of it go to pot. Do you be jolly, and never say die. What's the world compared to you? What is it, any how, but a lump of loam? Do you be jolly!"

Oh, noble cock!

"But my dear and glorious cock," mused I, upon second thought, "one can't so easily send this world to pot; one can't so easily be jolly with civil processes in his hat or hand."

Hark! the crow again. Plain as cock could speak, it said: "Hang the process, and hang the fellow that sent it! If you have not land or cash, go and thrash the fellow, and tell him you never mean to pay him. Be jolly!"

Now this was the way—through the imperative intimations of the cock—that I came to clap the added mortgage on my estate; paid all my debts by fusing them into this one added bond and mortgage. Thus made at ease again, I renewed my search for the noble cock. But in vain, though

I heard him every day. I began to think there was some sort of deception in this mysterious thing: some wonderful vent-riloquist prowled around my barns, or in my cellar, or on my roof, and was minded to be gayly mischievous. But no—what ventriloquist could so crow with such an heroic and celestial crow?

At last, one morning there came to me a certain singular man, who had sawed and split my wood in March—some five-and-thirty cords of it—and now he came for his pay. He was a singular man, I say. He was tall and spare, with a long saddish face, yet somehow a latently joyous eye, which offered the strangest contrast. His air seemed staid, but undepressed. He wore a long, gray, shabby coat, and a big battered hat. This man had sawed my wood at so much a cord. He would stand and saw all day long in a driving snow-storm, and never wink at it. He never spoke unless spoken to. He only sawed. Saw, saw, saw—snow, snow, snow. The saw and the snow went together like two nat-ural things. The first day this man came, he brought his dinner with him, and volunteered to eat it sitting on his buck in the snow-storm. From my window, where I was reading Burton's Anatomy of Melancholy,* I saw him in the act. I burst out of doors bare-headed. "Good heavens!" cried I; "what are you doing? Come in. *This* your dinner!"

He had a hunk of stale bread and another hunk of salt beef, wrapped in a wet newspaper, and washed his morsels down by melting a handful of fresh snow in his mouth. I took this rash man indoors, planted him by the fire, gave him a dish of hot pork and beans, and a mug of cider.

"Now," said I, "don't you bring any of your damp din-ners here. You work by the job, to be sure; but I'll dine you for all that."

He expressed his acknowledgments in a calm, proud, but not ungrateful way, and dispatched his meal with satisfac-tion to himself, and me also. It afforded me pleasure to per-ceive that he quaffed down his mug of cider like a man. I honored him. When I addressed him in the way of business at his buck, I did so in a guardedly respectful and deferential manner. Interested in his singular aspect, struck by his won-

drous intensity of application at his saw—a most wearisome
and disgustful occupation to most people—I often sought
to gather from him who he was, what sort of a life he led,
where he was born, and so on. But he was mum. He came
to saw my wood, and eat my dinners—if I chose to offer
them—but not to gabble. At first, I somewhat resented his
sullen silence under the circumstances. But better considering it, I honored him the more. I increased the respect-
fulness and deferentialness of my address toward him. I
concluded within myself that this man had experienced hard
times; that he had had many sore rubs in the world; that he
was of a solemn disposition; that he was of the mind of
Solomon;* that he lived calmly, decorously, temperately; and
though a very poor man, was, nevertheless, a highly respectable one. At times I imagined that he might even be an elder
or deacon of some small country church. I thought it would
not be a bad plan to run this excellent man for President
of the United States. He would prove a great reformer of
abuses.

His name was Merrymusk. I had often thought how jolly
a name for so unjolly a wight. I inquired of people whether
they knew Merrymusk. But it was some time before I learned
much about him. He was by birth a Marylander, it appeared,
who had long lived in the country round about; a wandering man; until within some ten years ago, a thriftless man,
though perfectly innocent of crime; a man who would work
hard a month with surprising soberness, and then spend all
his wages in one riotous night. In youth he had been a sailor,
and run away from his ship at Batavia,* where he caught the
fever, and came nigh dying. But he rallied, reshipped, landed
home, found all his friends dead, and struck for the Northern
interior, where he had since tarried. Nine years back he had
married a wife, and now had four children. His wife was
become a perfect invalid; one child had the white-swelling,
and the rest were rickety. He and his family lived in a shanty
on a lonely barren patch nigh the railroad-track, where it
passed close to the base of a mountain. He had bought a
fine cow to have plenty of wholesome milk for his children;
but the cow died during an accouchement, and he could

not afford to buy another. Still, his family never suffered for lack of food. He worked hard and brought it to them.

Now, as I said before, having long previously sawed my wood, this Merrymusk came for his pay.

"My friend," said I, "do you know of any gentleman hereabouts who owns an extraordinary cock?"

The twinkle glittered quite plain in the wood-sawyer's eye.

"I know of no *gentleman*," he replied, "who has what might well be called an extraordinary cock."

Oh, thought I, this Merrymusk is not the man to enlighten me. I am afraid I shall never discover this extraordinary cock.

Not having the full change to pay Merrymusk, I gave him his due, as nigh as I could make it, and told him that in a day or two I would take a walk and visit his place, and hand him the remainder. Accordingly one fine morning I sallied forth upon the errand. I had much ado finding the best road to the shanty. No one seemed to know where it was exactly. It lay in a very lonely part of the country, a densely-wooded mountain on one side (which I call October Mountain,* on account of its bannered aspect in that month), and a thicketed swamp on the other, the railroad cutting the swamp. Straight as a die the railroad cut it; many times a day tantalizing the wretched shanty with the sight of all the beauty, rank, fashion, health, trunks, silver and gold, dry-goods and groceries, brides and grooms, happy wives and husbands, flying by the lonely door—no time to stop—flash! here they are—and there they go!—out of sight at both ends—as if that part of the world were only made to fly over, and not to settle upon. And this was about all the shanty saw of what people call "life."

Though puzzled somewhat, yet I knew the general direction where the shanty lay, and on I trudged. As I advanced, I was surprised to hear the mysterious cock-crow with more and more distinctness. Is it possible, thought I, that any gentleman owning a Shanghai can dwell in such a lonesome, dreary region? Louder and louder, nigher and nigher, sounded the glorious and defiant clarion. Though somehow I may be out of the track to my wood-sawyer's, I said to myself, yet, thank heaven, I seem to be on the way toward that extraordinary cock. I was delighted with this auspicious accident. On I journeyed; while at intervals the crow sounded most invitingly, and jocundly, and superbly; and the last crow was ever nigher than the former one. At last, emerging from a thicket of alders, straight before me I saw the most resplendent creature that ever blessed the sight of man.

A cock, more like a golden eagle than a cock. A cock, more like a Field-Marshal than a cock. A cock, more like Lord Nelson with all his glittering arms on, standing on the Vanguard's quarter-deck going into battle, than a cock. A cock, more like the Emperor Charlemagne in his robes at Aix la Chapelle, than a cock.*

Such a cock!

He was of a haughty size, stood haughtily on his haughty legs. His colors were red, gold, and white. The red was on his crest alone, which was a mighty and symmetric crest, like unto Hector's helmet, as delineated on antique shields. His plumage was snowy, traced with gold. He walked in front of the shanty, like a peer of the realm; his crest lifted, his chest heaved out, his embroidered trappings flashing in the light. His pace was wonderful. He looked like some noble foreigner. He looked like some Oriental king in some magnificent Italian Opera.

Merrymusk advanced from the door.

"Pray is not that the Signor Beneventano?"*

"Sir?"

"That's the cock," said I, a little embarrassed. The truth was, my enthusiasm had betrayed me into a rather silly inadvertence. I had made a somewhat learned sort of allusion in the presence of an unlearned man. Consequently, upon discovering it by his honest stare, I felt foolish; but carried it off by declaring that *this was the cock*.

Now, during the preceding autumn I had been to the city, and had chanced to be present at a performance of the Italian Opera. In that Opera figured in some royal character a certain Signor Beneventano—a man of a tall, imposing person, clad in rich raiment, like to plumage, and with a most remarkable, majestic, scornful stride. The Signor Beneventano seemed on the point of tumbling over backward with exceeding haughtiness. And, for all the world, the proud pace of the cock seemed the very stage-pace of the Signor Beneventano.

Hark! Suddenly the cock paused, lifted his head still higher, ruffled his plumes, seemed inspired, and sent forth a lusty crow. October Mountain echoed it; other mountains sent it back; still others rebounded it; it overran the country round. Now I plainly perceived how it was I had chanced to hear the gladdening sound on my distant hill.

"Good Heavens! do you own the cock? Is that cock yours?"

"Is it my cock!" said Merrymusk, looking slyly gleeful out of the corner of his long, solemn face.

"Where did you get it?"

"It chipped the shell here. I raised it."

"You?"

Hark! Another crow. It might have raised the ghosts of all the pines and hemlocks ever cut down in that country. Marvelous cock! Having crowed, he strode on again, surrounded by a bevy of admiring hens.

"What will you take for Signor Beneventano?"

"Sir?"

"That magic cock!—what will you take for him?"

"I won't sell him."

"I will give you fifty dollars."

"Pooh!"

"One hundred!"

"Pish!"

"Five hundred!"

"Bah!"

"And you a poor man?"

"No; don't I own that cock, and haven't I refused five hundred dollars for him?"

"True," said I, in profound thought; "that's a fact. You won't sell him, then?"

"No."

"Will you give him?"

"No."

"Will you *keep* him, then!" I shouted, in a rage.

"Yes."

I stood awhile admiring the cock, and wondering at the man. At last I felt a redoubled admiration of the one, and a redoubled deference for the other.

"Won't you step in?" said Merrymusk.

"But won't the cock be prevailed upon to join us?" said I.

"Yes. Trumpet! hither, boy! hither!"

The cock turned round, and strode up to Merrymusk.

"Come!"

The cock followed us into the shanty.

"Crow!"

The roof jarred.

Oh, noble cock!

I turned in silence upon my entertainer. There he sat on an old battered chest, in his old battered gray coat, with patches at his knees and elbows, and a deplorably bunged hat. I glanced round the room. Bare rafters overhead, but solid junks of jerked beef hanging from them. Earth floor, but a heap of potatoes in one corner, and a sack of Indian meal in another. A blanket was strung across the apartment at the further end, from which came a woman's ailing voice and the voices of ailing children. But somehow in the ailing of these voices there seemed no complaint.

"Mrs. Merrymusk and children?"

"Yes."

I looked at the cock. There he stood majestically in the middle of the room. He looked like a Spanish grandee caught in a shower, and standing under some peasant's shed. There was a strange supernatural look of contrast about him. He irradiated the shanty; he glorified its meanness. He glorified the battered chest, and tattered gray coat, and the bunged hat. He glorified the very voices which came in ailing tones from behind the screen.

"Oh, father," cried a little sickly voice, "let Trumpet sound again."

"Crow," cried Merrymusk.

The cock threw himself into a posture.

The roof jarred.

"Does not this disturb Mrs. Merrymusk and the sick children?"

"Crow again, Trumpet."

The roof jarred.

"It does not disturb them, then?"

"Didn't you hear 'em *ask* for it?"

"How is it, that your sick family like this crowing?" said I. "The cock is a glorious cock, with a glorious voice, but not exactly the sort of thing for a sick chamber, one would suppose. Do they really like it?"

"Don't *you* like it? Don't it do *you* good? Ain't it inspiring? don't it impart pluck? give stuff against despair?"

"All true," said I, removing my hat with profound humility before the brave spirit disguised in the base coat.

"But then," said I still, with some misgivings, "so loud, so wonderfully clamorous a crow, methinks might be amiss to invalids, and retard their convalescence."

"Crow your best now, Trumpet!"

I leaped from my chair. The cock frightened me, like some overpowering angel in the Apocalypse. He seemed crowing over the fall of wicked Babylon, or crowing over the triumph of righteous Joshua in the vale of Ajalon.* When I regained my composure somewhat, an inquisitive thought occurred to me. I resolved to gratify it.

"Merrymusk, will you present me to your wife and children?"

"Yes. Wife, the gentleman wants to step in."

"He is very welcome," replied a weak voice.

Going behind the curtain, there lay a wasted, but strangely cheerful human face; and that was pretty much all; the body, hid by the counterpane and an old coat, seemed too shrunken to reveal itself through such impediments. At the bedside, sat a pale girl, ministering. In another bed lay three children, side by side: three more pale faces.

"Oh, father, we don't mislike the gentleman, but let us see Trumpet too."

At a word, the cock strode behind the screen, and perched himself on the children's bed. All their wasted eyes gazed at

him with a wild and spiritual delight. They seemed to sun
themselves in the radiant plumage of the cock.

"Better than a 'pothecary, eh?" said Merrymusk. "This is
Dr. Cock himself."

We retired from the sick ones, and I reseated myself again,
lost in thought, over this strange household.

"You seem a glorious independent fellow!" said I.

"And I don't think you a fool, and never did. Sir, you
are a trump."

"Is there any hope of your wife's recovery?" said I, modestly seeking to turn the conversation.

"Not the least."

"The children?"

"Very little."

"It must be a doleful life, then, for all concerned. This
lonely solitude—this shanty—hard work—hard times."

"Haven't I Trumpet? He's the cheerer. He crows through
all; crows at the darkest; 'Glory to God in the highest!' continually he crows it."

"Just the import I first ascribed to his crow, Merrymusk,
when first I heard it from my hill. I thought some rich nabob
owned some costly Shanghai; little weening any such poor
man as you owned this lusty cock of a domestic breed."

"*Poor* man like *me?* Why call *me* poor? Don't the cock *I*
own glorify this otherwise inglorious, lean, lantern-jawed
land? Didn't *my* cock encourage *you?* And *I* give you all this
glorification away gratis. I am a great philanthropist. I am
a rich man—a very rich man, and a very happy one. Crow,
Trumpet."

The roof jarred.

I returned home in a deep mood. I was not wholly at rest
concerning the soundness of Merrymusk's views of things,
though full of admiration for him. I was thinking on the
matter before my door, when I heard the cock crow again.
Enough. Merrymusk is right.

Oh, noble cock! oh, noble man!

I did not see Merrymusk for some weeks after this; but
hearing the glorious and rejoicing crow, I supposed that all
went as usual with him. My own frame of mind remained
a rejoicing one. The cock still inspired me. I saw another

mortgage piled on my plantation; but only bought another dozen of stout, and a dozen-dozen of Philadelphia porter. Some of my relatives died; I wore no mourning, but for three days drank stout in preference to porter, stout being of the darker color. I heard the cock crow the instant I received the unwelcome tidings.

"Your health in this stout, oh noble cock!"

I thought I would call on Merrymusk again, not having seen or heard of him for some time now. Approaching the place, there were no signs of motion about the shanty. I felt a strange misgiving. But the cock crew from within doors, and the boding vanished. I knocked at the door. A feeble voice bade me enter. The curtain was no longer drawn; the whole house was a hospital now. Merrymusk lay on a heap of old clothes; wife and children were all in their beds. The cock was perched on an old hogshead hoop, swung from the ridge-pole in the middle of the shanty.

"You are sick, Merrymusk," said I, mournfully.

"No, I am well," he feebly answered.—"Crow, Trumpet."

I shrunk. The strong soul in the feeble body appalled me. But the cock crew.

The roof jarred.

"How is Mrs. Merrymusk?"

"Well."

"And the children?"

"Well. All well."

The last two words he shouted forth in a kind of wild ecstasy of triumph over ill. It was too much. His head fell back. A white napkin seemed dropped upon his face. Merrymusk was dead.

An awful fear seized me.

But the cock crew.

The cock shook his plumage as if each feather were a banner. The cock hung from the shanty roof as erewhile the trophied flags from the dome of St. Paul's. The cock terrified me with exceeding wonder.

I drew nigh the bedsides of the woman and children. They marked my look of strange affright; they knew what had happened.

"My good man is just dead," breathed the woman lowly. "Tell me true?"

"Dead," said I.

The cock crew.

She fell back, without a sigh, and through long-loving sympathy was dead.

The cock crew.

The cock shook sparkles from his golden plumage. The cock seemed in a rapture of benevolent delight. Leaping from the hoop, he strode up majestically to the pile of old clothes, where the wood-sawyer lay, and planted himself, like an armorial supporter, at his side. Then raised one long, musical, triumphant, and final sort of crow, with throat heaved far back, as if he meant the blast to waft the wood-sawyer's soul sheer up to the seventh heavens. Then he strode, king-like, to the woman's bed. Another upturned and exultant crow, mated to the former.

The pallor of the children was changed to radiance. Their faces shone celestially through grime and dirt. They seemed children of emperors and kings, disguised. The cock sprang upon their bed, shook himself, and crowed, and crowed again, and still and still again. He seemed bent upon crowing the souls of the children out of their wasted bodies. He seemed bent upon rejoining instanter this whole family in the upper air. The children seemed to second his endeavors. Far, deep, intense longings for release transfigured them into spirits before my eyes. I saw angels where they lay.*

They were dead.

The cock shook his plumage over them. The cock crew. It was now like a Bravo! like a Hurrah! like a Three-times-three! hip! hip! He strode out of the shanty. I followed. He flew upon the apex of the dwelling, spread wide his wings, sounded one supernatural note, and dropped at my feet.

The cock was dead.

If now you visit that hilly region, you will see, nigh the railroad track, just beneath October Mountain, on the other side of the swamp—there you will see a grave-stone, not with skull and cross-bones, but with a lusty cock in act of crowing, chiseled on it, with the words beneath:

—"Oh! death, where is thy sting?
Oh! grave, where is thy victory?"*

The wood-sawyer and his family, with the Signor Beneventano,
lie in that spot; and I buried them, and planted the stone,
which was a stone made to order; and never since then have
I felt the doleful dumps, but under all circumstances crow
late and early with a continual crow.

COCK-A-DOODLE-DOO!—OO!—OO!—OO!—OO!

THE FIDDLER

So my poem is damned, and immortal fame is not for me! I am nobody forever and ever. Intolerable fate!

Snatching my hat, I dashed down the criticism, and rushed out into Broadway, where enthusiastic throngs were crowding to a circus in a side-street near by, very recently started, and famous for a capital clown.

Presently my old friend Standard rather boisterously accosted me.

"Well met, Helmstone, my boy! Ah! what's the matter? Haven't been committing murder? Ain't flying justice? You look wild!"

"You have seen it, then?" said I, of course referring to the criticism.

"Oh yes; I was there at the morning performance. Great clown, I assure you. But here comes Hautboy. Hautboy—Helmstone."

Without having time or inclination to resent so mortifying a mistake, I was instantly soothed as I gazed on the face of the new acquaintance so unceremoniously introduced. His person was short and full, with a juvenile, animated cast to it. His complexion rurally ruddy; his eye sincere, cheery, and gray. His hair alone betrayed that he was not an overgrown boy. From his hair I set him down as forty or more.

"Come, Standard," he gleefully cried to my friend, "are you not going to the circus? The clown is inimitable, they say. Come; Mr. Helmstone, too—come both; and circus over, we'll take a nice stew and punch at Taylor's."

The sterling content, good-humor, and extraordinary ruddy, sincere expression of this most singular new acquaintance acted upon me like magic. It seemed mere loyalty to human nature to accept an invitation from so unmistakably kind and honest a heart.

During the circus performance I kept my eye more on Hautboy than on the celebrated clown. Hautboy was the sight for me. Such genuine enjoyment as his struck me to the soul with a sense of the reality of the thing called happiness. The jokes of the clown he seemed to roll under his tongue as ripe magnum-bonums. Now the foot, now the hand, was employed to attest his grateful applause. At any hit more than ordinary, he turned upon Standard and me to see if his rare pleasure was shared. In a man of forty I saw a boy of twelve; and this too without the slightest abatement of my respect. Because all was so honest and natural, every expression and attitude so graceful with genuine good-nature, that the marvelous juvenility of Hautboy assumed a sort of divine and immortal air, like that of some forever youthful god of Greece.

But much as I gazed upon Hautboy, and much as I admired his air, yet that desperate mood in which I had first rushed from the house had not so entirely departed as not to molest me with momentary returns. But from these relapses I would rouse myself, and swiftly glance round the broad amphitheatre of eagerly interested and all-applauding human faces. Hark! claps, thumps, deafening huzzas; the vast assembly seemed frantic with acclamation; and what, mused I, has caused all this? Why, the clown only comically grinned with one of his extra grins.

Then I repeated in my mind that sublime passage in my poem, in which Cleothemes the Argive* vindicates the justice of the war. Ay, ay, thought I to myself, did I now leap into the ring there, and repeat that identical passage, nay, enact the whole tragic poem before them, would they applaud the poet as they applaud the clown? No! They would hoot me, and call me doting or mad. Then what does this prove? Your infatuation or their insensibility? Perhaps both; but indubitably the first. But why wail? Do you seek admiration from the admirers of a buffoon? Call to mind the saying of the Athenian, who, when the people vociferously applauded in the forum, asked his friend in a whisper, what foolish thing had he said?

Again my eye swept the circus, and fell on the ruddy radiance of the countenance of Hautboy. But its clear honest cheeriness disdained my disdain. My intolerant pride was rebuked. And yet Hautboy dreamed not what magic reproof to a soul like mine sat on his laughing brow. At the very instant I felt the dart of the censure, his eye twinkled, his hand waved, his voice was lifted in jubilant delight at another joke of the inexhaustible clown.

Circus over, we went to Taylor's. Among crowds of others, we sat down to our stews and punches at one of the small marble tables. Hautboy sat opposite to me. Though greatly subdued from its former hilarity, his face still shone with gladness. But added to this was a quality not so prominent before; a certain serene expression of leisurely, deep good sense. Good sense and good humor in him joined hands. As the conversation proceeded between the brisk Standard and him—for I said little or nothing—I was more and more struck with the excellent judgment he evinced. In most of his remarks upon a variety of topics Hautboy seemed intuitively to hit the exact line between enthusiasm and apathy. It was plain that while Hautboy saw the world pretty much as it was, yet he did not theoretically espouse its bright side nor its dark side.* Rejecting all solutions, he but acknowledged facts. What was sad in the world he did not superficially gainsay; what was glad in it he did not cynically slur; and all which was to him personally enjoyable, he gratefully took to his heart. It was plain, then—so it seemed at that moment, at least—that his extraordinary cheerfulness did not arise either from deficiency of feeling or thought.

Suddenly remembering an engagement, he took up his hat, bowed pleasantly, and left us.

"Well, Helmstone," said Standard, inaudibly drumming on the slab, "what do you think of your new acquaintance?"

The two last words tingled with a peculiar and novel significance.

"New acquaintance indeed," echoed I. "Standard, I owe you a thousand thanks for introducing me to one of the most singular men I have ever seen. It needed the optical sight of such a man to believe in the possibility of his existence."

"You rather like him, then," said Standard, with ironical dryness.

"I hugely love and admire him, Standard. I wish I were Hautboy."

"Ah? That's a pity now. There's only one Hautboy in the world."

This last remark set me to pondering again, and somehow it revived my dark mood.

"His wonderful cheerfulness, I suppose," said I, sneering with spleen, "originates not less in a felicitous fortune than in a felicitous temper. His great good sense is apparent; but great good sense may exist without sublime endowments. Nay, I take it, in certain cases, that good sense is simply owing to the absence of those. Much more, cheerfulness. Unpossessed of genius, Hautboy is eternally blessed."

"Ah? You would not think him an extraordinary genius then?"

"Genius? What! such a short, fat fellow a genius! Genius, like Cassius, is lank."*

"Ah? But could you not fancy that Hautboy might formerly have had genius, but luckily getting rid of it, at last fatted up?"

"For a genius to get rid of his genius is as impossible as for a man in the galloping consumption to get rid of that."

"Ah? You speak very decidedly."

"Yes, Standard," cried I, increasing in spleen,* "your cheery Hautboy, after all, is no pattern, no lesson for you and me. With average abilities; opinions clear, because circumscribed; passions docile, because they are feeble; a temper hilarious, because he was born to it—how can your Hautboy be made a reasonable example to a heady fellow like you, or an ambitious dreamer like me? Nothing tempts him beyond common limit; in himself he has nothing to restrain. By constitution he is exempted from all moral harm. Could ambition but prick him; had he but once heard applause, or endured contempt, a very different man would your Hautboy be. Acquiescent and calm from the cradle to the grave, he obviously slides through the crowd."

"Ah?"

"Why do you say ah to me so strangely whenever I speak?"

"Did you ever hear of Master Betty?"*

"The great English prodigy, who long ago ousted the Siddons and the Kembles from Drury Lane,* and made the whole town run mad with acclamation?"

"The same," said Standard, once more inaudibly drumming on the slab.

I looked at him perplexed. He seemed to be holding the master-key of our theme in mysterious reserve; seemed to be throwing out his Master Betty too, to puzzle me only the more.

"What under heaven can Master Betty, the great genius and prodigy, an English boy twelve years old, have to do with the poor common-place plodder Hautboy, an American of forty?"

"Oh, nothing in the least. I don't imagine that they ever saw each other. Besides, Master Betty must be dead and buried long ere this."

"Then why cross the ocean, and rifle the grave to drag his remains into this living discussion?"

"Absent-mindedness, I suppose. I humbly beg pardon. Proceed with your observations on Hautboy. You think he never had genius, quite too contented and happy, and fat for that—ah? You think him no pattern for men in general? affording no lesson of value to neglected merit, genius ignored, or impotent presumption rebuked?—all of which three amount to much the same thing. You admire his cheerfulness, while scorning his common-place soul. Poor Hautboy, how sad that your very cheerfulness should, by a by-blow, bring you despite!"

"I don't say I scorn him; you are unjust. I simply declare that he is no pattern for me."

A sudden noise at my side attracted my ear. Turning, I saw Hautboy again, who very blithely reseated himself on the chair he had left.

"I was behind time with my engagement," said Hautboy, "so thought I would run back and rejoin you. But come, you have sat long enough here. Let us go to my rooms. It is only a five minutes' walk."

"If you will promise to fiddle for us, we will," said Standard.

Fiddle! thought I—he's a jigembob *fiddler* then? No wonder genius declines to measure its pace to a fiddler's bow. My spleen was very strong on me now.

"I will gladly fiddle you your fill," replied Hautboy to Standard. "Come on."

In a few minutes we found ourselves in the fifth story of a sort of storehouse, in a lateral street to Broadway. It was curiously furnished with all sorts of odd furniture which seemed to have been obtained, piece by piece, at auctions of old-fashioned household stuff. But all was charmingly clean and cosy.

Pressed by Standard, Hautboy forthwith got out his dented old fiddle, and sitting down on a tall rickety stool, played away right merrily at Yankee Doodle and other off-handed, dashing, and disdainfully care-free airs. But common as were the tunes, I was transfixed by something miraculously superior in the style. Sitting there on the old stool, his rusty hat sideways cocked on his head, one foot dangling adrift, he plied the bow of an enchanter. All my moody discontent, every vestige of peevishness fled. My whole splenetic soul capitulated to the magical fiddle.

"Something of an Orpheus,* ah?" said Standard, archly nudging me beneath the left rib.

"And I, the charmed Bruin,"* murmured I.

The fiddle ceased. Once more, with redoubled curiosity, I gazed upon the easy, indifferent Hautboy. But he entirely baffled inquisition.

When, leaving him, Standard and I were in the street once more, I earnestly conjured him to tell me who, in sober truth, this marvelous Hautboy was.

"Why, haven't you seen him? And didn't you yourself lay his whole anatomy open on the marble slab at Taylor's? What more can you possibly learn? Doubtless your own masterly insight has already put you in possession of all."

"You mock me, Standard. There is some mystery here. Tell me, I entreat you, who is Hautboy?"

"An extraordinary genius, Helmstone," said Standard, with sudden ardor, "who in boyhood drained the whole flagon of glory; whose going from city to city was a going from triumph to triumph. One who has been an object of wonder to the wisest, been caressed by the loveliest, received the open homage of thousands on thousands of the rabble. But to-day he walks Broadway and no man knows him.* With you and me, the elbow of the hurrying clerk, and the pole of the remorseless omnibus, shove him. He who has a hundred times been crowned with laurels, now wears, as you see, a bunged beaver. Once fortune poured showers of gold into his lap, as showers of laurel leaves upon his brow. To-day, from house to house he hies, teaching fiddling for a living. Crammed once with fame, he is now hilarious without it. *With* genius and *without* fame, he is happier than a king. More a prodigy now than ever."

"His true name?"

"Let me whisper it in your ear."

"What! Oh Standard, myself, as a child, have shouted myself hoarse applauding that very name in the theatre."

"I have heard your poem was not very handsomely received," said Standard, now suddenly shifting the subject.

"Not a word of that, for heaven's sake!" cried I. "If Cicero, traveling in the East, found sympathetic solace for his grief in beholding the arid overthrow of a once gorgeous city, shall not my petty affair be as nothing, when I behold in Hautboy the vine and the rose climbing the shattered shafts of his tumbled temple of Fame?"

Next day I tore all my manuscripts, bought me a fiddle, and went to take regular lessons of Hautboy.

THE PARADISE OF BACHELORS
AND THE TARTARUS OF MAIDS

I. THE PARADISE OF BACHELORS

It lies not far from Temple-Bar.*

Going to it, by the usual way, is like stealing from a heated plain into some cool, deep glen, shady among harboring hills.

Sick with the din and soiled with the mud of Fleet Street* —where the Benedick* tradesmen are hurrying by, with ledger-lines ruled along their brows, thinking upon rise of bread and fall of babies—you adroitly turn a mystic corner —not a street—glide down a dim, monastic way, flanked by dark, sedate, and solemn piles, and still wending on, give the whole care-worn world the slip, and, disentangled, stand beneath the quiet cloisters of the Paradise of Bachelors.

Sweet are the oases in Sahara; charming the isle-groves of August prairies; delectable pure faith amidst a thousand perfidies: but sweeter, still more charming, most delectable, the dreamy Paradise of Bachelors, found in the stony heart of stunning London.

In mild meditation pace the cloisters; take your pleasure, sip your leisure, in the garden waterward; go linger in the ancient library; go worship in the sculptured chapel: but little have you seen, just nothing do you know, not the sweet kernel have you tasted, till you dine among the banded Bachelors, and see their convivial eyes and glasses sparkle. Not dine in bustling commons, during term-time, in the hall; but tranquilly, by private hint, at a private table; some fine Templar's hospitably invited guest.

Templar?* That's a romantic name. Let me see. Brian de Bois Guilbert* was a Templar, I believe. Do we understand you to insinuate that those famous Templars still survive in modern London? May the ring of their armed heels be heard, and the rattle of their shields, as in mailed prayer the monk-knights kneel before the consecrated Host? Surely a monk-knight were a curious sight picking his way along the Strand,* his gleaming corselet and snowy surcoat spattered by an omnibus. Long-bearded, too, according to his order's rule; his face fuzzy as a pard's;* how would the grim ghost look among the crop-haired, close-shaven citizens? We know indeed—sad history recounts it—that a moral blight tainted at last this sacred Brotherhood. Though no sworded foe might outskill them in the fence, yet the worm of luxury crawled beneath their guard, gnawing the core of knightly troth, nibbling the monastic vow, till at last the monk's austerity relaxed to wassailing, and the sworn knights-bachelors grew to be but hypocrites and rakes.

But for all this, quite unprepared were we to learn that Knights-Templars (if at all in being) were so entirely secularized as to be reduced from carving out immortal fame in glorious battling for the Holy Land, to the carving of roast-mutton at a dinner-board. Like Anacreon,* do these degenerate Templars now think it sweeter far to fall in banquet than in war? Or, indeed, how can there be any survival of that famous order? Templars in modern London! Templars in their red-cross mantles smoking cigars at the Divan! Templars crowded in a railway train, till, stacked with steel helmet, spear, and shield, the whole train looks like one elongated locomotive!

No. The genuine Templar is long since departed. Go view the wondrous tombs in the Temple Church; see there the rigidly-haughty forms stretched out, with crossed arms upon their stilly hearts, in everlasting and undreaming rest. Like the years before the flood, the bold Knights-Templars are no more. Nevertheless, the name remains, and the nominal society, and the ancient grounds, and some of the ancient edifices. But the iron heel is changed to a boot of patent-leather; the long two-handed sword to a one-handed quill; the monk-giver of gratuitous ghostly counsel now counsels for a fee; the defender of the sarcophagus (if in good practice with his weapon) now has more than one case to defend; the vowed opener and clearer of all highways leading to the Holy Sepulchre,* now has it in particular charge to check, to clog, to hinder, and embarrass all the courts and avenues of Law; the knight-combatant of the Saracen,* breasting spearpoints at Acre, now fights law-points in Westminster Hall. The helmet is a wig. Struck by Time's enchanter's wand, the Templar is to-day a Lawyer.

But, like many others tumbled from proud glory's height— like the apple, hard on the bough but mellow on the ground —the Templar's fall has but made him all the finer fellow.

I dare say those old warrior-priests were but gruff and grouty at the best; cased in Birmingham hardware, how could their crimped arms give yours or mine a hearty shake? Their proud, ambitious, monkish souls clasped shut, like horn-book missals; their very faces clapped in bombshells; what sort of genial men were these? But best of comrades, most affable of hosts, capital diner is the modern Templar. His wit and wine are both of sparkling brands.

The church and cloisters, courts and vaults, lanes and passages, banquet-halls, refectories, libraries, terraces, gardens, broad walks, domicils, and dessert-rooms, covering a very large space of ground, and all grouped in central neighborhood, and quite sequestered from the old city's surrounding din; and every thing about the place being kept in most bachelor-like particularity, no part of London offers to a quiet wight so agreeable a refuge.

The Temple is, indeed, a city by itself. A city with all the best appurtenances, as the above enumeration shows. A city with a park to it, and flower-beds, and a river-side— the Thames flowing by as openly, in one part, as by Eden's primal garden flowed the mild Euphrates. In what is now the Temple Garden the old Crusaders used to exercise their steeds and lances; the modern Templars now lounge on the benches beneath the trees, and, switching their patent-leather boots, in gay discourse exercise at repartee.

Long lines of stately portraits in the banquet-halls, show what great men of mark—famous nobles, judges, and Lord Chancellors—have in their time been Templars. But all Templars are not known to universal fame; though, if the having warm hearts and warmer welcomes, full minds and fuller cellars, and giving good advice and glorious dinners, spiced with rare divertisements of fun and fancy, merit immortal mention, set down, ye muses, the names of R. F. C. and his imperial brother.*

Though to be a Templar, in the one true sense, you must needs be a lawyer, or a student at the law, and be ceremoniously enrolled as member of the order, yet as many such, though Templars, do not reside within the Temple's precincts, though they may have their offices there, just so, on the other hand, there are many residents of the hoary old domicils who are not admitted Templars. If being, say, a lounging gentleman and bachelor, or a quiet, unmarried, literary man, charmed with the soft seclusion of the spot, you much desire to pitch your shady tent among the rest in this serene encampment, then you must make some special friend among the order, and procure him to rent, in his name but at your charge, whatever vacant chamber you may find to suit.

Thus, I suppose, did Dr. Johnson,* that nominal Benedick and widower but virtual bachelor, when for a space he resided here. So, too, did that undoubted bachelor and rare good soul, Charles Lamb.* And hundreds more, of sterling spirits, Brethren of the Order of Celibacy, from time to time have dined, and slept, and tabernacled here. Indeed, the place is all a honeycomb of offices and domicils. Like any cheese, it is quite perforated through and through in all directions with the snug cells of bachelors. Dear, delightful spot! Ah! when I bethink me of the sweet hours there passed, enjoying such genial hospitalities beneath those time-honored roofs, my heart only finds due utterance through poetry; and, with a sigh, I softly sing, "Carry me back to old Virginny!"*

Such then, at large, is the Paradise of Bachelors. And such I found it one pleasant afternoon in the smiling month of May, when, sallying from my hotel in Trafalgar Square, I went to keep my dinner-appointment with that fine Barrister, Bachelor, and Bencher, R. F. C. (he *is* the first and second, and *should be* the third; I hereby nominate him), whose card I kept fast pinched between my gloved forefinger and thumb, and every now and then snatched still another look at the pleasant address inscribed beneath the name, "No. —, Elm Court, Temple."

At the core he was a right bluff, care-free, right comfortable, and most companionable Englishman. If on a first
acquaintance he seemed reserved, quite icy in his air—
patience; this Champagne will thaw. And if it never do, better frozen Champagne than liquid vinegar.

There were nine gentlemen, all bachelors, at the dinner.
One was from "No. —, King's Bench Walk, Temple;" a second, third, and fourth, and fifth, from various courts or
passages christened with some similarly rich resounding syllables. It was indeed a sort of Senate of the Bachelors, sent
to this dinner from widely-scattered districts, to represent the
general celibacy of the Temple. Nay it was, by representation, a Grand Parliament of the best Bachelors in universal
London; several of those present being from distant quarters
of the town, noted immemorial seats of lawyers and unmarried men—Lincoln's Inn, Furnival's Inn; and one gentleman,
upon whom I looked with a sort of collateral awe, hailed
from the spot where Lord Verulam once abode a bachelor—
Gray's Inn.*

The apartment was well up toward heaven. I know not
how many strange old stairs I climbed to get to it. But a
good dinner, with famous company, should be well earned.
No doubt our host had his dining-room so high with a view
to secure the prior exercise necessary to the due relishing
and digesting of it.

The furniture was wonderfully unpretending, old, and snug.
No new shining mahogany, sticky with undried varnish; no
uncomfortably luxurious ottomans, and sofas too fine to use,
vexed you in this sedate apartment. It is a thing which every
sensible American should learn from every sensible Englishman,
that glare and glitter, gimcracks and gewgaws, are not indispensable to domestic solacement. The American Benedick
snatches, down-town, a tough chop in a gilded show-box; the
English bachelor leisurely dines at home on that incompar-
able South Down* of his, off a plain deal board.

The ceiling of the room was low. Who wants to dine
under the dome of St. Peter's? High ceilings! If that is your
demand, and the higher the better, and you be so very tall,
then go dine out with the topping giraffe in the open air.

In good time the nine gentlemen sat down to nine covers, and soon were fairly under way.

If I remember right, ox-tail soup inaugurated the affair. Of a rich russet hue, its agreeable flavor dissipated my first confounding of its main ingredient with teamster's gads and the raw-hides of ushers. (By way of interlude, we here drank a little claret.) Neptune's was the next tribute rendered— turbot coming second; snow-white, flaky, and just gelatinous enough, not too turtleish in its unctuousness.

(At this point we refreshed ourselves with a glass of sherry.) After these light skirmishers had vanished, the heavy artillery of the feast marched in, led by that well-known English generalissimo, roast beef. For aids-de-camp we had a saddle of mutton, a fat turkey, a chicken-pie, and endless other savory things; while for avant-couriers came nine silver flagons of humming ale. This heavy ordnance having departed on the track of the light skirmishers, a picked brigade of game-fowl encamped upon the board, their camp-fires lit by the ruddiest of decanters.

Tarts and puddings followed, with innumerable niceties; then cheese and crackers. (By way of ceremony, simply, only to keep up good old fashions, we here each drank a glass of good old port.)

The cloth was now removed; and like Blucher's army coming in at the death on the field of Waterloo,* in marched a fresh detachment of bottles, dusty with their hurried march.

All these manœuvrings of the forces were superintended by a surprising old field-marshal (I can not school myself to call him by the inglorious name of waiter), with snowy hair and napkin, and a head like Socrates. Amidst all the hilarity of the feast, intent on important business, he disdained to smile. Venerable man!

I have above endeavored to give some slight schedule of the general plan of operations. But any one knows that a good, genial dinner is a sort of pell-mell, indiscriminate affair, quite baffling to detail in all particulars. Thus, I spoke of taking a glass of claret, and a glass of sherry, and a glass of port, and a mug of ale—all at certain specific periods and times. But those were merely the state bumpers, so to speak.

Innumerable impromptu glasses were drained between the periods of those grand imposing ones.

The nine bachelors seemed to have the most tender concern for each other's health. All the time, in flowing wine, they most earnestly expressed their sincerest wishes for the entire well-being and lasting hygiene of the gentlemen on the right and on the left. I noticed that when one of these kind bachelors desired a little more wine (just for his stomach's sake, like Timothy), he would not help himself to it unless some other bachelor would join him. It seemed held something indelicate, selfish, and unfraternal, to be seen taking a lonely, unparticipated glass. Meantime, as the wine ran apace, the spirits of the company grew more and more to perfect genialness and unconstraint. They related all sorts of pleasant stories. Choice experiences in their private lives were now brought out, like choice brands of Moselle or Rhenish, only kept for particular company. One told us how mellowly he lived when a student at Oxford; with various spicy anecdotes of most frank-hearted noble lords, his liberal companions. Another bachelor, a gray-headed man, with a sunny face, who, by his own account, embraced every opportunity of leisure to cross over into the Low Countries, on sudden tours of inspection of the fine old Flemish architecture there—this learned, white-haired, sunny-faced old bachelor, excelled in his descriptions of the elaborate splendors of those old guild-halls, town-halls, and stadthold-houses, to be seen in the land of the ancient Flemings. A third was a great frequenter of the British Museum, and knew all about scores of wonderful antiquities, of Oriental manuscripts, and costly books without a duplicate. A fourth had lately returned from a trip to Old Granada,* and, of course, was full of Saracenic scenery. A fifth had a funny case in law to tell. A sixth was erudite in wines. A seventh had a strange characteristic anecdote of the private life of the Iron Duke,* never printed, and never before announced in any public or private company. An eighth had lately been amusing his evenings, now and then, with translating a comic poem of Pulci's.* He quoted for us the more amusing passages.

And so the evening slipped along, the hours told, not by a water-clock, like King Alfred's, but a wine-chronometer. Meantime the table seemed a sort of Epsom Heath;* a regular ring, where the decanters galloped round. For fear one decanter should not with sufficient speed reach his destination, another was sent express after him to hurry him; and then a third to hurry the second; and so on with a fourth and fifth. And throughout all this nothing loud, nothing unmannerly, nothing turbulent. I am quite sure, from the scrupulous gravity and austerity of his air, that had Socrates, the field-marshal, perceived aught of indecorum in the company he served, he would have forthwith departed without giving warning. I afterward learned that, during the repast, an invalid bachelor in an adjoining chamber enjoyed his first sound refreshing slumber in three long, weary weeks.

It was the very perfection of quiet absorption of good living, good drinking, good feeling, and good talk. We were a band of brothers. Comfort—fraternal, household comfort, was the grand trait of the affair. Also, you could plainly see that these easy-hearted men had no wives or children to give an anxious thought. Almost all of them were travelers, too; for bachelors alone can travel freely, and without any twinges of their consciences touching desertion of the fire-side.

The thing called pain, the bugbear styled trouble—those two legends seemed preposterous to their bachelor imaginations. How could men of liberal sense, ripe scholarship in the world, and capacious philosophical and convivial understandings—how could they suffer themselves to be imposed upon by such monkish fables? Pain! Trouble! As well talk of Catholic miracles. No such thing.—Pass the sherry, Sir. —Pooh, pooh! Can't be!—The port, Sir, if you please. Nonsense; don't tell me so.—The decanter stops with you, Sir, I believe.

And so it went.

Not long after the cloth was drawn our host glanced significantly upon Socrates, who, solemnly stepping to a stand, returned with an immense convolved horn, a regular Jericho horn,* mounted with polished silver, and otherwise chased and curiously enriched; not omitting two life-like goat's heads, with four more horns of solid silver, projecting from opposite sides of the mouth of the noble main horn.

Not having heard that our host was a performer on the bugle, I was surprised to see him lift this horn from the table, as if he were about to blow an inspiring blast. But I was relieved from this, and set quite right as touching the purposes of the horn, by his now inserting his thumb and forefinger into its mouth; whereupon a slight aroma was stirred up, and my nostrils were greeted with the smell of some choice Rappee. It was a mull of snuff. It went the rounds. Capital idea this, thought I, of taking snuff about this juncture. This goodly fashion must be introduced among my countrymen at home, further ruminated I.

The remarkable decorum of the nine bachelors—a decorum not to be affected by any quantity of wine—a decorum unassailable by any degree of mirthfulness—this was again set in a forcible light to me, by now observing that, though they took snuff very freely, yet not a man so far violated the proprieties, or so far molested the invalid bachelor in the adjoining room as to indulge himself in a sneeze. The snuff was snuffed silently, as if it had been some fine innoxious powder brushed off the wings of butterflies.

But fine though they be, bachelors' dinners, like bachelors' lives, can not endure forever. The time came for breaking up. One by one the bachelors took their hats, and two by two, and arm-in-arm they descended, still conversing, to the flagging of the court; some going to their neighboring chambers to turn over the Decameron* ere retiring for the night; some to smoke a cigar, promenading in the garden on the cool river-side; some to make for the street, call a hack, and be driven snugly to their distant lodgings.

I was the last lingerer.

"Well," said my smiling host, "what do you think of the Temple here, and the sort of life we bachelors make out to live in it?"

"Sir," said I, with a burst of admiring candor—"Sir, this is the very Paradise of Bachelors!"

II. THE TARTARUS OF MAIDS

IT lies not far from Woedolor Mountain* in New England. Turning to the east, right out from among bright farms and sunny meadows, nodding in early June with odorous grasses, you enter ascendingly among bleak hills. These gradually close in upon a dusky pass, which, from the violent Gulf Stream of air unceasingly driving between its cloven walls of haggard rock, as well as from the tradition of a crazy spinster's hut having long ago stood somewhere hereabouts, is called the Mad Maid's Bellows'-pipe.

Winding along at the bottom of the gorge is a dangerously narrow wheel-road, occupying the bed of a former torrent. Following this road to its highest point, you stand as within a Dantean gateway.* From the steepness of the walls here, their strangely ebon hue, and the sudden contraction of the gorge, this particular point is called the Black Notch. The ravine now expandingly descends into a great, purple, hopper-shaped hollow,* far sunk among many Plutonian, shaggy-wooded mountains. By the country people this hollow is called the Devil's Dungeon. Sounds of torrents fall on all sides upon the ear. These rapid waters unite at last in one turbid brick-colored stream, boiling through a flume among enormous boulders. They call this strange-colored torrent Blood River. Gaining a dark precipice it wheels suddenly to the west, and makes one maniac spring of sixty feet into the arms of a stunted wood of gray-haired pines, between which it thence eddies on its further way down to the invisible lowlands.

Conspicuously crowning a rocky bluff high to one side, at the cataract's verge, is the ruin of an old saw-mill, built in those primitive times when vast pines and hemlocks superabounded throughout the neighboring region. The black-mossed bulk of those immense, rough-hewn, and spike-knotted logs, here and there tumbled all together, in long abandonment and decay, or left in solitary, perilous projection over the cataract's gloomy brink, impart to this rude wooden ruin not only much of the aspect of one of rough-quarried stone, but also a sort of feudal, Rhineland,

and Thurmberg look, derived from the pinnacled wildness
of the neighboring scenery.

Not far from the bottom of the Dungeon stands a large
white-washed building, relieved, like some great whited sepulchre,* against the sullen background of mountain-side firs,
and other hardy evergreens, inaccessibly rising in grim terraces for some two thousand feet.

The building is a paper-mill.

Having embarked on a large scale in the seedsman's business* (so extensively and broadcast, indeed, that at length
my seeds were distributed through all the Eastern and Northern States, and even fell into the far soil of Missouri and the
Carolinas), the demand for paper at my place became so
great, that the expenditure soon amounted to a most important item in the general account. It need hardly be hinted
how paper comes into use with seedsmen, as envelopes.
These are mostly made of yellowish paper, folded square;
and when filled, are all but flat, and being stamped, and
superscribed with the nature of the seeds contained, assume
not a little the appearance of business-letters ready for the
mail. Of these small envelopes I used an incredible quantity—several hundreds of thousands in a year. For a time
I had purchased my paper from the wholesale dealers in a
neighboring town. For economy's sake, and partly for the
adventure of the trip, I now resolved to cross the mountains,
some sixty miles, and order my future paper at the Devil's
Dungeon paper-mill.

The sleighing being uncommonly fine toward the end of
January, and promising to hold so for no small period, in
spite of the bitter cold I started one gray Friday noon in my
pung,* well fitted with buffalo and wolf robes; and, spend-
ing one night on the road, next noon came in sight of
Woedolor Mountain.

The far summit fairly smoked with frost; white vapors
curled up from its white-wooded top, as from a chimney.
The intense congelation made the whole country look like
one petrifaction. The steel shoes of my pung craunched
and gritted over the vitreous, chippy snow, as if it had been
broken glass. The forests here and there skirting the route,
feeling the same all-stiffening influence, their inmost fibres

penetrated with the cold, strangely groaned—not in the swaying branches merely, but likewise in the vertical trunk—as
the fitful gusts remorselessly swept through them. Brittle with
excessive frost, many colossal tough-grained maples, snapped
in twain like pipe-stems, cumbered the unfeeling earth.

Flaked all over with frozen sweat, white as a milky ram,
his nostrils at each breath sending forth two horn-shaped
shoots of heated respiration, Black, my good horse, but six
years old, started at a sudden turn, where, right across the
track—not ten minutes fallen—an old distorted hemlock lay,
darkly undulatory as an anaconda.

Gaining the Bellows'-pipe, the violent blast, dead from
behind, all but shoved my high-backed pung up-hill. The
gust shrieked through the shivered pass, as if laden with lost
spirits bound to the unhappy world. Ere gaining the summit, Black, my horse, as if exasperated by the cutting wind,
slung out with his strong hind legs, tore the light pung
straight up-hill, and sweeping grazingly through the narrow
notch, sped downward madly past the ruined saw-mill. Into
the Devil's Dungeon horse and cataract rushed together.

With might and main, quitting my seat and robes, and
standing backward, with one foot braced against the dash-
board, I rasped and churned the bit, and stopped him just
in time to avoid collision, at a turn, with the bleak nozzle
of a rock, couchant like a lion in the way—a road-side rock.

At first I could not discover the paper-mill.

The whole hollow gleamed with the white, except, here
and there, where a pinnacle of granite showed one wind-
swept angle bare. The mountains stood pinned in shrouds—
a pass of Alpine corpses. Where stands the mill? Suddenly
a whirling, humming sound broke upon my ear. I looked,
and there, like an arrested avalanche, lay the large white-
washed factory. It was subordinately surrounded by a cluster of other and smaller buildings, some of which, from their
cheap, blank air, great length, gregarious windows, and com-
fortless expression, no doubt were boarding-houses of the
operatives. A snow-white hamlet amidst the snows. Various
rude, irregular squares and courts resulted from the somewhat picturesque clusterings of these buildings, owing to
the broken, rocky nature of the ground, which forbade all

method in their relative arrangement. Several narrow lanes and alleys, too, partly blocked with snow fallen from the roof, cut up the hamlet in all directions.

When, turning from the traveled highway, jingling with bells of numerous farmers—who, availing themselves of the fine sleighing, were dragging their wood to market—and frequently diversified with swift cutters dashing from inn to inn of the scattered villages—when, I say, turning from that bustling main-road, I by degrees wound into the Mad Maid's Bellows'-pipe, and saw the grim Black Notch beyond, then something latent, as well as something obvious in the time and scene, strangely brought back to my mind my first sight of dark and grimy Temple-Bar. And when Black, my horse, went darting through the Notch, perilously grazing its rocky wall, I remembered being in a runaway London omnibus, which in much the same sort of style, though by no means at an equal rate, dashed through the ancient arch of Wren.* Though the two objects did by no means completely correspond, yet this partial inadequacy but served to tinge the similitude not less with the vividness than the disorder of a dream. So that, when upon reining up at the protruding rock I at last caught sight of the quaint groupings of the factory-buildings, and with the traveled highway and the Notch behind, found myself all alone, silently and privily stealing through deep-cloven passages into this sequestered spot, and saw the long, high-gabled main factory edifice, with a rude tower—for hoisting heavy boxes—at one end, standing among its crowded outbuildings and boarding-houses, as the Temple Church amidst the surrounding offices and dormitories, and when the marvelous retirement of this mysterious mountain nook fastened its whole spell upon me, then, what memory lacked, all tributary imagination furnished, and I said to myself, "This is the very counterpart of the Paradise of Bachelors, but snowed upon, and frost-painted to a sepulchre."

Dismounting, and warily picking my way down the dangerous declivity—horse and man both sliding now and then upon the icy ledges—at length I drove, or the blast drove me, into the largest square, before one side of the main edifice.

Piercingly and shrilly the shotted blast blew by the corner; and redly and demoniacally boiled Blood River at one side. A long wood-pile, of many scores of cords, all glittering in mail of crusted ice, stood crosswise in the square. A row of horse-posts, their north sides plastered with adhesive snow, flanked the factory wall. The bleak frost packed and paved the square as with some ringing metal.

The inverted similitude recurred—"The sweet, tranquil Temple garden, with the Thames bordering its green beds," strangely meditated I.

But where are the gay bachelors?

Then, as I and my horse stood shivering in the wind-spray, a girl ran from a neighboring dormitory door, and throwing her thin apron over her bare head, made for the opposite building.

"One moment, my girl; is there no shed hereabouts which I may drive into?"

Pausing, she turned upon me a face pale with work, and blue with cold; an eye supernatural with unrelated misery.

"Nay," faltered I, "I mistook you. Go on; I want nothing."

Leading my horse close to the door from which she had come, I knocked. Another pale, blue girl appeared, shivering in the doorway as, to prevent the blast, she jealously held the door ajar.

"Nay, I mistake again. In God's name shut the door. But hold, is there no man about?"

That moment a dark-complexioned well-wrapped personage passed, making for the factory door, and spying him coming, the girl rapidly closed the other one.

"Is there no horse-shed here, Sir?"

"Yonder, to the wood-shed," he replied, and disappeared inside the factory.

With much ado I managed to wedge in horse and pung between the scattered piles of wood all sawn and split. Then, blanketing my horse, and piling my buffalo on the blanket's top, and tucking in its edges well around the breast-band and breeching, so that the wind might not strip him bare, I tied him fast, and ran lamely for the factory door, stiff with frost, and cumbered with my driver's dread-naught.*

Immediately I found myself standing in a spacious place, intolerably lighted by long rows of windows, focusing inward the snowy scene without.

At rows of blank-looking counters sat rows of blank-looking girls, with blank, white folders in their blank hands, all blankly folding blank paper.

In one corner stood some huge frame of ponderous iron, with a vertical thing like a piston periodically rising and falling upon a heavy wooden block. Before it—its tame minister —stood a tall girl, feeding the iron animal with half-quires of rose-hued note paper, which, at every downward dab of the piston-like machine, received in the corner the impress of a wreath of roses. I looked from the rosy paper to the pallid cheek, but said nothing.

Seated before a long apparatus, strung with long, slender strings like any harp, another girl was feeding it with foolscap sheets, which, so soon as they curiously traveled from her on the cords, were withdrawn at the opposite end of the machine by a second girl. They came to the first girl blank; they went to the second girl ruled.

I looked upon the first girl's brow, and saw it was young and fair; I looked upon the second girl's brow, and saw it was ruled and wrinkled. Then, as I still looked, the two— for some small variety to the monotony—changed places; and where had stood the young, fair brow, now stood the ruled and wrinkled one.

Perched high upon a narrow platform, and still higher upon a high stool crowning it, sat another figure serving some other iron animal; while below the platform sat her mate in some sort of reciprocal attendance.

Not a syllable was breathed. Nothing was heard but the low, steady, overruling hum of the iron animals. The human voice was banished from the spot. Machinery—that vaunted slave of humanity—here stood menially served by human beings, who served mutely and cringingly as the slave serves the Sultan. The girls did not so much seem accessory wheels to the general machinery as mere cogs to the wheels.

All this scene around me was instantaneously taken in at one sweeping glance—even before I had proceeded to

unwind the heavy fur tippet from around my neck. But
as soon as this fell from me the dark-complexioned man,
standing close by, raised a sudden cry, and seizing my arm,
dragged me out into the open air, and without pausing for
a word instantly caught up some congealed snow and began
rubbing both my cheeks.

"Two white spots like the whites of your eyes," he said;
"man, your cheeks are frozen."

"That may well be," muttered I; "'tis some wonder the
frost of the Devil's Dungeon strikes in no deeper. Rub
away."

Soon a horrible, tearing pain caught at my reviving cheeks.
Two gaunt blood-hounds, one on each side, seemed mum-
bling them. I seemed Actæon.*

Presently, when all was over, I re-entered the factory, made
known my business, concluded it satisfactorily, and then
begged to be conducted throughout the place to view it.

"Cupid is the boy for that," said the dark-complexioned
man. "Cupid!" and by this odd fancy-name calling a dimpled, red-cheeked, spirited-looking, forward little fellow, who
was rather impudently, I thought, gliding about among the
passive-looking girls—like a gold fish through hueless waves
—yet doing nothing in particular that I could see, the man
bade him lead the stranger through the edifice.

"Come first and see the water-wheel," said this lively lad,
with the air of boyishly-brisk importance.

Quitting the folding-room, we crossed some damp, cold
boards, and stood beneath a great wet shed, incessantly
showering with foam, like the green barnacled bow of some
East Indiaman in a gale. Round and round here went the
enormous revolutions of the dark colossal water-wheel, grim
with its one immutable purpose.

"This sets our whole machinery a-going, Sir; in every part
of all these buildings; where the girls work and all."

I looked, and saw that the turbid waters of Blood River
had not changed their hue by coming under the use of man.

"You make only blank paper; no printing of any sort, I
suppose? All blank paper, don't you?"

"Certainly; what else should a paper-factory make?"

The lad here looked at me as if suspicious of my common-sense.

"Oh, to be sure!" said I, confused and stammering; "it only struck me as so strange that red waters should turn out pale chee—paper, I mean."

He took me up a wet and rickety stair to a great light room, furnished with no visible thing but rude, manger-like receptacles running all round its sides; and up to these mangers, like so many mares haltered to the rack, stood rows of girls. Before each was vertically thrust up a long, glittering scythe, immovably fixed at bottom to the manger-edge. The curve of the scythe, and its having no snath to it, made it look exactly like a sword. To and fro, across the sharp edge, the girls forever dragged long strips of rags, washed white, picked from baskets at one side; thus ripping asunder every seam, and converting the tatters almost into lint. The air swam with the fine, poisonous particles, which from all sides darted, subtilely, as motes in sun-beams, into the lungs.

"This is the rag-room," coughed the boy.

"You find it rather stifling here," coughed I, in answer; "but the girls don't cough."

"Oh, they are used to it."

"Where do you get such hosts of rags?" picking up a handful from a basket.

"Some from the country round about; some from far over sea—Leghorn and London."

" 'Tis not unlikely, then," murmured I, "that among these heaps of rags there may be some old shirts, gathered from the dormitories of the Paradise of Bachelors. But the buttons are all dropped off. Pray, my lad, do you ever find any bachelor's buttons* hereabouts?"

"None grow in this part of the country. The Devil's Dungeon is no place for flowers."

"Oh! you mean the *flowers* so called—the Bachelor's Buttons?"

"And was not that what you asked about? Or did you mean the gold bosom-buttons of our boss, Old Bach, as our whispering girls all call him?"

"The man, then, I saw below is a bachelor, is he?"

"Oh, yes, he's a Bach."

"The edges of those swords, they are turned outward from the girls, if I see right; but their rags and fingers fly so, I can not distinctly see."

"Turned outward."

Yes, murmured I to myself; I see it now; turned outward; and each erected sword is so borne, edge-outward, before each girl. If my reading fails me not, just so, of old, condemned state-prisoners went from the hall of judgment to their doom: an officer before, bearing a sword, its edge turned outward, in significance of their fatal sentence. So, through consumptive pallors of this blank, raggy life, go these white girls to death.

"Those scythes look very sharp," again turning toward the boy.

"Yes; they have to keep them so. Look!"

That moment two of the girls, dropping their rags, plied each a whet-stone up and down the sword-blade. My unaccustomed blood curdled at the sharp shriek of the tormented steel.

Their own executioners; themselves whetting the very swords that slay them; meditated I.

"What makes those girls so sheet-white, my lad?"

"Why"—with a roguish twinkle, pure ignorant drollery, not knowing heartlessness—"I suppose the handling of such white bits of sheets all the time makes them so sheety."

"Let us leave the rag-room now, my lad."

More tragical and more inscrutably mysterious than any mystic sight, human or machine, throughout the factory, was the strange innocence of cruel-heartedness in this usage-hardened boy.

"And now," said he, cheerily, "I suppose you want to see our great machine, which cost us twelve thousand dollars only last autumn. That's the machine that makes the paper, too. This way, Sir."

Following him, I crossed a large, bespattered place, with two great round vats in it, full of a white, wet, woolly-looking stuff, not unlike the albuminous part of an egg, soft-boiled.

"There," said Cupid, tapping the vats carelessly, "these are the first beginnings of the paper; this white pulp you see. Look how it swims bubbling round and round, moved by the paddle here. From hence it pours from both vats into that one common channel yonder; and so goes, mixed up and leisurely, to the great machine. And now for that."

He led me into a room, stifling with a strange, blood-like, abdominal heat, as if here, true enough, were being finally developed the germinous particles lately seen.

Before me, rolled out like some long Eastern manuscript, lay stretched one continuous length of iron frame-work—multitudinous and mystical, with all sorts of rollers, wheels, and cylinders, in slowly-measured and unceasing motion.

"Here first comes the pulp now," said Cupid, pointing to the nighest end of the machine. "See; first it pours out and spreads itself upon this wide, sloping board; and then —look—slides, thin and quivering, beneath the first roller there. Follow on now, and see it as it slides from under that to the next cylinder. There; see how it has become just a very little less pulpy now. One step more, and it grows still more to some slight consistence. Still another cylinder, and it is so knitted—though as yet mere dragon-fly wing— that it forms an air-bridge here, like a suspended cobweb, between two more separated rollers; and flowing over the last one, and under again, and doubling about there out of sight for a minute among all those mixed cylinders you indistinctly see, it reappears here, looking now at last a little less like pulp and more like paper, but still quite delicate and defective yet awhile. But—a little further onward, Sir, if you please—here now, at this further point, it puts on something of a real look, as if it might turn out to be something you might possibly handle in the end. But it's not yet done, Sir. Good way to travel yet, and plenty more of cylinders must roll it."

"Bless my soul!" said I, amazed at the elongation, interminable convolutions, and deliberate slowness of the machine; "it must take a long time for the pulp to pass from end to end, and come out paper."

"Oh! not so long," smiled the precocious lad, with a superior and patronizing air; "only nine minutes. But look; you may try it for yourself. Have you a bit of paper? Ah! here's a bit on the floor. Now mark that with any word you please, and let me dab it on here, and we'll see how long before it comes out at the other end."

"Well, let me see," said I, taking out my pencil; "come, I'll mark it with your name."

Bidding me take out my watch, Cupid adroitly dropped the inscribed slip on an exposed part of the incipient mass.

Instantly my eye marked the second-hand on my dial-plate.

Slowly I followed the slip, inch by inch; sometimes pausing for full half a minute as it disappeared beneath inscrutable groups of the lower cylinders, but only gradually to emerge again; and so, on, and on, and on—inch by inch; now in open sight, sliding along like a freckle on the quivering sheet; and then again wholly vanished; and so, on, and on, and on—inch by inch; all the time the main sheet growing more and more to final firmness—when, suddenly, I saw a sort of paper-fall, not wholly unlike a water-fall; a scissory sound smote my ear, as of some cord being snapped; and down dropped an unfolded sheet of perfect foolscap, with my "Cupid" half faded out of it, and still moist and warm.

My travels were at an end, for here was the end of the machine.

"Well, how long was it?" said Cupid.

"Nine minutes to a second," replied I, watch in hand.

"I told you so."

For a moment a curious emotion filled me, not wholly unlike that which one might experience at the fulfillment of some mysterious prophecy. But how absurd, thought I again; the thing is a mere machine, the essence of which is unvarying punctuality and precision.

Previously absorbed by the wheels and cylinders, my attention was now directed to a sad-looking woman standing by.

"That is rather an elderly person so silently tending the machine-end here. She would not seem wholly used to it either."

"Oh," knowingly whispered Cupid, through the din, "she only came last week. She was a nurse formerly. But the business is poor in these parts, and she's left it. But look at the paper she is piling there."

"Ay, foolscap," handling the piles of moist, warm sheets, which continually were being delivered into the woman's waiting hands. "Don't you turn out any thing but foolscap at this machine?"

"Oh, sometimes, but not often, we turn out finer work —cream-laid and royal sheets, we call them. But foolscap being in chief demand, we turn out foolscap most."

It was very curious. Looking at that blank paper continually dropping, dropping, dropping, my mind ran on in wonderings of those strange uses to which those thousand sheets eventually would be put. All sorts of writings would be writ on those now vacant things—sermons, lawyers' briefs, physicians' prescriptions, love-letters, marriage certificates, bills of divorce, registers of births, death-warrants, and so on, without end. Then, recurring back to them as they here lay all blank, I could not but bethink me of that celebrated comparison of John Locke, who, in demonstration of his theory that man had no innate ideas, compared the human mind at birth to a sheet of blank paper;* something destined to be scribbled on, but what sort of characters no soul might tell.

Pacing slowly to and fro along the involved machine, still humming with its play, I was struck as well by the inevitability as the evolvement-power in all its motions.

"Does that thin cobweb there," said I, pointing to the sheet in its more imperfect stage, "does that never tear or break? It is marvelous fragile, and yet this machine it passes through is so mighty."

"It never is known to tear a hair's point."

"Does it never stop—get clogged?"

"No. It *must* go. The machinery makes it go just *so*; just that very way, and at that very pace you there plainly *see* it go. The pulp can't help going."

Something of awe now stole over me, as I gazed upon this inflexible iron animal. Always, more or less, machinery of this ponderous, elaborate sort strikes, in some moods, strange dread into the human heart, as some living, panting Behemoth might.* But what made the thing I saw so specially terrible to me was the metallic necessity, the unbudging fatality which governed it. Though, here and there, I could not follow the thin, gauzy vail of pulp in the course of its more mysterious or entirely invisible advance, yet it was indubitable that, at those points where it eluded me, it still marched on in unvarying docility to the autocratic cunning of the machine. A fascination fastened on me. I stood spell-bound and wandering in my soul. Before my eyes—there, passing in slow procession along the wheeling cylinders, I seemed to see, glued to the pallid incipience of the pulp, the yet more pallid faces of all the pallid girls I had eyed that heavy day. Slowly, mournfully, beseechingly, yet unresistingly, they gleamed along, their agony dimly outlined on the imperfect paper, like the print of the tormented face on the handkerchief of Saint Veronica.*

"Halloa! the heat of the room is too much for you," cried Cupid, staring at me.

"No—I am rather chill, if any thing."

"Come out, Sir—out—out," and, with the protecting air of a careful father, the precocious lad hurried me outside.

In a few moments, feeling revived a little, I went into the folding-room—the first room I had entered, and where the desk for transacting business stood, surrounded by the blank counters and blank girls engaged at them.

"Cupid here has led me a strange tour," said I to the dark-complexioned man before mentioned, whom I had ere this discovered not only to be an old bachelor, but also the principal proprietor. "Yours is a most wonderful factory. Your great machine is a miracle of inscrutable intricacy."

"Yes, all our visitors think it so. But we don't have many. We are in a very out-of-the-way corner here. Few inhabitants, too. Most of our girls come from far-off villages."

"The girls," echoed I, glancing round at their silent forms. "Why is it, Sir, that in most factories, female operatives, of whatever age, are indiscriminately called girls, never women?"

"Oh! as to that—why, I suppose, the fact of their being generally unmarried—that's the reason, I should think. But it never struck me before. For our factory here, we will not have married women; they are apt to be off-and-on too much. We want none but steady workers: twelve hours to the day, day after day, through the three hundred and sixty-five days, excepting Sundays, Thanksgiving, and Fast-days. That's our rule. And so, having no married women, what females we have are rightly enough called girls."

"Then these are all maids," said I, while some pained homage to their pale virginity made me involuntarily bow.

"All maids."

Again the strange emotion filled me.

"Your cheeks look whitish yet, Sir," said the man, gazing at me narrowly. "You must be careful going home. Do they pain you at all now? It's a bad sign, if they do."

"No doubt, Sir," answered I, "when once I have got out of the Devil's Dungeon, I shall feel them mending."

"Ah, yes; the winter air in valleys, or gorges, or any sunken place, is far colder and more bitter than elsewhere. You would hardly believe it now, but it is colder here than at the top of Woedolor Mountain."

"I dare say it is, Sir. But time presses me; I must depart."

With that, remuffling myself in dread-naught and tippet, thrusting my hands into my huge seal-skin mittens, I sallied out into the nipping air, and found poor Black, my horse, all cringing and doubled up with the cold.

Soon, wrapped in furs and meditations, I ascended from the Devil's Dungeon.

At the Black Notch I paused, and once more bethought me of Temple-Bar. Then, shooting through the pass, all alone with inscrutable nature, I exclaimed—Oh! Paradise of Bachelors! and oh! Tartarus of Maids!

THE LIGHTNING-ROD MAN

WHAT grand irregular thunder, thought I, standing on my hearthstone among the Acroceraunian hills,* as the scattered bolts boomed overhead and crashed down among the valleys, every bolt followed by zig-zag irradiations, and swift slants of sharp rain, which audibly rang, like a charge of spear-points, on my low shingled roof. I suppose, though, that the mountains hereabouts break and churn up the thunder, so that it is far more glorious here than on the plain. Hark!—some one at the door. Who is this that chooses a time of thunder for making calls? And why don't he, man-fashion, use the knocker, instead of making that doleful undertaker's clatter with his fist against the hollow panel? But let him in. Ah, here he comes. "Good day, sir:" an entire stranger. "Pray be seated." What is that strange-looking walking-stick he carries:—"A fine thunder-storm, sir."

"Fine?—Awful!"

"You are wet. Stand here on the hearth before the fire."

"Not for worlds!"

The stranger still stood in the exact middle of the cottage, where he had first planted himself. His singularity impelled a closer scrutiny. A lean, gloomy figure. Hair dark and lank, mattedly streaked over his brow. His sunken pitfalls of eyes were ringed by indigo halos, and played with an innocuous sort of lightning: the gleam without the bolt. The whole man was dripping. He stood in a puddle on the bare oak floor; his strange walking-stick vertically resting at his side.

It was a polished copper rod, four feet long, lengthwise attached to a neat wooden staff, by insertion into two balls of greenish glass, ringed with copper bands. The metal rod terminated at the top tripodwise, in three keen tines, brightly gilt. He held the thing by the wooden part alone.

"Sir," said I, bowing politely, "have I the honor of a visit from that illustrious god, Jupiter Tonans?* So stood he in the Greek statue of old, grasping the lightning-bolt. If you be he, or his viceroy, I have to thank you for this noble storm you have brewed among our mountains. Listen: That was a glorious peal. Ah, to a lover of the majestic, it is a good thing to have the Thunderer himself in one's cottage. The thunder grows finer for that. But pray be seated. This old rush-bottomed arm-chair, I grant, is a poor substitute for your evergreen throne on Olympus; but, condescend to be seated."

While I thus pleasantly spoke, the stranger eyed me, half in wonder and half in a strange sort of horror; but did not move a foot.

"Do, sir, be seated; you need to be dried ere going forth again."

I planted the chair invitingly on the broad hearth, where a little fire had been kindled that afternoon to dissipate the dampness, not the cold; for it was early in the month of September.

But without heeding my solicitation, and still standing in the middle of the floor, the stranger gazed at me portentously and spoke.

"Sir," said he, "excuse me, but instead of my accepting your invitation to be seated on the hearth there, I solemnly warn *you*, that you had best accept *mine*, and stand with me in the middle of the room. Good heavens!" he cried, starting—"there's another of those awful crashes. I warn you, sir, quit the hearth."

"Mr. Jupiter Tonans," said I, quietly rolling my body on the stone, "I stand very well here."

"Are you so horridly ignorant, then," he cried, "as not to know, that by far the most dangerous part of a house during such a terrific tempest as this, is the fire-place?"

"Nay, I did not know that," involuntarily stepping upon the first board next to the stone.

The stranger now assumed such an unpleasant air of successful admonition, that—quite involuntarily again—I stepped back upon the hearth, and threw myself into the erectest, proudest posture I could command. But I said nothing.

"For Heaven's sake," he cried, with a strange mixture of alarm and intimidation—"for Heaven's sake, get off of the hearth! Know you not, that the heated air and soot are conductors;—to say nothing of those immense iron fire-dogs? Quit the spot,—I conjure,—I command you."

"Mr. Jupiter Tonans, I am not accustomed to be commanded in my own house."

"Call me not by that pagan name. You are profane in this time of terror."

"Sir, will you be so good as to tell me your business? If you seek shelter from the storm, you are welcome, so long as you be civil; but if you come on business, open it forthwith. Who are you?"

"I am a dealer in lightning-rods,"* said the stranger, softening his tone; "my special business is—— Merciful heaven! what a crash!—Have you ever been struck—your premises, I mean? No? It's best to be provided;"—significantly rattling his metallic staff on the floor;—"by nature, there are no castles in thunder-storms; yet, say but the word, and of this cottage I can make a Gibraltar by a few waves of this wand. Hark, what Himmalayas of concussions!"

"You interrupted yourself; your special business you were about to speak of."

"My special business is to travel the country for orders for lightning-rods. This is my specimen-rod;" tapping his staff; "I have the best of references"—fumbling in his pockets. "In Criggan last month, I put up three-and-twenty rods on only five buildings."

"Let me see. Was it not at Criggan last week, about midnight on Saturday, that the steeple, the big elm and the Assembly-room cupola were struck?* Any of your rods there?"

"Not on the tree and cupola, but the steeple."

"Of what use is your rod then?"*

"Of life-and-death use. But my workman was heedless. In fitting the rod at top to the steeple, he allowed a part of the metal to graze the tin sheeting. Hence the accident. Not my fault, but his. Hark!"

"Never mind. That clap burst quite loud enough to be heard without finger-pointing. Did you hear of the event at Montreal last year? A servant girl struck at her bed-side with a rosary in her hand; the beads being metal. Does your beat extend into the Canadas?"

"No. And I hear that there, iron rods only are in use. They should have *mine*, which are copper. Iron is easily fused. Then they draw out the rod so slender, that it has not body enough to conduct the full electric current. The metal melts; the building is destroyed. My copper rods never act so. Those Canadians are fools. Some of them knob the rod at the top, which risks a deadly explosion, instead of imperceptibly carrying down the current into the earth, as this sort of rod does. *Mine* is the only true rod.* Look at it. Only one dollar a foot."

"This abuse of your own calling in another might make one distrustful with respect to yourself."

"Hark! The thunder becomes less muttering. It is nearing us, and nearing the earth, too. Hark! One crammed crash! All the vibrations made one by nearness. Another flash. Hold!"

"What do you?" I said, seeing him now, instantaneously relinquishing his staff, lean intently forward towards the window, with his right fore and middle fingers on his left wrist.

But ere the words had well escaped me, another exclamation escaped him.

"Crash! only three pulses—less than a third of a mile off— yonder, somewhere in that wood. I passed three stricken oaks there, ripped out new and glittering. The oak draws lightning more than other timber, having iron in solution in its sap. Your floor here seems oak."

"Heart-of-oak. From the peculiar time of your call upon me, I suppose you purposely select stormy weather for your journeys. When the thunder is roaring, you deem it an hour peculiarly favorable for producing impressions favorable to your trade."

"Hark!—Awful!"

"For one who would arm others with fearlessness, you seem unbeseemingly timorous yourself. Common men choose fair weather for their travels: you choose thunder-storms; and yet——"

"That I travel in thunder-storms, I grant; but not without particular precautions, such as only a lightning-rod man may know. Hark! Quick—look at my specimen rod. Only one dollar a foot."

"A very fine rod, I dare say. But what are these particular precautions of yours? Yet first let me close yonder shutters; the slanting rain is beating through the sash. I will bar up."

"Are you mad? Know you not that yon iron bar is a swift conductor? Desist."

"I will simply close the shutters then, and call my boy to bring me a wooden bar. Pray, touch the bell-pull there."

"Are you frantic? That bell-wire might blast you. Never touch bell-wire in a thunder-storm, nor ring a bell of any sort."

"Nor those in belfries? Pray, will you tell me where and how one may be safe in a time like this? Is there any part of my house I may touch with hopes of my life?"

"There is; but not where you now stand. Come away from the wall. The current will sometimes run down a wall, and—a man being a better conductor than a wall—it would leave the wall and run into him. Swoop! *That* must have fallen very nigh. That must have been globular lightning."

"Very probably. Tell me at once, which is, in your opinion, the safest part of this house?"

"This room, and this one spot in it where I stand. Come hither."

"The reasons first."

"Hark!—after the flash the gust—the sashes shiver—the house, the house!—Come hither to me!"

"The reasons, if you please."

"Come hither to me!"

"Thank you again, I think I will try my old stand,—the hearth. And now Mr. Lightning-rod-man, in the pauses of the thunder, be so good as to tell me your reasons for esteeming this one room of the house the safest, and your own one stand-point there the safest spot in it."

There was now a little cessation of the storm for a while. The Lightning-rod man seemed relieved, and replied:—

"Your house is a one-storied house, with an attic and a cellar; this room is between. Hence its comparative safety. Because lightning sometimes passes from the clouds to the earth, and sometimes from the earth to the clouds. Do you comprehend?—and I choose the middle of the room, because, if the lightning should strike the house at all, it would come down the chimney or walls; so, obviously, the further you are from them, the better. Come hither to me, now."

"Presently. Something you just said, instead of alarming me, has strangely inspired confidence."

"What have I said?"

"You said that sometimes lightning flashes from the earth to the clouds."

"Aye, the returning-stroke, as it is called; when the earth, being overcharged with the fluid, flashes its surplus upward."

"The returning-stroke; that is, from earth to sky. Better and better. But come here on the hearth and dry yourself."

"I am better here, and better wet."

"How?"

"It is the safest thing you can do—Hark, again!—to get yourself thoroughly drenched in a thunder-storm. Wet clothes are better conductors than the body; and so, if the lightning strike, it might pass down the wet clothes without touching the body. The storm deepens again. Have you a rug in the house? Rugs are non-conductors. Get one, that I may stand on it here, and you too. The skies blacken—it is dusk at noon. Hark!—the rug, the rug!"

I gave him one; while the hooded mountains seemed closing and tumbling into the cottage.

"And now, since our being dumb will not help us," said I, resuming my place, "let me hear your precautions in travelling during thunder-storms."

"Wait till this one is passed."

"Nay, proceed with the precautions. You stand in the safest possible place according to your own account. Go on."

"Briefly then. I avoid pine-trees, high houses, lonely barns, upland pastures, running water, flocks of cattle and sheep, a crowd of men. If I travel on foot,—as to-day—I do not walk fast; if in my buggy, I touch not its back or sides; if on horseback, I dismount and lead the horse. But of all things, I avoid tall men."

"Do I dream? Man avoid man? and in danger-time too?"

"Tall men in a thunder-storm I avoid. Are you so grossly ignorant as not to know, that the height of a six-footer is sufficient to discharge an electric cloud upon him? Are not lonely Kentuckians, ploughing, smit in the unfinished furrow? Nay, if the six-footer stand by running water, the cloud will sometimes *select* him as its conductor to that running water. Hark! Sure, yon black pinnacle is split. Yes, a man is a good conductor. The lightning goes through and through a man, but only peels a tree. But sir, you have kept me so long answering your questions, that I have not yet come to business. Will you order one of my rods? Look at this specimen one? See: it is of the best of copper. Copper's the best conductor. Your house is low; but being upon the mountains, that lowness does not one whit depress it. You mountaineers are most exposed. In mountainous countries the lightning-rod man should have most business. Look at the specimen, sir. One rod will answer for a house so small as this. Look over these recommendations. Only one rod, sir; cost, only twenty dollars. Hark! There go all the granite Taconics and Hoosics* dashed together like pebbles. By the sound, that must have struck something. An elevation of five feet above the house, will protect twenty feet radius all about the rod. Only twenty dollars, sir—a dollar a foot. Hark!—Dreadful!—Will you order? Will you buy? Shall I put down your name? Think of being a heap of charred offal, like a haltered horse burnt in his stall;—and all in one flash!"

"You pretended envoy extraordinary and minister plenipotentiary to and from Jupiter Tonans," laughed I; "you mere man who come here to put you and your pipestem between clay and sky, do you think that because you can strike a bit of green light from the Leyden jar,* that you can thoroughly avert the supernal bolt? Your rod rusts, or breaks, and where are you? Who has empowered you, you Tetzel,* to peddle round your indulgences from divine ordinations? The hairs of our heads are numbered, and the days of our lives. In thunder as in sunshine, I stand at ease in the hands of my God. False negotiator, away! See, the scroll of the storm is rolled back;* the house is unharmed; and in the blue heavens I read in the rainbow, that the Deity will not, of purpose, make war on man's earth."

"Impious wretch!" foamed the stranger, blackening in the face as the rainbow beamed, "I will publish your infidel notions."

"Begone! move quickly! if quickly you can, you that shine forth into sight in moist times like the worm."

The scowl grew blacker on his face; the indigo-circles enlarged round his eyes as the storm rings round the midnight moon. He sprang upon me; his tri-forked thing at my heart.

I seized it; I snapped it; I dashed it; I trod it; and dragging the dark lightning-king out of my door, flung his elbowed, copper sceptre after him.

But spite of my treatment, and spite of my dissuasive talk of him to my neighbors, the Lightning-rod man still dwells in the land; still travels in storm-time, and drives a brave trade with the fears of man.

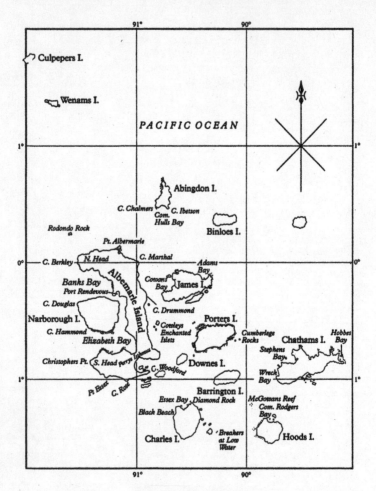

Culpepers I.

Wenams I.

PACIFIC OCEAN

Abingdon I.

C. Chalmers   C. Ibetson
              Com.
              Hulls Bay

Rodondo Rock   Binloes I.

Pt. Albemarle

C. Berkley   N. Head   C. Marshal
                                      Adams
                                      Bay
Banks Bay   Cowans   James I.
Port Rendevous   Bay
C. Douglas
Narborough I.   C. Drummond
C. Hammond   Cotoleys   Porters I.
                              Enchanted
              Elizabeth Bay   Islets   Cumberlege   Chathams I.   Hobbes
                                                        Rocks   Bay
                              Perrys Island   Stephens
Christophers Pt. S. Head   Bay
                              C. Woodford   Downes I.
                                                                      Wreck
              Pt Essex   C. Rose   Bay
                                      Barrington I.   McGowans Reef
                              Essex Bay Diamond Rock   Com. Rodgers
                              Black Beach   Bay
                                              Breakers
                          Charles I.   at Low   Hoods I.
                                              Water

Gallapagos [*sic*] Islands

Source: Captain David Porter, *Journal of a Cruise Made to the Pacific*

THE ENCANTADAS,
OR ENCHANTED ISLES

By Salvator R. Tarnmoor*

SKETCH FIRST

THE ISLES AT LARGE

—"That may not be, said then the ferryman,
Least we unweeting hap to be fordonne;
For those same islands seeming now and than,
Are not firme land, nor any certein wonne,
But stragling plots which to and fro do ronne
In the wide waters; therefore are they hight
The Wandering Islands; therefore do them shonne;
For they have oft drawne many a wandring wight
Into most deadly daunger and distressed plight;
For whosoever once hath fastened
His foot thereon may never it recure
But wandreth evermore uncertein and unsure."

"Darke, dolefull, dreary, like a greedy grave,
That still for carrion carcasses doth crave;
On top whereof ay dwelt the ghastly owl,
Shrieking his balefull note, which ever drave
Far from that haunt all other cheerful fowl,
And all about it wandring ghosts did wayle and howl."*

TAKE five-and-twenty heaps of cinders dumped here and
there in an outside city lot; imagine some of them magni-
fied into mountains, and the vacant lot the sea; and you
will have a fit idea of the general aspect of the Encantadas,
or Enchanted Isles. A group rather of extinct volcanoes than
of isles; looking much as the world at large might, after a
penal conflagration.

It is to be doubted whether any spot of earth can, in des-
olateness, furnish a parallel to this group. Abandoned cemet-
eries of long ago, old cities by piecemeal tumbling to their

ruin, these are melancholy enough; but, like all else which has but once been associated with humanity they still awaken in us some thoughts of sympathy, however sad. Hence, even the Dead Sea, along with whatever other emotions it may at times inspire, does not fail to touch in the pilgrim some of his less unpleasurable feelings.

And as for solitariness; the great forests of the north, the expanses of unnavigated waters, the Greenland ice-fields, are the profoundest of solitudes to a human observer; still the magic of their changeable tides and seasons mitigates their terror; because, though unvisited by men, those forests are visited by the May; the remotest seas reflect familiar stars even as Lake Erie does; and in the clear air of a fine Polar day, the irradiated, azure ice shows beautifully as malachite.

But the special curse, as one may call it, of the Encantadas, that which exalts them in desolation above Idumea* and the Pole, is that to them change never comes; neither the change of seasons nor of sorrows. Cut by the Equator, they know not autumn and they know not spring; while already reduced to the lees of fire, ruin itself can work little more upon them. The showers refresh the deserts, but in these isles, rain never falls. Like split Syrian gourds left withering in the sun, they are cracked by an everlasting drought beneath a torrid sky. "Have mercy upon me," the wailing spirit of the Encantadas seems to cry, "and send Lazarus that he may dip the tip of his finger in water and cool my tongue, for I am tormented in this flame."*

Another feature in these isles is their emphatic uninhabitableness. It is deemed a fit type of all-forsaken overthrow, that the jackal should den in the wastes of weedy Babylon;* but the Encantadas refuse to harbor even the outcasts of the beasts. Man and wolf alike disown them. Little but reptile life is here found:—tortoises, lizards, immense spiders, snakes, and that strangest anomaly of outlandish nature, the *iguana*. No voice, no low, no howl is heard; the chief sound of life here is a hiss.

On most of the isles where vegetation is found at all, it is more ungrateful than the blankness of Atacama.* Tangled thickets of wiry bushes, without fruit and without a name,

springing up among deep fissures of calcined rock, and treacherously masking them; or a parched growth of distorted cactus trees.

In many places the coast is rock-bound, or more properly,
clinker-bound; tumbled masses of blackish or greenish stuff
like the dross of an iron-furnace, forming dark clefts and
caves here and there, into which a ceaseless sea pours a fury
of foam; overhanging them with a swirl of gray, haggard
mist, amidst which sail screaming flights of unearthly birds
heightening the dismal din. However calm the sea without,
there is no rest for these swells and those rocks; they lash
and are lashed, even when the outer ocean is most at peace
with itself. On the oppressive, clouded days, such as are peculiar to this part of the watery Equator, the dark, vitrified
masses, many of which raise themselves among white whirl-
pools and breakers in detached and perilous places off the
shore, present a most Plutonian sight. In no world but a
fallen one could such lands exist.

Those parts of the strand free from the marks of fire,
stretch away in wide level beaches of multitudinous dead
shells, with here and there decayed bits of sugar-cane, bam-
boos, and cocoanuts, washed upon this other and darker
world from the charming palm isles to the westward and
southward; all the way from Paradise to Tartarus; while
mixed with the relics of distant beauty you will sometimes
see fragments of charred wood and mouldering ribs of wrecks.
Neither will any one be surprised at meeting these last, after
observing the conflicting currents which eddy throughout
nearly all the wide channels of the entire group. The capriciousness of the tides of air sympathizes with those of the
sea. Nowhere is the wind so light, baffling, and every way
unreliable, and so given to perplexing calms, as at the
Encantadas. Nigh a month has been spent by a ship going
from one isle to another, though but ninety miles between;
for owing to the force of the current, the boats employed
to tow barely suffice to keep the craft from sweeping upon
the cliffs, but do nothing towards accelerating her voyage.
Sometimes it is impossible for a vessel from afar to fetch up
with the group itself, unless large allowances for prospective

lee-way have been made ere its coming in sight. And yet, at other times, there is a mysterious indraft, which irresistibly draws a passing vessel among the isles, though not bound to them.

True, at one period, as to some extent at the present day, large fleets of whalemen cruised for Spermaceti upon what some seamen call the Enchanted Ground. But this, as in due place will be described, was off the great outer isle of Albemarle, away from the intricacies of the smaller isles, where there is plenty of sea-room; and hence, to that vicinity, the above remarks do not altogether apply; though even there the current runs at times with singular force, shifting, too, with as singular a caprice. Indeed, there are seasons when currents quite unaccountable prevail for a great distance round about the total group, and are so strong and irregular as to change a vessel's course against the helm, though sailing at the rate of four or five miles the hour. The difference in the reckonings of navigators produced by these causes, along with the light and variable winds, long nourished a persuasion that there existed two distinct clusters of isles in the parallel of the Encantadas, about a hundred leagues apart. Such was the idea of their earlier visitors, the Buccaneers; and as late as 1750, the charts of that part of the Pacific accorded with the strange delusion. And this apparent fleetingness and unreality of the locality of the isles was most probably one reason for the Spaniards calling them the Encantada, or Enchanted Group.

But not uninfluenced by their character, as they now confessedly exist, the modern voyager will be inclined to fancy that the bestowal of this name might have in part originated in that air of spell-bound desertness which so significantly invests the isles. Nothing can better suggest the aspect of once living things malignly crumbled from ruddiness into ashes. Apples of Sodom,* after touching, seem these isles.

However wavering their place may seem by reason of the currents, they themselves, at least to one upon the shore, appear invariably the same: fixed, cast, glued into the very body of cadaverous death.

Nor would the appellation, enchanted, seem misapplied in still another sense. For concerning the peculiar reptile

inhabitant of these wilds—whose presence gives the group
its second Spanish name, Gallipagos—concerning the tortoises found here, most mariners have long cherished a superstition, not more frightful than grotesque. They earnestly
believe that all wicked sea-officers, more especially commo-
dores and captains, are at death (and in some cases, before
death) transformed into tortoises; thenceforth dwelling upon
these hot aridities, sole solitary Lords of Asphaltum.

Doubtless so quaintly dolorous a thought was originally inspired by the woe-begone landscape itself, but more
particularly, perhaps, by the tortoises. For apart from their
strictly physical features, there is something strangely self-
condemned in the appearance of these creatures. Lasting
sorrow and penal hopelessness are in no animal form so
suppliantly expressed as in theirs; while the thought of their
wonderful longevity does not fail to enhance the impression.

Nor even at the risk of meriting the charge of absurdly
believing in enchantments, can I restrain the admission that
sometimes, even now, when leaving the crowded city to wander out July and August among the Adirondack Mountains,
far from the influences of towns and proportionally nigh to
the mysterious ones of nature; when at such times I sit me
down in the mossy head of some deep-wooded gorge, surrounded by prostrate trunks of blasted pines, and recall, as in
a dream, my other and far-distant rovings in the baked heart
of the charmed isles; and remember the sudden glimpses of
dusky shells, and long languid necks protruded from the
leafless thickets; and again have beheld the vitreous inland
rocks worn down and grooved into deep ruts by ages and
ages of the slow draggings of tortoises in quest of pools of
scanty water; I can hardly resist the feeling that in my time
I have indeed slept upon evilly enchanted ground.*

Nay, such is the vividness of my memory, or the magic
of my fancy, that I know not whether I am not the occasional victim of optical delusion concerning the Gallipagos.
For often in scenes of social merriment, and especially at
revels held by candle-light in old-fashioned mansions, so that
shadows are thrown into the further recesses of an angular
and spacious room, making them put on a look of haunted
undergrowth of lonely woods, I have drawn the attention of

my comrades by my fixed gaze and sudden change of air, as I have seemed to see, slowly emerging from those imagined solitudes, and heavily crawling along the floor, the ghost of a gigantic tortoise, with "Memento ****"* burning in live letters upon his back.

SKETCH SECOND

TWO SIDES TO A TORTOISE

"Most ugly shapes and horrible aspects,
Such as Dame Nature selfe mote feare to see,
Or shame, that ever should so fowle defects
From her most cunning hand escaped bee;
All dreadfull pourtraicts of deformitee.
Ne wonder if these do a man appall;
For all that here at home we dreadfull hold
Be but as bugs to fearen babes withall
Compared to the creatures in these isles' entrall.

Fear naught, then said the palmer, well avized,
For these same monsters are not these indeed,
But are into these fearful shapes disguized.

And lifting up his vertuous staffe on high,
Then all that dreadful armie fast gan flye
*Into great Tethys' bosom, where they hidden lye."**

IN view of the description given, may one be gay upon the Encantadas? Yes: that is, find one the gayety, and he will be gay. And indeed, sackcloth and ashes as they are, the isles are not perhaps unmitigated gloom. For while no spectator can deny their claims to a most solemn and superstitious consideration, no more than my firmest resolutions can decline to behold the spectre-tortoise when emerging from its shadowy recess; yet even the tortoise, dark and melancholy as it is upon the back, still possesses a bright side; its calapee or breast-plate being sometimes of a faint yellowish or golden tinge. Moreover, every one knows that tortoises as well as turtle are of such a make, that if you but put them on their backs you thereby expose their bright sides without the possibility of their recovering themselves, and turning into view the other. But after you have done this, and because you have done this, you should not swear that the tortoise has no dark side. Enjoy the bright, keep it turned up perpetually if you can, but be honest and don't deny the black.* Neither should he who cannot turn the tortoise from its natural position so as to hide the darker and expose his livelier aspect, like a great October pumpkin in the sun, for that cause declare the creature to be one total inky blot. The tortoise is both black and bright. But let us to particulars.

Some months before my first stepping ashore upon the group, my ship was cruising in its close vicinity. One noon we found ourselves off the South Head of Albemarle, and not very far from the land. Partly by way of freak, and partly by way of spying out so strange a country, a boat's crew was sent ashore, with orders to see all they could, and besides, bring back whatever tortoises they could conveniently transport.

It was after sunset when the adventurers returned. I looked down over the ship's high side as if looking down over the curb of a well, and dimly saw the damp boat deep in the sea with some unwonted weight. Ropes were dropt over, and presently three huge antediluvian-looking tortoises after much straining were landed on deck. They seemed hardly of the seed of earth. We had been broad upon the waters for five long months, a period amply sufficient to make all things of the land wear a fabulous hue to the dreamy mind. Had three Spanish custom-house officers boarded us then, it is not unlikely that I should have curiously stared at them, felt of them, and stroked them much as savages serve civilized guests. But instead of three custom-house officers, behold these really wondrous tortoises—none of your schoolboy mud-turtles—but black as widower's weeds, heavy as chests of plate, with vast shells medallioned and orbed like shields, and dented and blistered like shields that have breasted a battle, shaggy too, here and there, with dark green moss, and slimy with the spray of the sea. These mystic creatures suddenly translated by night from unutterable solitudes to our peopled deck, affected me in a manner not easy to unfold. They seemed newly crawled forth from beneath the foundations of the world. Yea, they seemed the identical tortoises whereon the Hindoo plants this total sphere.* With a lantern I inspected them more closely. Such worshipful venerableness of aspect! Such furry greenness mantling the rude peelings and healing the fissures of their shattered shells. I no more saw three tortoises. They expanded—became transfigured. I seemed to see three Roman Coliseums in magnificent decay.

Ye oldest inhabitants of this, or any other isle, said I, pray, give me the freedom of your three walled towns.

The great feeling inspired by these creatures was that of age:—dateless, indefinite endurance. And in fact that any other creature can live and breathe as long as the tortoise of the Encantadas, I will not readily believe. Not to hint of their known capacity of sustaining life, while going without food for an entire year, consider that impregnable armor of their living mail. What other bodily being possesses such a citadel wherein to resist the assaults of Time?

As, lantern in hand, I scraped among the moss and beheld the ancient scars of bruises received in many a sullen fall among the marly mountains of the isle—scars strangely widened, swollen, half obliterate, and yet distorted like those sometimes found in the bark of very hoary trees, I seemed an antiquary of a geologist, studying the bird-tracks and ciphers upon the exhumed slates trod by incredible creatures whose very ghosts are now defunct.

As I lay in my hammock that night, overhead I heard the slow weary draggings of the three ponderous strangers along the encumbered deck. Their stupidity or their resolution was so great, that they never went aside for any impediment. One ceased his movements altogether just before the midwatch. At sunrise I found him butted like a battering-ram against the immovable foot of the foremast, and still striving, tooth and nail, to force the impossible passage. That these tortoises are the victims of a penal, or malignant, or perhaps a downright diabolical enchanter, seems in nothing more likely than in that strange infatuation of hopeless toil which so often possesses them. I have known them in their journeyings ram themselves heroically against rocks, and long abide there, nudging, wriggling, wedging, in order to displace them, and so hold on their inflexible path. Their crowning curse is their drudging impulse to straightforwardness in a belittered world.*

Meeting with no such hinderance as their companion did, the other tortoises merely fell foul of small stumbling-blocks; buckets, blocks, and coils of rigging; and at times in the act of crawling over them would slip with an astounding rattle to the deck. Listening to these draggings and concussions, I thought me of the haunt from which they came; an isle full of metallic ravines and gulches, sunk bottomlessly into the hearts of splintered mountains, and covered for many miles with inextricable thickets. I then pictured these three straightforward monsters, century after century, writhing through the shades, grim as blacksmiths; crawling so slowly and ponderously, that not only did toadstools and all fungous things grow beneath their feet, but a sooty moss sprouted upon their backs. With them I lost myself in volcanic mazes; brushed away endless boughs of rotting thickets; till finally in a dream I found myself sitting cross-legged upon the foremost, a Brahmin similarly mounted upon either side, forming a tripod of foreheads which upheld the universal cope.

Such was the wild nightmare begot by my first impression of the Encantadas tortoise. But next evening, strange to say, I sat down with my shipmates, and made a merry repast from tortoise steaks and tortoise stews;* and supper over, out knife, and helped convert the three mighty concave shells into three fanciful soup-tureens, and polished the three flat yellowish calapees into three gorgeous salvers.

SKETCH THIRD

ROCK RODONDO*

"*Forthy this hight the Rock of vile Reproach,
A dangerous and dreadful place,
To which nor fish nor fowl did once approach,*

But yelling meaws with sea-gulls hoars and bace
And cormoyrants with birds of ravenous race,
Which still sit waiting on that dreadful clift."

"With that the rolling sea resounding soft
In his big base them fitly answered,
And on the Rock, the waves breaking aloft,
A solemn meane unto them measured."

"Then he the boteman bad row easily,
And let him heare some part of that rare melody."

"Suddeinly an innumerable flight
Of harmefull fowles about them fluttering cride,
And with their wicked wings them oft did smight
And sore annoyed, groping in that griesly night."

"Even all the nation of unfortunate
And fatal birds about them flocked were."*

To go up into a high stone tower is not only a very fine thing in itself, but the very best mode of gaining a comprehensive view of the region round about. It is all the better if this tower stand solitary and alone, like that mysterious Newport one, or else be sole survivor of some perished castle.

Now, with reference to the Enchanted Isles, we are fortunately supplied with just such a noble point of observation in a remarkable rock, from its peculiar figure called of old by the Spaniards, Rock Rodondo, or Round Rock. Some two hundred and fifty feet high, rising straight from the sea ten miles from land, with the whole mountainous group to the south and east, Rock Rodondo occupies, on a large scale, very much the position which the famous Campanile or detached Bell Tower of St. Mark* does with respect to the tangled group of hoary edifices around it.

Ere ascending, however, to gaze abroad upon the Encantadas, this sea-tower itself claims attention. It is visible at the distance of thirty miles; and, fully participating in that enchantment which pervades the group, when first seen afar invariably is mistaken for a sail. Four leagues away, of a golden, hazy noon, it seems some Spanish Admiral's ship, stacked up with glittering canvas. Sail ho! Sail ho! Sail ho! from all three masts. But coming nigh, the enchanted frigate is transformed apace into a craggy keep.

My first visit to the spot was made in the gray of the morning. With a view of fishing, we had lowered three boats, and pulling some two miles from our vessel, found ourselves just before dawn of day close under the moon-shadow of Rodondo. Its aspect was heightened, and yet softened, by the strange double twilight of the hour. The great full moon burnt in the low west like a half-spent beacon, casting a soft mellow tinge upon the sea like that cast by a waning fire of embers upon a midnight hearth; while along the entire east the invisible sun sent pallid intimations of his coming. The wind was light; the waves languid; the stars twinkled with a faint effulgence; all nature seemed supine with the long night watch, and half-suspended in jaded expectation of the sun. This was the critical hour to catch Rodondo in his perfect mood. The twilight was just enough to reveal every striking point, without tearing away the dim investiture of wonder.

From a broken, stair-like base, washed, as the steps of a water-palace, by the waves, the tower rose in entablatures of strata to a shaven summit. These uniform layers which compose the mass form its most peculiar feature. For at their lines of junction they project flatly into encircling shelves, from top to bottom, rising one above another in graduated series. And as the eaves of any old barn or abbey are alive with swallows, so were all these rocky ledges with unnumbered sea-fowl. Eaves upon eaves, and nests upon nests. Here and there were long birdlime streaks of a ghostly white staining the tower from sea to air, readily accounting for its sail-like look afar. All would have been bewitchingly quiescent, were it not for the demoniac din created by the birds. Not only were the eaves rustling with them, but they flew densely overhead, spreading themselves into a winged and continually shifting canopy. The tower is the resort of aquatic birds for hundreds of leagues around. To the north, to the east, to the west, stretches nothing but eternal ocean; so that the man-of-war hawk coming from the coasts of North America, Polynesia, or Peru, makes his first land at Rodondo. And yet though Rodondo be terra-firma, no land-bird ever lighted on it. Fancy a red-robbin or a canary there! What a falling into the hands of the Philistines, when the poor warbler should be surrounded by such locust-flights of strong bandit birds, with long bills cruel as daggers.

I know not where one can better study the Natural History of strange sea-fowl* than at Rodondo. It is the aviary of Ocean. Birds light here which never touched mast or tree; hermit-birds, which ever fly alone, cloud-birds, familiar with unpierced zones of air.

Let us first glance low down to the lowermost shelf of all, which is the widest too, and but a little space from high-water mark. What outlandish beings are these? Erect as men, but hardly as symmetrical, they stand all round the rock like sculptured caryatides, supporting the next range of eaves above. Their bodies are grotesquely misshapen; their bills short; their feet seemingly legless; while the members at their sides are neither fin, wing, nor arm. And truly neither fish, flesh, nor fowl is the penguin; as an edible, pertaining neither to Carnival nor Lent; without exception the most ambiguous and least lovely creature yet discovered by man. Though dabbling in all three elements, and indeed possessing some rudimental claims to all, the penguin is at home in none. On land it stumps; afloat it sculls; in the air it flops. As if ashamed of her failure, Nature keeps this ungainly child hidden away at the ends of the earth, in the Straits of Magellan, and on the abased sea-story of Rodondo.

But look, what are yon wobegone regiments drawn up on the next shelf above? what rank and file of large strange fowl? what sea Friars of Orders Gray? Pelicans. Their elongated bills, and heavy leathern pouches suspended thereto, give them the most lugubrious expression. A pensive race, they stand for hours together without motion. Their dull, ashy plumage imparts an aspect as if they had been powdered over with cinders. A penitential bird indeed, fitly haunting the shores of the clinkered Encantadas, whereon tormented Job himself might have well sat down and scraped himself with potsherds.

Higher up now we mark the gony, or gray albatross, anomalously so called, an unsightly unpoetic bird, unlike its storied kinsman, which is the snow-white ghost of the haunted Capes of Hope and Horn.

As we still ascend from shelf to shelf, we find the tenants of the tower serially disposed in order of their magnitude:— gannets, black and speckled haglets, jays, sea-hens, sperm-whale-birds, gulls of all varieties:—thrones, princedoms, powers, dominating one above another in senatorial array; while sprinkled over all, like an ever-repeated fly in a great piece of broidery, the stormy petrel or Mother Cary's chicken sounds his continual challenge and alarm. That this mys-terious humming-bird of ocean, which had it but brilliancy of hue might from its evanescent liveliness be almost called its butterfly, yet whose chirrup under the stern is ominous to mariners as to the peasant the death-tick sounding from behind the chimney jam—should have its special haunt at the Encantadas, contributes in the seaman's mind, not a little to their dreary spell.

As day advances the dissonant din augments. With ear-splitting cries the wild birds celebrate their matins. Each moment, flights push from the tower, and join the aerial choir hovering overhead, while their places below are sup-plied by darting myriads. But down through all this discord of commotion, I hear clear silver bugle-like notes unbrokenly falling, like oblique lines of swift slanting rain in a cascading shower. I gaze far up, and behold a snow-white angelic thing, with one long lance-like feather thrust out behind. It is the bright inspiriting chanticleer of ocean, the beauteous bird, from its bestirring whistle of musical invocation, fitly styled the "Boatswain's Mate."

The winged life clouding Rodondo on that well-remembered morning, I saw had its full counterpart in the finny hosts which peopled the waters at its base. Below the water-line, the rock seemed one honeycomb of grottoes, affording laby-rinthine lurking places for swarms of fairy fish. All were strange; many exceedingly beautiful; and would have well graced the costliest glass globes in which gold-fish are kept for a show. Nothing was more striking than the complete novelty of many individuals of this multitude. Here hues were seen as yet unpainted, and figures which are unengraved.

To show the multitude, avidity, and nameless fearlessness and tameness of these fish, let me say, that often, marking through clear spaces of water—temporarily made so by the concentric dartings of the fish above the surface—certain larger and less unwary wights, which swam slow and deep; our anglers would cautiously essay to drop their lines down to these last. But in vain; there was no passing the uppermost zone. No sooner did the hook touch the sea, than a hundred infatuates contended for the honor of capture. Poor fish of Rodondo! in your victimized confidence, you are of the number of those who inconsiderately trust, while they do not understand, human nature.

But the dawn is now fairly day. Band after band, the seafowl sail away to forage the deep for their food. The tower is left solitary, save the fish caves at its base. Its birdlime gleams in the golden rays like the white-wash of a tall lighthouse, or the lofty sails of a cruiser. This moment, doubtless, while we know it to be a dead desert rock, other voyagers are taking oaths it is a glad populous ship.

But ropes now, and let us ascend. Yet soft, this is not so easy.

SKETCH FOURTH

A PISGAH VIEW FROM THE ROCK*

—*"That done, he leads him to the highest mount,*
From whence, far off he unto him did show:"——*

IF you seek to ascend Rock Rodondo, take the following prescription. Go three voyages round the world as a mainroyal-man of the tallest frigate that floats; then serve a year or two apprenticeship to the guides who conduct strangers up the Peak of Teneriffe;* and as many more, respectively, to a rope-dancer, an Indian Juggler, and a chamois. This done, come and be rewarded by the view from our tower. How we get there, we alone know. If we sought to tell others, what the wiser were they? Suffice it, that here at the summit you and I stand. Does any balloonist, does the outlooking man in the moon, take a broader view of space? Much thus,

one fancies, looks the universe from Milton's celestial bat-
tlements. A boundless watery Kentucky. Here Daniel Boone
would have dwelt content.

Never heed for the present yonder Burnt District of the
Enchanted Isles. Look edgeways, as it were, past them, to
the south. You see nothing; but permit me to point out
the direction, if not the place, of certain interesting objects
in the vast sea, which kissing this tower's base, we behold
unscrolling itself towards the Antarctic Pole.

We stand now ten miles from the Equator. Yonder, to the
East, some six hundred miles, lies the continent; this Rock
being just about on the parallel of Quito.*

Observe another thing here. We are at one of three uninhabited clusters, which, at pretty nearly uniform distances from
the main, sentinel, at long intervals from each other, the entire coast of South America. In a peculiar manner, also, they
terminate the South American character of country. Of the
unnumbered Polynesian chains to the westward, not one
partakes of the qualities of the Encantadas or Gallipagos,
the isles St. Felix and St. Ambrose, the isles Juan Fernandes
and Massafuero.* Of the first it needs not here to speak. The
second lie a little above the Southern Tropic; lofty, inhospitable, and uninhabitable rocks, one of which, presenting two
round hummocks connected by a low reef, exactly resembles
a huge double-headed shot. The last lie in the latitude of
33°; high, wild and cloven. Juan Fernandes is sufficiently
famous without further description. Massafuero is a Spanish
name, expressive of the fact, that the isle so called lies *more
without*, that is, further off the main than its neighbor Juan.
This isle Massafuero has a very imposing aspect at a distance
of eight or ten miles. Approached in one direction, in cloudy
weather, its great overhanging height and rugged contour, and
more especially a peculiar slope of its broad summits, give
it much the air of a vast iceberg drifting in tremendous poise.
Its sides are split with dark cavernous recesses, as an old
cathedral with its gloomy lateral chapels. Drawing nigh one
of these gorges from sea after a long voyage, and beholding
some tatterdemallion outlaw, staff in hand, descending its
steep rocks toward you, conveys a very queer emotion to a
lover of the picturesque.

On fishing parties from ships, at various times, I have chanced to visit each of these groups. The impression they give to the stranger pulling close up in his boat under their grim cliffs is, that surely he must be their first discoverer, such for the most part is the unimpaired . . . . . silence and solitude. And here, by the way, the mode in which these isles were really first lighted upon by Europeans is not unworthy mention, especially as what is about to be said, likewise applies to the original discovery of our Encantadas.

Prior to the year 1563, the voyages made by Spanish ships from Peru to Chili, were full of difficulty. Along this coast the winds from the South most generally prevail; and it had been an invariable custom to keep close in with the land, from a superstitious conceit on the part of the Spaniards, that were they to lose sight of it, the eternal trade wind would waft them into unending waters, from whence would be no return. Here, involved among tortuous capes and headlands, shoals and reefs, beating too against a continual head wind, often light, and sometimes for days and weeks sunk into utter calm, the provincial vessels, in many cases, suffered the extremest hardships, in passages, which at the present day seem to have been incredibly protracted. There is on record in some collections of nautical disasters, an account of one of these ships, which starting on a voyage whose duration was estimated at ten days, spent four months at sea, and indeed never again entered harbor, for in the end she was cast away. Singular to tell, this craft never encountered a gale, but was the vexed sport of malicious calms and currents. Thrice, out of provisions, she put back to an intermediate port, and started afresh, but only yet again to return. Frequent fogs enveloped her; so that no observation could be had of her place, and once, when all hands were joyously anticipating sight of their destination, lo! the vapors lifted and disclosed the mountains from which they had taken their first departure. In the like deceptive vapors she at last struck upon a reef, whence ensued a long series of calamities too sad to detail.

It was the famous pilot, Juan Fernandes, immortalized by the island named after him, who put an end to these coasting tribulations, by boldly venturing the experiment—as Da Gama did before him with respect to Europe—of standing broad out from land. Here he found the winds favorable for getting to the south, and by running westward till beyond the influence of the trades, he regained the coast without difficulty; making the passage which, though in a high degree circuitous, proved far more expeditious than the nominally direct one. Now it was upon these new tracks, and about the year 1670 or thereabouts, that the Enchanted Isles and the rest of the sentinel groups, as they may be called, were discovered. Though I know of no account as to whether any of them were found inhabited or no, it may be reasonably concluded that they have been immemorial solitudes. But let us return to Rodondo.

Southwest from our tower lies all Polynesia, hundreds of leagues away; but straight west, on the precise line of his parallel, no land rises till your keel is beached upon the Kingsmills, a nice little sail of say 5,000 miles.

Having thus by such distant references—with Rodondo the only possible ones—settled our relative place on the sea, let us consider objects not quite so remote. Behold the grim and charred Enchanted Isles. This nearest crater-shaped headland is part of Albemarle, the largest of the group, being some sixty miles or more long, and fifteen broad. Did you ever lay eye on the real genuine Equator? Have you ever, in the largest sense, toed the Line? Well, that identical crater-shaped headland there, all yellow lava, is cut by the Equator exactly as a knife cuts straight through the centre of a pumpkin pie. If you could only see so far, just to one side of that same headland, across yon low dykey ground, you would catch sight of the isle of Narborough, the loftiest land of the cluster; no soil whatever; one seamed clinker from top to bottom; abounding in black caves like smithies; its metallic shore ringing under foot like plates of iron; its central volcanoes standing grouped like a gigantic chimney-stack.

Narborough and Albemarle are neighbors after a quite curious fashion. A familiar diagram will illustrate this strange neighborhood:

Ǝ

Cut a channel at the above letter joint, and the middle transverse limb is Narborough, and all the rest is Albemarle. Volcanic Narborough lies in the black jaws of Albemarle like a wolf's red tongue in his open mouth.

If now you desire the population of Albemarle, I will give you, in round numbers, the statistics, according to the most reliable estimates made upon the spot:

Men, ...	none.
Ant-eaters, ...	unknown.
Man-haters, ...	unknown.
Lizards, ...	500,000.
Snakes, ...	500,000.
Spiders, ...	10,000,000.
Salamanders, ...	unknown.
Devils, ...	do.
Making a clean total of	11,000,000.

exclusive of an incomputable host of fiends, ant-eaters, man-haters, and salamanders.

Albemarle opens his mouth towards the setting sun. His distended jaws form a great bay, which Narborough, his tongue, divides into halves, one whereof is called Weather Bay, the other Lee Bay; while the volcanic promontories terminating his coasts are styled South Head and North Head. I note this, because these Bays are famous in the annals of the Sperm Whale Fishery. The whales come here at certain seasons to calve. When ships first cruised hereabouts, I am told, they used to blockade the entrance of Lee Bay, when their boats going round by Weather Bay, passed through Narborough channel, and so had the Leviathans very neatly in a pen.

The day after we took fish at the base of this Round Tower, we had a fine wind, and shooting round the north headland, suddenly descried a fleet of full thirty sail, all beating to windward like a squadron in line. A brave sight as ever man saw. A most harmonious concord of rushing keels. Their thirty kelsons* hummed like thirty harp-strings, and looked as straight whilst they left their parallel traces on the sea. But there proved too many hunters for the game. The fleet broke up, and went their separate ways out of sight, leaving my own ship and two trim gentlemen of London. These last, finding no luck either, likewise vanished; and Lee Bay, with all its appurtenances, and without a rival, devolved to us.

The way of cruising here is this. You keep hovering about the entrance of the bay, in one beat and out the next. But at times—not always, as in other parts of the group—a race-horse of a current sweeps right across its mouth. So, with all sails set, you carefully ply your tacks. How often, standing at the foremast head at sunrise, with our patient prow pointed in between these isles, did I gaze upon that land, not of cakes but of clinkers, not of streams of sparkling water, but arrested torrents of tormented lava.

As the ship runs in from the open sea, Narborough presents its side in one dark craggy mass, soaring up some five or six thousand feet, at which point it hoods itself in heavy clouds, whose lowest level fold is as clearly defined against the rocks, as the snow-line against the Andes. There is dire mischief going on in that upper dark. There toil the demons of fire, who at intervals irradiate the nights with a strange spectral illumination for miles and miles around, but unaccompanied by any further demonstration; or else, suddenly announce themselves by terrific concussions, and the full drama of a volcanic eruption. The blacker that cloud by day, the more may you look for light by night. Often whalemen have found themselves cruising nigh that burning mountain when all aglow with a ball-room blaze. Or, rather, glass-works, you may call this same vitreous isle of Narborough, with its tall chimney-stacks.

Where we still stand, here on Rodondo, we cannot see all the other isles, but it is a good place from which to point out where they lie. Yonder, though, to the E.N.E., I mark a distant dusky ridge. It is Abington Isle, one of the most northerly of the group; so solitary, remote, and blank, it looks like No-Man's Land seen off our northern shore. I doubt whether two human beings ever touched upon that spot. So far as yon Abington Isle is concerned, Adam and his billions of posterity remain uncreated.

Ranging south of Abington, and quite out of sight behind the long spine of Albemarle, lies James's Isle, so called by the early Buccaneers after the luckless Stuart, Duke of York.* Observe here, by the way, that, excepting the isles particularized in comparatively recent times, and which mostly received the names of famous Admirals, the Encantadas were first christened by the Spaniards; but these Spanish names were generally effaced on English charts by the subsequent christenings of the Buccaneers, who, in the middle of the seventeenth century, called them after English noblemen and kings. Of these loyal freebooters and the things which associate their name with the Encantadas, we shall hear anon. Nay, for one little item, immediately; for between James's Isle and Albemarle, lies a fantastic islet, strangely known as "Cowley's Enchanted Isle." But as all the group is deemed enchanted, the reason must be given for the spell within a spell involved by this particular designation. The name was bestowed by that excellent Buccaneer himself,* on his first visit here. Speaking in his published voyages of this spot, he says—"My fancy led me to call it Cowley's Enchanted Isle, for we having had a sight of it upon several points of the compass, it appeared always in so many different forms; sometimes like a ruined fortification; upon another point like a great city," &c. No wonder though, that among the Encantadas all sorts of ocular deceptions and mirages should be met.

That Cowley linked his name with this self-transforming and bemocking isle, suggests the possibility that it conveyed to him some meditative image of himself. At least, as is not impossible, if he were any relative of the mildly thoughtful, and self-upbraiding poet Cowley,* who lived about his time, the conceit might seem not unwarranted; for that sort of thing evinced in the naming of this isle runs in the blood, and may be seen in pirates as in poets.

Still south of James's Isle lie Jervis Isle, Duncan Isle, Crossman's Isle, Brattle Isle, Wood's Isle, Chatham Isle, and various lesser isles, for the most part an archipelago of aridities, without inhabitant, history, or hope of either in all time

to come. But not far from these are rather notable isles—
Barrington, Charles's, Norfolk, and Hood's. Succeeding chapters will reveal some ground for their notability.

SKETCH FIFTH

THE FRIGATE, AND SHIP FLYAWAY

> "Looking far forth into the ocean wide,
> A goodly ship with banners bravely dight,
> And flag in her top-gallant I espide,
> Through the main sea making her merry flight."*

ERE quitting Rodondo, it must not be omitted that here,
in 1813, the U.S. frigate Essex, Captain David Porter,*
came near leaving her bones. Lying becalmed one morning
with a strong current setting her rapidly towards the rock,
a strange sail was descried, which—not out of keeping with
alleged enchantments of the neighborhood—seemed to be
staggering under a violent wind, while the frigate lay lifeless
as if spell-bound. But a light air springing up, all sail was
made by the frigate in chase of the enemy, as supposed—
he being deemed an English whale-ship—but the rapidity of
the current was so great, that soon all sight was lost of him;
and at meridian the Essex, spite of her drags, was driven so
close under the foam-lashed cliffs of Rodondo that for a
time all hands gave her up. A smart breeze, however, at last
helped her off, though the escape was so critical as to seem
almost miraculous.

Thus saved from destruction herself, she now made use of
that salvation to destroy the other vessel, if possible. Renewing the chase in the direction in which the stranger had disappeared, sight was caught of him the following morning.
Upon being descried he hoisted American colors and stood
away from the Essex. A calm ensued; when, still confident
that the stranger was an Englishman, Porter despatched a
cutter, not to board the enemy, but drive back his boats
engaged in towing him. The cutter succeeded. Cutters were
subsequently sent to capture him; the stranger now showing

English colors in place of American. But when the frigate's boats were within a short distance of their hoped-for prize, another sudden breeze sprang up; the stranger under all sail bore off to the northward, and ere night was hull down ahead of the Essex, which all this time lay perfectly becalmed.

This enigmatic craft—American in the morning, and English in the evening—her sails full of wind in a calm—was never again beheld. An enchanted ship no doubt. So at least the sailors swore.

This cruise of the Essex in the Pacific during the war of 1812, is perhaps the strangest and most stirring to be found in the history of the American navy. She captured the furthest wandering vessels; visited the remotest seas and isles; long hovered in the charmed vicinity of the enchanted group; and finally valiantly gave up the ghost fighting two English frigates in the harbor of Valparaiso.* Mention is made of her here for the same reason that the buccaneers will likewise receive record; because, like them, by long cruising among the isles, tortoise-hunting upon their shores, and generally exploring them; for these and other reasons, the Essex is peculiarly associated with the Encantadas.

Here be it said that you have but three eye-witness authorities worth mentioning* touching the Enchanted Isles:— Cowley, the buccaneer (1684); Colnett, the whaling-ground explorer (1793); Porter, the post captain (1813). Other than these you have but barren, bootless allusions from some few passing voyagers or compilers.

SKETCH SIXTH

BARRINGTON ISLE AND THE BUCCANEERS

> *"Let us all servile base subjection scorn,*
> *And as we be sons of the earth so wide,*
> *Let us our father's heritage divide,*
> *And challenge to ourselves our portions dew*
> *Of all the patrimony, which a few*
> *Now hold in hugger-mugger in their hand."*

"Lords of the world, and so will wander free,
*Where-so us listeth, uncontroll'd of any."**

"How bravely now we live, how jocund, how near the first
*inheritance, without fears, how free from little troubles!"**

NEAR two centuries ago Barrington Isle was the resort of
that famous wing of the West Indian buccaneers, which,
upon their repulse from the Cuban waters, crossing the
Isthmus of Darien, ravaged the Pacific side of the Spanish
colonies, and, with the regularity and timing of a modern
mail, waylaid the royal treasure ships plying between Manilla
and Acapulco. After the toils of piratic war, here they came
to say their prayers, enjoy their free-and-easies, count their
crackers from the cask, their doubloons from the keg, and
measure their silks of Asia with long Toledos* for their
yard-sticks.

As a secure retreat, an undiscoverable hiding place, no spot
in those days could have been better fitted. In the centre of
a vast and silent sea, but very little traversed; surrounded
by islands, whose inhospitable aspect might well drive away
the chance navigator; and yet within a few days' sail of the
opulent countries which they made their prey; the unmolested buccaneers found here that tranquillity which they
fiercely denied to every civilized harbor in that part of the
world. Here, after stress of weather, or a temporary drubbing at the hands of their vindictive foes, or in swift flight
with golden booty, those old marauders came, and lay snugly
out of all harm's reach. But not only was the place a harbor
of safety, and a bower of ease, but for utility in other things
it was most admirable.

Barrington Isle is in many respects singularly adapted
to careening, refitting, refreshing, and other seamen's purposes. Not only has it good water, and good anchorage, well
sheltered from all winds by the high land of Albemarle, but
it is the least unproductive isle of the group. Tortoises good
for food, trees good for fuel, and long grass good for bed-
ding, abound here, and there are pretty natural walks, and
several landscapes to be seen. Indeed, though in its locality

belonging to the Enchanted group, Barrington Isle is so unlike most of its neighbors, that it would hardly seem of kin to them.

"I once landed on its western side," says a sentimental voyager* long ago, "where it faces the black buttress of Albemarle. I walked beneath groves of trees; not very lofty, and not palm trees, or orange trees, or peach trees, to be sure; but for all that, after long sea-faring very beautiful to walk under, even though they supplied no fruit. And here, in calm spaces at the heads of glades, and on the shaded tops of slopes commanding the most quiet scenery—what do you think I saw? Seats which might have served Brahmins and presidents of peace societies. Fine old ruins of what had once been symmetric lounges of stone and turf; they bore every mark both of artificialness and age, and were undoubtedly made by the buccaneers. One had been a long sofa, with back and arms, just such a sofa as the poet Gray might have loved to throw himself upon, his Crebillon* in hand.

"Though they sometimes tarried here for months at a time, and used the spot for a storing-place for spare spars, sails, and casks; yet it is highly improbable that the buccaneers ever erected dwelling-houses upon the isle. They never were here except their ships remained, and they would most likely have slept on board. I mention this, because I cannot avoid the thought, that it is hard to impute the construction of these romantic seats to any other motive than one of pure peacefulness and kindly fellowship with nature. That the buccaneers perpetrated the greatest outrages is very true; that some of them were mere cut-throats is not to be denied; but we know that here and there among their host was a Dampier, a Wafer, and a Cowley,* and likewise other men, whose worst reproach was their desperate fortunes; whom persecution, or adversity, or secret and unavengeable wrongs, had driven from Christian society to seek the melancholy solitude or the guilty adventures of the sea. At any rate, long as those ruins of seats on Barrington remain, the most singular monuments are furnished to the fact, that all of the buccaneers were not unmitigated monsters.

"But during my ramble on the isle I was not long in discovering other tokens, of things quite in accordance with those wild traits, popularly, and no doubt truly enough imputed to the freebooters at large. Had I picked up old nails and rusty hoops I would only have thought of the ship's carpenter and cooper. But I found old cutlasses and daggers reduced to mere threads of rust, which doubtless had stuck between Spanish ribs ere now. There were signs of the murderer and robber; the reveller likewise had left his trace. Mixed with shells, fragments of broken jars were lying here and there, high up upon the beach. They were precisely like the jars now used upon the Spanish coast for the wine and Pisco spirits of that country.

"With a rusty dagger-fragment in one hand, and a bit of a wine-jar in another, I sat me down on the ruinous green sofa I have spoken of, and bethought me long and deeply of these same buccaneers. Could it be possible, that they robbed and murdered one day, revelled the next, and rested themselves by turning meditative philosophers, rural poets, and seat-builders on the third? Not very improbable, after all. For consider the vacillations of a man. Still, strange as it may seem, I must also abide by the more charitable thought; namely, that among these adventurers were some gentlemanly, companionable souls, capable of genuine tranquillity and virtue."

SKETCH SEVENTH

CHARLES' ISLE AND THE DOG-KING

—— *So with outragious cry,*
A thousand villeins round about him swarmed
Out of the rocks and caves adjoining nye;
Vile caitive wretches, ragged, rude, deformed;
All threatning death, all in straunge manner armed;
Some with unweldy clubs, some with long speares,
Some rusty knives, some staves in fier warmd. *

> We will not be of any occupation,
> Let such vile vassals, born to base vocation,
> Drudge in the world, and for their living droyle,
> Which have no wit to live withouten toyle.*

SOUTHWEST of Barrington lies Charles' Isle. And hereby hangs a history which I gathered long ago from a shipmate learned in all the lore of outlandish life.

During the successful revolt of the Spanish provinces from Old Spain, there fought on behalf of Peru a certain Creole adventurer from Cuba, who by his bravery and good fortune at length advanced himself to high rank in the patriot army. The war being ended, Peru found itself like many valorous gentlemen, free and independent enough, but with few shot in the locker. In other words, Peru had not wherewithal to pay off its troops. But the Creole—I forget his name—volunteered to take his pay in lands. So they told him he might have his pick of the Enchanted Isles, which were then, as they still remain, the nominal appanage of Peru. The soldier straightway embarks thither, explores the group, returns to Callao,* and says he will take a deed of Charles' Isle. Moreover, this deed must stipulate that thenceforth Charles' Isle is not only the sole property of the Creole, but is for ever free of Peru, even as Peru of Spain. To be short, this adventurer procures himself to be made in effect Supreme Lord of the Island, one of the princes of the powers of the earth.[1]

He now sends forth a proclamation inviting subjects to his as yet unpopulated kingdom. Some eighty souls, men and women, respond; and being provided by their leader with necessaries, and tools of various sorts, together with a few cattle and goats, take ship for the promised land; the last arrival on board, prior to sailing, being the Creole himself, accompanied, strange to say, by a disciplined cavalry

---

[1] The American Spaniards have long been in the habit of making presents of islands to deserving individuals. The pilot Juan Fernandez procured a deed of the isle named after him, and for some years resided there before Selkirk* came. It is supposed, however, that he eventually contracted the blues upon his princely property, for after a time he returned to the main, and as report goes, became a very garrulous barber in the city of Lima.

company of large grim dogs. These, it was observed on the passage, refusing to consort with the emigrants, remained aristocratically grouped around their master on the elevated quarter-deck, casting disdainful glances forward upon the inferior rabble there; much as from the ramparts, the soldiers of a garrison thrown into a conquered town, eye the inglorious citizen-mob over which they are set to watch.

Now Charles' Isle not only resembles Barrington Isle in being much more inhabitable than other parts of the group; but it is double the size of Barrington; say forty or fifty miles in circuit.

Safely debarked at last, the company under direction of their lord and patron, forthwith proceeded to build their capital city. They make considerable advance in the way of walls of clinkers, and lava floors, nicely sanded with cinders. On the least barren hills they pasture their cattle, while the goats, adventurers by nature, explore the far inland solitudes for a scanty livelihood of lofty herbage. Meantime, abundance of fish and tortoises supply their other wants.

The disorders incident to settling all primitive regions, in the present case were heightened by the peculiarly untoward character of many of the pilgrims. His Majesty was forced at last to proclaim martial law, and actually hunted and shot with his own hand several of his rebellious subjects, who, with most questionable intentions, had clandestinely encamped in the interior; whence they stole by night, to prowl barefooted on tiptoe round the precincts of the lava-palace. It is to be remarked, however, that prior to such stern proceedings, the more reliable men had been judiciously picked out for an infantry body-guard, subordinate to the cavalry body-guard of dogs. But the state of politics in this unhappy nation may be somewhat imagined from the circumstance, that all who were not of the body-guard were downright plotters and malignant traitors. At length the death penalty was tacitly abolished, owing to the timely thought, that were strict sportsman's justice to be dispensed among such subjects, ere long the Nimrod King would have little or no remaining game to shoot. The human part of the life-guard was now disbanded, and set to work cultivating the soil, and raising potatoes; the regular army now solely consisting of the dog-regiment. These, as I have heard, were of a singularly ferocious character, though by severe training rendered docile to their master. Armed to the teeth, the Creole now goes in state, surrounded by his canine janizaries, whose terrific bayings prove quite as serviceable as bayonets in keeping down the surgings of revolt.

But the census of the isle, sadly lessened by the dispensation of justice, and not materially recruited by matrimony, began to fill his mind with sad mistrust. Some way the population must be increased. Now, from its possessing a little water, and its comparative pleasantness of aspect, Charles' Isle at this period was occasionally visited by foreign whalers. These His Majesty had always levied upon for port charges, thereby contributing to his revenue. But now he had additional designs. By insidious arts he from time to time cajoles certain sailors to desert their ships and enlist beneath his banner. Soon as missed, their captains crave permission to go and hunt them up. Whereupon His Majesty first hides them very carefully away, and then freely permits the search. In consequence, the delinquents are never found, and the ships retire without them.

Thus, by a two-edged policy of this crafty monarch, foreign nations were crippled in the number of their subjects, and his own were greatly multiplied. He particularly petted these renegado strangers. But alas for the deep-laid schemes of ambitious princes, and alas for the vanity of glory. As the foreign-born Pretorians, unwisely introduced into the Roman state, and still more unwisely made favorites of the Emperors, at last insulted and overturned the throne, even so these lawless mariners, with all the rest of the body-guard and all the populace, broke out into a terrible mutiny, and defied their master. He marched against them with all his dogs. A deadly battle ensued upon the beach. It raged for three hours, the dogs fighting with determined valor, and the sailors reckless of every thing but victory. Three men and thirteen dogs were left dead upon the field, many on both sides were wounded, and the king was forced to fly with the remainder of his canine regiment. The enemy pursued, stoning the dogs with their master into the wilderness of the interior.

Discontinuing the pursuit, the victors returned to the village on the shore, stove the spirit-casks, and proclaimed a Republic. The dead men were interred with the honors of war, and the dead dogs ignominiously thrown into the sea. At last, forced by stress of suffering, the fugitive Creole came down from the hills and offered to treat for peace. But the rebels refused it on any other terms than his unconditional banishment. Accordingly, the next ship that arrived carried away the ex-king to Peru.

The history of the king of Charles' Island furnishes another illustration of the difficulty of colonizing barren islands with unprincipled pilgrims.

Doubtless for a long time the exiled monarch, pensively ruralizing in Peru, which afforded him a safe asylum in his calamity, watched every arrival from the Encantadas, to hear news of the failure of the Republic, the consequent penitence of the rebels, and his own recall to royalty. Doubtless he deemed the Republic but a miserable experiment which would soon explode. But no, the insurgents had confederated themselves into a democracy neither Grecian, Roman, nor American. Nay, it was no democracy at all, but a permanent *Riotocracy*, which gloried in having no law but lawlessness. Great inducements being offered to deserters, their ranks were swelled by accessions of scamps from every ship which touched their shores. Charles' Island was proclaimed the asylum of the oppressed of all navies. Each runaway tar was hailed as a martyr in the cause of freedom, and became immediately installed a ragged citizen of this universal nation. In vain the captains of absconding seamen strove to regain them. Their new compatriots were ready to give any number of ornamental eyes in their behalf. They had few cannon, but their fists were not to be trifled with. So at last it came to pass that no vessels acquainted with the character of that country durst touch there, however sorely in want of refreshment. It became Anathema—a sea Alsatia*—the unassailed lurking-place of all sorts of desperadoes, who in the name of liberty did just what they pleased. They continually fluctuated in their numbers. Sailors deserting ships at other islands, or in boats at sea any where in that vicinity, steered for Charles' Isle, as to their sure home of refuge; while sated with the life of the isle, numbers from time to time crossed the water to the neighboring ones, and there presenting themselves to strange captains as shipwrecked seamen, often succeeded in getting on board vessels bound to the Spanish coast; and having a compassionate purse made up for them on landing there.

One warm night during my first visit to the group, our ship was floating along in languid stillness, when some one on the forecastle shouted "Light ho!" We looked and saw a beacon burning on some obscure land off the beam. Our third mate was not intimate with this part of the world. Going to the captain he said, "Sir, shall I put off in a boat? These must be shipwrecked men."

The captain laughed rather grimly, as, shaking his fist towards the beacon, he rapped out an oath, and said—"No, no, you precious rascals, you don't juggle one of my boats ashore this blessed night. You do well, you thieves—you do benevolently to hoist a light yonder as on a dangerous shoal. It tempts no wise man to pull off and see what's the matter, but bids him steer small and keep off shore—that is Charles' Island; brace up, Mr. Mate, and keep the light astern."

SKETCH EIGHTH

NORFOLK ISLE AND THE CHOLA WIDOW

"At last they in an island did espy
A seemly woman sitting by the shore,
That with great sorrow and sad agony
Seemed some great misfortune to deplore,
*And loud to them for succor called evermore."**

"Black his eye as the midnight sky,
White his neck as the driven snow,
Red his cheek as the morning light;—
Cold he lies in the ground below.
My love is dead,
Gone to his death-bed,
*All under the cactus tree."**

"Each lonely scene shall thee restore,
For thee the tear be duly shed;
Belov'd till life can charm no more,
*And mourned till Pity's self be dead."**

FAR to the northeast of Charles' Isle,* sequestered from the rest, lies Norfolk Isle; and, however insignificant to most voyagers, to me, through sympathy, that lone island has become a spot made sacred by the strongest trials of humanity.

It was my first visit to the Encantadas. Two days had been spent ashore in hunting tortoises. There was not time to capture many; so on the third afternoon we loosed our sails. We were just in the act of getting under way, the uprooted anchor yet suspended and invisibly swaying beneath the wave, as the good ship gradually turned on her heel to leave the isle behind, when the seaman who heaved with me at the windlass paused suddenly, and directed my attention to something moving on the land, not along the beach, but somewhat back, fluttering from a height.

In view of the sequel of this little story, be it here narrated how it came to pass, that an object which partly from its being so small was quite lost to every other man on board, still caught the eye of my handspike companion. The rest of the crew, myself included, merely stood up to our spikes in heaving; whereas, unwontedly exhilarated at every turn of the ponderous windlass, my belted comrade leaped atop of it, with might and main giving a downward, thewey, perpendicular heave, his raised eye bent in cheery animation upon the slowly receding shore. Being high lifted above all others was the reason he perceived the object, otherwise unperceivable: and this elevation of his eye was owing to the elevation of his spirits; and this again—for truth must out—to a dram of Peruvian pisco,* in guerdon for some kindness done, secretly administered to him that morning by our mulatto steward. Now, certainly, pisco does a deal of mischief in the world; yet seeing that, in the present case, it was the means, though indirect, of rescuing a human being from the most dreadful fate, must we not also needs admit that sometimes pisco does a deal of good?

Glancing across the water in the direction pointed out, I saw some white thing hanging from an inland rock, perhaps half a mile from the sea.

"It is a bird; a white-winged bird; perhaps a——no; it is ——it is a handkerchief!"

"Aye, a handkerchief!" echoed my comrade, and with a louder shout apprised the captain.

Quickly now—like the running out and training of a great gun—the long cabin spy-glass was thrust through the mizzen rigging from the high platform of the poop; whereupon a human figure was plainly seen upon the inland rock, eagerly waving towards us what seemed to be the handkerchief.

Our captain was a prompt, good fellow. Dropping the glass, he lustily ran forward, ordering the anchor to be dropped again; hands to stand by a boat, and lower away.

In a half-hour's time the swift boat returned. It went with six and came with seven; and the seventh was a woman.

It is not artistic heartlessness, but I wish I could but draw in crayons; for this woman was a most touching sight; and crayons, tracing softly melancholy lines, would best depict the mournful image of the dark-damasked Chola widow.*

Her story was soon told, and though given in her own strange language was as quickly understood, for our captain from long trading on the Chilian coast was well versed in the Spanish. A Chola, or half-breed Indian woman of Payta in Peru, three years gone by, with her young new-wedded husband Felipe, of pure Castilian blood, and her one only Indian brother, Truxill, Hunilla had taken passage on the main in a French whaler, commanded by a joyous man; which vessel, bound to the cruising grounds beyond the Enchanted Isles, proposed passing close by their vicinity. The object of the little party was to procure tortoise oil, a fluid which for its great purity and delicacy is held in high estimation wherever known; and it is well known all along this part of the Pacific coast. With a chest of clothes, tools, cooking utensils, a rude apparatus for trying out the oil, some casks of biscuit, and other things, not omitting two favorite dogs, of which faithful animal all the Cholos are very fond,

Hunilla and her companions were safely landed at their chosen place; the Frenchman, according to the contract made ere sailing, engaged to take them off upon returning from a four months' cruise in the westward seas; which interval the three adventurers deemed quite sufficient for their purposes.

On the isle's lone beach they paid him in silver for their passage out, the stranger having declined to carry them at all except upon that condition; though willing to take every means to insure the due fulfilment of his promise. Felipe had striven hard to have this payment put off to the period of the ship's return. But in vain. Still, they thought they had, in another way, ample pledge of the good faith of the Frenchman. It was arranged that the expenses of the passage home should not be payable in silver, but in tortoises; one hundred tortoises ready captured to the returning captain's hand. These the Cholos meant to secure after their own work was done, against the probable time of the Frenchman's coming back; and no doubt in prospect already felt, that in those hundred tortoises—now somewhere ranging the isle's interior—they possessed one hundred hostages. Enough: the vessel sailed; the gazing three on shore answered the loud glee of the singing crew; and ere evening, the French craft was hull down in the distant sea, its masts three faintest lines which quickly faded from Hunilla's eye.

The stranger had given a blithesome promise, and anchored it with oaths; but oaths and anchors equally will drag; nought else abides on fickle earth but unkept promises of joy. Contrary winds from out unstable skies, or contrary moods of his more varying mind, or shipwreck and sudden death in solitary waves; whatever was the cause, the blithe stranger never was seen again.

Yet, however dire a calamity was here in store, misgivings of it ere due time never disturbed the Cholos' busy mind, now all intent upon the toilsome matter which had brought them hither. Nay, by swift doom coming like the thief at night, ere seven weeks went by, two of the little party were removed from all anxieties of land or sea. No more they sought to gaze with feverish fear, or still more feverish hope, beyond the present's horizon line; but into the furthest future their own silent spirits sailed. By persevering labor beneath that burning sun, Felipe and Truxill had brought down to their hut many scores of tortoises, and tried out the oil, when, elated with their good success, and to reward themselves for such hard work, they, too hastily, made a catamaran, or Indian raft, much used on the Spanish main, and merrily started on a fishing trip, just without a long reef with many jagged gaps, running parallel with the shore, about half a mile from it. By some bad tide or hap, or natural negligence of joyfulness (for though they could not be heard, yet by their gestures they seemed singing at the time), forced in deep water against that iron bar, the ill-made catamaran was overset, and came all to pieces; when, dashed by broad-chested swells between their broken logs and the sharp teeth of the reef, both adventurers perished before Hunilla's eyes.

Before Hunilla's eyes they sank. The real woe of this event passed before her sight as some sham tragedy on the stage. She was seated on a rude bower among the withered thickets, crowning a lofty cliff, a little back from the beach. The thickets were so disposed, that in looking upon the sea at large she peered out from among the branches as from the lattice of a high balcony. But upon the day we speak of here, the better to watch the adventure of those two hearts she loved, Hunilla had withdrawn the branches to one side, and held them so. They formed an oval frame, through which the bluely boundless sea rolled like a painted one. And there, the invisible painter painted to her view the wave-tossed and disjointed raft, its once level logs slantingly upheaved, as raking masts, and the four struggling arms undistinguishable among them; and then all subsided into smooth-flowing creamy waters, slowly drifting the splintered wreck; while first and last, no sound of any sort was heard. Death in a silent picture; a dream of the eye; such vanishing shapes as the mirage shows.

So instant was the scene, so trance-like its mild pictorial effect, so distant from her blasted bower and her common sense of things, that Hunilla gazed and gazed, nor raised a finger or a wail. But as good to sit thus dumb, in stupor staring on that dumb show, for all that otherwise might be done. With half a mile of sea between, how could her two enchanted arms aid those four fated ones? The distance long, the time one sand. After the lightning is beheld, what fool shall stay the thunderbolt? Felipe's body was washed ashore, but Truxill's never came; only his gay, braided hat of golden straw—that same sunflower thing he waved to her, pushing from the strand—and now, to the last gallant, it still saluted her. But Felipe's body floated to the marge, with one arm encirclingly outstretched. Lock-jawed in grim death, the lover-husband, softly clasped his bride, true to her even in death's dream. Ah, Heaven, when man thus keeps his faith, wilt thou be faithless who created the faithful one?* But they cannot break faith who never plighted it.

It needs not to be said what nameless misery now wrapped the lonely widow. In telling her own story she passed this almost entirely over, simply recounting the event. Construe the comment of her features, as you might; from her mere words little would you have weened that Hunilla was herself the heroine of her tale. But not thus did she defraud us of our tears. All hearts bled that grief could be so brave.

She but showed us her soul's lid, and the strange ciphers thereon engraved; all within, with pride's timidity, was withheld. Yet was there one exception. Holding out her small olive hand before our captain, she said in mild and slowest Spanish, "Señor, I buried him;" then paused, struggled as against the writhed coilings of a snake, and cringing suddenly, leaped up, repeating in impassioned pain, "I buried him, my life, my soul!"

Doubtless it was by half-unconscious, automatic motions of her hands, that this heavy-hearted one performed the final offices for Felipe, and planted a rude cross of withered sticks —no green ones might be had—at the head of that lonely grave, where rested now in lasting uncomplaint and quiet haven he whom untranquil seas had overthrown.

But some dull sense of another body that should be interred, of another cross that should hallow another grave— unmade as yet;—some dull anxiety and pain touching her undiscovered brother now haunted the oppressed Hunilla. Her hands fresh from the burial earth, she slowly went back to the beach, with unshaped purposes wandered there, her spellbound eye bent upon the incessant waves. But they bore nothing to her but a dirge, which maddened her to think that murderers should mourn. As time went by, and these things came less dreamingly to her mind, the strong persuasions of her Romish faith, which sets peculiar store by consecrated urns, prompted her to resume in waking earnest that pious search which had but been begun as in somnambulism. Day after day, week after week, she trod the cindery beach, till at length a double motive edged every eager glance. With equal longing she now looked for the living and the dead; the brother and the captain; alike vanished, never to return. Little accurate note of time had Hunilla taken under such emotions as were hers, and little, outside herself, served for calendar or dial. As to poor Crusoe in the self-same sea, no saint's bell pealed forth the lapse of week or month; each day went by unchallenged; no chanticleer announced those sultry dawns, no lowing herds those poisonous nights. All wonted and steadily recurring sounds, human, or humanized by sweet fellowship with man, but one stirred that torrid trance,—the cry of dogs; save which nought but the rolling sea invaded it, an all pervading monotone; and to the widow that was the least loved voice she could have heard.

No wonder that as her thoughts now wandered to the unreturning ship, and were beaten back again, the hope against hope so struggled in her soul, that at length she desperately said, "Not yet, not yet; my foolish heart runs on too fast." So she forced patience for some further weeks. But to those whom earth's sure indraft draws, patience or impatience is still the same.

Hunilla now sought to settle precisely in her mind, to an hour, how long it was since the ship had sailed; and then, with the same precision, how long a space remained to pass. But this proved impossible. What present day or month it was she could not say. Time was her labyrinth, in which Hunilla was entirely lost.

And now follows——

Against my own purposes a pause descends upon me here. One knows not whether nature doth not impose some secrecy upon him who has been privy to certain things. At least, it is to be doubted whether it be good to blazon such. If some books are deemed most baneful and their sale forbid, how then with deadlier facts, not dreams of doting men? Those whom books will hurt will not be proof against events. Events, not books, should be forbid. But in all things man sows upon the wind, which bloweth just there whither it listeth; for ill or good man cannot know. Often ill comes from the good, as good from ill.

When Hunilla——

Dire sight it is to see some silken beast long dally with a golden lizard ere she devour. More terrible, to see how feline Fate will sometimes dally with a human soul, and by a nameless magic make it repulse a sane despair with a hope which is but mad. Unwittingly I imp this cat-like thing, sporting with the heart of him who reads; for if he feel not, he reads in vain.

——"The ship sails this day, to-day," at last said Hunilla to herself; "this gives me certain time to stand on; without certainty I go mad. In loose ignorance I have hoped and hoped; now in firm knowledge I will but wait. Now I live and no longer perish in bewilderings. Holy Virgin, aid me! Thou wilt waft back the ship. Oh, past length of weary weeks—all to be dragged over—to buy the certainty of to-day, I freely give ye, though I tear ye from me!"

As mariners tossed in tempest on some desolate ledge patch them a boat out of the remnants of their vessel's wreck, and launch it in the selfsame waves, see here Hunilla, this lone shipwrecked soul, out of treachery invoking trust. Humanity, thou strong thing, I worship thee, not in the laurelled victor, but in this vanquished one.

Truly Hunilla leaned upon a reed, a real one; no metaphor; a real Eastern reed. A piece of hollow cane, drifted from unknown isles, and found upon the beach, its once jagged ends rubbed smoothly even as by sand-paper; its golden glazing gone. Long ground between the sea and land, upper and nether stone, the unvarnished substance was filed bare, and wore another polish now, one with itself, the polish of its agony. Circular lines at intervals cut all round this surface, divided it into six panels of unequal length. In the first were scored the days, each tenth one marked by a longer and deeper notch; the second was scored for the number of sea-fowl eggs for sustenance, picked out from the rocky nests; the third, how many fish had been caught from the shore; the fourth, how many small tortoises found inland; the fifth, how many days of sun; the sixth, of clouds; which last, of the two, was the greater one. Long night of busy number-ing, misery's mathematics, to weary her too-wakeful soul to sleep; yet sleep for that was none.

The panel of the days was deeply worn, the long tenth notches half effaced, as alphabets of the blind. Ten thou-sand times the longing widow had traced her finger over the bamboo; dull flute, which played on, gave no sound; as if counting birds flown by in air, would hasten tortoises creep-ing through the woods.

After the one hundred and eightieth day no further mark was seen; that last one was the faintest, as the first the deepest.

"There were more days," said our Captain; "many, many more; why did you not go on and notch them too, Hunilla?"

"Señor, ask me not."

"And meantime, did no other vessel pass the isle?"

"Nay, Señor;—but——"

"You do not speak; but *what*, Hunilla?"

"Ask me not, Señor."

"You saw ships pass, far away; you waved to them; they passed on;—was that it, Hunilla?"

"Señor, be it as you say."

Braced against her woe, Hunilla would not, durst not trust the weakness of her tongue. Then when our Captain asked whether any whale-boats had——

But no, I will not file this thing complete for scoffing souls to quote, and call it firm proof upon their side. The half shall here remain untold. Those two unnamed events which befell Hunilla on this isle, let them abide between her and her God. In nature, as in law, it may be libellous to speak some truths.

Still, how it was that although our vessel had lain three days anchored nigh the isle, its one human tenant should not have discovered us till just upon the point of sailing, never to revisit so lone and far a spot; this needs explaining ere the sequel come. ·

The place where the French captain had landed the little party was on the farther and opposite end of the isle. There too it was that they had afterwards built their hut. Nor did the widow in her solitude desert the spot where her loved ones had dwelt with her, and where the dearest of the twain now slept his last long sleep, and all her plaints awaked him not, and he of husbands the most faithful during life.

Now, high broken land rises between the opposite extremities of the isle. A ship anchored at one side is invisible from the other. Neither is the isle so small, but a considerable company might wander for days through the wilderness of one side, and never be seen, or their halloos heard, by any stranger holding aloof on the other. Hence Hunilla, who naturally associated the possible coming of ships with her own part of the isle, might to the end have remained quite ignorant of the presence of our vessel, were it not for a mysterious presentiment, borne to her, so our mariners averred, by this isle's enchanted air. Nor did the widow's answer undo the thought.

"How did you come to cross the isle this morning then, Hunilla?" said our Captain.

"Señor, something came flitting by me. It touched my cheek, my heart, Señor."

"What do you say, Hunilla?"

"I have said, Señor; something came through the air."

It was a narrow chance. For when in crossing the isle Hunilla gained the high land in the centre, she must then for the first have perceived our masts, and also marked that their sails were being loosed, perhaps even heard the echoing chorus of the windlass song. The strange ship was about to sail, and she behind. With all haste she now descends the height on the hither side, but soon loses sight of the ship among the sunken jungles at the mountain's base. She

struggles on through the withered branches, which seek at
every step to bar her path, till she comes to the isolated
rock, still some way from the water. This she climbs, to re-
assure herself. The ship is still in plainest sight. But now
worn out with over tension, Hunilla all but faints; she fears
to step down from her giddy perch; she is feign to pause,
there where she is, and as a last resort catches the turban from
her head, unfurls and waves it over the jungles towards us.

During the telling of her story the mariners formed a
voiceless circle round Hunilla and the Captain; and when
at length the word was given to man the fastest boat, and
pull round to the isle's thither side, to bring away Hunilla's
chest and the tortoise-oil; such alacrity of both cheery and
sad obedience seldom before was seen. Little ado was made.
Already the anchor had been recommitted to the bottom,
and the ship swung calmly to it.

But Hunilla insisted upon accompanying the boat as indispensable pilot to her hidden hut. So being refreshed with
the best the steward could supply, she started with us. Nor
did ever any wife of the most famous admiral in her husband's barge receive more silent reverence of respect, than
poor Hunilla from this boat's crew.

Rounding many a vitreous cape and bluff, in two hours'
time we shot inside the fatal reef; wound into a secret cove,
looked up along a green many-gabled lava wall, and saw the
island's solitary dwelling.

It hung upon an impending cliff, sheltered on two sides
by tangled thickets, and half-screened from view in front by
juttings of the rude stairway, which climbed the precipice
from the sea. Built of canes, it was thatched with long, mil-
dewed grass. It seemed an abandoned hay-rick whose hay-
makers were now no more. The roof inclined but one way;
the eaves coming to within two feet of the ground. And here
was a simple apparatus to collect the dews, or rather doubly-
distilled and finest winnowed rains, which, in mercy or in
mockery, the night-skies sometimes drop upon these blighted
Encantadas. All along beneath the eaves, a spotted sheet,
quite weather-stained, was spread, pinned to short, upright
stakes, set in the shallow sand. A small clinker, thrown into

the cloth, weighed its middle down, thereby straining all moisture into a calabash placed below. This vessel supplied each drop of water ever drunk upon the isle by the Cholos. Hunilla told us the calabash would sometimes, but not often, be half filled over-night. It held six quarts, perhaps. "But," said she, "we were used to thirst. At sandy Payta, where I live, no shower from heaven ever fell; all the water there is brought on mules from the inland vales."

Tied among the thickets were some twenty moaning tortoises, supplying Hunilla's lonely larder; while hundreds of vast tableted black bucklers, like displaced, shattered tombstones of dark slate, were also scattered round. These were the skeleton backs of those great tortoises from which Felipe and Truxill had made their precious oil. Several large calabashes and two goodly kegs were filled with it. In a pot near by were the caked crusts of a quantity which had been permitted to evaporate. "They meant to have strained it off next day," said Hunilla, as she turned aside.

I forgot to mention the most singular sight of all, though the first that greeted us after landing.

Some ten small, soft-haired, ringleted dogs, of a beautiful breed, peculiar to Peru, set up a concert of glad welcomings when we gained the beach, which was responded to by Hunilla. Some of these dogs had, since her widowhood, been born upon the isle, the progeny of the two brought from Payta. Owing to the jagged steeps and pitfalls, tortuous thickets, sunken clefts and perilous intricacies of all sorts in the interior; Hunilla, admonished by the loss of one favorite among them, never allowed these delicate creatures to follow her in her occasional birds'-nests climbs and other wanderings; so that, through long habituation, they offered not to follow, when that morning she crossed the land; and her own soul was then too full of other things to heed their lingering behind. Yet, all along she had so clung to them, that, besides what moisture they lapped up at early daybreak from the small scoop-holes among the adjacent rocks, she had shared the dew of her calabash among them; never laying by any considerable store against those prolonged and utter droughts, which in some disastrous seasons warp these isles.

Having pointed out, at our desire, what few things she would like transported to the ship—her chest, the oil, not omitting the live tortoises which she intended for a grateful present to our Captain—we immediately set to work, carrying them to the boat down the long, sloping stair of deeply-shadowed rock. While my comrades were thus employed, I looked, and Hunilla had disappeared.

It was not curiosity alone, but, it seems to me, something different mingled with it, which prompted me to drop my tortoise, and once more gaze slowly around. I remembered the husband buried by Hunilla's hands. A narrow pathway led into a dense part of the thickets. Following it through many mazes, I came out upon a small, round, open space, deeply chambered there.

The mound rose in the middle; a bare heap of finest sand, like that unverdured heap found at the bottom of an hour-glass run out. At its head stood the cross of withered sticks; the dry, peeled bark still fraying from it; its transverse limb tied up with rope, and forlornly adroop in the silent air.

Hunilla was partly prostrate upon the grave; her dark head bowed, and lost in her long, loosened Indian hair; her hands extended to the cross-foot, with a little brass crucifix clasped between; a crucifix worn featureless, like an ancient graven knocker long plied in vain. She did not see me, and I made no noise, but slid aside, and left the spot.

A few moments ere all was ready for our going, she re-appeared among us. I looked into her eyes, but saw no tear. There was something which seemed strangely haughty in her air, and yet it was the air of woe. A Spanish and an Indian grief, which would not visibly lament. Pride's height in vain abased to proneness on the rack; nature's pride subduing nature's torture.

Like pages the small and silken dogs surrounded her, as she slowly descended towards the beach. She caught the two most eager creatures in her arms:—"Mia Teeta! Mia Tomoteeta!" and fondling them, inquired how many could we take on board.

The mate commanded the boat's crew; not a hard-hearted man, but his way of life had been such that in most things, even in the smallest, simple utility was his leading motive.

"We cannot take them all, Hunilla; our supplies are short; the winds are unreliable; we may be a good many days going to Tombez. So take those you have, Hunilla; but no more."

She was in the boat; the oarsmen too were seated; all save one, who stood ready to push off and then spring himself. With the sagacity of their race, the dogs now seemed aware that they were in the very instant of being deserted upon a barren strand. The gunwales of the boat were high; its prow—presented inland—was lifted; so owing to the water, which they seemed instinctively to shun, the dogs could not well leap into the little craft. But their busy paws hard scraped the prow, as it had been some farmer's door shutting them out from shelter in a winter storm. A clamorous agony of alarm. They did not howl, or whine; they all but spoke.

"Push off! Give way!" cried the mate. The boat gave one heavy drag and lurch, and next moment shot swiftly from the beach, turned on her heel, and sped. The dogs ran howling along the water's marge; now pausing to gaze at the flying boat, then motioning as if to leap in chase, but mysteriously withheld themselves; and again ran howling along the beach. Had they been human beings hardly would they have more vividly inspired the sense of desolation. The oars were plied as confederate feathers of two wings. No one spoke. I looked back upon the beach, and then upon Hunilla, but her face was set in a stern dusky calm. The dogs crouching in her lap vainly licked her rigid hands. She never looked behind her; but sat motionless, till we turned a promontory of the coast and lost all sights and sounds astern. She seemed as one, who having experienced the sharpest of mortal pangs, was henceforth content to have all lesser heart-strings riven, one by one. To Hunilla, pain seemed so necessary, that pain in other beings, though by love and sympathy made her own, was unrepiningly to be borne. A heart of yearning in a frame of steel. A heart of earthly yearning, frozen by the frost which falleth from the sky.

The sequel is soon told. After a long passage, vexed by calms and baffling winds, we made the little port of Tombez in Peru, there to recruit the ship. Payta was not very distant. Our captain sold the tortoise oil to a Tombez merchant;

and adding to the silver a contribution from all hands, gave it to our silent passenger, who knew not what the mariners had done.

The last seen of lone Hunilla she was passing into Payta town, riding upon a small gray ass; and before her on the ass's shoulders, she eyed the jointed workings of the beast's armorial cross.

SKETCH NINTH

HOOD'S ISLE AND THE HERMIT OBERLUS

"*That darkesome glen they enter, where they find*
That cursed man low sitting on the ground,
Musing full sadly in his sullein mind;
His griesly lockes long growen and unbound,
Disordered hong about his shoulders round,
And hid his face, through which his hollow eyne
Lookt deadly dull, and stared as astound;
His raw-bone cheekes, through penurie and pine,
Were shronke into the jawes, as he did never dine.
His garments nought but many ragged clouts,
With thornes together pind and patched was,
The which his naked sides he wrapt abouts."*

SOUTHEAST of Crossman's Isle lies Hood's Isle, or McCain's Beclouded Isle; and upon its south side is a vitreous cove with a wide strand of dark pounded black lava, called Black Beach, or Oberlus's Landing. It might fitly have been styled Charon's.

It received its name from a wild white creature who spent many years here; in the person of a European bringing into this savage region qualities more diabolical than are to be found among any of the surrounding cannibals.

About half a century ago, Oberlus* deserted at the above-named island, then, as now, a solitude. He built himself a den of lava and clinkers, about a mile from the Landing, subsequently called after him, in a vale, or expanded gulch, containing here and there among the rocks about two acres of soil capable of rude cultivation; the only place on the isle not too blasted for that purpose. Here he succeeded in raising a sort of degenerate potatoes and pumpkins, which from time to time he exchanged with needy whalemen passing, for spirits or dollars.

His appearance, from all accounts, was that of the victim of some malignant sorceress; he seemed to have drunk of Circe's cup;* beast-like; rags insufficient to hide his nakedness; his befreckled skin blistered by continual exposure to the sun; nose flat; countenance contorted, heavy, earthy; hair and beard unshorn, profuse, and of a fiery red. He struck strangers much as if he were a volcanic creature thrown up by the same convulsion which exploded into sight the isle. All bepatched and coiled asleep in his lonely lava den among the mountains, he looked, they say, as a heaped drift of withered leaves, torn from autumn trees, and so left in some hidden nook by the whirling halt for an instant of a fierce night-wind, which then ruthlessly sweeps on, somewhere else to repeat the capricious act. It is also reported to have been the strangest sight, this same Oberlus, of a sultry, cloudy morning, hidden under his shocking old black tarpaulin hat, hoeing potatoes among the lava. So warped and crooked was his strange nature, that the very handle of his hoe seemed gradually to have shrunk and twisted in his grasp, being a wretched bent stick, elbowed more like a savage's war-sickle than a civilized hoe-handle. It was his mysterious custom upon a first encounter with a stranger ever to present his back; possibly, because that was his better side, since it revealed the least. If the encounter chanced in his garden, as it sometimes did—the new-landed strangers going from the sea-side straight through the gorge, to hunt up the queer green-grocer reported doing business here— Oberlus for a time hoed on, unmindful of all greeting, jovial or bland; as the curious stranger would turn to face him, the recluse, hoe in hand, as diligently would avert himself; bowed over, and sullenly revolving round his murphy hill. Thus far for hoeing. When planting, his whole aspect and all his gestures were so malevolently and uselessly sinister and secret, that he seemed rather in act of dropping poison into wells than potatoes into soil. But among his lesser and more harmless marvels was an idea he ever had, that his visitors came equally as well led by longings to behold the mighty hermit Oberlus in his royal state of solitude, as simply to obtain potatoes, or find whatever company might be upon a barren isle. It seems incredible that such a being should possess such vanity; a misanthrope be conceited; but he really had his notion; and upon the strength of it, often gave himself amusing airs to captains. But after all, this is somewhat of a piece with the well-known eccentricity of some convicts, proud of that very hatefulness which makes them notorious. At other times, another unaccountable whim would seize him, and he would long dodge advancing strangers round the clinkered corners of his hut; sometimes like a stealthy bear, he would slink through the withered thickets up the mountains, and refuse to see the human face.

Except his occasional visitors from the sea, for a long period, the only companions of Oberlus were the crawling tortoises; and he seemed more than degraded to their level, having no desires for a time beyond theirs, unless it were for the stupor brought on by drunkenness. But sufficiently debased as he appeared, there yet lurked in him, only await-ing occasion for discovery, a still further proneness. Indeed the sole superiority of Oberlus over the tortoises was his pos-session of a larger capacity of degradation; and along with that, something like an intelligent will to it. Moreover, what is about to be revealed, perhaps will show, that selfish ambi-tion, or the love of rule for its own sake, far from being the peculiar infirmity of noble minds, is shared by beings which have no mind at all. No creatures are so selfishly tyrannical as some brutes; as any one who has observed the tenants of the pasture must occasionally have observed.

"This island's mine by Sycorax my mother;"* said Oberlus to himself, glaring round upon his haggard solitude. By some means, barter or theft—for in those days ships at intervals still kept touching at his Landing—he obtained an old musket, with a few charges of powder and ball. Possessed of arms, he was stimulated to enterprise, as a tiger that first feels the coming of its claws. The long habit of sole dominion over every object round him, his almost unbroken solitude, his never encountering humanity except on terms of misanthropic independence, or mercantile craftiness, and even such encounters being comparatively but rare; all this must have gradually nourished in him a vast idea of his own importance, together with a pure animal sort of scorn for all the rest of the universe.

The unfortunate Creole, who enjoyed his brief term of royalty at Charles's Isle was perhaps in some degree influenced by not unworthy motives; such as prompt other adventurous spirits to lead colonists into distant regions and assume political pre-eminence over them. His summary execution of many of his Peruvians is quite pardonable, considering the desperate characters he had to deal with; while his offering canine battle to the banded rebels seems under the circumstances altogether just. But for this King Oberlus and what shortly follows, no shade of palliation can be given. He acted out of mere delight in tyranny and cruelty, by virtue of a quality in him inherited from Sycorax his mother. Armed now with that shocking blunderbuss, strong in the thought of being master of that horrid isle, he panted for a chance to prove his potency upon the first specimen of humanity which should fall unbefriended into his hands.

Nor was he long without it. One day he spied a boat upon the beach, with one man, a negro, standing by it. Some distance off was a ship, and Oberlus immediately knew how matters stood. The vessel had put in for wood, and the boat's crew had gone into the thickets for it. From a convenient spot he kept watch of the boat, till presently a straggling company appeared loaded with billets. Throwing these on the beach, they again went into the thickets, while the negro proceeded to load the boat.

Oberlus now makes all haste and accosts the negro, who aghast at seeing any living being inhabiting such a solitude, and especially so horrific a one, immediately falls into a panic, not at all lessened by the ursine suavity of Oberlus, who begs the favor of assisting him in his labors. The negro stands with several billets on his shoulder, in act of shouldering others; and Oberlus, with a short cord concealed in his bosom, kindly proceeds to lift those other billets to their place. In so doing he persists in keeping behind the negro, who rightly suspicious of this, in vain dodges about to gain the front of Oberlus; but Oberlus dodges also; till at last, weary of this bootless attempt at treachery, or fearful of being surprised by the remainder of the party, Oberlus runs off a little space to a bush, and fetching his blunderbuss, savagely commands the negro to desist work and follow him. He refuses. Whereupon, presenting his piece, Oberlus snaps at him. Luckily the blunderbuss misses fire; but by this time, frightened out of his wits, the negro, upon a second intrepid summons drops his billets, surrenders at discretion, and follows on. By a narrow defile familiar to him, Oberlus speedily removes out of sight of the water.

On their way up the mountains, he exultingly informs the negro, that henceforth he is to work for him, and be his slave, and that his treatment would entirely depend on his future conduct. But Oberlus, deceived by the first impulsive cowardice of the black, in an evil moment slackens his vigilance. Passing through a narrow way, and perceiving his leader quite off his guard, the negro, a powerful fellow, suddenly grasps him in his arms, throws him down, wrests his musketoon from him, ties his hands with the monster's own cord, shoulders him, and returns with him down to the boat. When the rest of the party arrive, Oberlus is carried on board the ship. This proved an Englishman, and a smuggler; a sort of craft not apt to be over-charitable. Oberlus is severely whipped, then handcuffed, taken ashore, and compelled to make known his habitation and produce his property. His potatoes, pumpkins, and tortoises, with a pile of dollars he had hoarded from his mercantile operations were secured on the spot. But while the too vindictive smugglers were busy destroying his hut and garden, Oberlus makes his escape into the mountains, and conceals himself there in impenetrable recesses, only known to himself, till the ship sails, when he ventures back, and by means of an old file which he sticks into a tree, contrives to free himself from his handcuffs.

Brooding among the ruins of his hut, and the desolate clinkers and extinct volcanoes of this outcast isle, the insulted misanthrope now meditates a signal revenge upon humanity, but conceals his purposes. Vessels still touch the Landing at times; and by and by Oberlus is enabled to supply them with some vegetables.

Warned by his former failure in kidnapping strangers, he now pursues a quite different plan. When seamen come ashore, he makes up to them like a free-and-easy comrade, invites them to his hut, and with whatever affability his red-haired grimness may assume, entreats them to drink his liquor and be merry. But his guests need little pressing; and so, soon as rendered insensible, are tied hand and foot, and pitched among the clinkers, are there concealed till the ship departs, when finding themselves entirely dependent upon Oberlus, alarmed at his changed demeanor, his savage threats, and above all, that shocking blunderbuss, they willingly enlist under him, becoming his humble slaves, and Oberlus the most incredible of tyrants. So much so, that two or three perish beneath his initiating process. He sets the remainder—four of them—to breaking the caked soil; transporting upon their backs loads of loamy earth, scooped up in moist clefts among the mountains; keeps them on the roughest fare; presents his piece at the slightest hint of insurrection; and in all respects converts them into reptiles at his feet; plebeian garter-snakes to this Lord Anaconda.

At last, Oberlus contrives to stock his arsenal with four rusty cutlasses, and an added supply of powder and ball intended for his blunderbuss. Remitting in good part the labor of his slaves, he now approves himself a man, or rather devil, of great abilities in the way of cajoling or coercing others into acquiescence with his own ulterior designs, however at first abhorrent to them. But indeed, prepared for almost any eventual evil by their previous lawless life, as a sort of ranging Cow-Boys of the sea, which had dissolved within them the whole moral man, so that they were ready to concrete in the first offered mould of baseness now; rotted down from manhood by their hopeless misery on the isle; wonted to cringe in all things to their lord, himself the worst of slaves; these wretches were now become wholly corrupted to his hands. He used them as creatures of an inferior race; in short, he gaffles his four animals, and makes murderers of them; out of cowards fitly manufacturing bravos.

Now, sword or dagger, human arms are but artificial claws and fangs, tied on like false spurs to the fighting cock. So, we repeat, Oberlus, czar of the isle, gaffles his four subjects; that is, with intent of glory, puts four rusty cutlasses into their hands. Like any other autocrat, he had a noble army now.

It might be thought a servile war would hereupon ensue. Arms in the hands of trodden slaves? how indiscreet of Emperor Oberlus! Nay, they had but cutlasses—sad old scythes enough—he a blunderbuss, which by its blind scatterings of all sorts of boulders, clinkers and other scoria would annihilate all four mutineers, like four pigeons at one shot. Besides, at first he did not sleep in his accustomed hut; every lurid sunset, for a time, he might have been seen wending his way among the riven mountains, there to secret himself till dawn in some sulphurous pitfall, undiscoverable to his gang; but finding this at last too troublesome, he now each evening tied his slaves hand and foot, hid the cutlasses, and thrusting them into his barracks, shut to the door, and lying down before it, beneath a rude shed lately added, slept out the night, blunderbuss in hand.

It is supposed that not content with daily parading over a cindery solitude at the head of his fine army, Oberlus now meditated the most active mischief; his probable object being to surprise some passing ship touching at his dominions, massacre the crew, and run away with her to parts unknown. While these plans were simmering in his head, two ships touch in company at the isle, on the opposite side to his; when his designs undergo a sudden change.

The ships are in want of vegetables, which Oberlus promises in great abundance, provided they send their boats round to his landing, so that the crews may bring the vegetables from his garden; informing the two captains, at the same time, that his rascals—slaves and soldiers—had become so abominably lazy and good-for-nothing of late, that he could not make them work by ordinary inducements, and did not have the heart to be severe with them.

The arrangement was agreed to, and the boats were sent and hauled upon the beach. The crews went to the lava hut; but to their surprise nobody was there. After waiting till their patience was exhausted, they returned to the shore, when lo, some stranger—not the Good Samaritan either—seems to have very recently passed that way. Three of the boats were broken in a thousand pieces, and the fourth was missing. By hard toil over the mountains and through the clinkers, some of the strangers succeeded in returning to that side of the isle where the ships lay, when fresh boats are sent to the relief of the rest of the hapless party.

However amazed at the treachery of Oberlus, the two captains afraid of new and still more mysterious atrocities, —and indeed, half imputing such strange events to the enchantments associated with these isles,—perceive no security but in instant flight; leaving Oberlus and his army in quiet possession of the stolen boat.

On the eve of sailing they put a letter in a keg, giving the Pacific Ocean intelligence of the affair, and moored the keg in the bay. Some time subsequent, the keg was opened by another captain chancing to anchor there, but not until after he had dispatched a boat round to Oberlus's Landing. As may be readily surmised, he felt no little inquietude till the boat's return; when another letter was handed him, giving Oberlus's version of the affair. This precious document had been found pinned half-mildewed to the clinker wall of the sulphurous and deserted hut. It ran as follows; showing that Oberlus was at least an accomplished writer, and no mere boor; and what is more, was capable of the most tristful eloquence.

"Sir: I am the most unfortunate ill-treated gentleman that lives. I am a patriot, exiled from my country by the cruel hand of tyranny.

"Banished to these Enchanted Isles, I have again and again besought captains of ships to sell me a boat, but always have been refused, though I offered the handsomest prices in Mexican dollars. At length an opportunity presented of possessing myself of one, and I did not let it slip.

"I have been long endeavoring by hard labor and much solitary suffering to accumulate something to make myself comfortable in a virtuous though unhappy old age; but at various times have been robbed and beaten by men professing to be Christians.

"To-day I sail from the Enchanted group in the good boat Charity bound to the Feejee Isles.

"FATHERLESS OBERLUS.

"P.S.—Behind the clinkers, nigh the oven, you will find the old fowl. Do not kill it; be patient; I leave it setting; if it shall have any chicks, I hereby bequeathe them to you, whoever you may be. But don't count your chicks before they are hatched."

The fowl proved a starveling rooster, reduced to a sitting posture by sheer debility.

Oberlus declares that he was bound to the Feejee Isles; but this was only to throw pursuers on a false scent. For after a long time he arrived, alone in his open boat, at Guayaquil.* As his miscreants were never again beheld on Hood's Isle, it is supposed, either that they perished for want of water on the passage to Guayaquil, or, what is quite as probable, were thrown overboard by Oberlus, when he found the water growing scarce.

From Guayaquil Oberlus proceeded to Payta; and there, with that nameless witchery peculiar to some of the ugliest animals, wound himself into the affections of a tawny damsel; prevailing upon her to accompany him back to his Enchanted Isle; which doubtless he painted as a Paradise of flowers, not a Tartarus of clinkers.

But unfortunately for the colonization of Hood's Isle with a choice variety of animated nature, the extraordinary and devilish aspect of Oberlus made him to be regarded in Payta as a highly suspicious character. So that being found concealed one night, with matches in his pocket, under the hull of a small vessel just ready to be launched, he was seized and thrown into jail.

The jails in most South American towns are generally of the least wholesome sort. Built of huge cakes of sun-burnt brick, and containing but one room, without windows or yard, and but one door heavily grated with wooden bars, they present both within and without the grimmest aspect. As public edifices they conspicuously stand upon the hot and dusty Plaza, offering to view, through the gratings, their villanous and hopeless inmates, burrowing in all sorts of tragic squalor. And here, for a long time Oberlus was seen; the central figure of a mongrel and assassin band; a creature whom it is religion to detest, since it is philanthropy to hate a misanthrope.

Note.—They who may be disposed to question the possibility of the character above depicted, are referred to the 1st vol. of Porter's Voyage into the Pacific, where they will recognize many sentences, for expedition's sake derived verbatim from thence, and incorporated here; the main difference—save a few passing reflections—between the two accounts being, that the present writer has added to Porter's facts accessory ones picked up in the Pacific from reliable sources; and where facts conflict, has naturally preferred his own authorities to Porter's. As, for instance, *his* authorities place Oberlus on Hood's Isle: Porter's, on Charles's Isle. The letter found in the hut is also somewhat different, for while at the Encantadas he was informed that not only did it evince a certain clerkliness, but was full of the strangest satiric effrontery which does not adequately appear in Porter's version. I accordingly altered it to suit the general character of its author.

SKETCH TENTH

RUNAWAYS, CASTAWAYS, SOLITARIES, GRAVE-STONES, ETC.

> *"And all about old stocks and stubs of trees,*
> *Whereon nor fruit nor leaf was ever seen,*
> *Did hang upon the ragged knotty knees,*
> *On which had many wretches hanged been."**

SOME relics of the hut of Oberlus partially remain to this day at the head of the clinkered valley. Nor does the stranger wandering among other of the Enchanted Isles fail to stumble upon still other solitary abodes, long abandoned to the tortoise and the lizard. Probably few parts of earth have in modern times sheltered so many solitaries. The reason is, that these isles are situated in a distant sea, and the vessels which occasionally visit them are mostly all whalers, or ships bound on dreary and protracted voyages, exempting them in a good degree from both the oversight and the memory of human law. Such is the character of some commanders and some seamen, that under these untoward circumstances, it is quite impossible but that scenes of unpleasantness and discord should occur between them. A sullen hatred of the tyrannic ship will seize the sailor, and he gladly exchanges it for isles, which though blighted as by a continual sirocco and burning breeze, still offer him in their labyrinthine interior, a retreat beyond the possibility of capture. To flee the ship in any Peruvian or Chilian port, even the smallest and most rustical, is not unattended with great risk of apprehension, not to speak of jaguars. A reward of five pesos sends fifty dastardly Spaniards into the woods, who with long knives scour them day and night in eager hopes of securing their prey. Neither is it, in general, much easier to escape pursuit at the isles of Polynesia. Those of them which have felt a civilizing influence present the same difficulty to the runaway with the Peruvian ports, the advanced natives being quite as mercenary and keen of knife and scent, as the retrograde Spaniards; while, owing to the bad odor in which all Europeans lie in the minds of aboriginal savages who have chanced to hear aught of them, to desert the ship among primitive Polynesians, is, in most cases, a hope not unforlorn. Hence the Enchanted Isles become the voluntary tarrying places of all sorts of refugees; some of whom too sadly experience the fact that flight from tyranny does not of itself insure a safe asylum, far less a happy home.

Moreover, it has not seldom happened that hermits have been made upon the isles by the accidents incident to tortoise-hunting. The interior of most of them is tangled and difficult of passage beyond description; the air is sultry and stifling; an intolerable thirst is provoked, for which no running stream offers its kind relief. In a few hours, under an equatorial sun, reduced by these causes to entire exhaustion, woe betide the straggler at the Enchanted Isles! Their extent is such as to forbid an adequate search unless weeks are devoted to it. The impatient ship waits a day or two; when the missing man remaining undiscovered, up goes a stake on the beach, with a letter of regret, and a keg of crackers and another of water tied to it, and away sails the craft.

Nor have there been wanting instances where the inhumanity of some captains has led them to wreak a secure revenge upon seamen who have given their caprice or pride some singular offence. Thrust ashore upon the scorching marl, such mariners are abandoned to perish outright, unless by solitary labors they succeed in discovering some precious dribblets of moisture oozing from a rock or stagnant in a mountain pool.

I was well acquainted with a man, who, lost upon the Isle of Narborough, was brought to such extremes by thirst, that at last he only saved his life by taking that of another being. A large hair-seal came upon the beach. He rushed upon it, stabbed it in the neck, and then throwing himself upon the panting body quaffed at the living wound; the palpitations of the creature's dying heart injecting life into the drinker.

Another seaman thrust ashore in a boat upon an isle at which no ship ever touched, owing to its peculiar sterility and the shoals about it, and from which all other parts of the group were hidden; this man feeling that it was sure death to remain there, and that nothing worse than death menaced him in quitting it, killed two seals, and inflating their skins, made a float, upon which he transported himself to Charles's Island, and joined the republic there.

But men not endowed with courage equal to such desperate attempts, find their only resource in forthwith seeking for some watering-place, however precarious or scanty; building a hut; catching tortoises and birds; and in all respects preparing for hermit life, till tide or time, or a passing ship arrives to float them off.

At the foot of precipices on many of the isles, small rude basins in the rocks are found, partly filled with rotted rubbish or vegetable decay, or overgrown with thickets, and sometimes a little moist; which, upon examination, reveal plain tokens of artificial instruments employed in hollowing them out, by some poor castaway or still more miserable runaway. These basins are made in places where it was supposed some scanty drops of dew might exude into them from the upper crevices.

The relics of hermitages and stone basins, are not the only signs of vanishing humanity to be found upon the isles. And curious to say, that spot which of all others in settled communities is most animated, at the Enchanted Isles presents the most dreary of aspects. And though it may seem very strange to talk of post-offices in this barren region, yet post-offices are occasionally to be found there. They consist of a stake and bottle. The letters being not only sealed, but corked. They are generally deposited by captains of Nantucketers for the benefit of passing fishermen; and contain statements as to what luck they had in whaling or tortoise-hunting. Frequently, however, long months and months, whole years glide by and no applicant appears. The stake rots and falls, presenting no very exhilarating object.

If now it be added that grave-stones, or rather grave-boards, are also discovered upon some of the isles, the picture will be complete.

Upon the beach of James's Isle for many years, was to be seen a rude finger-post pointing inland. And perhaps taking it for some signal of possible hospitality in this otherwise desolate spot—some good hermit living there with his maple dish—the stranger would follow on in the path thus indicated, till at last he would come out in a noiseless nook, and find his only welcome, a dead man; his sole greeting the inscription over a grave: "Here, in 1813, fell in a daybreak duel, a Lieutenant of the U.S. frigate Essex, aged twenty-one: attaining his majority in death."

It is but fit that like those old monastic institutions of Europe, whose inmates go not out of their own walls to be inurned, but are entombed there where they die; the Encantadas too should bury their own dead, even as the great general monastery of earth does hers.

It is known that burial in the ocean is a pure necessity of sea-faring life, and that it is only done when land is far astern, and not clearly visible from the bow. Hence to vessels cruising in the vicinity of the Enchanted Isles, they afford a convenient Potter's Field.* The interment over, some good-natured forecastle poet and artist seizes his paint-brush, and inscribes a doggerel epitaph. When after a long lapse of time, other good-natured seamen chance to come upon the spot, they usually make a table of the mound, and quaff a friendly can to the poor soul's repose.

As a specimen of these epitaphs, take the following, found in a bleak gorge of Chatham Isle:—

"Oh Brother Jack, as you pass by,
As you are now, so once was I.
Just so game and just so gay,
But now, alack, they've stopped my pay.
No more I peep out of my blinkers,
Here I be—tucked in with clinkers!"*

BENITO CERENO

In the year 1799, Captain Amasa Delano, of Duxbury, in Massachusetts, commanding a large sealer and general trader, lay at anchor, with a valuable cargo, in the harbor of St. Maria—a small, desert, uninhabited island toward the southern extremity of the long coast of Chili. There he had touched for water.*

On the second day, not long after dawn, while lying in his berth, his mate came below, informing him that a strange sail was coming into the bay. Ships were then not so plenty in those waters as now. He rose, dressed, and went on deck.

The morning was one peculiar to that coast. Everything was mute and calm; everything gray. The sea, though undulated into long roods of swells, seemed fixed, and was sleeked at the surface like waved lead that has cooled and set in the smelter's mould. The sky seemed a gray surtout. Flights of troubled gray fowl, kith and kin with flights of troubled gray vapors among which they were mixed, skimmed low and fitfully over the waters, as swallows over meadows before storms. Shadows present, foreshadowing deeper shadows to come.*

To Captain Delano's surprise, the stranger, viewed through the glass, showed no colors; though to do so upon entering a haven, however uninhabited in its shores, where but a single other ship might be lying, was the custom among peaceful seamen of all nations. Considering the lawlessness and loneliness of the spot, and the sort of stories, at that day, associated with those seas, Captain Delano's surprise might have deepened into some uneasiness had he not been a person of a singularly undistrustful good nature,* not liable, except on extraordinary and repeated incentives, and hardly then, to indulge in personal alarms, any way involving the imputation of malign evil in man. Whether, in view of what humanity is capable, such a trait implies, along with a benevolent heart, more than ordinary quickness and accuracy of intellectual perception, may be left to the wise to determine.

But whatever misgivings might have obtruded on first seeing the stranger, would almost, in any seaman's mind, have
been dissipated by observing that, the ship, in navigating
into the harbor, was drawing too near the land, for her own
safety's sake, owing to a sunken reef making out off her bow.
This seemed to prove her a stranger, indeed, not only to the
sealer, but the island; consequently, she could be no wonted
freebooter on that ocean. With no small interest, Captain
Delano continued to watch her—a proceeding not much
facilitated by the vapors partly mantling the hull, through
which the far matin light from her cabin streamed equivocally enough; much like the sun—by this time hemisphered
on the rim of the horizon, and apparently, in company with
the strange ship, entering the harbor—which, wimpled by
the same low, creeping clouds, showed not unlike a Lima
intriguante's one sinister eye peering across the Plaza from
the Indian loop-hole of her dusk *saya-y-manta.**
    It might have been but a deception of the vapors, but, the
longer the stranger was watched, the more singular appeared
her maneuvers. Ere long it seemed hard to decide whether
she meant to come in or no—what she wanted, or what she
was about. The wind, which had breezed up a little during
the night, was now extremely light and baffling, which the
more increased the apparent uncertainty of her movements.
    Surmising, at last, that it might be a ship in distress, Cap-
tain Delano ordered his whale-boat to be dropped, and, much
to the wary opposition of his mate, prepared to board her, and,
at the least, pilot her in. On the night previous, a fishing-
party of the seamen had gone a long distance to some detached rocks out of sight from the sealer, and, an hour or two
before day-break, had returned, having met with no small success. Presuming that the stranger might have been long off
soundings, the good captain put several baskets of the fish,
for presents, into his boat, and so pulled away. From her continuing too near the sunken reef, deeming her in danger, calling to his men, he made all haste to apprise those on board
of their situation. But, some time ere the boat came up, the
wind, light though it was, having shifted, had headed the vessel off, as well as partly broken the vapors from about her.

Upon gaining a less remote view, the ship, when made signally visible on the verge of the leaden-hued swells, with the shreds of fog here and there raggedly furring her, appeared like a white-washed monastery* after a thunder-storm, seen perched upon some dun cliff among the Pyrenees. But it was no purely fanciful resemblance which now, for a moment, almost led Captain Delano to think that nothing less than a ship-load of monks was before him. Peering over the bulwarks were what really seemed, in the hazy distance, throngs of dark cowls; while, fitfully revealed through the open portholes, other dark moving figures were dimly descried, as of Black Friars* pacing the cloisters.

Upon a still nigher approach, this appearance was modified, and the true character of the vessel was plain—a Spanish merchantman of the first class; carrying negro slaves, amongst other valuable freight, from one colonial port to another. A very large, and, in its time, a very fine vessel, such as in those days were at intervals encountered along that main; sometimes superseded Acapulco treasure-ships, or retired frigates of the Spanish king's navy, which, like superannuated Italian palaces, still, under a decline of masters, preserved signs of former state.

As the whale-boat drew more and more nigh, the cause of the peculiar pipe-clayed aspect of the stranger was seen in the slovenly neglect pervading her. The spars, ropes, and great part of the bulwarks, looked woolly, from long unacquaintance with the scraper, tar, and the brush. Her keel seemed laid, her ribs put together, and she launched, from Ezekiel's Valley of Dry Bones.*

In the present business in which she was engaged, the ship's general model and rig appeared to have undergone no material change from their original war-like and Froissart pattern. However, no guns were seen.

The tops were large, and were railed about with what had once been octagonal net-work, all now in sad disrepair. These tops hung overhead like three ruinous aviaries, in one of which was seen perched, on a ratlin, a white noddy,* a strange fowl, so called from its lethargic, somnambulistic character, being frequently caught by hand at sea. Battered and mouldy, the castellated forecastle seemed some ancient turret, long ago taken by assault, and then left to decay. Toward the stern, two high-raised quarter galleries—the balustrades here and there covered with dry, tindery sea-moss—opening out from the unoccupied state-cabin, whose dead lights, for all the mild weather, were hermetically closed and calked—these tenantless balconies hung over the sea as if it were the grand Venetian canal. But the principal relic of faded grandeur was the ample oval of the shield-like stern-piece, intricately carved with the arms of Castile and Leon, medallioned about by groups of mythological or symbolical devices; uppermost and central of which was a dark satyr in a mask, holding his foot on the prostrate neck of a writhing figure, likewise masked.

Whether the ship had a figure-head, or only a plain beak, was not quite certain, owing to canvas wrapped about that part, either to protect it while undergoing a re-furbishing, or else decently to hide its decay. Rudely painted or chalked, as in a sailor freak, along the forward side of a sort of pedestal below the canvas, was the sentence, "*Seguid vuestro jefe,*" (follow your leader); while upon the tarnished head-boards, near by, appeared, in stately capitals, once gilt, the ship's name, "San Dominick,"* each letter streakingly corroded with tricklings of copper-spike rust; while, like mourning weeds, dark festoons of sea-grass slimily swept to and fro over the name, with every hearse-like roll of the hull.

As at last the boat was hooked from the bow along toward the gangway amidship, its keel, while yet some inches separated from the hull, harshly grated as on a sunken coral reef. It proved a huge bunch of conglobated barnacles adhering below the water to the side like a wen; a token of baffling airs and long calms passed somewhere in those seas.

Climbing the side, the visitor was at once surrounded by a clamorous throng of whites and blacks, but the latter out-numbering the former more than could have been expected, negro transportation-ship as the stranger in port was. But, in one language, and as with one voice, all poured out a common tale of suffering; in which the negresses, of whom there were not a few, exceeded the others in their dolorous vehe-mence. The scurvy, together with a fever, had swept off a great part of their number, more especially the Spaniards.

Off Cape Horn, they had narrowly escaped shipwreck; then, for days together, they had lain tranced without wind; their provisions were low; their water next to none; their lips that moment were baked.

While Captain Delano was thus made the mark of all eager tongues, his one eager glance took in all the faces, with every other object about him.

Always upon first boarding a large and populous ship at sea, especially a foreign one, with a nondescript crew such as Lascars* or Manilla men, the impression varies in a peculiar way from that produced by first entering a strange house with strange inmates in a strange land. Both house and ship, the one by its walls and blinds, the other by its high bulwarks like ramparts, hoard from view their interiors till the last moment; but in the case of the ship there is this addition; that the living spectacle it contains, upon its sudden and complete disclosure, has, in contrast with the blank ocean which zones it, something of the effect of enchantment. The ship seems unreal; these strange costumes, gestures, and faces, but a shadowy tableau just emerged from the deep, which directly must receive back what it gave.

Perhaps it was some such influence as above is attempted to be described, which, in Captain Delano's mind, heightened whatever, upon a staid scrutiny, might have seemed unusual; especially the conspicuous figures of four elderly grizzled negroes, their heads like black, doddered willow tops, who, in venerable contrast to the tumult below them, were couched sphynx-like, one on the starboard cat-head, another on the larboard, and the remaining pair face to face on the opposite bulwarks above the main-chains. They each had bits of unstranded old junk in their hands, and, with a sort of stoical self-content, were picking the junk into oakum, a small heap of which lay by their sides. They accompanied the task with a continuous, low, monotonous chant; droning and druling away like so many gray-headed bag-pipers playing a funeral march.

The quarter-deck rose into an ample elevated poop, upon the forward verge of which, lifted, like the oakum-pickers, some eight feet above the general throng, sat along in a row,

separated by regular spaces, the cross-legged figures of six
other blacks; each with a rusty hatchet in his hand, which,
with a bit of brick and a rag, he was engaged like a scul-
lion in scouring; while between each two was a small stack
of hatchets, their rusted edges turned forward awaiting a
like operation. Though occasionally the four oakum-pickers
would briefly address some person or persons in the crowd
below, yet the six hatchet-polishers neither spoke to others,
nor breathed a whisper among themselves, but sat intent
upon their task, except at intervals, when, with the peculiar
love in negroes of uniting industry with pastime, two and
two they sideways clashed their hatchets together, like cym-
bals, with a barbarous din. All six, unlike the generality, had
the raw aspect of unsophisticated Africans.

But that first comprehensive glance which took in those
ten figures, with scores less conspicuous, rested but an instant
upon them, as, impatient of the hubbub of voices, the visitor
turned in quest of whomsoever it might be that commanded
the ship.

But as if not unwilling to let nature make known her own
case among his suffering charge, or else in despair of restrain-
ing it for the time, the Spanish captain, a gentlemanly, reserved-
looking, and rather young man to a stranger's eye, dressed
with singular richness, but bearing plain traces of recent
sleepless cares and disquietudes, stood passively by, leaning
against the main-mast, at one moment casting a dreary, spir-
itless look upon his excited people, at the next an unhappy
glance toward his visitor. By his side stood a black of small
stature, in whose rude face, as occasionally, like a shepherd's
dog, he mutely turned it up into the Spaniard's, sorrow and
affection were equally blended.

Struggling through the throng, the American advanced to
the Spaniard, assuring him of his sympathies, and offering
to render whatever assistance might be in his power. To
which the Spaniard returned, for the present, but grave and
ceremonious acknowledgments, his national formality dusked
by the saturnine mood of ill health.

But losing no time in mere compliments, Captain Delano
returning to the gangway, had his baskets of fish brought

up; and as the wind still continued light, so that some hours at least must elapse ere the ship could be brought to the anchorage, he bade his men return to the sealer, and fetch back as much water as the whale-boat could carry, with whatever soft bread the steward might have, all the remaining pumpkins on board, with a box of sugar, and a dozen of his private bottles of cider.

Not many minutes after the boat's pushing off, to the vexation of all, the wind entirely died away, and the tide turning, began drifting back the ship helplessly seaward. But trusting this would not long last, Captain Delano sought with good hopes to cheer up the strangers, feeling no small satisfaction that, with persons in their condition he could— thanks to his frequent voyages along the Spanish main— converse with some freedom in their native tongue.

While left alone with them, he was not long in observing some things tending to heighten his first impressions; but surprise was lost in pity, both for the Spaniards and blacks, alike evidently reduced from scarcity of water and provisions; while long-continued suffering seemed to have brought out the less good-natured qualities of the negroes, besides, at the same time, impairing the Spaniard's authority over them. But, under the circumstances, precisely this condition of things was to have been anticipated. In armies, navies, cities, or families, in nature herself, nothing more relaxes good order than misery. Still, Captain Delano was not without the idea, that had Benito Cereno been a man of greater energy, misrule would hardly have come to the present pass. But the debility, constitutional or induced by the hardships, bodily and mental, of the Spanish captain, was too obvious to be overlooked. A prey to settled dejection, as if long mocked with hope he would not now indulge it, even when it had ceased to be a mock, the prospect of that day or evening at furthest, lying at anchor, with plenty of water for his people, and a brother captain to counsel and befriend, seemed in no perceptible degree to encourage him. His mind appeared unstrung, if not still more seriously affected. Shut up in these oaken walls, chained to one dull round of command, whose unconditionality cloyed him, like some hypochondriac abbot he moved slowly about, at times suddenly pausing, starting, or staring, biting his lip, biting his finger-nail, flushing, paling, twitching his beard, with other symptoms of an absent or moody mind. This distempered spirit was lodged, as before hinted, in as distempered a frame. He was rather tall, but seemed never to have been robust, and now with nervous suffering was almost worn to a skeleton. A tendency to some pulmonary complaint appeared to have been lately confirmed. His voice was like that of one with lungs half gone, hoarsely suppressed, a husky whisper. No wonder that, as in this state he tottered about, his private servant apprehensively followed him. Sometimes the negro gave his master his arm, or took his handkerchief out of his pocket for him; performing these and similar offices with that affectionate zeal which transmutes into something filial or fraternal acts in themselves but menial; and which has gained for the negro the repute of making the most pleasing body servant in the world; one, too, whom a master need be on no stiffly superior terms with, but may treat with familiar trust; less a servant than a devoted companion.

Marking the noisy indocility of the blacks in general, as well as what seemed the sullen inefficiency of the whites, it was not without humane satisfaction that Captain Delano witnessed the steady good conduct of Babo.*

But the good conduct of Babo, hardly more than the ill-behavior of others, seemed to withdraw the half-lunatic Don Benito from his cloudy languor. Not that such precisely was the impression made by the Spaniard on the mind of his visitor. The Spaniard's individual unrest was, for the present, but noted as a conspicuous feature in the ship's general affliction. Still, Captain Delano was not a little concerned at what he could not help taking for the time to be Don Benito's unfriendly indifference towards himself. The Spaniard's manner, too, conveyed a sort of sour and gloomy disdain, which he seemed at no pains to disguise. But this the American in charity ascribed to the harassing effects of sickness, since, in former instances, he had noted that there are peculiar natures on whom prolonged physical suffering seems to cancel every social instinct of kindness; as if forced to black bread themselves, they deemed it but equity that each person coming nigh them should, indirectly, by some slight or affront, be made to partake of their fare.

But ere long Captain Delano bethought him that, indulgent as he was at the first, in judging the Spaniard, he might not, after all, have exercised charity enough. At bottom it was Don Benito's reserve which displeased him; but the same reserve was shown towards all but his faithful personal attendant. Even the formal reports which, according to sea-usage, were, at stated times, made to him by some petty underling, either a white, mulatto or black, he hardly had patience enough to listen to, without betraying contemptuous aversion. His manner upon such occasions was, in its degree, not unlike that which might be supposed to have been his imperial countryman's, Charles V.,* just previous to the anchoritish retirement of that monarch from the throne.

This splenetic disrelish of his place was evinced in almost every function pertaining to it. Proud as he was moody, he condescended to no personal mandate. Whatever special orders were necessary, their delivery was delegated to his body-servant, who in turn transferred them to their ultimate destination, through runners, alert Spanish boys or slave boys, like pages or pilot-fish within easy call continually hovering round Don Benito. So that to have beheld this undemonstrative invalid gliding about, apathetic and mute, no landsman could have dreamed that in him was lodged a dictatorship beyond which, while at sea, there was no earthly appeal.

Thus, the Spaniard, regarded in his reserve, seemed as the involuntary victim of mental disorder. But, in fact, his reserve might, in some degree, have proceeded from design. If so, then here was evinced the unhealthy climax of that icy though conscientious policy, more or less adopted by all commanders of large ships, which, except in signal emergencies, obliterates alike the manifestation of sway with every trace of sociality; transforming the man into a block, or rather into a loaded cannon, which, until there is call for thunder, has nothing to say.

Viewing him in this light, it seemed but a natural token of the perverse habit induced by a long course of such hard self-restraint, that, notwithstanding the present condition of his ship, the Spaniard should still persist in a demeanor, which, however harmless, or, it may be, appropriate, in a well appointed vessel, such as the San Dominick might have been at the outset of the voyage, was anything but judicious now. But the Spaniard perhaps thought that it was with captains as with gods: reserve, under all events, must still be their cue. But more probably this appearance of slumbering dominion might have been but an attempted disguise to conscious imbecility—not deep policy, but shallow device. But be all this as it might, whether Don Benito's manner was designed or not, the more Captain Delano noted its pervading reserve, the less he felt uneasiness at any particular manifestation of that reserve towards himself.

Neither were his thoughts taken up by the captain alone. Wonted to the quiet orderliness of the sealer's comfortable family of a crew, the noisy confusion of the San Dominick's suffering host repeatedly challenged his eye. Some prominent breaches not only of discipline but of decency were observed. These Captain Delano could not but ascribe, in the main, to the absence of those subordinate deck-officers to whom, along with higher duties, is entrusted what may be styled the police department of a populous ship. True, the old oakum-pickers appeared at times to act the part of monitorial constables to their countrymen, the blacks; but though occasionally succeeding in allaying trifling outbreaks now and then between man and man, they could do little or nothing toward establishing general quiet. The San Dominick was in the condition of a transatlantic emigrant ship, among whose multitude of living freight are some individuals, doubtless, as little troublesome as crates and bales; but the friendly remonstrances of such with their ruder companions are of not so much avail as the unfriendly arm of the mate. What the San Dominick wanted was, what the emigrant ship has, stern superior officers. But on these decks not so much as a fourth mate was to be seen.

The visitor's curiosity was roused to learn the particulars of those mishaps which had brought about such absentee-ism, with its consequences; because, though deriving some ink-ling of the voyage from the wails which at the first moment had greeted him, yet of the details no clear understanding had been had. The best account would, doubtless, be given by the captain. Yet at first the visitor was loth to ask it, un-willing to provoke some distant rebuff. But plucking up courage, he at last accosted Don Benito, renewing the expression of his benevolent interest, adding, that did he (Captain Delano) but know the particulars of the ship's misfortunes, he would, perhaps, be better able in the end to relieve them. Would Don Benito favor him with the whole story?

Don Benito faltered; then, like some somnambulist sud-denly interfered with, vacantly stared at his visitor, and ended by looking down on the deck. He maintained this posture so long, that Captain Delano, almost equally disconcerted, and involuntarily almost as rude, turned suddenly from him, walking forward to accost one of the Spanish seamen for the desired information. But he had hardly gone five paces, when with a sort of eagerness Don Benito invited him back, regret-ting his momentary absence of mind, and professing readi-ness to gratify him.

While most part of the story was being given, the two cap-tains stood on the after part of the main-deck, a privileged spot, no one being near but the servant.

"It is now a hundred and ninety days," began the Spaniard, in his husky whisper, "that this ship, well officered and well manned, with several cabin passengers—some fifty Spaniards in all—sailed from Buenos Ayres bound to Lima, with a gen-eral cargo, hardware, Paraguay tea and the like—and," point-ing forward, "that parcel of negroes, now not more than a hundred and fifty, as you see, but then numbering over three hundred souls. Off Cape Horn we had heavy gales. In one moment, by night, three of my best officers, with fifteen sailors, were lost, with the main-yard; the spar snapping under them in the slings, as they sought, with heavers, to beat down the icy sail. To lighten the hull, the heavier sacks of mate* were thrown into the sea, with most of the water-pipes lashed on deck at the time. And this last necessity it was, combined with the prolonged detentions afterwards experienced, which eventually brought about our chief causes of suffering. When——"

Here there was a sudden fainting attack of his cough, brought on, no doubt, by his mental distress. His servant sustained him, and drawing a cordial from his pocket placed it to his lips. He a little revived. But unwilling to leave him unsupported while yet imperfectly restored, the black with one arm still encircled his master, at the same time keeping his eye fixed on his face, as if to watch for the first sign of complete restoration, or relapse, as the event might prove.

The Spaniard proceeded, but brokenly and obscurely, as one in a dream.

—"Oh, my God! rather than pass through what I have, with joy I would have hailed the most terrible gales; but——"

His cough returned and with increased violence; this subsiding, with reddened lips and closed eyes he fell heavily against his supporter.

"His mind wanders. He was thinking of the plague that followed the gales," plaintively sighed the servant; "my poor, poor master!" wringing one hand, and with the other wiping the mouth. "But be patient, Señor," again turning to Captain Delano, "these fits do not last long; master will soon be himself."

Don Benito reviving, went on; but as this portion of the story was very brokenly delivered, the substance only will here be set down.

It appeared that after the ship had been many days tossed in storms off the Cape, the scurvy broke out, carrying off numbers of the whites and blacks. When at last they had worked round into the Pacific, their spars and sails were so damaged, and so inadequately handled by the surviving mariners, most of whom were become invalids, that, unable to lay her northerly course by the wind, which was powerful, the unmanageable ship for successive days and nights was blown northwestward, where the breeze suddenly deserted her, in unknown waters, to sultry calms. The absence of the water-pipes now proved as fatal to life as before their presence had menaced it. Induced, or at least aggravated, by the more than scanty allowance of water, a malignant fever followed the scurvy; with the excessive heat of the lengthened calm, making such short work of it as to sweep away, as by billows, whole families of the Africans, and a yet larger number, proportionably, of the Spaniards, including, by a luckless fatality, every remaining officer on board. Consequently, in the smart west winds eventually following the calm, the already rent sails having to be simply dropped, not furled, at need, had been gradually reduced to the beggar's rags they were now. To procure substitutes for his lost sailors, as well as supplies of water and sails, the captain at the earliest opportunity had made for Baldivia, the southermost civilized port of Chili and South America; but upon nearing the coast the thick weather had prevented him from so much as sighting that harbor. Since which period, almost without a crew, and almost without canvas and almost without water, and at intervals giving its added dead to the sea, the San Dominick had been battle-dored about by contrary winds, inveigled by currents, or grown weedy in calms. Like a man lost in woods, more than once she had doubled upon her own track.

"But throughout these calamities," huskily continued Don Benito, painfully turning in the half embrace of his servant, "I have to thank those negroes you see, who, though to your inexperienced eyes appearing unruly, have, indeed, conducted themselves with less of restlessness than even their owner could have thought possible under such circumstances."

Here he again fell faintly back. Again his mind wandered: but he rallied, and less obscurely proceeded.

"Yes, their owner was quite right in assuring me that no fetters would be needed with his blacks; so that while, as is wont in this transportation, those negroes have always remained upon deck—not thrust below, as in the Guinea-men —they have, also, from the beginning, been freely permitted to range within given bounds at their pleasure."

Once more the faintness returned—his mind roved—but, recovering, he resumed:

"But it is Babo here to whom, under God, I owe not only my own preservation, but likewise to him, chiefly, the merit is due, of pacifying his more ignorant brethren, when at intervals tempted to murmurings."

"Ah, master," sighed the black, bowing his face, "don't speak of me; Babo is nothing; what Babo has done was but duty."

"Faithful fellow!" cried Capt. Delano. "Don Benito, I envy you such a friend; slave I cannot call him."

As master and man stood before him, the black upholding the white, Captain Delano could not but bethink him of the beauty of that relationship which could present such a spectacle of fidelity on the one hand and confidence on the other. The scene was heightened by the contrast in dress, denoting their relative positions. The Spaniard wore a loose Chili jacket of dark velvet; white small clothes and stockings, with silver buckles at the knee and instep; a high-crowned sombrero, of fine grass; a slender sword, silver mounted, hung from a knot in his sash; the last being an almost invariable adjunct, more for utility than ornament, of a South American gentleman's dress to this hour. Excepting when his occasional nervous contortions brought about disarray, there was a certain precision in his attire, curiously at variance with the unsightly disorder around; especially in the belittered Ghetto, forward of the main-mast, wholly occupied by the blacks.

The servant wore nothing but wide trowsers, apparently, from their coarseness and patches, made out of some old topsail; they were clean, and confined at the waist by a bit of unstranded rope, which, with his composed, deprecatory air at times, made him look something like a begging friar of St. Francis.

However unsuitable for the time and place, at least in the blunt-thinking American's eyes, and however strangely surviving in the midst of all his afflictions, the toilette of Don Benito might not, in fashion at least, have gone beyond the style of the day among South Americans of his class.

Though on the present voyage sailing from Buenos Ayres, he had avowed himself a native and resident of Chili, whose inhabitants had not so generally adopted the plain coat and once plebeian pantaloons; but, with a becoming modification, adhered to their provincial costume, picturesque as any in the world. Still, relatively to the pale history of the voyage, and his own pale face, there seemed something so incongruous in the Spaniard's apparel, as almost to suggest the image of an invalid courtier tottering about London streets in the time of the plague.

The portion of the narrative which, perhaps, most excited interest, as well as some surprise, considering the latitudes in question, was the long calms spoken of, and more particularly the ship's so long drifting about. Without communicating the opinion, of course, the American could not but impute at least part of the detentions both to clumsy seamanship and faulty navigation. Eying Don Benito's small, yellow hands, he easily inferred that the young captain had not got into command at the hawse-hole,* but the cabin-window; and if so, why wonder at incompetence, in youth, sickness, and gentility united?

But drowning criticism in compassion, after a fresh repetition of his sympathies, Captain Delano having heard out his story, not only engaged, as in the first place, to see Don Benito and his people supplied in their immediate bodily needs, but, also, now further promised to assist him in procuring a large permanent supply of water, as well as some sails and rigging; and, though it would involve no small embarrassment to himself, yet he would spare three of his best seamen for temporary deck officers; so that without delay the ship might proceed to Conception,* there fully to refit for Lima, her destined port.

Such generosity was not without its effect, even upon the invalid. His face lighted up; eager and hectic, he met the honest glance of his visitor. With gratitude he seemed overcome.

"This excitement is bad for master," whispered the servant, taking his arm, and with soothing words gently drawing him aside.

When Don Benito returned, the American was pained to observe that his hopefulness, like the sudden kindling in his cheek, was but febrile and transient.

Ere long, with a joyless mien, looking up towards the poop, the host invited his guest to accompany him there, for the benefit of what little breath of wind might be stirring.

As during the telling of the story, Captain Delano had once or twice started at the occasional cymballing of the hatchet-polishers, wondering why such an interruption should be allowed, especially in that part of the ship, and in the ears of an invalid; and moreover, as the hatchets had anything but an attractive look, and the handlers of them still less so, it was, therefore, to tell the truth, not without some lurking reluctance, or even shrinking, it may be, that Captain Delano, with apparent complaisance, acquiesced in his host's invitation. The more so, since with an untimely caprice of punctilio, rendered distressing by his cadaverous aspect, Don Benito, with Castilian bows, solemnly insisted upon his guest's preceding him up the ladder leading to the elevation; where, one on each side of the last step, sat for armorial supporters and sentries two of the ominous file. Gingerly enough stepped good Captain Delano between them, and in the instant of leaving them behind, like one running the gauntlet, he felt an apprehensive twitch in the calves of his legs.

But when, facing about, he saw the whole file, like so many organ-grinders, still stupidly intent on their work, unmindful of everything beside, he could not but smile at his late fidgeting panic.

Presently, while standing with his host, looking forward upon the decks below, he was struck by one of those instances of insubordination previously alluded to. Three black boys, with two Spanish boys, were sitting together on the hatches, scraping a rude wooden platter, in which some scanty mess had recently been cooked. Suddenly, one of the black boys, enraged at a word dropped by one of his white companions, seized a knife, and though called to forbear by one of the oakum-pickers, struck the lad over the head, inflicting a gash from which blood flowed.

In amazement, Captain Delano inquired what this meant. To which the pale Don Benito dully muttered, that it was merely the sport of the lad.

"Pretty serious sport, truly," rejoined Captain Delano. "Had such a thing happened on board the Bachelor's Delight, instant punishment would have followed."

At these words the Spaniard turned upon the American one of his sudden, staring, half-lunatic looks; then relapsing into his torpor, answered, "Doubtless, doubtless, Señor."

Is it, thought Captain Delano, that this hapless man is one of those paper captains I've known, who by policy wink at what by power they cannot put down? I know no sadder sight than a commander who has little of command but the name.

"I should think, Don Benito," he now said, glancing towards the oakum-picker who had sought to interfere with the boys, "that you would find it advantageous to keep all your blacks employed, especially the younger ones, no matter at what useless task, and no matter what happens to the ship. Why, even with my little band, I find such a course indispensable. I once kept a crew on my quarter-deck thrumming mats for my cabin, when, for three days, I had given up my ship—mats, men, and all—for a speedy loss, owing to the violence of a gale, in which we could do nothing but helplessly drive before it."

"Doubtless, doubtless," muttered Don Benito.

"But," continued Captain Delano, again glancing upon the oakum-pickers and then at the hatchet-polishers, near by, "I see you keep some at least of your host employed."

"Yes," was again the vacant response.

"Those old men there, shaking their pows from their pulpits," continued Captain Delano, pointing to the oakum-pickers, "seem to act the part of old dominies to the rest, little heeded as their admonitions are at times. It this voluntary on their part, Don Benito, or have you appointed them shepherds to your flock of black sheep?"

"What posts they fill, I appointed them," rejoined the Spaniard, in an acrid tone, as if resenting some supposed satiric reflection.

"And these others, these Ashantee* conjurors here," continued Captain Delano, rather uneasily eying the brandished steel of the hatchet-polishers, where in spots it had been brought to a shine, "this seems a curious business they are at, Don Benito?"

"In the gales we met," answered the Spaniard, "what of our general cargo was not thrown overboard was much damaged by the brine. Since coming into calm weather, I have had several cases of knives and hatchets daily brought up for overhauling and cleaning."

"A prudent idea, Don Benito. You are part owner of ship and cargo, I presume; but not of the slaves, perhaps?"

"I am owner of all you see," impatiently returned Don Benito, "except the main company of blacks, who belonged to my late friend, Alexandro Aranda."*

As he mentioned this name, his air was heart-broken; his knees shook: his servant supported him.

Thinking he divined the cause of such unusual emotion, to confirm his surmise, Captain Delano, after a pause, said, "And may I ask, Don Benito, whether—since awhile ago you spoke of some cabin passengers—the friend, whose loss so afflicts you at the outset of the voyage accompanied his blacks?"

"Yes."

"But died of the fever?"

"Died of the fever.—Oh, could I but——"

Again quivering, the Spaniard paused.

"Pardon me," said Captain Delano lowly, "but I think that, by a sympathetic experience, I conjecture, Don Benito, what it is that gives the keener edge to your grief. It was once my hard fortune to lose at sea a dear friend, my own brother, then supercargo. Assured of the welfare of his spirit, its departure I could have borne like a man; but that honest eye, that honest hand—both of which had so often met mine—and that warm heart; all, all—like scraps to the dogs—to throw all to the sharks! It was then I vowed never to have for fellow-voyager a man I loved, unless, unbeknown to him, I had provided every requisite, in case of a fatality, for embalming his mortal part for interment on shore. Were your friend's remains now on board this ship, Don Benito, not thus strangely would the mention of his name affect you."

"On board this ship?" echoed the Spaniard. Then, with horrified gestures, as directed against some specter, he unconsciously fell into the ready arms of his attendant, who, with a silent appeal toward Captain Delano, seemed beseeching him not again to broach a theme so unspeakably distressing to his master.

This poor fellow now, thought the pained American, is the victim of that sad superstition which associates goblins with the deserted body of man, as ghosts with an abandoned house. How unlike are we made! What to me, in like case, would have been a solemn satisfaction, the bare suggestion, even, terrifies the Spaniard into this trance. Poor Alexandro Aranda! what would you say could you here see your friend —who, on former voyages, when you for months were left behind, has, I dare say, often longed, and longed, for one peep at you—now transported with terror at the least thought of having you anyway nigh him.

At this moment, with a dreary grave-yard toll, betokening a flaw, the ship's forecastle bell, smote by one of the grizzled oakum-pickers, proclaimed ten o'clock through the leaden calm; when Captain Delano's attention was caught by the moving figure of a gigantic black, emerging from the general crowd below, and slowly advancing towards the elevated poop. An iron collar was about his neck, from which depended a chain, thrice wound round his body; the terminating links padlocked together at a broad band of iron, his girdle.

"How like a mute Atufal moves," murmured the servant.

The black mounted the steps of the poop, and, like a brave prisoner, brought up to receive sentence, stood in unquailing muteness before Don Benito, now recovered from his attack.

At the first glimpse of his approach, Don Benito had started, a resentful shadow swept over his face; and, as with the sudden memory of bootless rage, his white lips glued together.

This is some mulish mutineer, thought Captain Delano, surveying, not without a mixture of admiration, the colossal form of the negro.

"See, he waits your question, master," said the servant.

Thus reminded, Don Benito, nervously averting his glance, as if shunning, by anticipation, some rebellious response, in a disconcerted voice, thus spoke:—

"Atufal, will you ask my pardon now?"

The black was silent.

"Again, master," murmured the servant, with bitter upbraiding eying his countryman, "Again, master; he will bend to master yet."

"Answer," said Don Benito, still averting his glance, "say but the one word *pardon*, and your chains shall be off."

Upon this, the black, slowly raising both arms, let them lifelessly fall, his links clanking, his head bowed; as much as to say, "no, I am content."

"Go," said Don Benito, with inkept and unknown emotion.

Deliberately as he had come, the black obeyed.

"Excuse me, Don Benito," said Captain Delano, "but this scene surprises me; what means it, pray?"

"It means that that negro alone, of all the band, has given me peculiar cause of offense. I have put him in chains; I——"

Here he paused; his hand to his head, as if there were a swimming there, or a sudden bewilderment of memory had come over him; but meeting his servant's kindly glance seemed reassured, and proceeded:—

"I could not scourge such a form. But I told him he must ask my pardon. As yet he has not. At my command, every two hours he stands before me."

"And how long has this been?"

"Some sixty days."

"And obedient in all else? And respectful?"

"Yes."

"Upon my conscience, then," exclaimed Captain Delano, impulsively, "he has a royal spirit in him, this fellow."

"He may have some right to it," bitterly returned Don Benito, "he says he was king in his own land."

"Yes," said the servant, entering a word, "those slits in Atufal's ears once held wedges of gold; but poor Babo here, in his own land, was only a poor slave; a black man's slave was Babo, who now is the white's."

Somewhat annoyed by these conversational familiarities, Captain Delano turned curiously upon the attendant, then glanced inquiringly at his master; but, as if long wonted to these little informalities, neither master nor man seemed to understand him.

"What, pray, was Atufal's offense, Don Benito?" asked Captain Delano; "if it was not something very serious, take a fool's advice, and, in view of his general docility, as well as in some natural respect for his spirit, remit him his penalty."

"No, no, master never will do that," here murmured the servant to himself, "proud Atufal must first ask master's pardon. The slave there carries the padlock, but master here carries the key."

His attention thus directed, Captain Delano now noticed for the first time that, suspended by a slender silken cord, from Don Benito's neck hung a key. At once, from the servant's muttered syllables divining the key's purpose, he smiled and said:—"So, Don Benito—padlock and key—significant symbols, truly."

Biting his lip, Don Benito faltered.

Though the remark of Captain Delano, a man of such native simplicity as to be incapable of satire or irony, had been dropped in playful allusion to the Spaniard's singularly evidenced lordship over the black; yet the hypochondriac seemed in some way to have taken it as a malicious reflection upon his confessed inability thus far to break down, at least, on a verbal summons, the entrenched will of the slave. Deploring this supposed misconception, yet despairing of correcting it, Captain Delano shifted the subject; but finding his companion more than ever withdrawn, as if still sourly digesting the lees of the presumed affront above-mentioned, by-and-by Captain Delano likewise became less talkative, oppressed, against his own will, by what seemed the secret vindictiveness of the morbidly sensitive Spaniard. But the good sailor himself, of a quite contrary disposition, refrained, on his part, alike from the appearance as from the feeling of resentment, and if silent, was only so from contagion.

Presently the Spaniard, assisted by his servant, somewhat discourteously crossed over from his guest; a procedure which, sensibly enough, might have been allowed to pass for idle caprice of ill-humor, had not master and man, lingering round the corner of the elevated skylight, began whispering together in low voices. This was unpleasing. And more: the moody air of the Spaniard, which at times had not been without a sort of valetudinarian stateliness, now seemed anything but dignified; while the menial familiarity of the servant lost its original charm of simple-hearted attachment.

In his embarrassment, the visitor turned his face to the other side of the ship. By so doing, his glance accidentally fell on a young Spanish sailor, a coil of rope in his hand, just stepped from the deck to the first round of the mizzen-rigging. Perhaps the man would not have been particularly noticed, were it not that, during his ascent to one of the yards, he, with a sort of covert intentness, kept his eye fixed on Captain Delano, from whom, presently, it passed, as if by a natural sequence, to the two whisperers.

His own attention thus redirected to that quarter, Captain Delano gave a slight start. From something in Don Benito's manner just then, it seemed as if the visitor had, at least partly, been the subject of the withdrawn consultation going on—a conjecture as little agreeable to the guest as it was little flattering to the host.

The singular alternations of courtesy and ill-breeding in the Spanish captain were unaccountable, except on one of two suppositions—innocent lunacy, or wicked imposture.

But the first idea, though it might naturally have occurred to an indifferent observer, and, in some respect, had not hitherto been wholly a stranger to Captain Delano's mind, yet, now that, in an incipient way, he began to regard the stranger's conduct something in the light of an intentional affront, of course the idea of lunacy was virtually vacated. But if not a lunatic, what then? Under the circumstances, would a gentleman, nay, any honest boor, act the part now

acted by his host? The man was an impostor. Some low-
born adventurer, masquerading as an oceanic grandee; yet
so ignorant of the first requisites of mere gentlemanhood
as to be betrayed into the present remarkable indecorum.
That strange ceremoniousness, too, at other times evinced,
seemed not uncharacteristic of one playing a part above his
real level. Benito Cereno—Don Benito Cereno—a sounding
name. One, too, at that period, not unknown, in the surname, to supercargoes and sea captains trading along the
Spanish Main, as belonging to one of the most enterprising and extensive mercantile families in all those provinces;
several members of it having titles; a sort of Castilian Rothschild,* with a noble brother, or cousin, in every great trading town of South America. The alleged Don Benito was in
early manhood, about twenty-nine or thirty. To assume a sort
of roving cadetship in the maritime affairs of such a house,
what more likely scheme for a young knave of talent and
spirit? But the Spaniard was a pale invalid. Never mind. For
even to the degree of simulating mortal disease, the craft of
some tricksters had been known to attain. To think that,
under the aspect of infantile weakness, the most savage
energies might be couched—those velvets of the Spaniard
but the silky paw to his fangs.

From no train of thought did these fancies come; not from
within, but from without; suddenly, too, and in one throng,
like hoar frost; yet as soon to vanish as the mild sun of
Captain Delano's good-nature regained its meridian.

Glancing over once more towards his host—whose side-
face, revealed above the skylight, was now turned towards
him—he was struck by the profile, whose clearness of cut
was refined by the thinness incident to ill-health, as well as
ennobled about the chin by the beard. Away with suspicion.
He was a true off-shoot of a true hidalgo Cereno.

Relieved by these and other better thoughts, the visitor,
lightly humming a tune, now began indifferently pacing
the poop, so as not to betray to Don Benito that he had at
all mistrusted incivility, much less duplicity; for such mistrust would yet be proved illusory, and by the event; though,
for the present, the circumstance which had provoked that

distrust remained unexplained. But when that little mystery should have been cleared up, Captain Delano thought he might extremely regret it, did he allow Don Benito to become aware that he had indulged in ungenerous surmises. In short, to the Spaniard's black-letter text, it was best, for awhile, to leave open margin.

Presently, his pale face twitching and overcast, the Spaniard, still supported by his attendant, moved over towards his guest, when, with even more than his usual embarrassment, and a strange sort of intriguing intonation in his husky whisper, the following conversation began:—

"Señor, may I ask how long you have lain at this isle?"

"Oh, but a day or two, Don Benito."

"And from what port are you last?"

"Canton."

"And there, Señor, you exchanged your seal-skins for teas and silks, I think you said?"

"Yes. Silks, mostly."

"And the balance you took in specie, perhaps?"

Captain Delano, fidgeting a little, answered—

"Yes; some silver; not a very great deal, though."

"Ah—well. May I ask how many men have you, Señor?"

Captain Delano slightly started, but answered—

"About five-and-twenty, all told."

"And at present, Señor, all on board, I suppose?"

"All on board, Don Benito," replied the Captain, now with satisfaction.

"And will be to-night, Señor?"

At this last question, following so many pertinacious ones, for the soul of him Captain Delano could not but look very earnestly at the questioner, who, instead of meeting the glance, with every token of craven discomposure dropped his eyes to the deck; presenting an unworthy contrast to his servant, who, just then, was kneeling at his feet, adjusting a loose shoe-buckle; his disengaged face meantime, with humble curiosity, turned openly up into his master's downcast one.

The Spaniard, still with a guilty shuffle, repeated his question:—

"And—and will be to-night, Señor?"

"Yes, for aught I know," returned Captain Delano,—"but nay," rallying himself into fearless truth, "some of them talked of going off on another fishing party about midnight."

"Your ships generally go—go more or less armed, I believe, Señor?"

"Oh, a six-pounder or two, in case of emergency," was the intrepidly indifferent reply, "with a small stock of muskets, sealing-spears, and cutlasses, you know."

As he thus responded, Captain Delano again glanced at Don Benito, but the latter's eyes were averted; while abruptly and awkwardly shifting the subject, he made some peevish allusion to the calm, and then, without apology, once more, with his attendant, withdrew to the opposite bulwarks, where the whispering was resumed.

At this moment, and ere Captain Delano could cast a cool thought upon what had just passed, the young Spanish sailor before mentioned was seen descending from the rigging. In act of stooping over to spring inboard to the deck, his voluminous, unconfined frock, or shirt, of coarse woollen, much spotted with tar, opened out far down the chest, revealing a soiled under garment of what seemed the finest linen, edged, about the neck, with a narrow blue ribbon, sadly faded and worn. At this moment the young sailor's eye was again fixed on the whisperers, and Captain Delano thought he observed a lurking significance in it, as if silent signs of some Freemason sort had that instant been interchanged.

This once more impelled his own glance in the direction of Don Benito, and, as before, he could not but infer that himself formed the subject of the conference. He paused. The sound of the hatchet-polishing fell on his ears. He cast another swift side-look at the two. They had the air of conspirators. In connection with the late questionings and the incident of the young sailor, these things now begat such return of involuntary suspicion, that the singular guilelessness of the American could not endure it. Plucking up a gay and humorous expression, he crossed over to the two rapidly, saying:—"Ha, Don Benito, your black here seems high in your trust; a sort of privy-counselor, in fact."

Upon this, the servant looked up with a good-natured grin, but the master started as from a venomous bite. It was a moment or two before the Spaniard sufficiently recovered himself to reply; which he did, at last, with cold constraint: —"Yes, Señor, I have trust in Babo."

Here Babo, changing his previous grin of mere animal humor into an intelligent smile, not ungratefully eyed his master.

Finding that the Spaniard now stood silent and reserved, as if involuntarily, or purposely giving hint that his guest's proximity was inconvenient just then, Captain Delano, unwilling to appear uncivil even to incivility itself, made some trivial remark and moved off; again and again turning over in his mind the mysterious demeanor of Don Benito Cereno.

He had descended from the poop, and, wrapped in thought, was passing near a dark hatchway, leading down into the steerage, when, perceiving motion there, he looked to see what moved. The same instant there was a sparkle in the shadowy hatchway, and he saw one of the Spanish sailors prowling there hurriedly placing his hand in the bosom of his frock, as if hiding something. Before the man could have been certain who it was that was passing, he slunk below out of sight. But enough was seen of him to make it sure that he was the same young sailor before noticed in the rigging.

What was that which so sparkled? thought Captain Delano. It was no lamp—no match—no live coal. Could it have been a jewel? But how come sailors with jewels?—or with silk-trimmed under-shirts either? Has he been robbing the trunks of the dead cabin passengers? But if so, he would hardly wear one of the stolen articles on board ship here. Ah, ah— if now that was, indeed, a secret sign I saw passing between this suspicious fellow and his captain awhile since; if I could only be certain that in my uneasiness my senses did not deceive me, then——

Here, passing from one suspicious thing to another, his mind revolved the point of the strange questions put to him concerning his ship.

By a curious coincidence, as each point was recalled, the black wizards of Ashantee would strike up with their hatchets, as in ominous comment on the white stranger's thoughts. Pressed by such enigmas and portents, it would have been almost against nature, had not, even into the least distrustful heart, some ugly misgivings obtruded.

Observing the ship now helplessly fallen into a current, with enchanted sails, drifting with increased rapidity seaward; and noting that, from a lately intercepted projection of the land, the sealer was hidden, the stout mariner began to quake at thoughts which he barely durst confess to himself. Above all, he began to feel a ghostly dread of Don Benito. And yet when he roused himself, dilated his chest, felt himself strong on his legs, and coolly considered it— what did all these phantoms amount to?

Had the Spaniard any sinister scheme, it must have reference not so much to him (Captain Delano) as to his ship (the Bachelor's Delight). Hence the present drifting away of the one ship from the other, instead of favoring any such possible scheme, was, for the time at least, opposed to it. Clearly any suspicion, combining such contradictions, must need be delusive. Beside, was it not absurd to think of a vessel in distress—a vessel by sickness almost dismanned of her crew—a vessel whose inmates were parched for water— was it not a thousand times absurd that such a craft should, at present, be of a piratical character; or her commander, either for himself or those under him, cherish any desire but for speedy relief and refreshment? But then, might not general distress, and thirst in particular, be affected? And might not that same undiminished Spanish crew, alleged to have perished off to a remnant, be at that very moment lurking in the hold? On heart-broken pretense of entreating a cup of cold water, fiends in human form had got into lonely dwellings, nor retired until a dark deed had been done. And among the Malay pirates, it was no unusual thing to lure ships after them into their treacherous harbors, or entice boarders from a declared enemy at sea, by the spectacle of thinly manned or vacant decks, beneath which prowled a hundred spears with yellow arms ready to upthrust them through the mats. Not that Captain Delano had entirely credited such things. He had heard of them—and now, as stories, they recurred. The present destination of the ship was the anchorage. There she would be near his own vessel. Upon gaining that vicinity, might not the San Dominick, like a slumbering volcano, suddenly let loose energies now hid?

He recalled the Spaniard's manner while telling his story. There was a gloomy hesitancy and subterfuge about it. It was just the manner of one making up his tale for evil purposes, as he goes. But if that story was not true, what was the truth? That the ship had unlawfully come into the Spaniard's possession? But in many of its details, especially in reference to the more calamitous parts, such as the fatalities among the seamen, the consequent prolonged beating about, the past sufferings from obstinate calms, and still continued suffering from thirst; in all these points, as well as others, Don Benito's story had been corroborated not only by the wailing ejaculations of the indiscriminate multitude, white and black, but likewise—what seemed impossible to be counterfeit—by the very expression and play of every human feature, which Captain Delano saw. If Don Benito's story was throughout an invention, then every soul on board, down to the youngest negress, was his carefully drilled recruit in the plot: an incredible inference. And yet, if there was ground for mistrusting his veracity, that inference was a legitimate one.

But those questions of the Spaniard. There, indeed, one might pause. Did they not seem put with much the same object with which the burglar or assassin, by day-time, reconnoitres the walls of a house? But, with ill purposes, to solicit such information openly of the chief person endangered, and so, in effect, setting him on his guard; how unlikely a procedure was that? Absurd, then, to suppose that those questions had been prompted by evil designs. Thus, the same conduct, which, in this instance, had raised the alarm, served to dispel it. In short, scarce any suspicion or uneasiness, however apparently reasonable at the time, which was not now, with equal apparent reason, dismissed.

At last he began to laugh at his former forebodings; and laugh at the strange ship for, in its aspect someway siding with them, as it were; and laugh, too, at the odd-looking blacks, particularly those old scissors-grinders, the Ashantees;

and those bed-ridden old knitting-women, the oakum-pickers; and almost at the dark Spaniard himself, the central hobgoblin of all.

For the rest, whatever in a serious way seemed enigmatical, was now good-naturedly explained away by the thought that, for the most part, the poor invalid scarcely knew what he was about; either sulking in black vapors, or putting idle questions without sense or object. Evidently, for the present, the man was not fit to be entrusted with the ship. On some benevolent plea withdrawing the command from him, Captain Delano would yet have to send her to Conception, in charge of his second mate, a worthy person and good navigator—a plan not more convenient for the San Dominick than for Don Benito; for, relieved from all anxiety, keeping wholly to his cabin, the sick man, under the good nursing of his servant, would probably, by the end of the passage, be in a measure restored to health, and with that he should also be restored to authority.

Such were the American's thoughts. They were tranquilizing. There was a difference between the idea of Don Benito's darkly pre-ordaining Captain Delano's fate, and Captain Delano's lightly arranging Don Benito's. Nevertheless, it was not without something of relief that the good seaman presently perceived his whale-boat in the distance. Its absence had been prolonged by unexpected detention at the sealer's side, as well as its returning trip lengthened by the continual recession of the goal.

The advancing speck was observed by the blacks. Their shouts attracted the attention of Don Benito, who, with a return of courtesy, approaching Captain Delano, expressed satisfaction at the coming of some supplies, slight and temporary as they must necessarily prove.

Captain Delano responded; but while doing so, his attention was drawn to something passing on the deck below: among the crowd climbing the landward bulwarks, anxiously watching the coming boat, two blacks, to all appearances accidentally incommoded by one of the sailors, flew out against him with horrible curses, which the sailor someway resenting, the two blacks dashed him to the deck and jumped upon him, despite the earnest cries of the oakum-pickers.

"Don Benito," said Captain Delano quickly, "do you see what is going on there? Look!"

But, seized by his cough, the Spaniard staggered, with both hands to his face, on the point of falling. Captain Delano would have supported him, but the servant was more alert, who, with one hand sustaining his master, with the other applied the cordial. Don Benito restored, the black withdrew his support, slipping aside a little, but dutifully remaining within call of a whisper. Such discretion was here evinced as quite wiped away, in the visitor's eyes, any blemish of impropriety which might have attached to the attendant, from the indecorous conferences before mentioned; showing, too, that if the servant were to blame, it might be more the master's fault than his own, since when left to himself he could conduct thus well.

His glance thus called away from the spectacle of disorder to the more pleasing one before him, Captain Delano could not avoid again congratulating his host upon possessing such a servant, who, though perhaps a little too forward now and then, must upon the whole be invaluable to one in the invalid's situation.

"Tell me, Don Benito," he added, with a smile—"I should like to have your man here myself—what will you take for him? Would fifty doubloons be any object?"

"Master wouldn't part with Babo for a thousand doubloons," murmured the black, overhearing the offer, and taking it in earnest, and, with the strange vanity of a faithful slave appreciated by his master, scorning to hear so paltry a valuation put upon him by a stranger. But Don Benito, apparently hardly yet completely restored, and again interrupted by his cough, made but some broken reply.

Soon his physical distress became so great, affecting his mind, too, apparently, that, as if to screen the sad spectacle, the servant gently conducted his master below.

Left to himself, the American, to while away the time till his boat should arrive, would have pleasantly accosted some one of the few Spanish seamen he saw; but recalling something that Don Benito had said touching their ill conduct, he refrained, as a ship-master indisposed to countenance cowardice or unfaithfulness in seamen.

While, with these thoughts, standing with eye directed forward towards that handful of sailors, suddenly he thought that one or two of them returned the glance and with a sort of meaning. He rubbed his eyes, and looked again; but again seemed to see the same thing. Under a new form, but more obscure than any previous one, the old suspicions recurred, but, in the absence of Don Benito, with less of panic than before. Despite the bad account given of the sailors, Captain Delano resolved forthwith to accost one of them. Descending the poop, he made his way through the blacks, his movement drawing a queer cry from the oakum-pickers, prompted by whom, the negroes, twitching each other aside, divided before him; but, as if curious to see what was the object of this deliberate visit to their Ghetto, closing in behind, in tolerable order, followed the white stranger up. His progress thus proclaimed as by mounted kings-at-arms, and escorted as by a Caffre guard of honor,* Captain Delano, assuming a good humored, off-handed air, continued to advance; now and then saying a blithe word to the negroes, and his eye curiously surveying the white faces, here and there sparsely mixed in with the blacks, like stray white pawns venturously involved in the ranks of the chess-men opposed.

While thinking which of them to select for his purpose, he chanced to observe a sailor seated on the deck engaged in tarring the strap of a large block, with a circle of blacks squatted round him inquisitively eying the process.

The mean employment of the man was in contrast with something superior in his figure. His hand, black with continually thrusting it into the tar-pot held for him by a negro, seemed not naturally allied to his face, a face which would have been a very fine one but for its haggardness. Whether this haggardness had aught to do with criminality, could not be determined; since, as intense heat and cold, though unlike, produce like sensations, so innocence and guilt, when, through casual association with mental pain, stamping any visible impress, use one seal—a hacked one.

Not again that this reflection occurred to Captain Delano at the time, charitable man as he was. Rather another idea. Because observing so singular a haggardness combined with a dark eye, averted as in trouble and shame, and then again recalling Don Benito's confessed ill opinion of his crew, insensibly he was operated upon by certain general notions, which, while disconnecting pain and abashment from virtue, invariably link them with vice.

If, indeed, there be any wickedness on board this ship, thought Captain Delano, be sure that man there has fouled his hand in it, even as now he fouls it in the pitch. I don't like to accost him. I will speak to this other, this old Jack here on the windlass.

He advanced to an old Barcelona tar, in ragged red breeches and dirty night-cap, cheeks trenched and bronzed, whiskers dense as thorn hedges. Seated between two sleepy-looking Africans, this mariner, like his younger shipmate, was employed upon some rigging—splicing a cable—the sleepy-looking blacks performing the inferior function of holding the outer parts of the ropes for him.

Upon Captain Delano's approach, the man at once hung his head below its previous level; the one necessary for business. It appeared as if he desired to be thought absorbed, with more than common fidelity, in his task. Being addressed, he glanced up, but with what seemed a furtive, diffident air, which sat strangely enough on his weather-beaten visage, much as if a grizzly bear, instead of growling and biting, should simper and cast sheep's eyes. He was asked several questions concerning the voyage, questions purposely referring to several particulars in Don Benito's narrative, not previously corroborated by those impulsive cries greeting the visitor on first coming on board. The questions were briefly answered, confirming all that remained to be confirmed of the story. The negroes about the windlass joined in with the old sailor, but, as they became talkative, he by degrees became mute, and at length quite glum, seemed morosely unwilling to answer more questions, and yet, all the while, this ursine air was somehow mixed with his sheepish one.

Despairing of getting into unembarrassed talk with such a centaur, Captain Delano, after glancing round for a more promising countenance, but seeing none, spoke pleasantly to the blacks to make way for him; and so, amid various

grins and grimaces, returned to the poop, feeling a little
strange at first, he could hardly tell why, but upon the whole
with regained confidence in Benito Cereno.

How plainly, thought he, did that old whiskerando yonder betray a consciousness of ill-desert. No doubt, when he
saw me coming, he dreaded lest I, apprised by his Captain
of the crew's general misbehavior, came with sharp words
for him, and so down with his head. And yet—and yet, now
that I think of it, that very old fellow, if I err not, was one
of those who seemed so earnestly eying me here awhile since.
Ah, these currents spin one's head round almost as much as
they do the ship. Ha, there now's a pleasant sort of sunny
sight; quite sociable, too.

His attention had been drawn to a slumbering negress,
partly disclosed through the lace-work of some rigging, lying,
with youthful limbs carelessly disposed, under the lee of
the bulwarks, like a doe in the shade of a woodland rock.
Sprawling at her lapped breasts was her wide-awake fawn,
stark naked, its black little body half lifted from the deck,
crosswise with its dam's; its hands, like two paws, clamber-
ing upon her; its mouth and nose ineffectually rooting to
get at the mark; and meantime giving a vexatious half-grunt,
blending with the composed snore of the negress.

The uncommon vigor of the child at length roused the
mother. She started up, at distance facing Captain Delano.
But as if not at all concerned at the attitude in which she
had been caught, delightedly she caught the child up, with
maternal transports, covering it with kisses.

There's naked nature, now; pure tenderness and love,
thought Captain Delano, well pleased.

This incident prompted him to remark the other negresses
more particularly than before. He was gratified with their
manners; like most uncivilized women, they seemed at once
tender of heart and tough of constitution; equally ready to
die for their infants or fight for them. Unsophisticated as
leopardesses; loving as doves. Ah! thought Captain Delano,
these perhaps are some of the very women whom Mungo
Park* saw in Africa, and gave such a noble account of.

These natural sights somehow insensibly deepened his
confidence and ease. At last he looked to see how his boat

was getting on; but it was still pretty remote. He turned to see if Don Benito had returned; but he had not.

To change the scene, as well as to please himself with a leisurely observation of the coming boat, stepping over into the mizzen-chains he clambered his way into the starboard quarter-gallery; one of those abandoned Venetian-looking water-balconies previously mentioned; retreats cut off from the deck. As his foot pressed the half-damp, half-dry sea-mosses matting the place, and a chance phantom cats-paw*—an islet of breeze, unheralded, unfollowed—as this ghostly cats-paw came fanning his cheek, as his glance fell upon the row of small, round dead-lights, all closed like coppered eyes of the coffined, and the state-cabin door, once connecting with the gallery, even as the dead-lights had once looked out upon it, but now calked fast like a sarcophagus lid, to a purple-black, tarred-over panel, threshold, and post; and he bethought him of the time, when that state-cabin and this state-balcony had heard the voices of the Spanish king's officers, and the forms of the Lima viceroy's daughters had perhaps leaned where he stood—as these and other images flitted through his mind, as the cats-paw through the calm, gradually he felt rising a dreamy inquietude, like that of one who alone on the prairie feels unrest from the repose of the noon.

He leaned against the carved balustrade, again looking off toward his boat; but found his eye falling upon the ribbon grass, trailing along the ship's water-line, straight as a border of green box; and parterres of seaweed, broad ovals and crescents, floating nigh and far, with what seemed long formal alleys between, crossing the terraces of swells, and sweeping round as if leading to the grottoes below. And overhanging all was the balustrade by his arm, which, partly stained with pitch and partly embossed with moss, seemed the charred ruin of some summer-house in a grand garden long running to waste.

Trying to break one charm, he was but becharmed anew. Though upon the wide sea, he seemed in some far inland country; prisoner in some deserted château, left to stare at empty grounds, and peer out at vague roads, where never wagon or wayfarer passed.

But these enchantments were a little disenchanted as his
eye fell on the corroded main-chains. Of an ancient style,
massy and rusty in link, shackle and bolt, they seemed even
more fit for the ship's present business than the one for
which probably she had been built.

Presently he thought something moved nigh the chains.
He rubbed his eyes, and looked hard. Groves of rigging were
about the chains; and there, peering from behind a great
stay, like an Indian from behind a hemlock, a Spanish
sailor, a marlingspike* in his hand, was seen, who made what
seemed an imperfect gesture towards the balcony, but immediately, as if alarmed by some advancing step along the deck
within, vanished into the recesses of the hempen forest, like
a poacher.

What meant this? Something the man had sought to com-
municate, unbeknown to any one, even to his captain. Did
the secret involve aught unfavorable to his captain? Were
those previous misgivings of Captain Delano's about to be
verified? Or, in his haunted mood at the moment, had some
random, unintentional motion of the man, while busy with
the stay, as if repairing it, been mistaken for a significant
beckoning?

Not unbewildered, again he gazed off for his boat. But it
was temporarily hidden by a rocky spur of the isle. As with
some eagerness he bent forward, watching for the first shooting view of its beak, the balustrade gave way before him like
charcoal. Had he not clutched an outreaching rope he would
have fallen into the sea. The crash, though feeble, and the
fall, though hollow, of the rotten fragments, must have been
overheard. He glanced up. With sober curiosity peering down
upon him was one of the old oakum-pickers, slipped from
his perch to an outside boom; while below the old negro,
and, invisible to him, reconnoitering from a port-hole like
a fox from the mouth of its den, crouched the Spanish sailor
again. From something suddenly suggested by the man's air,
the mad idea now darted into Captain Delano's mind, that
Don Benito's plea of indisposition, in withdrawing below,
was but a pretense: that he was engaged there maturing
some plot, of which the sailor, by some means gaining an

inkling, had a mind to warn the stranger against; incited, it may be, by gratitude for a kind word on first boarding the ship. Was it from foreseeing some possible interference like this, that Don Benito had, beforehand, given such a bad character of his sailors, while praising the negroes; though, indeed, the former seemed as docile as the latter the contrary? The whites, too, by nature, were the shrewder race.* A man with some evil design, would he not be likely to speak well of that stupidity which was blind to his depravity, and malign that intelligence from which it might not be hidden? Not unlikely, perhaps. But if the whites had dark secrets concerning Don Benito, could then Don Benito be any way in complicity with the blacks? But they were too stupid. Besides, who ever heard of a white so far a renegade as to apostatize from his very species almost, by leaguing in against it with negroes? These difficulties recalled former ones. Lost in their mazes, Captain Delano, who had now regained the deck, was uneasily advancing along it, when he observed a new face; an aged sailor seated cross-legged near the main hatchway. His skin was shrunk up with wrinkles like a pelican's empty pouch; his hair frosted; his countenance grave and composed. His hands were full of ropes, which he was working into a large knot. Some blacks were about him obligingly dipping the strands for him, here and there, as the exigencies of the operation demanded.

Captain Delano crossed over to him, and stood in silence surveying the knot; his mind, by a not uncongenial transition, passing from its own entanglements to those of the hemp. For intricacy such a knot he had never seen in an American ship, or indeed any other. The old man looked like an Egyptian priest, making gordian knots for the temple of Ammon.* The knot seemed a combination of double-bowline-knot, treble-crown-knot, back-handed-well-knot, knot-in-and-out-knot, and jamming-knot.

At last, puzzled to comprehend the meaning of such a knot, Captain Delano addressed the knotter:—

"What are you knotting there, my man?"

"The knot," was the brief reply, without looking up.

"So it seems; but what is it for?"

"For some one else to undo," muttered back the old man, plying his fingers harder than ever, the knot being now nearly completed.

While Captain Delano stood watching him, suddenly the old man threw the knot towards him, saying in broken English, —the first heard in the ship,—something to this effect—"Undo it, cut it, quick." It was said lowly, but with such condensation of rapidity, that the long, slow words in Spanish, which had preceded and followed, almost operated as covers to the brief English between.

For a moment, knot in hand, and knot in head, Captain Delano stood mute; while, without further heeding him, the old man was now intent upon other ropes. Presently there was a slight stir behind Captain Delano. Turning, he saw the chained negro, Atufal, standing quietly there. The next moment the old sailor rose, muttering, and, followed by his subordinate negroes, removed to the forward part of the ship, where in the crowd he disappeared.

An elderly negro, in a clout like an infant's, and with a pepper and salt head, and a kind of attorney air, now approached Captain Delano. In tolerable Spanish, and with a good-natured, knowing wink, he informed him that the old knotter was simple-witted, but harmless; often playing his old tricks. The negro concluded by begging the knot, for of course the stranger would not care to be troubled with it. Unconsciously, it was handed to him. With a sort of congé,* the negro received it, and turning his back, ferreted into it like a detective Custom House officer after smuggled laces. Soon, with some African word, equivalent to pshaw, he tossed the knot overboard.

All this is very queer now, thought Captain Delano, with a qualmish sort of emotion; but as one feeling incipient sea-sickness, he strove, by ignoring the symptoms, to get rid of the malady. Once more he looked off for his boat. To his delight, it was now again in view, leaving the rocky spur astern.

The sensation here experienced, after at first relieving his uneasiness, with unforeseen efficacy, soon began to remove it. The less distant sight of that well-known boat—showing it, not as before, half blended with the haze, but with outline defined, so that its individuality, like a man's, was manifest; that boat, Rover by name, which, though now in strange seas, had often pressed the beach of Captain Delano's home, and, brought to its threshold for repairs, had familiarly lain there, as a Newfoundland dog; the sight of that household boat evoked a thousand trustful associations, which, contrasted with previous suspicions, filled him not only with lightsome confidence, but somehow with half humorous self-reproaches at his former lack of it.

"What, I, Amasa Delano—Jack of the Beach, as they called me when a lad—I, Amasa; the same that, duck-satchel in hand, used to paddle along the waterside to the schoolhouse made from the old hulk;—I, little Jack of the Beach, that used to go berrying with cousin Nat and the rest; I to be murdered here at the ends of the earth, on board a haunted pirate-ship by a horrible Spaniard?—Too nonsensical to think of! Who would murder Amasa Delano? His conscience is clean. There is some one above. Fie, fie, Jack of the Beach! you are a child indeed; a child of the second childhood, old boy; you are beginning to dote and drule, I'm afraid."

Light of heart and foot, he stepped aft, and there was met by Don Benito's servant, who, with a pleasing expression, responsive to his own present feelings, informed him that his master had recovered from the effects of his coughing fit, and had just ordered him to go present his compliments to his good guest, Don Amasa, and say that he (Don Benito) would soon have the happiness to rejoin him.

There now, do you mark that? again thought Captain Delano, walking the poop. What a donkey I was. This kind gentleman who here sends me his kind compliments, he, but ten minutes ago, dark-lantern in hand, was dodging round some old grind-stone in the hold, sharpening a hatchet for me, I thought. Well, well; these long calms have a morbid effect on the mind, I've often heard, though I never believed it before. Ha! glancing towards the boat; there's Rover; good dog; a white bone in her mouth. A pretty big bone though,

seems to me.—What? Yes, she has fallen afoul of the bubbling tide-rip there. It sets her the other way, too, for the
time. Patience.

It was now about noon, though, from the grayness of
everything, it seemed to be getting towards dusk.

The calm was confirmed. In the far distance, away from
the influence of land, the leaden ocean seemed laid out and
leaded up, its course finished, soul gone, defunct. But the
current from landward, where the ship was, increased; silently
sweeping her further and further towards the tranced waters
beyond.

Still, from his knowledge of those latitudes, cherishing hopes
of a breeze, and a fair and fresh one, at any moment, Captain
Delano, despite present prospects, buoyantly counted upon
bringing the San Dominick safely to anchor ere night. The
distance swept over was nothing; since, with a good wind,
ten minutes' sailing would retrace more than sixty minutes'
drifting. Meantime, one moment turning to mark "Rover"
fighting the tide-rip, and the next to see Don Benito approaching, he continued walking the poop.

Gradually he felt a´ vexation arising from the delay of his
boat; this soon merged into uneasiness; and at last, his eye
falling continually, as from a stage-box into the pit, upon
the strange crowd before and below him, and by and by
recognising there the face—now composed to indifference—
of the Spanish sailor who had seemed to beckon from the
main chains, something of his old trepidations returned.

Ah, thought he—gravely enough—this is like the ague:
because it went off, it follows not that it won't come back.

Though ashamed of the relapse, he could not altogether
subdue it; and so, exerting his good nature to the utmost,
insensibly he came to a compromise.

Yes, this is a strange craft; a strange history, too, and
strange folks on board. But—nothing more.

By way of keeping his mind out of mischief till the boat
should arrive, he tried to occupy it with turning over and
over, in a purely speculative sort of way, some lesser peculiarities of the captain and crew. Among others, four curious points recurred.

First, the affair of the Spanish lad assailed with a knife
by the slave boy; an act winked at by Don Benito. Second,
the tyranny in Don Benito's treatment of Atufal, the black;
as if a child should lead a bull of the Nile by the ring in his
nose. Third, the trampling of the sailor by the two negroes;
a piece of insolence passed over without so much as a rep-
rimand. Fourth, the cringing submission to their master of
all the ship's underlings, mostly blacks; as if by the least inadvertence they feared to draw down his despotic displeasure.

Coupling these points, they seemed somewhat contra-
dictory. But what then, thought Captain Delano, glancing
towards his now nearing boat,—what then? Why, Don Benito
is a very capricious commander. But he is not the first of
the sort I have seen; though it's true he rather exceeds any
other. But as a nation—continued he in his reveries—these
Spaniards are all an odd set; the very word Spaniard has
a curious, conspirator, Guy-Fawkish* twang to it. And yet,
I dare say, Spaniards in the main are as good folks as any
in Duxbury, Massachusetts. Ah good! At last "Rover" has
come.

As, with its welcome freight, the boat touched the side,
the oakum-pickers, with venerable gestures, sought to restrain
the blacks, who, at the sight of three gurried* water-casks
in its bottom, and a pile of wilted pumpkins in its bow,
hung over the bulwarks in disorderly raptures.

Don Benito with his servant now appeared; his coming,
perhaps, hastened by hearing the noise. Of him Captain
Delano sought permission to serve out the water, so that
all might share alike, and none injure themselves by unfair
excess. But sensible, and, on Don Benito's account, kind as
this offer was, it was received with what seemed impatience;
as if aware that he lacked energy as a commander, Don
Benito, with the true jealousy of weakness, resented as an
affront any interference. So, at least, Captain Delano inferred.

In another moment the casks were being hoisted in,
when some of the eager negroes accidentally jostled Captain
Delano, where he stood by the gangway; so that, unmindful of Don Benito, yielding to the impulse of the moment,
with good-natured authority he bade the blacks stand back;

to enforce his words making use of a half-mirthful, half-menacing gesture. Instantly the blacks paused, just where they were, each negro and negress suspended in his or her posture, exactly as the word had found them—for a few seconds continuing so—while, as between the responsive posts of a telegraph, an unknown syllable ran from man to man among the perched oakum-pickers. While the visitor's attention was fixed by this scene, suddenly the hatchet-polishers half rose, and a rapid cry came from Don Benito.

Thinking that at the signal of the Spaniard he was about to be massacred, Captain Delano would have sprung for his boat, but paused, as the oakum-pickers, dropping down into the crowd with earnest exclamations, forced every white and every negro back, at the same moment, with gestures friendly and familiar, almost jocose, bidding him, in substance, not be a fool. Simultaneously the hatchet-polishers resumed their seats, quietly as so many tailors, and at once, as if nothing had happened, the work of hoisting in the casks was resumed, whites and blacks singing at the tackle.

Captain Delano glanced towards Don Benito. As he saw his meager form in the act of recovering itself from reclining in the servant's arms, into which the agitated invalid had fallen, he could not but marvel at the panic by which himself had been surprised on the darting supposition that such a commander, who upon a legitimate occasion, so trivial, too, as it now appeared, could lose all self-command, was, with energetic iniquity, going to bring about his murder.

The casks being on deck, Captain Delano was handed a number of jars and cups by one of the steward's aids, who, in the name of his captain, entreated him to do as he had proposed: dole out the water. He complied, with republican impartiality as to this republican element, which always seeks one level, serving the oldest white no better than the youngest black; excepting, indeed, poor Don Benito, whose condition, if not rank, demanded an extra allowance. To him, in the first place, Captain Delano presented a fair pitcher of the fluid; but, thirsting as he was for it, the Spaniard quaffed not a drop until after several grave bows and salutes. A reciprocation of courtesies which the sight-loving Africans hailed with clapping of hands.

Two of the less wilted pumpkins being reserved for the cabin table, the residue were minced up on the spot for the general regalement. But the soft bread, sugar, and bottled cider, Captain Delano would have given the whites alone, and in chief Don Benito; but the latter objected; which disinterestedness, on his part, not a little pleased the American; and so mouthfuls all around were given alike to whites and blacks; excepting one bottle of cider, which Babo insisted upon setting aside for his master.

Here it may be observed that as, on the first visit of the boat, the American had not permitted his men to board the ship, neither did he now; being unwilling to add to the confusion of the decks.

Not uninfluenced by the peculiar good humor at present prevailing, and for the time oblivious of any but benevolent thoughts, Captain Delano, who from recent indications counted upon a breeze within an hour or two at furthest, dispatched the boat back to the sealer with orders for all the hands that could be spared immediately to set about rafting casks to the watering-place and filling them. Likewise he bade word be carried to his chief officer, that if against present expectation the ship was not brought to anchor by sunset, he need be under no concern, for as there was to be a full moon that night, he (Captain Delano) would remain on board ready to play the pilot, come the wind soon or late.

As the two Captains stood together, observing the departing boat—the servant as it happened having just spied a spot on his master's velvet sleeve, and silently engaged rubbing it out—the American expressed his regrets that the San Dominick had no boats; none, at least, but the unseaworthy old hulk of the long-boat, which, warped as a camel's skeleton in the desert, and almost as bleached, lay pot-wise inverted amidships, one side a little tipped, furnishing a subterraneous sort of den for family groups of the blacks, mostly women and small children; who, squatting on old mats below, or perched above in the dark dome, on the elevated seats, were descried, some distance within, like a social circle of bats, sheltering in some friendly cave; at intervals, ebon flights of naked boys and girls, three or four years old, darting in and out of the den's mouth.

"Had you three or four boats now, Don Benito," said Captain Delano, "I think that, by tugging at the oars, your negroes here might help along matters some.—Did you sail from port without boats, Don Benito?"

"They were stove in the gales, Señor."

"That was bad. Many men, too, you lost then. Boats and men.—Those must have been hard gales, Don Benito."

"Past all speech," cringed the Spaniard.

"Tell me, Don Benito," continued his companion with increased interest, "tell me, were these gales immediately off the pitch of Cape Horn?"

"Cape Horn?—who spoke of Cape Horn?"

"Yourself did, when giving me an account of your voyage," answered Captain Delano with almost equal astonishment at this eating of his own words, even as he ever seemed eating his own heart, on the part of the Spaniard. "You yourself, Don Benito, spoke of Cape Horn," he emphatically repeated.

The Spaniard turned, in a sort of stooping posture, pausing an instant, as one about to make a plunging exchange of elements, as from air to water.

At this moment a messenger-boy, a white, hurried by, in the regular performance of his function carrying the last expired half hour forward to the forecastle, from the cabin time-piece, to have it struck at the ship's large bell.

"Master," said the servant, discontinuing his work on the coat sleeve, and addressing the rapt Spaniard with a sort of timid apprehensiveness, as one charged with a duty, the discharge of which, it was foreseen, would prove irksome to the very person who had imposed it, and for whose benefit it was intended, "master told me never mind where he was, or how engaged, always to remind him, to a minute, when shaving-time comes. Miguel has gone to strike the half-hour afternoon. It is *now*, master. Will master go into the cuddy?"*

"Ah—yes," answered the Spaniard, starting, somewhat as from dreams into realities; then turning upon Captain Delano, he said that ere long he would resume the conversation.

"Then if master means to talk more to Don Amasa," said the servant, "why not let Don Amasa sit by master in the cuddy, and master can talk, and Don Amasa can listen, while Babo here lathers and strops."

"Yes," said Captain Delano, not unpleased with this sociable plan, "yes, Don Benito, unless you had rather not, I will go with you."

"Be it so, Señor."

As the three passed aft, the American could not but think it another strange instance of his host's capriciousness, this being shaved with such uncommon punctuality in the middle of the day. But he deemed it more than likely that the servant's anxious fidelity had something to do with the matter; inasmuch as the timely interruption served to rally his master from the mood which had evidently been coming upon him.

The place called the cuddy was a light deck-cabin formed by the poop, a sort of attic to the large cabin below. Part of it had formerly been the quarters of the officers; but since their death all the partitionings had been thrown down, and the whole interior converted into one spacious and airy marine hall; for absence of fine furniture and picturesque disarray, of odd appurtenances, somewhat answering to the wide, cluttered hall of some eccentric bachelor-squire in the country, who hangs his shooting-jacket and tobacco-pouch on deer antlers, and keeps his fishing-rod, tongs, and walking-stick in the same corner.

The similitude was heightened, if not originally suggested, by glimpses of the surrounding sea; since, in one aspect, the country and the ocean seem cousins-german.

The floor of the cuddy was matted. Overhead, four or five old muskets were stuck into horizontal holes along the beams. On one side was a claw-footed old table lashed to the deck; a thumbed missal on it, and over it a small, meager crucifix attached to the bulk-head. Under the table lay a dented cutlass or two, with a hacked harpoon, among some melancholy old rigging, like a heap of poor friar's girdles. There were also two long, sharp-ribbed settees of malacca cane, black with age, and uncomfortable to look at as inquisitors' racks, with a large, misshapen arm-chair, which, furnished with a rude barber's crutch at the back, working with

a screw, seemed some grotesque, middle-age engine of torment. A flag locker was in one corner, open, exposing various colored bunting, some rolled up, others half unrolled,
still others tumbled. Opposite was a cumbrous washstand,
of black mahogany, all of one block, with a pedestal, like a
font, and over it a railed shelf, containing combs, brushes,
and other implements of the toilet. A torn hammock of stained
grass swung near; the sheets tossed, and the pillow wrinkled
up like a brow, as if whoever slept here slept but illy, with
alternate visitations of sad thoughts and bad dreams.

The further extremity of the cuddy, overhanging the ship's
stern, was pierced with three openings, windows or port
holes, according as men or cannon might peer, socially or
unsocially, out of them. At present neither men nor cannon
were seen, though huge ring-bolts and other rusty iron fixtures of the wood-work hinted of twenty-four-pounders.

Glancing towards the hammock as he entered, Captain
Delano said, "You sleep here, Don Benito?"

"Yes, Señor, since we got into mild weather."

"This seems a sort of dormitory, sitting-room, sail-loft,
chapel, armory, and private closet all together, Don Benito,"
added Captain Delano, looking round.

"Yes, Señor; events have not been favorable to much
order in my arrangements."

Here the servant, napkin on arm, made a motion as if
waiting his master's good pleasure. Don Benito signified his
readiness, when, seating him in the malacca arm-chair, and
for the guest's convenience drawing opposite it one of the
settees, the servant commenced operations by throwing back
his master's collar and loosening his cravat.

There is something in the negro which, in a peculiar way,
fits him for avocations about one's person. Most negroes are
natural valets and hairdressers; taking to the comb and brush
congenially as to the castinets, and flourishing them apparently with almost equal satisfaction. There is, too, a smooth
tact about them in this employment, with a marvelous, noiseless, gliding briskness, not ungraceful in its way, singularly
pleasing to behold, and still more so to be the manipulated
subject of. And above all is the great gift of good humor.

Not the mere grin or laugh is here meant. Those were unsuitable. But a certain easy cheerfulness, harmonious in every glance and gesture; as though God had set the whole negro to some pleasant tune.

When to all this is added the docility arising from the unaspiring contentment of a limited mind, and that suscept-ibility of blind attachment sometimes inhering in indisput-able inferiors, one readily perceives why those hypochondriacs, Johnson and Byron*—it may be something like the hypochon-driac, Benito Cereno—took to their hearts, almost to the exclu-sion of the entire white race, their serving men, the negroes, Barber and Fletcher. But if there be that in the negro which exempts him from the inflicted sourness of the morbid or cynical mind, how, in his most prepossessing aspects, must he appear to a benevolent one? When at ease with respect to exterior things, Captain Delano's nature was not only benign, but familiarly and humorously so. At home, he had often taken rare satisfaction in sitting in his door, watching some free man of color at his work or play. If on a voyage he chanced to have a black sailor, invariably he was on chatty, and half-gamesome terms with him. In fact, like most men of a good, blithe heart, Captain Delano took to negroes, not philanthropically, but genially, just as other men to New-foundland dogs.

Hitherto the circumstances in which he found the San Dominick had repressed the tendency. But in the cuddy, relieved from his former uneasiness, and, for various rea-sons, more sociably inclined than at any previous period of the day, and seeing the colored servant, napkin on arm, so debonair about his master, in a business so familiar as that of shaving, too, all his old weakness for negroes returned.

Among other things, he was amused with an odd instance of the African love of bright colors and fine shows, in the black's informally taking from the flag-locker a great piece of bunting of all hues, and lavishly tucking it under his mas-ter's chin for an apron.

The mode of shaving among the Spaniards is a little different from what it is with other nations. They have a basin, specifically called a barber's basin, which on one side is scooped out, so as accurately to receive the chin, against which it is closely held in lathering; which is done, not with a brush, but with soap dipped in the water of the basin and rubbed on the face.

In the present instance salt-water was used for lack of better; and the parts lathered were only the upper lip, and low down under the throat, all the rest being cultivated beard.

The preliminaries being somewhat novel to Captain Delano, he sat curiously eying them, so that no conversation took place, nor for the present did Don Benito appear disposed to renew any.

Setting down his basin, the negro searched among the razors, as for the sharpest, and having found it, gave it an additional edge by expertly strapping it on the firm, smooth, oily skin of his open palm; he then made a gesture as if to begin, but midway stood suspended for an instant, one hand elevating the razor, the other professionally dabbling among the bubbling suds on the Spaniard's lank neck. Not unaffected by the close sight of the gleaming steel, Don Benito nervously shuddered; his usual ghastliness was heightened by the lather, which lather, again, was intensified in its hue by the contrasting sootiness of the negro's body. Altogether the scene was somewhat peculiar, at least to Captain Delano, nor, as he saw the two thus postured, could he resist the vagary, that in the black he saw a headsman, and in the white, a man at the block. But this was one of those antic conceits, appearing and vanishing in a breath, from which, perhaps, the best regulated mind is not always free.

Meantime the agitation of the Spaniard had a little loosened the bunting from around him, so that one broad fold swept curtain-like over the chair-arm to the floor, revealing, amid a profusion of armorial bars and ground-colors— black, blue, and yellow—a closed castle in a blood-red field diagonal with a lion rampant in a white.

"The castle and the lion," exclaimed Captain Delano— "why, Don Benito, this is the flag of Spain you use here. It's well it's only I, and not the King, that sees this," he added with a smile, "but"—turning towards the black,— "it's all one, I suppose, so the colors be gay;" which playful remark did not fail somewhat to tickle the negro.

"Now, master," he said, readjusting the flag, and pressing the head gently further back into the crotch of the chair; "now master," and the steel glanced nigh the throat.

Again Don Benito faintly shuddered.

"You must not shake so, master.—See, Don Amasa, master always shakes when I shave him. And yet master knows I never yet have drawn blood, though it's true, if master will shake so, I may some of these times. Now master," he continued. "And now, Don Amasa, please go on with your talk about the gale, and all that, master can hear, and between times master can answer."

"Ah yes, these gales," said Captain Delano; "but the more I think of your voyage, Don Benito, the more I wonder, not at the gales, terrible as they must have been, but at the disastrous interval following them. For here, by your account, have you been these two months and more getting from Cape Horn to St. Maria, a distance which I myself, with a good wind, have sailed in a few days. True, you had calms, and long ones, but to be becalmed for two months, that is, at least, unusual. Why, Don Benito, had almost any other gentleman told me such a story, I should have been half disposed to a little incredulity."

Here an involuntary expression came over the Spaniard, similar to that just before on the deck, and whether it was the start he gave, or a sudden gawky roll of the hull in the calm, or a momentary unsteadiness of the servant's hand; however it was, just then the razor drew blood, spots of which stained the creamy lather under the throat; immediately the black barber drew back his steel, and remaining in his professional attitude, back to Captain Delano, and face to Don Benito, held up the trickling razor, saying, with a sort of half humorous sorrow, "See, master,—you shook so—here's Babo's first blood."

No sword drawn before James the First of England,* no assassination in that timid King's presence, could have produced a more terrified aspect than was now presented by Don Benito.

Poor fellow, thought Captain Delano, so nervous he can't even bear the sight of barber's blood; and this unstrung, sick man, is it credible that I should have imagined he meant

to spill all my blood, who can't endure the sight of one little
drop of his own? Surely, Amasa Delano, you have been
beside yourself this day. Tell it not when you get home,
sappy Amasa. Well, well, he looks like a murderer, doesn't
he? More like as if himself were to be done for. Well, well,
this day's experience shall be a good lesson.

Meantime, while these things were running through the
honest seaman's mind, the servant had taken the napkin
from his arm, and to Don Benito had said—"But answer
Don Amasa, please, master, while I wipe this ugly stuff off
the razor, and strop it again."

As he said the words, his face was turned half round, so
as to be alike visible to the Spaniard and the American, and
seemed by its expression to hint, that he was desirous, by
getting his master to go on with the conversation, consider-
ately to withdraw his attention from the recent annoying
accident. As if glad to snatch the offered relief, Don Benito
resumed, rehearsing to Captain Delano, that not only were
the calms of unusual duration, but the ship had fallen in
with obstinate currents; and other things he added, some of
which were but repetitions of former statements, to explain
how it came to pass that the passage from Cape Horn to
St. Maria had been so exceedingly long, now and then ming-
ling with his words, incidental praises, less qualified than
before, to the blacks, for their general good conduct.

These particulars were not given consecutively, the servant, at convenient times, using his razor, and so, between
the intervals of shaving, the story and panegyric went on
with more than usual huskiness.

To Captain Delano's imagination, now again not wholly
at rest, there was something so hollow in the Spaniard's manner, with apparently some reciprocal hollowness in the servant's dusky comment of silence, that the idea flashed across
him, that possibly master and man, for some unknown purpose, were acting out, both in word and deed, nay, to the
very tremor of Don Benito's limbs, some juggling play before him. Neither did the suspicion of collusion lack apparent support, from the fact of those whispered conferences
before mentioned. But then, what could be the object of

enacting this play of the barber before him? At last, regarding the notion as a whimsy, insensibly suggested, perhaps, by the theatrical aspect of Don Benito in his harlequin ensign, Captain Delano speedily banished it.

The shaving over, the servant bestirred himself with a small bottle of scented waters, pouring a few drops on the head, and then diligently rubbing; the vehemence of the exercise causing the muscles of his face to twitch rather strangely.

His next operation was with comb, scissors and brush; going round and round, smoothing a curl here, clipping an unruly whisker-hair there, giving a graceful sweep to the temple-lock, with other impromptu touches evincing the hand of a master; while, like any resigned gentleman in barber's hands, Don Benito bore all, much less uneasily, at least, than he had done the razoring; indeed, he sat so pale and rigid now, that the negro seemed a Nubian* sculptor finishing off a white statue-head.

All being over at last, the standard of Spain removed, tumbled up, and tossed back into the flag-locker, the negro's warm breath blowing away any stray hair which might have lodged down his master's neck; collar and cravat readjusted; a speck of lint whisked off the velvet lapel; all this being done; backing off a little space, and pausing with an expression of subdued self-complacency, the servant for a moment surveyed his master, as, in toilet at least, the creature of his own tasteful hands.

Captain Delano playfully complimented him upon his achievement; at the same time congratulating Don Benito.

But neither sweet waters, nor shampooing, nor fidelity, nor sociality, delighted the Spaniard. Seeing him relapsing into forbidding gloom, and still remaining seated, Captain Delano, thinking that his presence was undesired just then, withdrew, on pretense of seeing whether, as he had prophecied, any signs of a breeze were visible.

Walking forward to the mainmast, he stood awhile thinking over the scene, and not without some undefined misgivings, when he heard a noise near the cuddy, and turning, saw the negro, his hand to his cheek. Advancing, Captain Delano perceived that the cheek was bleeding. He was about to ask the cause, when the negro's wailing soliloquy enlightened him.

"Ah, when will master get better from his sickness; only the sour heart that sour sickness breeds made him serve Babo so; cutting Babo with the razor, because, only by accident, Babo had given master one little scratch; and for the first time in so many a day, too. Ah, ah, ah," holding his hand to his face.

Is it possible, thought Captain Delano; was it to wreak in private his Spanish spite against this poor friend of his, that Don Benito, by his sullen manner, impelled me to withdraw? Ah, this slavery breeds ugly passions in man.—Poor fellow!

He was about to speak in sympathy to the negro, but with a timid reluctance he now reëntered the cuddy.

Presently master and man came forth; Don Benito leaning on his servant as if nothing had happened.

But a sort of love-quarrel, after all, thought Captain Delano.

He accosted Don Benito, and they slowly walked together. They had gone but a few paces, when the steward—a tall, rajah-looking mulatto, orientally set off with a pagoda turban formed by three or four Madras handkerchiefs wound about his head, tier on tier—approaching with a salaam, announced lunch in the cabin.

On their way thither, the two Captains were preceded by the mulatto, who, turning round as he advanced, with continual smiles and bows, ushered them on, a display of elegance which quite completed the insignificance of the small bare-headed Babo, who, as if not unconscious of inferiority, eyed askance the graceful steward. But in part, Captain Delano imputed his jealous watchfulness to that peculiar feeling which the full-blooded African entertains for the adulterated one. As for the steward, his manner, if not bespeaking much dignity of self-respect, yet evidenced his extreme desire to please; which is doubly meritorious, as at once Christian and Chesterfieldian.*

Captain Delano observed with interest that while the complexion of the mulatto was hybrid, his physiognomy was European; classically so.

"Don Benito," whispered he, "I am glad to see this usher-of-the-golden-rod of yours; the sight refutes an ugly remark once made to me by a Barbadoes planter; that when a mulatto has a regular European face, look out for him; he is a devil. But see, your steward here has features more regular than King George's of England; and yet there he nods, and bows, and smiles; a king, indeed—the king of kind hearts and polite fellows. What a pleasant voice he has, too!"

"He has, Señor."

"But, tell me, has he not, so far as you have known him, always proved a good, worthy fellow?" said Captain Delano, pausing, while with a final genuflexion the steward disappeared into the cabin; "come, for the reason just mentioned, I am curious to know."

"Francesco is a good man," a sort of sluggishly responded Don Benito, like a phlegmatic appreciator, who would neither find fault nor flatter.

"Ah, I thought so. For it were strange indeed, and not very creditable to us white-skins, if a little of our blood mixed with the African's, should, far from improving the latter's quality, have the sad effect of pouring vitriolic acid into black broth; improving the hue, perhaps, but not the wholesomeness."

"Doubtless, doubtless, Señor, but"—glancing at Babo—"not to speak of negroes, your planter's remark I have heard applied to the Spanish and Indian intermixtures in our provinces. But I know nothing about the matter," he listlessly added.

And here they entered the cabin.

The lunch was a frugal one. Some of Captain Delano's fresh fish and pumpkins, biscuit and salt beef, the reserved bottle of cider, and the San Dominick's last bottle of Canary.*

As they entered, Francesco, with two or three colored aids, was hovering over the table giving the last adjustments. Upon perceiving their master they withdrew, Francesco making a smiling congé, and the Spaniard, without condescending to notice it, fastidiously remarking to his companion that he relished not superfluous attendance.

Without companions, host and guest sat down, like a child-
less married couple, at opposite ends of the table, Don Benito
waving Captain Delano to his place, and, weak as he was,
insisting upon that gentleman being seated before himself.

The negro placed a rug under Don Benito's feet, and a
cushion behind his back, and then stood behind, not his
master's chair, but Captain Delano's. At first, this a little
surprised the latter. But it was soon evident that, in taking
his position, the black was still true to his master; since by
facing him he could the more readily anticipate his slightest
want.

"This is an uncommonly intelligent fellow of yours, Don
Benito," whispered Captain Delano across the table.

"You say true, Señor."

During the repast, the guest again reverted to parts of
Don Benito's story, begging further particulars here and
there. He inquired how it was that the scurvy and fever
should have committed such wholesale havoc upon the
whites, while destroying less than half of the blacks. As if
this question reproduced the whole scene of plague before
the Spaniard's eyes, miserably reminding him of his solitude
in a cabin where before he had had so many friends and
officers round him, his hand shook, his face became hueless, broken words escaped; but directly the sane memory
of the past seemed replaced by insane terrors of the present. With starting eyes he stared before him at vacancy. For
nothing was to be seen but the hand of his servant* pushing the Canary over towards him. At length a few sips served
partially to restore him. He made random reference to the
different constitution of races, enabling one to offer more
resistance to certain maladies than another. The thought was
new to his companion.

Presently Captain Delano, intending to say something to
his host concerning the pecuniary part of the business he
had undertaken for him, especially—since he was strictly
accountable to his owners—with reference to the new suit
of sails, and other things of that sort; and naturally prefer-
ring to conduct such affairs in private, was desirous that
the servant should withdraw; imagining that Don Benito
for a few minutes could dispense with his attendance. He,

however, waited awhile; thinking that, as the conversation proceeded, Don Benito, without being prompted, would perceive the propriety of the step.

But it was otherwise. At last catching his host's eye, Captain Delano, with a slight backward gesture of his thumb, whispered, "Don Benito, pardon me, but there is an interference with the full expression of what I have to say to you."

Upon this the Spaniard changed countenance; which was imputed to his resenting the hint, as in some way a reflection upon his servant. After a moment's pause, he assured his guest that the black's remaining with them could be of no disservice; because since losing his officers he had made Babo (whose original office, it now appeared, had been captain of the slaves) not only his constant attendant and companion, but in all things his confidant.

After this, nothing more could be said; though, indeed, Captain Delano could hardly avoid some little tinge of irritation upon being left ungratified in so inconsiderable a wish, by one, too, for whom he intended such solid services. But it is only his querulousness, thought he; and so filling his glass he proceeded to business.

The price of the sails and other matters was fixed upon. But while this was being done, the American observed that, though his original offer of assistance had been hailed with hectic animation, yet now when it was reduced to a business transaction, indifference and apathy were betrayed. Don Benito, in fact, appeared to submit to hearing the details more out of regard to common propriety, than from any impression that weighty benefit to himself and his voyage was involved.

Soon, this manner became still more reserved. The effort was vain to seek to draw him into social talk. Gnawed by his splenetic mood, he sat twitching his beard, while to little purpose the hand of his servant, mute as that on the wall,* slowly pushed over the Canary.

Lunch being over, they sat down on the cushioned transom; the servant placing a pillow behind his master. The long continuance of the calm had now affected the atmosphere. Don Benito sighed heavily, as if for breath.

"Why not adjourn to the cuddy," said Captain Delano; "there is more air there." But the host sat silent and motionless.

Meantime his servant knelt before him, with a large fan of feathers. And Francesco coming in on tiptoes, handed the negro a little cup of aromatic waters, with which at intervals he chafed his master's brow; smoothing the hair along the temples as a nurse does a child's. He spoke no word. He only rested his eye on his master's, as if, amid all Don Benito's distress, a little to refresh his spirit by the silent sight of fidelity.

Presently the ship's bell sounded two o'clock; and through the cabin-windows a slight rippling of the sea was discerned; and from the desired direction.

"There," exclaimed Captain Delano, "I told you so, Don Benito, look!"

He had risen to his feet, speaking in a very animated tone, with a view the more to rouse his companion. But though the crimson curtain of the stern-window near him that moment fluttered against his pale cheek, Don Benito seemed to have even less welcome for the breeze than the calm.

Poor fellow, thought Captain Delano, bitter experience has taught him that one ripple does not make a wind, any more than one swallow a summer. But he is mistaken for once. I will get his ship in for him, and prove it.

Briefly alluding to his weak condition, he urged his host to remain quietly where he was, since he (Captain Delano) would with pleasure take upon himself the responsibility of making the best use of the wind.

Upon gaining the deck, Captain Delano started at the unexpected figure of Atufal, monumentally fixed at the threshold, like one of those sculptured porters of black marble guarding the porches of Egyptian tombs.

But this time the start was, perhaps, purely physical. Atufal's presence, singularly attesting docility even in sullenness, was contrasted with that of the hatchet-polishers, who in patience evinced their industry; while both spectacles showed, that lax as Don Benito's general authority might be, still, whenever he chose to exert it, no man so savage or colossal but must, more or less, bow.

Snatching a trumpet which hung from the bulwarks, with a free step Captain Delano advanced to the forward edge of the poop, issuing his orders in his best Spanish. The few sailors and many negroes, all equally pleased, obediently set about heading the ship towards the harbor.

While giving some directions about setting a lower stu'n'-sail, suddenly Captain Delano heard a voice faithfully repeating his orders. Turning, he saw Babo, now for the time acting, under the pilot, his original part of captain of the slaves. This assistance proved valuable. Tattered sails and warped yards were soon brought into some trim. And no brace or halyard was pulled but to the blithe songs of the inspirited negroes.

Good fellows, thought Captain Delano, a little training would make fine sailors of them. Why see, the very women pull and sing too. These must be some of those Ashantee negresses that make such capital soldiers, I've heard. But who's at the helm. I must have a good hand there.

He went to see.

The San Dominick steered with a cumbrous tiller, with large horizontal pullies attached. At each pully-end stood a subordinate black, and between them, at the tiller-head, the responsible post, a Spanish seaman, whose countenance evinced his due share in the general hopefulness and confidence at the coming of the breeze.

He proved the same man who had behaved with so shamefaced an air on the windlass.

"Ah,—it is you, my man," exclaimed Captain Delano—"well, no more sheep's-eyes now;—look straight forward and keep the ship so. Good hand, I trust? And want to get into the harbor, don't you?"

The man assented with an inward chuckle, grasping the tiller-head firmly. Upon this, unperceived by the American, the two blacks eyed the sailor intently.

Finding all right at the helm, the pilot went forward to the forecastle, to see how matters stood there.

The ship now had way enough to breast the current. With the approach of evening, the breeze would be sure to freshen.

Having done all that was needed for the present, Captain Delano, giving his last orders to the sailors, turned aft to

report affairs to Don Benito in the cabin; perhaps additionally
incited to rejoin him by the hope of snatching a moment's
private chat while his servant was engaged upon deck.

From opposite sides, there were, beneath the poop, two
approaches to the cabin; one further forward than the other,
and consequently communicating with a longer passage. Marking the servant still above, Captain Delano, taking the nighest
entrance—the one last named, and at whose porch Atufal
still stood—hurried on his way, till, arrived at the cabin
threshold, he paused an instant, a little to recover from his
eagerness. Then, with the words of his intended business
upon his lips, he entered. As he advanced toward the seated
Spaniard, he heard another footstep, keeping time with his.
From the opposite door, a salver in hand, the servant was
likewise advancing.

"Confound the faithful fellow," thought Captain Delano;
"what a vexatious coincidence."

Possibly, the vexation might have been something different, were it not for the brisk confidence inspired by the
breeze. But even as it was, he felt a slight twinge, from a sudden indefinite association in his mind of Babo with Atufal.

"Don Benito," said he, "I give you joy; the breeze will
hold, and will increase. By the way, your tall man and time-
piece, Atufal, stands without. By your order, of course?"

Don Benito recoiled, as if at some bland satirical touch,
delivered with such adroit garnish of apparent good-breeding
as to present no handle for retort.

He is like one flayed alive, thought Captain Delano; where
may one touch him without causing a shrink?

The servant moved before his master, adjusting a cushion; recalled to civility, the Spaniard stiffly replied: "you are
right. The slave appears where you saw him, according to
my command; which is, that if at the given hour I am below,
he must take his stand and abide my coming."

"Ah now, pardon me, but that is treating the poor fellow
like an ex-king indeed. Ah, Don Benito," smiling, "for all
the license you permit in some things, I fear lest, at bottom, you are a bitter hard master."

Again Don Benito shrank; and this time, as the good sailor
thought, from a genuine twinge of his conscience.

Again conversation became constrained. In vain Captain Delano called attention to the now perceptible motion of the keel gently cleaving the sea; with lack-lustre eye, Don Benito returned words few and reserved.

By-and-by, the wind having steadily risen, and still blowing right into the harbor, bore the San Dominick swiftly on. Rounding a point of land, the sealer at distance came into open view.

Meantime Captain Delano had again repaired to the deck, remaining there some time. Having at last altered the ship's course, so as to give the reef a wide berth, he returned for a few moments below.

I will cheer up my poor friend, this time, thought he.

"Better and better, Don Benito," he cried as he blithely reëntered; "there will soon be an end to your cares, at least for awhile. For when, after a long, sad voyage, you know, the anchor drops into the haven, all its vast weight seems lifted from the captain's heart. We are getting on famously, Don Benito. My ship is in sight. Look through this side-light here; there she is; all a-taunt-o! The Bachelor's Delight, my good friend. Ah, how this wind braces one up. Come, you must take a cup of coffee with me this evening. My old steward will give you as fine a cup as ever any sultan tasted. What say you, Don Benito, will you?"

At first, the Spaniard glanced feverishly up, casting a longing look towards the sealer, while with mute concern his servant gazed into his face. Suddenly the old ague of coldness returned, and dropping back to his cushions he was silent.

"You do not answer. Come, all day you have been my host; would you have hospitality all on one side?"

"I cannot go," was the response.

"What? it will not fatigue you. The ships will lie together as near as they can, without swinging foul. It will be little more than stepping from deck to deck; which is but as from room to room. Come, come, you must not refuse me."

"I cannot go," decisively and repulsively repeated Don Benito.

Renouncing all but the last appearance of courtesy, with a sort of cadaverous sullenness, and biting his thin nails to the quick, he glanced, almost glared, at his guest; as if impatient that a stranger's presence should interfere with the full indulgence of his morbid hour. Meantime the sound of the parted waters came more and more gurglingly and merrily in at the windows; as reproaching him for his dark spleen; as telling him that, sulk as he might, and go mad with it, nature cared not a jot; since, whose fault was it, pray?

But the foul mood was now at its depth, as the fair wind at its height.

There was something in the man so far beyond any mere unsociality or sourness previously evinced, that even the forbearing good-nature of his guest could no longer endure it. Wholly at a loss to account for such demeanor, and deeming sickness with eccentricity, however extreme, no adequate excuse, well satisfied, too, that nothing in his own conduct could justify it, Captain Delano's pride began to be roused. Himself became reserved. But all seemed one to the Spaniard. Quitting him, therefore, Captain Delano once more went to the deck.

The ship was now within less than two miles of the sealer. The whale-boat was seen darting over the interval.

To be brief, the two vessels, thanks to the pilot's skill, ere long in neighborly style lay anchored together.

Before returning to his own vessel, Captain Delano had intended communicating to Don Benito the smaller details of the proposed services to be rendered. But, as it was, unwilling anew to subject himself to rebuffs, he resolved, now that he had seen the San Dominick safely moored, immediately to quit her, without further allusion to hospitality or business. Indefinitely postponing his ulterior plans, he would regulate his future actions according to future circumstances. His boat was ready to receive him; but his host still tarried below. Well, thought Captain Delano, if he has little breeding, the more need to show mine. He descended to the cabin to bid a ceremonious, and, it may be, tacitly rebukeful adieu. But to his great satisfaction, Don Benito, as if he began to feel the weight of that treatment with which his slighted guest had, not indecorously, retaliated upon him, now supported by his servant, rose to his feet, and grasping Captain

Delano's hand, stood tremulous; too much agitated to speak. But the good augury hence drawn was suddenly dashed, by his resuming all his previous reserve, with augmented gloom, as, with half-averted eyes, he silently reseated himself on his cushions. With a corresponding return of his own chilled feelings, Captain Delano bowed and withdrew.

He was hardly midway in the narrow corridor, dim as a tunnel, leading from the cabin to the stairs, when a sound, as of the tolling for execution in some jail-yard, fell on his ears. It was the echo of the ship's flawed bell, striking the hour, drearily reverberated in this subterranean vault. Instantly, by a fatality not to be withstood, his mind, responsive to the portent, swarmed with superstitious suspicions. He paused. In images far swifter than these sentences, the minutest details of all his former distrusts swept through him.

Hitherto, credulous good-nature had been too ready to furnish excuses for reasonable fears. Why was the Spaniard, so superfluously punctilious at times, now heedless of common propriety in not accompanying to the side his departing guest? Did indisposition forbid? Indisposition had not forbidden more irksome exertion that day. His last equivocal demeanor recurred. He had risen to his feet, grasped his guest's hand, motioned toward his hat; then, in an instant, all was eclipsed in sinister muteness and gloom. Did this imply one brief, repentent relenting at the final moment, from some iniquitous plot, followed by remorseless return to it? His last glance seemed to express a calamitous, yet acquiescent farewell to Captain Delano forever. Why decline the invitation to visit the sealer that evening? Or was the Spaniard less hardened than the Jew,* who refrained not from supping at the board of him whom the same night he meant to betray? What imported all those day-long enigmas and contradictions, except they were intended to mystify, preliminary to some stealthy blow? Atufal, the pretended rebel, but punctual shadow, that moment lurked by the threshold without. He seemed a sentry, and more. Who, by his own confession, had stationed him there? Was the negro now lying in wait?

The Spaniard behind—his creature before: to rush from darkness to light was the involuntary choice.

The next moment, with clenched jaw and hand, he passed Atufal, and stood unharmed in the light. As he saw his trim ship lying peacefully at her anchor, and almost within ordinary call; as he saw his household boat, with familiar faces in it, patiently rising and falling on the short waves by the San Dominick's side; and then, glancing about the decks where he stood, saw the oakum-pickers still gravely plying their fingers; and heard the low, buzzing whistle and industrious hum of the hatchet-polishers, still bestirring themselves over their endless occupation; and more than all, as he saw the benign aspect of nature, taking her innocent repose in the evening; the screened sun in the quiet camp of the west shining out like the mild light from Abraham's tent; as charmed eye and ear took in all these, with the chained figure of the black, clenched jaw and hand relaxed. Once again he smiled at the phantoms which had mocked him, and felt something like a tinge of remorse, that, by harboring them even for a moment, he should, by implication, have betrayed an almost atheist doubt of the ever-watchful Providence above.

There was a few minutes' delay, while, in obedience to his orders, the boat was being hooked along to the gangway. During this interval, a sort of saddened satisfaction stole over Captain Delano, at thinking of the kindly offices he had that day discharged for a stranger. Ah, thought he, after good actions one's conscience is never ungrateful, however much so the benefited party may be.

Presently, his foot, in the first act of descent into the boat, pressed the first round of the side-ladder, his face presented inward upon the deck. In the same moment, he heard his name courteously sounded; and, to his pleased surprise, saw Don Benito advancing—an unwonted energy in his air, as if, at the last moment, intent upon making amends for his recent discourtesy. With instinctive good feeling, Captain Delano, withdrawing his foot, turned and reciprocally advanced. As he did so, the Spaniard's nervous eagerness increased, but his vital energy failed; so that, the better to support him, the servant, placing his master's hand on his naked shoulder, and gently holding it there, formed himself into a sort of crutch.

When the two captains met, the Spaniard again fervently took the hand of the American, at the same time casting an earnest glance into his eyes, but, as before, too much overcome to speak.

I have done him wrong, self-reproachfully thought Captain Delano; his apparent coldness has deceived me; in no instance has he meant to offend.

Meantime, as if fearful that the continuance of the scene might too much unstring his master, the servant seemed anxious to terminate it. And so, still presenting himself as a crutch, and walking between the two captains, he advanced with them towards the gangway; while still, as if full of kindly contrition, Don Benito would not let go the hand of Captain Delano, but retained it in his, across the black's body.

Soon they were standing by the side, looking over into the boat, whose crew turned up their curious eyes. Waiting a moment for the Spaniard to relinquish his hold, the now embarrassed Captain Delano lifted his foot, to overstep the threshold of the open gangway; but still Don Benito would not let go his hand. And yet, with an agitated tone, he said, "I can go no further; here I must bid you adieu. Adieu, my dear, dear Don Amasa. Go—go!" suddenly tearing his hand loose, "go, and God guard you better than me, my best friend."

Not unaffected, Captain Delano would now have lingered; but catching the meekly admonitory eye of the servant, with a hasty farewell he descended into his boat, followed by the continual adieus of Don Benito, standing rooted in the gangway.

Seating himself in the stern, Captain Delano, making a last salute, ordered the boat shoved off. The crew had their oars on end. The bowsman pushed the boat a sufficient distance for the oars to be lengthwise dropped. The instant that was done, Don Benito sprang over the bulwarks, falling at the feet of Captain Delano; at the same time, calling towards his ship, but in tones so frenzied, that none in the boat could understand him. But, as if not equally obtuse, three sailors, from three different and distant parts of the ship, splashed into the sea, swimming after their captain, as if intent upon his rescue.

The dismayed officer of the boat eagerly asked what this meant. To which, Captain Delano, turning a disdainful smile upon the unaccountable Spaniard, answered that, for his part, he neither knew nor cared; but it seemed as if Don Benito had taken it into his head to produce the impression among his people that the boat wanted to kidnap him. "Or else—give way for your lives," he wildly added, starting at a clattering hubbub in the ship, above which rang the tocsin of the hatchet-polishers; and seizing Don Benito by the throat he added, "this plotting pirate means murder!" Here, in apparent verification of the words, the servant, a dagger in his hand, was seen on the rail overhead, poised, in the act of leaping, as if with desperate fidelity to befriend his master to the last; while, seemingly to aid the black, the three white sailors were trying to clamber into the hampered bow. Meantime, the whole host of negroes, as if inflamed at the sight of their jeopardized captain, impended in one sooty avalanche over the bulwarks.

All this, with what preceded, and what followed, occurred with such involutions of rapidity, that past, present, and future seemed one.

Seeing the negro coming, Captain Delano had flung the Spaniard aside, almost in the very act of clutching him, and, by the unconscious recoil, shifting his place, with arms thrown up, so promptly grappled the servant in his descent, that with dagger presented at Captain Delano's heart, the black seemed of purpose to have leaped there as to his mark. But the weapon was wrenched away, and the assailant dashed down into the bottom of the boat, which now, with disentangled oars, began to speed through the sea.

At this juncture, the left hand of Captain Delano, on one side, again clutched the half-reclined Don Benito, heedless that he was in a speechless faint, while his right foot, on the other side, ground the prostrate negro;* and his right arm pressed for added speed on the after oar, his eye bent forward, encouraging his men to their utmost.

But here, the officer of the boat, who had at last succeeded in beating off the towing sailors, and was now, with face turned aft, assisting the bowsman at his oar, suddenly called to Captain Delano, to see what the black was about; while a Portuguese oarsman shouted to him to give heed to what the Spaniard was saying.

Glancing down at his feet, Captain Delano saw the freed hand of the servant aiming with a second dagger—a small one, before concealed in his wool—with this he was snakishly writhing up from the boat's bottom, at the heart of his master, his countenance lividly vindictive, expressing the centred purpose of his soul; while the Spaniard, half-choked, was vainly shrinking away, with husky words, incoherent to all but the Portuguese.

That moment, across the long-benighted mind of Captain Delano, a flash of revelation swept, illuminating in unanticipated clearness his host's whole mysterious demeanor, with every enigmatic event of the day, as well as the entire past voyage of the San Dominick. He smote Babo's hand down, but his own heart smote him harder. With infinite pity he withdrew his hold from Don Benito. Not Captain Delano, but Don Benito, the black, in leaping into the boat, had intended to stab.

Both the black's hands were held, as, glancing up towards the San Dominick, Captain Delano, now with the scales dropped from his eyes, saw the negroes, not in misrule, not in tumult, not as if frantically concerned for Don Benito, but with mask torn away, flourishing hatchets and knives, in ferocious piratical revolt. Like delirious black dervishes, the six Ashantees danced on the poop. Prevented by their foes from springing into the water, the Spanish boys were hurrying up to the topmost spars, while such of the few Spanish sailors, not already in the sea, less alert, were descried, helplessly mixed in, on deck, with the blacks.

Meantime Captain Delano hailed his own vessel, ordering the ports up, and the guns run out. But by this time the cable of the San Dominick had been cut; and the fag-end, in lashing out, whipped away the canvas shroud about the beak, suddenly revealing, as the bleached hull swung round towards the open ocean, death for the figurehead, in a human skeleton; chalky comment on the chalked words below, *"Follow your leader."*

At the sight, Don Benito, covering his face, wailed out: "'Tis he, Aranda! my murdered, unburied friend!"

Upon reaching the sealer, calling for ropes, Captain Delano bound the negro, who made no resistance, and had him hoisted to the deck. He would then have assisted the now almost helpless Don Benito up the side; but Don Benito, wan as he was, refused to move, or be moved, until the negro should have been first put below out of view. When, presently assured that it was done, he no more shrank from the ascent.

The boat was immediately dispatched back to pick up the three swimming sailors. Meantime, the guns were in readiness, though, owing to the San Dominick having glided somewhat astern of the sealer, only the aftermost one could be brought to bear. With this, they fired six times; thinking to cripple the fugitive ship by bringing down her spars. But only a few inconsiderable ropes were shot away. Soon the ship was beyond the gun's range, steering broad out of the bay; the blacks thickly clustering round the bowsprit, one moment with taunting cries towards the whites, the next with upthrown gestures hailing the now dusky moors of ocean— cawing crows escaped from the hand of the fowler.

The first impulse was to slip the cables and give chase. But, upon second thoughts, to pursue with whale-boat and yawl seemed more promising.

Upon inquiring of Don Benito what fire arms they had on board the San Dominick, Captain Delano was answered that they had none that could be used; because, in the earlier stages of the mutiny, a cabin-passenger, since dead, had secretly put out of order the locks of what few muskets there were. But with all his remaining strength, Don Benito entreated the American not to give chase, either with ship or boat; for the negroes had already proved themselves such desperadoes, that, in case of a present assault, nothing but a total massacre of the whites could be looked for. But, regarding this warning as coming from one whose spirit had been crushed by misery, the American did not give up his design.

The boats were got ready and armed. Captain Delano ordered his men into them. He was going himself when Don Benito grasped his arm.

"What! have you saved my life, señor, and are you now going to throw away your own?"

The officers also, for reasons connected with their interests and those of the voyage, and a duty owing to the owners, strongly objected against their commander's going. Weighing their remonstrances a moment, Captain Delano felt bound to remain; appointing his chief mate—an athletic and resolute man, who had been a privateer's-man, and, as his enemies whispered, a pirate—to head the party. The more to encourage the sailors, they were told, that the Spanish captain considered his ship as good as lost; that she and her cargo, including some gold and silver, were worth more than a thousand doubloons. Take her, and no small part should be theirs. The sailors replied with a shout.

The fugitives had now almost gained an offing. It was nearly night; but the moon was rising. After hard, prolonged pulling, the boats came up on the ship's quarters, at a suitable distance laying upon their oars to discharge their muskets. Having no bullets to return, the negroes sent their yells. But, upon the second volley, Indian-like, they hurtled their hatchets. One took off a sailor's fingers. Another struck the whale-boat's bow, cutting off the rope there, and remaining stuck in the gunwale like a woodman's axe. Snatching it, quivering from its lodgment, the mate hurled it back. The returned gauntlet now stuck in the ship's broken quarter-gallery, and so remained.

The negroes giving too hot a reception, the whites kept a more respectful distance. Hovering now just out of reach of the hurtling hatchets, they, with a view to the close encounter which must soon come, sought to decoy the blacks into entirely disarming themselves of their most murderous weapons in a hand-to-hand fight, by foolishly flinging them,

as missiles, short of the mark, into the sea. But ere long
perceiving the stratagem, the negroes desisted, though not
before many of them had to replace their lost hatchets with
handspikes; an exchange which, as counted upon, proved in
the end favorable to the assailants.

Meantime, with a strong wind, the ship still clove the
water; the boats alternately falling behind, and pulling up,
to discharge fresh volleys.

The fire was mostly directed towards the stern, since
there, chiefly, the negroes, at present, were clustering. But
to kill or maim the negroes was not the object. To take
them, with the ship, was the object. To do it, the ship must
be boarded; which could not be done by boats while she
was sailing so fast.

A thought now struck the mate. Observing the Spanish
boys still aloft, high as they could get, he called to them to
descend to the yards, and cut adrift the sails. It was done.
About this time, owing to causes hereafter to be shown, two
Spaniards, in the dress of sailors and conspicuously showing themselves, were killed; not by volleys, but by deliberate marksman's shots; while, as it afterwards appeared,
by one of the general discharges, Atufal, the black, and the
Spaniard at the helm likewise were killed. What now, with
the loss of the sails, and loss of leaders, the ship became
unmanageable to the negroes.

With creaking masts, she came heavily round to the wind;
the prow slowly swinging, into view of the boats, its skeleton
gleaming in the horizontal moonlight, and casting a gigantic
ribbed shadow upon the water. One extended arm of the ghost
seemed beckoning the whites to avenge it.

"Follow your leader!" cried the mate; and, one on each
bow, the boats boarded. Sealing-spears and cutlasses crossed
hatchets and handspikes. Huddled upon the long-boat amidships, the negresses raised a wailing chant, whose chorus was
the clash of the steel.

For a time, the attack wavered; the negroes wedging themselves to beat it back; the half-repelled sailors, as yet unable
to gain a footing, fighting as troopers in the saddle, one leg
sideways flung over the bulwarks, and one without, plying

their cutlasses like carters' whips. But in vain. They were almost overborne, when, rallying themselves into a squad as one man, with a huzza, they sprang inboard; where, entangled, they involuntarily separated again. For a few breaths' space, there was a vague, muffled, inner sound, as of submerged sword-fish rushing hither and thither through shoals of black-fish. Soon, in a reunited band, and joined by the Spanish seamen, the whites came to the surface, irresistibly driving the negroes toward the stern. But a barricade of casks and sacks, from side to side, had been thrown up by the mainmast. Here the negroes faced about, and though scorning peace or truce, yet fain would have had a respite. But, without pause, overleaping the barrier, the unflagging sailors again closed. Exhausted, the blacks now fought in despair. Their red tongues lolled, wolf-like, from their black mouths. But the pale sailors' teeth were set; not a word was spoken; and, in five minutes more, the ship was won.

Nearly a score of the negroes were killed. Exclusive of those by the balls, many were mangled; their wounds—mostly inflicted by the long-edged sealing-spears—resembling those shaven ones of the English at Preston Pans,* made by the poled scythes of the Highlanders. On the other side, none were killed, though several were wounded; some severely, including the mate. The surviving negroes were temporarily secured, and the ship, towed back into the harbor at midnight, once more lay anchored.

Omitting the incidents and arrangements ensuing, suffice it that, after two days spent in refitting, the two ships sailed in company for Conception, in Chili, and thence for Lima, in Peru; where, before the vice-regal courts, the whole affair, from the beginning, underwent investigation.

Though, midway on the passage, the ill-fated Spaniard, relaxed from constraint, showed some signs of regaining health with free-will; yet, agreeably to his own foreboding, shortly before arriving at Lima, he relapsed, finally becoming so reduced as to be carried ashore in arms. Hearing of his story and plight, one of the many religious institutions of the City of Kings opened an hospitable refuge to him, where both physician and priest were his nurses, and a member of the order volunteered to be his one special guardian and consoler, by night and by day.

The following extracts, translated from one of the official Spanish documents, will it is hoped, shed light on the preceding narrative, as well as, in the first place, reveal the true port of departure and true history of the San Dominick's voyage, down to the time of her touching at the island of St. Maria.

But, ere the extracts come, it may be well to preface them with a remark.

The document selected, from among many others, for partial translation, contains the deposition of Benito Cereno; the first taken in the case. Some disclosures therein were, at the time, held dubious for both learned and natural reasons. The tribunal inclined to the opinion that the deponent, not undisturbed in his mind by recent events, raved of some things which could never have happened. But subsequent depositions of the surviving sailors, bearing out the revelations of their captain in several of the strangest particulars, gave credence to the rest. So that the tribunal, in its final decision, rested its capital sentences upon statements which, had they lacked confirmation, it would have deemed it but duty to reject.

I, Don Jose de Abos and Padilla, His Majesty's Notary for the Royal Revenue, and Register of this Province, and Notary Public of the Holy Crusade of this Bishopric, etc.

Do certify and declare, as much as is requisite in law, that, in the criminal cause commenced the twenty-fourth of the month of September, in the year seventeen hundred and ninety-nine, against the negroes of the ship San Dominick, the following declaration before me was made.

Declaration of the first witness, DON BENITO CERENO.

The same day, and month, and year, His Honor, Doctor Juan Martinez de Rozas, Councilor of the Royal Audience of this Kingdom, and learned in the law of this Intendency, ordered the captain of the ship San Dominick, Don Benito Cereno, to appear; which he did in his litter, attended by the monk Infelez; of whom

he received the oath, which he took by God, our Lord, and a sign
of the Cross; under which he promised to tell the truth of whatever he should know and should be asked;—and being interrogated agreeably to the tenor of the act commencing the process, he
said, that on the twentieth of May last, he set sail with his ship
from the port of Valparaiso, bound to that of Callao; loaded with
the produce of the country beside thirty cases of hardware and one
hundred and sixty blacks, of both sexes, mostly belonging to Don
Alexandro Aranda, gentleman, of the city of Mendoza; that the
crew of the ship consisted of thirty-six men, beside the persons
who went as passengers; that the negroes were in part as follows:

*[Here, in the original, follows a list of some fifty names, descriptions,
and ages, compiled from certain recovered documents of Aranda's, and
also from recollections of the deponent, from which portions only are
extracted.]*

—One, from about eighteen to nineteen years, named José, and
this was the man that waited upon his master, Don Alexandro,
and who speaks well the Spanish, having served him four or five
years; * * * a mulatto, named Francesco, the cabin steward, of a
good person and voice, having sung in the Valparaiso churches,
native of the province of Buenos Ayres, aged about thirty-five years.
* * * A smart negro, named Dago, who had been for many years
a grave-digger among the Spaniards, aged forty-six years. * * *
Four old negroes, born in Africa, from sixty to seventy, but sound,
calkers by trade, whose names are as follows:—the first was named
Mure, and he was killed (as was also his son named Diamelo); the
second, Natu; the third, Yola, likewise killed; the fourth, Ghofan;
and six full-grown negroes, aged from thirty to forty-five, all raw,
and born among the Ashantees—Matiluqui, Yau, Lecbe, Mapenda,
Yambaio, Akim; four of whom were killed; * * * a powerful negro
named Atufal, who, being supposed to have been a chief in Africa,
his owners set great store by him. * * * And a small negro of
Senegal, but some years among the Spaniards, aged about thirty,
which negro's name was Babo; * * * that he does not remember
the names of the others, but that still expecting the residue of Don
Alexandro's papers will be found, will then take due account of
them all, and remit to the court; * * * and thirty-nine women and
children of all ages.

*[The catalogue over, the deposition goes on:]**

* * * That all the negroes slept upon deck, as is customary in
this navigation, and none wore fetters, because the owner, his friend

Aranda, told him that they were all tractable; * * * that on the seventh day after leaving port, at three o'clock in the morning, all the Spaniards being asleep except the two officers on the watch, who were the boatswain, Juan Robles, and the carpenter, Juan Bautista Gayete, and the helmsman and his boy, the negroes revolted suddenly, wounded dangerously the boatswain and the carpenter, and successively killed eighteen men of those who were sleeping upon deck, some with hand-spikes and hatchets, and others by throwing them alive overboard, after tying them; that of the Spaniards upon deck, they left about seven, as he thinks, alive and tied, to manœuvre the ship, and three or four more, who hid themselves, remained also alive. Although in the act of revolt the negroes made themselves masters of the hatchway, six or seven wounded went through it to the cockpit, without any hindrance on their part; that during the act of revolt, the mate and another person, whose name he does not recollect, attempted to come up through the hatchway, but being quickly wounded, they were obliged to return to the cabin; that the deponent resolved at break of day to come up the companion-way, where the negro Babo was, being the ringleader, and Atufal, who assisted him, and having spoken to them, exhorted them to cease committing such atrocities, asking them, at the same time, what they wanted and intended to do, offering, himself, to obey their commands; that, notwithstanding this, they threw, in his presence, three men, alive and tied, overboard; that they told the deponent to come up, and that they would not kill him; which having done, the negro Babo asked him whether there were in those seas any negro countries where they might be carried, and he answered them, No; that the negro Babo afterwards told him to carry them to Senegal,* or to the neighboring islands of St. Nicolas; and he answered, that this was impossible, on account of the great distance, the necessity involved of rounding Cape Horn, the bad condition of the vessel, the want of provisions, sails, and water; but that the negro Babo replied to him he must carry them in any way; that they would do and conform themselves to everything the deponent should require as to eating and drinking; that after a long conference, being absolutely compelled to please them, for they threatened him to kill all the whites if they were not, at all events, carried to Senegal, he told them that what was most wanting for the voyage was water; that they would go near the coast to take it, and thence they would proceed on their course; that the negro Babo agreed to it; and the deponent steered towards the intermediate ports, hoping to meet some Spanish or foreign vessel that would save them; that within ten or eleven days

they saw the land, and continued their course by it in the vicinity
of Nasca; that the deponent observed that the negroes were now
restless and mutinous, because he did not effect the taking in of
water, the negro Babo having required, with threats, that it should
be done, without fail, the following day; he told him they saw plainly
that the coast was steep, and the rivers designated in the maps
were not to be found, with other reasons suitable to the circumstances; that the best way would be to go to the island of Santa
Maria, where they might water and victual easily, it being a solitary island, as the foreigners did; that the deponent did not go to
Pisco, that was near, nor make any other port of the coast, because
the negro Babo had intimated to him several times, that he would
kill all the whites the very moment he should perceive any city,
town, or settlement of any kind on the shores to which they should
be carried: that having determined to go to the island of Santa
Maria, as the deponent had planned, for the purpose of trying
whether, on the passage or near the island itself, they could find
any vessel that should favor them, or whether he could escape from
it in a boat to the neighboring coast of Arauco; to adopt the necessary means he immediately changed his course, steering for the
island; that the negroes Babo and Atufal held daily conferences, in
which they discussed what was necessary for their design of returning to Senegal, whether they were to kill all the Spaniards, and
particularly the deponent; that eight days after parting from the
coast of Nasca, the deponent being on the watch a little after day-
break, and soon after the negroes had their meeting, the negro
Babo came to the place where the deponent was, and told him that
he had determined to kill his master, Don Alexandro Aranda, both
because he and his companions could not otherwise be sure of their
liberty, and that, to keep the seamen in subjection, he wanted to
prepare a warning of what road they should be made to take did
they or any of them oppose him; and that, by means of the death
of Don Alexandro, that warning would best be given; but, that
what this last meant, the deponent did not at the time comprehend, nor could not, further than that the death of Don Alexandro
was intended; and moreover, the negro Babo proposed to the deponent to call the mate Raneds, who was sleeping in the cabin, before
the thing was done, for fear, as the deponent understood it, that
the mate, who was a good navigator, should be killed with Don
Alexandro and the rest; that the deponent, who was the friend,
from youth, of Don Alexandro, prayed and conjured, but all was
useless; for the negro Babo answered him that the thing could not
be prevented, and that all the Spaniards risked their death if they

should attempt to frustrate his will in this matter, or any other; that, in this conflict, the deponent called the mate, Raneds, who was forced to go apart, and immediately the negro Babo commanded the Ashantee Matiluqui and the Ashantee Lecbe to go and commit the murder; that those two went down with hatchets to the berth of Don Alexandro; that, yet half alive and mangled, they dragged him on deck; that they were going to throw him overboard in that state, but the negro Babo stopped them, bidding the murder be completed on the deck before him, which was done, when, by his orders, the body was carried below, forward; that nothing more was seen of it by the deponent for three days; * * * that Don Alonzo Sidonia, an old man, long resident at Valparaiso, and lately appointed to a civil office in Peru, whither he had taken passage, was at the time sleeping in the berth opposite Don Alexandro's; that, awakening at his cries, surprised by them, and at the sight of the negroes with their bloody hatchets in their hands, he threw himself into the sea through a window which was near him, and was drowned, without it being in the power of the deponent to assist or take him up; * * * that, a short time after killing Aranda, they brought upon deck his german-cousin, of middle-age, Don Francisco Masa, of Mendoza, and the young Don Joaquin, Marques de Arambaolaza, then lately from Spain, with his Spanish servant Ponce, and the three young clerks of Aranda, José Morairi, Lorenzo Bargas, and Hermenegildo Gandix, all of Cadiz; that Don Joaquin and Hermenegildo Gandix, the negro Babo for purposes hereafter to appear, preserved alive; but Don Francisco Masa, José Morairi, and Lorenzo Bargas, with Ponce the servant, beside the boatswain, Juan Robles, the boatswain's mates, Manuel Viscaya and Roderigo Hurta, and four of the sailors, the negro Babo ordered to be thrown alive into the sea, although they made no resistance, nor begged for anything else but mercy; that the boatswain, Juan Robles, who knew how to swim, kept the longest above water, making acts of contrition, and, in the last words he uttered, charged this deponent to cause mass to be said for his soul to our Lady of Succor; * * * that, during the three days which followed, the deponent, uncertain what fate had befallen the remains of Don Alexandro, frequently asked the negro Babo where they were, and, if still on board, whether they were to be preserved for interment ashore, entreating him so to order it; that the negro Babo answered nothing till the fourth day, when at sunrise, the deponent coming on deck, the negro Babo showed him a skeleton, which had been substituted for the ship's proper figure-head, the image of Christopher Colon,* the discoverer of the New World; that the negro Babo

asked him whose skeleton that was, and whether, from its whiteness, he should not think it a white's; that, upon his covering his
face, the negro Babo, coming close, said words to this effect: "Keep
faith with the blacks from here to Senegal, or you shall in spirit,
as now in body, follow your leader," pointing to the prow; * * *
that the same morning the negro Babo took by succession each
Spaniard forward, and asked him whose skeleton that was, and
whether, from its whiteness, he should not think it a white's; that
each Spaniard covered his face; that then to each the negro Babo
repeated the words in the first place said to the deponent; * * *
that they (the Spaniards), being then assembled aft, the negro
Babo harangued them, saying that he had now done all; that the
deponent (as navigator for the negroes) might pursue his course,
warning him and all of them that they should, soul and body, go
the way of Don Alexandro if he saw them (the Spaniards) speak
or plot anything against them (the negroes)—a threat which was
repeated every day; that, before the events last mentioned, they had
tied the cook to throw him overboard, for it is not known what
thing they heard him speak, but finally the negro Babo spared his
life, at the request of the deponent; that a few days after, the deponent, endeavoring not to omit any means to preserve the lives of the
remaining whites, spoke to the negroes peace and tranquillity, and
agreed to draw up a paper, signed by the deponent and the sailors
who could write, as also by the negro Babo, for himself and all the
blacks, in which the deponent obliged himself to carry them to
Senegal, and they not to kill any more, and he formally to make
over to them the ship, with the cargo, with which they were for
that time satisfied and quieted. * * * But the next day, the more
surely to guard against the sailors' escape, the negro Babo commanded all the boats to be destroyed but the long-boat, which was
unseaworthy, and another, a cutter in good condition, which, knowing it would yet be wanted for towing the water casks, he had it
lowered down into the hold.

*

*[Various particulars of the prolonged and perplexed navigation ensu-
ing here follow, with incidents of a calamitous calm, from which portion
one passage is extracted, to wit:]*

—That on the fifth day of the calm, all on board suffering much
from the heat, and want of water, and five having died in fits, and
mad, the negroes became irritable, and for a chance gesture, which
they deemed suspicious—though it was harmless—made by the
mate, Raneds, to the deponent, in the act of handing a quadrant,

they killed him; but that for this they afterwards were sorry, the mate being the only remaining navigator on board, except the deponent.

*

—That omitting other events, which daily happened, and which can only serve uselessly to recall past misfortunes and conflicts, after seventy-three days' navigation, reckoned from the time they sailed from Nasca, during which they navigated under a scanty allowance of water, and were afflicted with the calms before mentioned, they at last arrived at the island of Santa Maria, on the seventeenth of the month of August, at about six o'clock in the afternoon, at which hour they cast anchor very near the American ship, Bachelor's Delight, which lay in the same bay, commanded by the generous Captain Amasa Delano; but at six o'clock in the morning, they had already descried the port, and the negroes became uneasy, as soon as at distance they saw the ship, not having expected to see one there; that the negro Babo pacified them, assuring them that no fear need be had; that straightway he ordered the figure on the bow to be covered with canvas, as for repairs, and had the decks a little set in order; that for a time the negro Babo and the negro Atufal conferred; that the negro Atufal was for sailing away, but the negro Babo would not, and, by himself, cast about what to do; that at last he came to the deponent, proposing to him to say and do all that the deponent declares to have said and done to the American captain; * * * * * * that the negro Babo warned him that if he varied in the least, or uttered any word, or gave any look that should give the least intimation of the past events or present state, he would instantly kill him, with all his companions, showing a dagger, which he carried hid, saying something which, as he understood it, meant that that dagger would be alert as his eye; that the negro Babo then announced the plan to all his companions, which pleased them; that he then, the better to disguise the truth, devised many expedients, in some of them uniting deceit and defense; that of this sort was the device of the six Ashantees before named, who were his bravoes; that them he stationed on the break of the poop, as if to clean certain hatchets (in cases, which were part of the cargo), but in reality to use them, and distribute them at need, and at a given word he told them; that, among other devices, was the device of presenting Atufal, his right-hand man, as chained, though in a moment the chains could be dropped; that in every particular he informed the deponent what part he was expected to enact in every device, and what story he was to tell on every occasion, always threatening him with instant death if he varied in the least: that, conscious that many of the negroes would be turbulent, the negro Babo appointed the four aged negroes, who were calkers, to keep what domestic order they could on the decks; that again and again he harangued the Spaniards and his companions, informing them of his intent, and of his devices, and of the invented story that this deponent was to tell, charging them lest any of them varied from that story; that these arrangements were made and matured during the interval of two or three hours, between their first sighting the ship and the arrival on board of Captain Amasa Delano; that this happened about half-past seven o'clock in the morning, Captain Amasa Delano coming in his boat, and all gladly receiving him; that the deponent, as well as he could force himself, acting then the part of principal owner, and a free captain of the ship, told Captain Amasa Delano, when called upon, that he came from Buenos Ayres, bound to Lima, with three hundred negroes; that off Cape Horn, and in a subsequent fever, many negroes had died; that also, by similar casualties, all the sea officers and the greatest part of the crew had died.

*

[And so the deposition goes on, circumstantially recounting the fictitious story dictated to the deponent by Babo, and through the deponent imposed upon Captain Delano; and also recounting the friendly offers of Captain Delano, with other things, but all of which is here omitted. After the fictitious, strange story, etc., the deposition proceeds:]

—that the generous Captain Amasa Delano remained on board all the day, till he left the ship anchored at six o'clock in the evening, deponent speaking to him always of his pretended misfortunes, under the forementioned principles, without having had it in his power to tell a single word, or give him the least hint, that he might know the truth and state of things; because the negro Babo, performing the office of an officious servant with all the appearance of submission of the humble slave, did not leave the deponent one moment; that this was in order to observe the deponent's actions and words, for the negro Babo understands well the Spanish; and besides, there were thereabout some others who were constantly on the watch, and likewise understood the Spanish; * * * that upon one occasion, while deponent was standing on the deck conversing with Amasa Delano, by a secret sign the negro Babo drew him (the deponent) aside, the act appearing as if originating with the deponent; that then, he being drawn aside, the negro Babo proposed to him to gain from Amasa Delano full particulars about his ship, and crew, and arms; that the deponent asked "For what?"

that the negro Babo answered he might conceive; that, grieved at
the prospect of what might overtake the generous Captain Amasa
Delano, the deponent at first refused to ask the desired questions,
and used every argument to induce the negro Babo to give up this
new design; that the negro Babo showed the point of his dagger;
that, after the information had been obtained, the negro Babo again
drew him aside, telling him that that very night he (the deponent)
would be captain of two ships, instead of one, for that, great part
of the American's ship's crew being to be absent fishing, the six
Ashantees, without any one else, would easily take it; that at this
time he said other things to the same purpose; that no entreaties
availed; that, before Amasa Delano's coming on board, no hint
had been given touching the capture of the American ship: that to
prevent this project the deponent was powerless; * * * —that in
some things his memory is confused, he cannot distinctly recall
every event; * * * —that as soon as they had cast anchor at six of
the clock in the evening, as has before been stated, the American
Captain took leave to return to his vessel; that upon a sudden
impulse, which the deponent believes to have come from God
and his angels, he, after the farewell had been said, followed the
generous Captain Amasa Delano as far as the gunwale, where he
stayed, under pretense of taking leave, until Amasa Delano should
have been seated in his boat; that on shoving off, the deponent
sprang from the gunwale into the boat, and fell into it, he knows
not how, God guarding him; that—

*

*[Here, in the original, follows the account of what further happened
at the escape, and how the San Dominick was retaken, and of the passage to the coast; including in the recital many expressions of "eternal
gratitude" to the "generous Captain Amasa Delano." The deposition
then proceeds with recapitulatory remarks, and a partial renumeration
of the negroes, making record of their individual part in the past events,
with a view to furnishing, according to command of the court, the data
whereon to found the criminal sentences to be pronounced. From this
portion is the following:]*

—That he believes that all the negroes, though not in the first
place knowing to the design of revolt, when it was accomplished,
approved it. * * * That the negro, José, eighteen years old, and in
the personal service of Don Alexandro, was the one who communicated the information to the negro Babo, about the state of things
in the cabin, before the revolt; that this is known, because, in the
preceding midnights, he used to come from his berth, which was

under his master's, in the cabin, to the deck where the ringleader and his associates were, and had secret conversations with the negro Babo, in which he was several times seen by the mate; that, one night, the mate drove him away twice; * * that this same negro José, was the one who, without being commanded to do so by the negro Babo, as Lecbe and Matiluqui were, stabbed his master, Don Alexandro, after he had been dragged half-lifeless to the deck; * * that the mulatto steward, Francesco, was of the first band of revolters, that he was, in all things, the creature and tool of the negro Babo; that, to make his court, he, just before a repast in the cabin, proposed, to the negro Babo, poisoning a dish for the generous Captain Amasa Delano; this is known and believed, because the negroes have said it; but that the negro Babo, having another design, forbade Francesco; * * that the Ashantee Lecbe was one of the worst of them; for that, on the day the ship was retaken, he assisted in the defense of her, with a hatchet in each hand, with one of which he wounded, in the breast, the chief mate of Amasa Delano, in the first act of boarding; this all knew; that, in sight of the deponent, Lecbe struck, with a hatchet, Don Francisco Masa when, by the negro Babo's orders, he was carrying him to throw him overboard, alive; beside participating in the murder, before mentioned, of Don Alexandro Aranda, and others of the cabin-passengers; that, owing to the fury with which the Ashantees fought in the engagement with the boats, but this Lecbe and Yau survived; that Yau was bad as Lecbe; that Yau was the man who, by Babo's command, willingly prepared the skeleton of Don Alexandro, in a way the negroes afterwards told the deponent, but which he, so long as reason is left him, can never divulge; that Yau and Lecbe were the two who, in a calm by night, riveted the skeleton to the bow; this also the negroes told him; that the negro Babo was he who traced the inscription below it; that the negro Babo was the plotter from first to last; he ordered every murder, and was the helm and keel of the revolt; that Atufal was his lieutenant in all; but Atufal, with his own hand, committed no murder; nor did the negro Babo; * * that Atufal was shot, being killed in the fight with the boats, ere boarding; * * that the negresses, of age, were knowing to the revolt, and testified themselves satisfied at the death of their master, Don Alexandro; that, had the negroes not restrained them, they would have tortured to death, instead of simply killing, the Spaniards slain by command of the negro Babo; that the negresses used their utmost influence to have the deponent made away with; that, in the various acts of murder, they sang songs and danced—not gaily, but solemnly; and before the engagement with

the boats, as well as during the action, they sang melancholy songs
to the negroes, and that this melancholy tone was more inflaming
than a different one would have been, and was so intended; that
all this is believed, because the negroes have said it.

—that of the thirty-six men of the crew exclusive of the passengers,
(all of whom are now dead), which the deponent had knowledge
of, six only remained alive, with four cabin-boys and ship-boys, not
included with the crew; * * —that the negroes broke an arm of
one of the cabin-boys and gave him strokes with hatchets.

*[Then follow various random disclosures referring to various periods
of time. The following are extracted:]*

—That during the presence of Captain Amasa Delano on board,
some attempts were made by the sailors, and one by Hermenegildo
Gandix, to convey hints to him of the true state of affairs; but
that these attempts were ineffectual, owing to fear of incurring
death, and furthermore owing to the devices which offered contradictions to the true state of affairs; as well as owing to the generosity and piety of Amasa Delano incapable of sounding such
wickedness; * * * that Luys Galgo, a sailor about sixty years of
age, and formerly of the king's navy, was one of those who sought
to convey tokens to Captain Amasa Delano; but his intent, though
undiscovered, being suspected, he was, on a pretense, made to
retire out of sight, and at last into the hold, and there was made
away with. This the negroes have since said; * * * that one of the
ship-boys feeling, from Captain Amasa Delano's presence, some
hopes of release, and not having enough prudence, dropped some
chance-word respecting his expectations, which being overheard
and understood by a slave-boy with whom he was eating at the
time, the latter struck him on the head with a knife, inflicting a
bad wound, but of which the boy is now healing; that likewise,
not long before the ship was brought to anchor, one of the seamen, steering at the time, endangered himself by letting the blacks
remark some expression in his countenance, arising from a cause
similar to the above; but this sailor, by his heedful after conduct,
escaped; * * * that these statements are made to show the court
that from the beginning to the end of the revolt, it was impossible for the deponent and his men to act otherwise than they did;
* * * —that the third clerk, Hermenegildo Gandix, who before
had been forced to live among the seamen, wearing a seaman's
habit, and in all respects appearing to be one for the time; he,
Gandix, was killed by a musket-ball fired through a mistake from
the American boats before boarding; having in his fright ran up

the mizzen-rigging, calling to the boats—"don't board," lest upon
their boarding the negroes should kill him; that this inducing the
Americans to believe he some way favored the cause of the negroes,
they fired two balls at him, so that he fell wounded from the rigging, and was drowned in the sea; * * * —that the young Don
Joaquin, Marques de Arambaolaza, like Hermenegildo Gandix, the
third clerk, was degraded to the office and appearance of a common seaman; that upon one occasion when Don Joaquin shrank,
the negro Babo commanded the Ashantee Lecbe to take tar and
heat it, and pour it upon Don Joaquin's hands; * * * —that Don
Joaquin was killed owing to another mistake of the Americans,
but one impossible to be avoided, as upon the approach of the
boats, Don Joaquin, with a hatchet tied edge out and upright to
his hand, was made by the negroes to appear on the bulwarks;
whereupon, seen with arms in his hands and in a questionable attitude, he was shot for a renegade seaman; * * * —that on the person of Don Joaquin was found secreted a jewel, which, by papers
that were discovered, proved to have been meant for the shrine of
our Lady of Mercy in Lima; a votive offering, beforehand prepared
and guarded, to attest his gratitude, when he should have landed
in Peru, his last destination, for the safe conclusion of his entire
voyage from Spain;* * * * —that the jewel, with the other effects
of the late Don Joaquin, is in the custody of the brethren of the
Hospital de Sacerdotes, awaiting the disposition of the honorable
court; * * * —that, owing to the condition of the deponent, as
well as the haste in which the boats departed for the attack, the
Americans were not forewarned that there were, among the apparent crew, a passenger and one of the clerks disguised by the negro
Babo; * * * —that, beside the negroes killed in the action, some
were killed after the capture and re-anchoring at night, when shackled to the ring-bolts on deck; that these deaths were committed by
the sailors, ere they could be prevented. That so soon as informed
of it, Captain Amasa Delano used all his authority, and, in particular with his own hand, struck down Martinez Gola, who, having found a razor in the pocket of an old jacket of his, which one
of the shackled negroes had on, was aiming it at the negro's throat;*
that the noble Captain Amasa Delano also wrenched from the hand
of Bartholomew Barlo, a dagger secreted at the time of the massacre of the whites, with which he was in the act of stabbing a
shackled negro, who, the same day, with another negro, had thrown
him down and jumped upon him; * * * —that, for all the events,
befalling through so long a time, during which the ship was in the
hands of the negro Babo, he cannot here give account; but that,

what he has said is the most substantial of what occurs to him at present, and is the truth under the oath which he has taken; which declaration he affirmed and ratified, after hearing it read to him.

He said that he is twenty-nine years of age, and broken in body and mind; that when finally dismissed by the court, he shall not return home to Chili, but betake himself to the monastery on Mount Agonia* without; and signed with his honor, and crossed himself, and, for the time, departed as he came, in his litter, with the monk Infelez, to the Hospital de Sacerdotes.

                                                            BENITO CERENO.

DOCTOR ROZAS.

If the Deposition have served as the key to fit into the lock of the complications which precede it, then, as a vault whose door has been flung back, the San Dominick's hull lies open to-day.

Hitherto the nature of this narrative, besides rendering the intricacies in the beginning unavoidable, has more or less required that many things, instead of being set down in the order of occurrence, should be retrospectively, or irregularly given; this last is the case with the following passages, which will conclude the account:

During the long, mild voyage to Lima, there was, as before hinted, a period during which the sufferer a little recovered his health, or, at least in some degree, his tranquillity. Ere the decided relapse which came, the two captains had many cordial conversations—their fraternal unreserve in singular contrast with former withdrawments.

Again and again, it was repeated, how hard it had been to enact the part forced on the Spaniard by Babo.

"Ah, my dear friend," Don Benito once said, "at those very times when you thought me so morose and ungrateful, nay, when, as you now admit, you half thought me plotting your murder, at those very times my heart was frozen; I could not look at you, thinking of what, both on board this ship and your own, hung, from other hands, over my kind benefactor. And as God lives, Don Amasa, I know not whether desire for my own safety alone could have nerved me to that leap into your boat, had it not been for the thought that, did you, unenlightened, return to your ship, you, my best friend, with all who might be with you, stolen upon, that night, in your hammocks, would never in this world have wakened again. Do but think how you walked this deck, how you sat in this cabin, every inch of ground mined into honey-combs under you. Had I dropped the least hint, made the least advance towards an understanding between us, death, explosive death—yours as mine— would have ended the scene."

"True, true," cried Captain Delano, starting, "you have saved my life, Don Benito, more than I yours; saved it, too, against my knowledge and will."

"Nay, my friend," rejoined the Spaniard, courteous even to the point of religion, "God charmed your life, but you saved mine. To think of some things you did—those smilings and chattings, rash pointings and gesturings. For less than these, they slew my mate, Raneds; but you had the Prince of Heaven's safe conduct through all ambuscades."

"Yes, all is owing to Providence, I know; but the temper of my mind that morning was more than commonly pleasant, while the sight of so much suffering, more apparent than real, added to my good nature, compassion, and charity, happily interweaving the three. Had it been otherwise, doubtless, as you hint, some of my interferences might have ended unhappily enough. Besides that, those feelings I spoke of enabled me to get the better of momentary distrust, at times when acuteness might have cost me my life, without saving another's. Only at the end did my suspicions get the better of me, and you know how wide of the mark they then proved."

"Wide, indeed," said Don Benito, sadly; "you were with me all day; stood with me, sat with me, talked with me, looked at me, ate with me, drank with me; and yet, your last act was to clutch for a monster, not only an innocent man, but the most pitiable of all men. To such degree may malign machinations and deceptions impose. So far may even the best man err, in judging the conduct of one with the recesses of whose condition he is not acquainted. But you were forced to it; and you were in time undeceived. Would that, in both respects, it was so ever, and with all men."

"You generalize, Don Benito; and mournfully enough. But the past is passed; why moralize upon it? Forget it. See, yon bright sun has forgotten it all, and the blue sea, and the blue sky; these have turned over new leaves."

"Because they have no memory," he dejectedly replied; "because they are not human."

"But these mild trades that now fan your cheek, do they not come with a human-like healing to you? Warm friends, steadfast friends are the trades."

"With their steadfastness they but waft me to my tomb, señor," was the foreboding response.

"You are saved," cried Captain Delano, more and more astonished and pained; "you are saved; what has cast such a shadow upon you?"

"The negro."

There was silence, while the moody man sat, slowly and unconsciously gathering his mantle about him, as if it were a pall.

There was no more conversation that day.

But if the Spaniard's melancholy sometimes ended in muteness upon topics like the above, there were others upon which he never spoke at all; on which, indeed, all his old reserves were piled. Pass over the worst, and, only to elucidate, let an item or two of these be cited. The dress so precise and costly, worn by him on the day whose events have been narrated, had not willingly been put on. And that silver-mounted sword, apparent symbol of despotic command, was not, indeed, a sword, but the ghost of one. The scabbard, artificially stiffened, was empty.

As for the black—whose brain, not body, had schemed and led the revolt, with the plot—his slight frame, inadequate to that which it held, had at once yielded to the superior muscular strength of his captor, in the boat. Seeing all was over, he uttered no sound, and could not be forced to. His aspect seemed to say, since I cannot do deeds, I will not speak words. Put in irons in the hold, with the rest, he was carried to Lima. During the passage Don Benito did not visit him. Nor then, nor at any time after, would he look at him. Before the tribunal he refused. When pressed by the judges he fainted. On the testimony of the sailors alone rested the legal identity of Babo.

Some months after, dragged to the gibbet at the tail of a mule, the black met his voiceless end. The body was burned to ashes; but for many days, the head, that hive of subtlety, fixed on a pole in the Plaza, met, unabashed, the gaze of the whites; and across the Plaza looked towards St. Bartholomew's church, in whose vaults slept then, as now, the recovered bones of Aranda; and across the Rimac bridge looked towards the monastery, on Mount Agonia without; where, three months after being dismissed by the court, Benito Cereno, borne on the bier, did, indeed, follow his leader.

I AND MY CHIMNEY

I AND my chimney, two grey-headed old smokers, reside in the country. We are, I may say, old settlers here; particularly my old chimney, which settles more and more every day.

Though I always say, *I and my chimney*, as Cardinal Wolsey* used to say, *I and my King*, yet this egotistic way of speaking, wherein I take precedence of my chimney, is hardly borne out by the facts; in everything, except the above phrase, my chimney taking precedence of me.

Within thirty feet of the turf-sided road, my chimney—a huge, corpulent old Harry VIII. of a chimney*—rises full in front of me and all my possessions. Standing well up a hill-side, my chimney, like Lord Rosse's monster telescope,* swung vertical to hit the meridian moon, is the first object to greet the approaching traveler's eye, nor is it the last which the sun salutes. My chimney, too, is before me in receiving the first-fruits of the seasons. The snow is on its head ere on my hat; and every spring, as in a hollow beech tree, the first swallows build their nests in it.

But it is within doors that the preëminence of my chimney is most manifest. When in the rear room, set apart for that object, I stand to receive my guests (who, by the way call more, I suspect, to see my chimney than me), I then stand, not so much before, as, strictly speaking, behind my chimney, which is, indeed, the true host. Not that I demur. In the presence of my betters, I hope I know my place.

From this habitual precedence of my chimney over me, some even think that I have got into a sad rearward way altogether; in short, from standing behind my old-fashioned chimney so much, I have got to be quite behind the age too, as well as running behind-hand in everything else. But to tell the truth, I never was a very forward old fellow, nor what my farming neighbors call a forehanded one. Indeed, those rumors about my behindhandedness are so far correct, that I have an odd sauntering way with me sometimes of going about with my hands behind my back. As for my belonging to the rear-guard in general, certain it is, I bring up the rear of my chimney—which, by the way, is this moment before me—and that, too, both in fancy and fact. In brief, my chimney is my superior; my superior by I know not how many heads and shoulders; my superior, too, in that humbly bowing over with shovel and tongs, I much minister to it; yet never does it minister, or incline over to me; but, if any thing, in its settlings, rather leans the other way.

My chimney is grand seignior here—the one great domineering object, not more of the landscape, than of the house; all the rest of which house, in each architectural arrangement, as may shortly appear, is, in the most marked manner, accommodated, not to my wants, but to my chimney's, which, among other things, has the centre of the house to himself, leaving but the odd holes and corners to me.

But I and my chimney must explain; and as we are both rather obese, we may have to expatiate.

In those houses which are strictly double houses—that is, where the hall is in the middle—the fire-places usually are on opposite sides; so that while one member of the household is warming himself at a fire built into a recess of the north wall, say another member, the former's own brother, perhaps, may be holding his feet to the blaze before a hearth in the south wall—the two thus fairly sitting back to back. Is this well? Be it put to any man who has a proper fraternal feeling. Has it not a sort of sulky appearance? But very probably this style of chimney building originated with some architect afflicted with a quarrelsome family.*

Then again, almost every modern fire-place has its separate flue—separate throughout, from hearth to chimney-top. At least such an arrangement is deemed desirable. Does not this look egotistical, selfish? But still more, all these separate flues, instead of having independent masonry establishments of their own, or instead of being grouped together in one federal stock in the middle of the house—instead of this, I say, each flue is surreptitiously honeycombed into the walls; so that these last are here and there, or indeed almost anywhere, treacherously hollow, and, in consequence, more or less weak. Of course, the main reason of this style of chimney building is to economize room. In cities, where lots are sold by the inch, small space is to spare for a chimney constructed on magnanimous principles; and, as with most thin men, who are generally tall, so with such houses, what is lacking in breadth must be made up in height. This remark holds true even with regard to many very stylish abodes, built by the most stylish of gentlemen. And yet, when that stylish gentleman, Louis le Grand of France, would build a palace for his lady friend, Madame de Maintenon, he built it but one story high—in fact in the cottage style. But then how uncommonly quadrangular, spacious, and broad—horizontal acres, not vertical ones. Such is the palace, which, in all its one-storied magnificence of Languedoc marble, in the garden of Versailles, still remains to this day. Any man can buy a square foot of land and plant a liberty-pole on it; but it takes a king to set apart whole acres for a grand Trianon.

But nowadays it is different; and furthermore, what originated in a necessity has been mounted into a vaunt. In towns there is large rivalry in building tall houses. If one gentleman builds his house four stories high, and another gentleman comes next door and builds five stories high, then the former, not to be looked down upon that way, immediately sends for his architect and claps a fifth and a sixth story on top of his previous four. And, not till the gentleman has achieved his aspiration, not till he has stolen over the way by twilight and observed how his sixth story soars beyond his neighbor's fifth—not till then does he retire to his rest with satisfaction.

Such folks, it seems to me, need mountains for neighbors, to take this emulous conceit of soaring out of them.

If, considering that mine is a very wide house, and by no means lofty, aught in the above may appear like interested pleading, as if I did but fold myself about in the cloak of a general proposition, cunningly to tickle my individual vanity beneath it, such misconception must vanish upon my frankly conceding, that land adjoining my alder swamp was sold last month for ten dollars an acre, and thought a rash purchase at that; so that for wide houses hereabouts there is plenty of room, and cheap. Indeed so cheap—dirt cheap— is the soil, that our elms thrust out their roots in it, and hang their great boughs over it, in the most lavish and reckless way. Almost all our crops, too, are sown broadcast, even peas and turnips. A farmer among us, who should go about his twenty-acre field, poking his finger into it here and there, and dropping down a mustard seed, would be thought a penurious, narrow-minded husbandman. The dandelions in the river-meadows, and the forget-me-nots along the mountain roads, you see at once they are put to no economy in space. Some seasons, too, our rye comes up, here and there a spear, sole and single like a church-spire. It doesn't care to crowd itself where it knows there is such a deal of room. The world is wide, the world is all before us, says the rye. Weeds, too, it is amazing how they spread. No such thing as arresting them—some of our pastures being a sort of Alsatia for the weeds. As for the grass, every spring it is like Kossuth's rising* of what he calls the peoples. Mountains, too, a regular camp-meeting of them. For the same reason, the same all-sufficiency of room, our shadows march and countermarch, going through their various drills and masterly evolutions, like the old imperial guard on the Champs de Mars.* As for the hills, especially where the roads cross them, the supervisors of our various towns have given notice to all concerned, that they can come and dig them down and cart them off, and never a cent to pay, no more than for the privilege of picking blackberries. The stranger who is buried here, what liberal-hearted landed proprietor among us grudges him his six feet of rocky pasture?

Nevertheless, cheap, after all, as our land is, and much as it is trodden under foot, I, for one, am proud of it for what it bears; and chiefly for its three great lions—the Great Oak, Ogg Mountain, and my chimney.

Most houses, here, are but one and a half stories high; few exceed two. That in which I and my chimney dwell,* is in width nearly twice its height, from sill to eaves—which accounts for the magnitude of its main content—besides, showing that in this house, as in this country at large, there is abundance of space, and to spare, for both of us.

The frame of the old house is of wood—which but the more sets forth the solidity of the chimney, which is of brick. And as the great wrought nails, binding the clapboards, are unknown in these degenerate days, so are the huge bricks in the chimney walls. The architect of the chimney must have had the pyramid of Cheops* before him; for, after that famous structure, it seems modeled, only its rate of decrease towards the summit is considerably less, and it is truncated. From the exact middle of the mansion it soars from the cellar, right up through each successive floor, till, four feet square, it breaks water from the ridge-pole of the roof, like an anvil-headed whale, through the crest of a billow. Most people, though, liken it, in that part, to a razeed observatory, masoned up.

The reason for its peculiar appearance above the roof touches upon rather delicate ground. How shall I reveal that, forasmuch as many years ago the original gable roof of the old house had become very leaky, a temporary proprietor hired a band of woodmen, with their huge, cross-cut saws, and went to sawing the old gable roof clean off. Off it went, with all its birds' nests, and dormer windows. It was replaced with a modern roof, more fit for a railway wood-house than an old country gentleman's abode. This operation—razeeing the structure some fifteen feet—was, in effect upon the chimney, something like the falling of the great spring tides. It left uncommon low water all about the chimney—to abate which appearance, the same person now proceeds to slice fifteen feet off the chimney itself, actually beheading my royal old chimney—a regicidal act,* which, were it not for the palliating fact, that he was a poulterer by trade, and, therefore, hardened to such neck-wringings, should send that former proprietor down to posterity in the same cart with Cromwell.

Owing to its pyramidal shape, the reduction of the chimney inordinately widened its razeed summit. Inordinately, I say, but only in the estimation of such as have no eye to the picturesque. What care I, if, unaware that my chimney, as a free citizen of this free land, stands upon an independent basis of its own, people passing it, wonder how such a brick-kiln, as they call it, is supported upon mere joists and rafters? What care I? I will give a traveler a cup of switchel, if he want it; but am I bound to supply him with a sweet taste? Men of cultivated minds see, in my old house and chimney, a goodly old elephant-and-castle.*

All feeling hearts will sympathize with me in what I am now about to add. The surgical operation, above referred to, necessarily brought into the open air a part of the chimney previously under cover, and intended to remain so, and, therefore, not built of what are called weather-bricks. In consequence, the chimney, though of a vigorous constitution, suffered not a little, from so naked an exposure; and, unable to acclimate itself, ere long began to fail—showing blotchy symptoms akin to those in measles. Whereupon travelers, passing my way, would wag their heads, laughing: "See that wax nose—how it melts off!" But what cared I? The same travelers would travel across the sea to view Kenilworth* peeling away, and for a very good reason; that of all artists of the picturesque, decay wears the palm—I would say, the ivy. In fact, I've often thought that the proper place for my old chimney is ivied old England.

In vain my wife—with what probable ulterior intent will, ere long, appear—solemnly warned me, that unless something were done, and speedily, we should be burnt to the ground, owing to the holes crumbling through the aforesaid blotchy parts, where the chimney joined the roof. "Wife," said I, "far better that my house should burn down, than that my chimney should be pulled down, though but a few feet. They call it a wax nose; very good; not for me to tweak the nose of my superior." But at last the man who has a mortgage on the house dropped me a note, reminding me that, if my chimney was allowed to stand in that invalid condition, my policy of insurance would be void. This was a sort of hint not to be neglected. All the world over, the picturesque yields to the pocketesque. The mortgagor cared not, but the mortgagee did.

So another operation was performed. The wax nose was taken off, and a new one fitted on. Unfortunately for the expression—being put up by a squint-eyed mason, who, at the time, had a bad stitch in the same side—the new nose stands a little awry, in the same direction.

Of one thing, however, I am proud. The horizontal dimensions of the new part are unreduced.

Large as the chimney appears upon the roof, that is nothing to its spaciousness below. At its base in the cellar, it is precisely twelve feet square; and hence covers precisely one hundred and forty-four superficial feet. What an appropriation of terra firma for a chimney, and what a huge load for this earth! In fact, it was only because I and my chimney formed no part of his ancient burden, that that stout peddler, Atlas* of old, was enabled to stand up so bravely under his pack. The dimensions given may, perhaps, seem fabulous. But, like those stones at Gilgal,* which Joshua set up for a memorial of having passed over Jordan, does not my chimney remain, even unto this day?

Very often I go down into my cellar, and attentively survey that vast square of masonry. I stand long, and ponder over, and wonder at it. It has a druidical look, away down in the umbrageous cellar there, whose numerous vaulted passages, and far glens of gloom, resemble the dark, damp depths of primeval woods. So strongly did this conceit steal over me, so deeply was I penetrated with wonder at the chimney, that one day—when I was a little out of my mind, I now think—getting a spade from the garden, I set to work, digging round the foundation, especially at the corners thereof, obscurely prompted by dreams of striking upon some old, earthen-worn memorial of that by-gone day, when, into all this gloom, the light of heaven entered, as the masons laid the foundation-stones, peradventure sweltering under an August sun, or pelted by a March storm. Plying my blunted spade, how vexed was I by that ungracious interruption of a neighbor, who, calling to see me upon some business, and being informed that I was below, said I need not be troubled to come up, but he would go down to me; and so, without ceremony, and without my having been forewarned, suddenly discovered me, digging in my cellar.

"Gold digging, sir?"

"Nay, sir," answered I, starting, "I was merely—ahem!—merely—I say I was merely digging—round my chimney."

"Ah, loosening the soil, to make it grow. Your chimney, sir, you regard as too small, I suppose; needing further development, especially at the top?"

"Sir!" said I, throwing down the spade, "do not be personal. I and my chimney—"

"Personal?"

"Sir, I look upon this chimney less as a pile of masonry than as a personage. It is the king of the house. I am but a suffered and inferior subject."

In fact, I would permit no gibes to be cast at either myself or my chimney; and never again did my visitor refer to it in my hearing, without coupling some compliment with the mention. It well deserves a respectful consideration. There it stands, solitary and alone—not a council of ten flues, but, like his sacred majesty of Russia, a unit of an autocrat.

Even to me, its dimensions, at times, seem incredible. It does not look so big—no, not even in the cellar. By the mere eye, its magnitude can be but imperfectly comprehended, because only one side can be received at one time; and said side can only present twelve feet, linear measure. But then, each other side also is twelve feet long; and the whole obviously forms a square; and twelve times twelve is one hundred and forty-four. And so, an adequate conception of the magnitude of this chimney is only to be got at by a sort of process in the higher mathematics, by a method somewhat akin to those whereby the surprising distances of fixed stars are computed.

It need hardly be said, that the walls of my house are entirely free from fire-places. These all congregate in the middle—in the one grand central chimney, upon all four sides of which are hearths—two tiers of hearths—so that when, in the various chambers, my family and guests are warming themselves of a cold winter's night, just before retiring, then, though at the time they may not be thinking so, all their faces mutually look towards each other, yea, all their feet point to one centre; and, when they go to sleep in their beds, they all sleep round one warm chimney, like so many Iroquois Indians, in the woods, round their one heap of embers. And just as the Indians' fire serves, not only to keep them comfortable, but also to keep off wolves, and other savage monsters, so my chimney, by its obvious smoke at top, keeps off prowling burglars from the towns —for what burglar or murderer would dare break into an abode from whose chimney issues such a continual smoke— betokening that if the inmates are not stirring, at least fires are, and in case of an alarm, candles may readily be lighted, to say nothing of muskets.

But stately as is the chimney—yea, grand high altar as it is, right worthy for the celebration of high mass before the Pope of Rome, and all his cardinals—yet what is there perfect in this world? Caius Julius Cæsar, had he not been so inordinately great, they say that Brutus, Cassius, Antony, and the rest, had been greater. My chimney, were it not so mighty in its magnitude, my chambers had been larger. How often has my wife ruefully told me, that my chimney, like the English aristocracy, casts a contracting shade all round it. She avers that endless domestic inconveniences arise— more particularly from the chimney's stubborn central locality. The grand objection with her is, that it stands midway in the place where a fine entrance-hall ought to be. In truth, there is no hall whatever to the house—nothing but a sort of square landing-place, as you enter from the wide front door. A roomy enough landing-place, I admit, but not attaining to the dignity of a hall. Now, as the front door is precisely in the middle of the front of the house, inwards it faces the chimney. In fact, the opposite wall of the landing-place is formed solely by the chimney; and hence—owing to the gradual tapering of the chimney—is a little less than twelve feet in width. Climbing the chimney in this part, is the principal stair-case—which, by three abrupt turns, and three minor landing-places, mounts to the second floor, where, over the front door, runs a sort of narrow gallery, something less than twelve feet long, leading to chambers on either hand. This gallery, of course, is railed; and so, looking down upon the stairs, and all those landing-places together, with the main one at bottom, resembles not a little a balcony for musicians, in some jolly old abode, in times Elizabethan.

Shall I tell a weakness? I cherish the cobwebs there, and many a time arrest Biddy in the act of brushing them with her broom, and have many a quarrel with my wife and daughters about it.

Now the ceiling, so to speak, of the place where you enter the house, that ceiling is, in fact, the ceiling of the second floor, not the first. The two floors are made one here; so that ascending this turning stairs, you seem going up into a kind of soaring tower, or light-house. At the second landing, midway up the chimney, is a mysterious door, entering to a mysterious closet; and here I keep mysterious cordials, of a choice, mysterious flavor, made so by the constant nurturing and subtle ripening of the chimney's gentle heat, distilled through that warm mass of masonry. Better for wines is it than voyages to the Indies; my chimney itself a tropic. A chair by my chimney in a November day is as good for an invalid as a long season spent in Cuba. Often I think how grapes might ripen against my chimney. How my wife's geraniums bud there! Bud in December. Her eggs, too— can't keep them near the chimney, on account of hatching. Ah, a warm heart has my chimney.

How often my wife was at me about that projected grand entrance-hall of hers, which was to be knocked clean through the chimney, from one end of the house to the other, and astonish all guests by its generous amplitude. "But, wife," said I, "the chimney—consider the chimney: if you demolish the foundation, what is to support the superstructure?" "Oh, that will rest on the second floor." The truth is, women know next to nothing about the realities of architecture. However, my wife still talked of running her entries and partitions. She spent many long nights elaborating her plans; in imagination building her boasted hall through the chimney, as though its high mightiness were a mere spear of sorrel-top. At last, I gently reminded her that, little as she might fancy it, the chimney was a fact—a sober, substantial fact, which, in all her plannings, it would be well to take into full consideration. But this was not of much avail.

And here, respectfully craving her permission, I must say a few words about this enterprising wife of mine.* Though in years nearly old as myself, in spirit she is young as my little sorrel mare, Trigger, that threw me last fall. What is extraordinary, though she comes of a rheumatic family, she is straight as a pine, never has any aches; while for me with the sciatica,* I am sometimes as crippled up as any old apple tree. But she has not so much as a toothache. As for her hearing—let me enter the house in my dusty boots, and she away up in the attic. And for her sight—Biddy, the house-maid, tells other people's housemaids, that her mistress will spy a spot on the dresser straight through the pewter plat-ter, put up on purpose to hide it. Her faculties are alert as her limbs and her senses. No danger of my spouse dying of torpor. The longest night in the year I've known her lie awake, planning her campaign for the morrow. She is a nat-ural projector. The maxim, "Whatever is, is right," is not hers. Her maxim is, Whatever is, is wrong; and what is more, must be altered; and what is still more, must be altered right away. Dreadful maxim for the wife of a dozy old dreamer like me, who dote on seventh days as days of rest, and out of a sabbatical horror of industry, will, on a week day, go out of my road a quarter of a mile, to avoid the sight of a man at work.

That matches are made in heaven, may be, but my wife would have been just the wife for Peter the Great, or Peter the Piper. How she would have set in order that huge lit-tered empire of the one, and with indefatigable painstaking picked the peck of pickled peppers for the other.

But the most wonderful thing is, my wife never thinks of her end. Her youthful incredulity, as to the plain the-ory, and still plainer fact of death, hardly seems Christian. Advanced in years, as she knows she must be, my wife seems to think that she is to teem on, and be inexhaustible for-ever. She doesn't believe in old age. At that strange promise in the plain of Mamre, my old wife, unlike old Abraham's, would not have jeeringly laughed within herself.*

Judge how to me, who, sitting in the comfortable shadow of my chimney, smoking my comfortable pipe, with ashes not unwelcome at my feet, and ashes not unwelcome all but in my mouth; and who am thus in a comfortable sort of not unwelcome, though, indeed, ashy enough way, reminded of the ultimate exhaustion even of the most fiery life; judge how to me this unwarrantable vitality in my wife must come, sometimes, it is true, with a moral and a calm, but oftener with a breeze and a ruffle.

If the doctrine be true, that in wedlock contraries attract, by how cogent a fatality must I have been drawn to my wife! While spicily impatient of present and past, like a glass of ginger-beer she overflows with her schemes; and, with like energy as she puts down her foot, puts down her preserves and her pickles, and lives with them in a continual future; or ever full of expectations both from time and space, is ever restless for newspapers, and ravenous for letters. Content with the years that are gone, taking no thought for the morrow, and looking for no new thing from any person or quarter whatever, I have not a single scheme or expectation on earth, save in unequal resistance of the undue encroachment of hers.

Old myself, I take to oldness in things; for that cause mainly loving old Montaigne,* and old cheese, and old wine; and eschewing young people, hot rolls, new books, and early potatoes, and very fond of my old claw-footed chair, and old club-footed Deacon White, my neighbor, and that still nigher old neighbor, my betwisted old grape-vine, that of a summer evening leans in his elbow for cosy company at my window-sill, while I, within doors, lean over mine to meet his; and above all, high above all, am fond of my high-mantled old chimney. But she, out of that infatuate juvenility of hers, takes to nothing but newness; for that cause mainly, loving new cider in autumn, and in spring, as if she were own daughter of Nebuchadnezzar, fairly raving after all sorts of salads and spinages, and more particularly green cucumbers (though all the time nature rebukes such unsuitable young hankerings in so elderly a person, by never permitting such things to agree with her), and has an itch after recently-discovered fine prospects (so no grave-yard be in the background), and also after Swedenborgianism, and the Spirit Rapping philosophy,* with other new views, alike in things natural and unnatural; and immortally hopeful, is forever making new flower-beds even on the north side of the house, where the bleak mountain wind would scarce allow the wiry weed called hard-hack to gain a thorough footing; and on the road-side sets out mere pipe-stems of young elms; though there is no hope of any shade from them, except over the ruins of her great granddaughters' gravestones; and won't wear caps, but plaits her gray hair; and takes the Ladies' Magazine* for the fashions; and always buys her new almanac a month before the new year; and rises at dawn; and to the warmest sunset turns a cold shoulder; and still goes on at odd hours with her new course of history, and her French, and her music; and likes young company; and offers to ride young colts; and sets out young suckers in the orchard; and has a spite against my elbowed old grape-vine, and my club-footed old neighbor, and my claw-footed old chair, and above all, high above all, would fain persecute, unto death, my high-mantled old chimney. By what perverse magic, I a thousand times think, does such a very autumnal old lady have such a very vernal young soul? When I would remonstrate at times, she spins round on me with, "Oh, don't you grumble, old man (she always calls me old man), it's I, young I, that keep you from stagnating." Well, I suppose it is so. Yea, after all, these things are well ordered. My wife, as one of her poor relations, good soul, intimates, is the salt of the earth, and none the less the salt of my sea, which otherwise were unwholesome. She is its monsoon, too, blowing a brisk gale over it, in the one steady direction of my chimney.

Not insensible of her superior energies, my wife has frequently made me propositions to take upon herself all the responsibilities of my affairs. She is desirous that, domestically, I should abdicate; that, renouncing further rule, like the venerable Charles V.,* I should retire into some sort of monastery. But indeed, the chimney excepted, I have little authority to lay down. By my wife's ingenious application of the principle that certain things belong of right to female jurisdiction, I find myself, through my easy compliances, insensibly stripped by degrees of one masculine prerogative after another. In a dream I go about my fields, a sort of lazy, happy-go-lucky, good-for-nothing, loafing, old Lear.

Only by some sudden revelation am I reminded who is over me; as year before last, one day seeing in one corner of the premises fresh deposits of mysterious boards and timbers, the oddity of the incident at length begat serious meditation. "Wife," said I, "whose boards and timbers are those I see near the orchard there? Do you know any thing about them, wife? Who put them there? You know I do not like the neighbors to use my land that way; they should ask permission first."

She regarded me with a pitying smile.

"Why, old man, don't you know I am building a new barn? Didn't you know that, old man?"

This is the poor old lady that was accusing me of tyrannizing over her.

To return now to the chimney. Upon being assured of the futility of her proposed hall, so long as the obstacle remained, for a time my wife was for a modified project. But I could never exactly comprehend it. As far as I could see through it, it seemed to involve the general idea of a sort of irregular archway, or elbowed tunnel, which was to penetrate the chimney at some convenient point under the staircase, and carefully avoiding dangerous contact with the fire-places, and particularly steering clear of the great interior flue, was to conduct the enterprising traveler from the front door all the way into the dining-room in the remote rear of the mansion. Doubtless it was a bold stroke of genius, that plan of hers, and so was Nero's when he schemed his grand canal through the Isthmus of Corinth. Nor will I take oath, that, had her project been accomplished, then, by help of lights hung at judicious intervals through the tunnel, some Belzoni* or other might not have succeeded in future ages in penetrating through the masonry, and actually emerging into the dining-room, and once there, it would have been inhospitable treatment of such a traveler to have denied him a recruiting meal.

But my bustling wife did not restrict her objections, nor in the end confine her proposed alterations to the first floor. Her ambition was of the mounting order. She ascended with her schemes to the second floor, and so to the attic. Perhaps there was some small ground for her discontent with things as they were. The truth is, there was no regular passage-way up stairs or down, unless we again except that little orchestra-gallery before mentioned. And all this was owing to the chimney, which my gamesome spouse seemed despitefully to regard as the bully of the house. On all its four sides, nearly all the chambers sidled up to the chimney for the benefit of a fire-place. The chimney would not go to them; they must needs go to it. The consequence was, almost every room, like a philosophical system, was in itself an entry, or passage-way to other rooms, and systems of rooms—a whole suite of entries, in fact. Going through the house, you seem to be forever going somewhere, and getting nowhere. It is like losing one's self in the woods; round and round the chimney you go, and if you arrive at all, it is just where you started, and so you begin again, and again get nowhere. Indeed—though I say it not in the way of fault-finding at all—never was there so labyrinthine an abode. Guests will tarry with me several weeks and every now and then, be anew astonished at some unforeseen apartment.

The puzzling nature of the mansion, resulting from the chimney, is peculiarly noticeable in the dining-room, which has no less than nine doors, opening in all directions, and into all sorts of places. A stranger for the first time entering this dining-room, and naturally taking no special heed at what door he entered, will, upon rising to depart, commit the strangest blunders. Such, for instance, as opening the first door that comes handy, and finding himself stealing up stairs by the back passage. Shutting that door, he will proceed to another, and be aghast at the cellar yawning at his feet. Trying a third, he surprises the housemaid at her work. In the end, no more relying on his own unaided efforts, he procures a trusty guide in some passing person, and in good time successfully emerges. Perhaps as curious a blunder as any, was that of a certain stylish young gentleman, a great exquisite, in whose judicious eyes my daughter Anna had found especial favor. He called upon the young lady one evening, and found her alone in the dining-room at her needle-work. He stayed rather late; and after abund-

ance of superfine discourse, all the while retaining his hat
and cane, made his profuse adieus, and with repeated graceful bows proceeded to depart, after the fashion of courtiers
from the Queen, and by so doing, opening a door at random, with one hand placed behind, very effectually succeeded in backing himself into a dark pantry, where he
carefully shut himself up, wondering there was no light in
the entry. After several strange noises as of a cat among the
crockery, he reappeared through the same door, looking uncommonly crest-fallen, and, with a deeply embarrassed air,
requested my daughter to designate at which of the nine he
should find exit. When the mischievous Anna told me the
story, she said it was surprising how unaffected and matter-
of-fact the young gentleman's manner was after his re-
appearance. He was more candid than ever, to be sure;
having inadvertently thrust his white kids into an open
drawer of Havana sugar, under the impression, probably,
that being what they call "a sweet fellow," his route might
possibly lie in that direction.

Another inconvenience resulting from the chimney is,
the bewilderment of a guest in gaining his chamber, many
strange doors lying between him and it. To direct him by
finger-posts would look rather queer; and just as queer in
him to be knocking at every door on his route, like London's
city guest, the king, at Temple Bar.

Now, of all these things and many, many more, my family continually complained. At last my wife came out with
her sweeping proposition—in toto to abolish the chimney.

"What!" said I, "abolish the chimney? To take out the
back-bone of anything, wife, is a hazardous affair. Spines
out of backs, and chimneys out of houses, are not to be
taken like frosted lead-pipes from the ground. Besides,"
added I, "the chimney is the one grand permanence of this
abode. If undisturbed by innovators, then in future ages,
when all the house shall have crumbled from it, this chimney will still survive—a Bunker Hill monument.* No, no,
wife, I can't abolish my back-bone."

So said I then. But who is sure of himself, especially an
old man, with both wife and daughters ever at his elbow

and ear? In time, I was persuaded to think a little better of it; in short, to take the matter into preliminary consideration. At length it came to pass that a master-mason—a rough sort of architect—one Mr. Scribe,* was summoned to a conference. I formally introduced him to my chimney. A previous introduction from my wife had introduced him to myself. He had been not a little employed by that lady, in preparing plans and estimates for some of her extensive operations in drainage. Having, with much ado, extorted from my spouse the promise that she would leave us to an unmolested survey, I began by leading Mr. Scribe down to the root of the matter, in the cellar. Lamp in hand, I descended; for though up stairs it was noon, below it was night.

We seemed in the pyramids; and I, with one hand holding my lamp over head, and with the other pointing out, in the obscurity, the hoar mass of the chimney, seemed some Arab guide, showing the cobwebbed mausoleum of the great god Apis.

"This is a most remarkable structure, sir," said the master-mason, after long contemplating it in silence, "a most remarkable structure, sir."

"Yes," said I complacently, "every one says so."

"But large as it appears above the roof, I would not have inferred the magnitude of this foundation, sir," eyeing it critically.

Then taking out his rule, he measured it.

"Twelve feet square; one hundred and forty-four square feet! sir, this house would appear to have been built simply for the accommodation of your chimney."

"Yes, my chimney and me. Tell me candidly, now," I added, "would you have such a famous chimney abolished?"

"I wouldn't have it in a house of mine, sir, for a gift," was the reply. "It's a losing affair altogether, sir. Do you know, sir, that in retaining this chimney, you are losing, not only one hundred and forty-four square feet of good ground, but likewise a considerable interest upon a considerable principal?"

"How?"

"Look, sir," said he, taking a bit of red chalk from his pocket, and figuring against a whitewashed wall, "twenty times eight is so and so; then forty-two times thirty-nine is so and so—aint it, sir? Well, add those together, and subtract this here, then that makes so and so," still chalking away.

To be brief, after no small ciphering, Mr. Scribe informed me that my chimney contained, I am ashamed to say how many thousand and odd valuable bricks.

"No more," said I fidgeting. "Pray now, let us have a look above."

In that upper zone we made two more circumnavigations for the first and second floors. That done, we stood together at the foot of the stairway by the front door; my hand upon the knob, and Mr. Scribe hat in hand.

"Well, sir," said he, a sort of feeling his way, and, to help himself, fumbling with his hat, "well, sir, I think it can be done."

"What, pray, Mr. Scribe; *what* can be done?"

"Your chimney, sir; it can without rashness be removed, I think."

"*I* will think of it, too, Mr. Scribe," said I, turning the knob, and bowing him towards the open space without, "I will *think* of it, sir; it demands consideration; much obliged to ye; good morning, Mr. Scribe."

"It is all arranged, then," cried my wife with great glee, bursting from the nighest room.

"When will they begin?" demanded my daughter Julia.

"To-morrow?" asked Anna.

"Patience, patience, my dears," said I, "such a big chimney is not to be abolished in a minute."

Next morning it began again.

"You remember the chimney," said my wife.

"Wife," said I, "it is never out of my house, and never out of my mind."

"But when is Mr. Scribe to begin to pull it down?" asked Anna.

"Not to-day, Anna," said I.

"*When*, then?" demanded Julia, in alarm.

Now, if this chimney of mine was, for size, a sort of belfry, for ding-donging at me about it, my wife and daughters were a sort of bells, always chiming together, or taking up each other's melodies at every pause, my wife the key-clapper of all. A very sweet ringing, and pealing, and chiming, I confess; but then, the most silvery of bells may, sometimes, dismally toll, as well as merrily play. And as touching the subject in question, it became so now. Perceiving a strange relapse of opposition in me, wife and daughters began a soft and dirge-like, melancholy tolling over it.

At length my wife, getting much excited, declared to me, with pointed finger, that so long as that chimney stood, she should regard it as the monument of what she called my broken pledge. But finding this did not answer, the next day, she gave me to understand that either she or the chimney must quit the house.

Finding matters coming to such a pass, I and my pipe philosophized over them awhile, and finally concluded between us, that little as our hearts went with the plan, yet for peace' sake, I might write out the chimney's death-warrant, and, while my hand was in, scratch a note to Mr. Scribe.

Considering that I, and my chimney, and my pipe, from having been so much together, were three great cronies, the facility with which my pipe consented to a project so fatal to the goodliest of our trio; or rather, the way in which I and my pipe, in secret, conspired together, as it were, against our unsuspicious old comrade—this may seem rather strange, if not suggestive of sad reflections upon us two. But, indeed, we, sons of clay, that is my pipe and I, are no whit better than the rest. Far from us, indeed, to have volunteered the betrayal of our crony. We are of a peaceable nature, too. But that love of peace it was which made us false to a mutual friend, as soon as his cause demanded a vigorous vindication. But I rejoice to add, that better and braver thoughts soon returned, as will now briefly be set forth.

To my note, Mr. Scribe replied in person.

Once more we made a survey, mainly now with a view to a pecuniary estimate.

"I will do it for five hundred dollars," said Mr. Scribe at last, again hat in hand.

"Very well, Mr. Scribe, I will think of it," replied I, again bowing him to the door.

Not unvexed by this, for the second time, unexpected response, again he withdrew, and from my wife and daughters again burst the old exclamations.

The truth is, resolve how I would, at the last pinch I and my chimney could not be parted.

"So Holofernes* will have his way, never mind whose heart breaks for it," said my wife next morning, at breakfast, in that half-didactic, half-reproachful way of hers, which is harder to bear than her most energetic assault. Holofernes, too, is with her a pet name for any fell domestic despot. So, whenever, against her most ambitious innovations, those which saw me quite across the grain, I, as in the present instance, stand with however little steadfastness on the defence, she is sure to call me Holofernes, and ten to one takes the first opportunity to read aloud, with a suppressed emphasis, of an evening, the first newspaper paragraph about some tyrannic day-laborer, who, after being for many years the Caligula* of his family, ends by beating his long-suffering spouse to death, with a garret door wrenched off its hinges, and then, pitching his little innocents out of the window, suicidally turns inward towards the broken wall scored with the butcher's and baker's bills, and so rushes headlong to his dreadful account.

Nevertheless, for a few days, not a little to my surprise, I heard no further reproaches. An intense calm pervaded my wife, but beneath which, as in the sea, there was no knowing what portentous movements might be going on. She frequently went abroad, and in a direction which I thought not unsuspicious; namely, in the direction of New Petra, a griffin-like house of wood and stucco, in the highest style of ornamental art, graced with four chimneys in the form of erect dragons spouting smoke from their nostrils; the elegant modern residence of Mr. Scribe, which he had built for the purpose of a standing advertisement, not more of his taste as an architect, than his solidity as a master-mason.

At last, smoking my pipe one morning, I heard a rap at the door, and my wife, with an air unusually quiet for her, brought me a note. As I have no correspondents except Solomon, with whom, in his sentiments, at least, I entirely correspond, the note occasioned me some little surprise, which was not diminished upon reading the following:—

"NEW PETRA, April 1st.

"SIR:—During my last examination of your chimney, possibly you may have noted that I frequently applied my rule to it in a manner apparently unnecessary. Possibly also, at the same time, you might have observed in me more or less of perplexity, to which, however, I refrained from giving any verbal expression.

"I now feel it obligatory upon me to inform you of what was then but a dim suspicion, and as such would have been unwise to give utterance to, but which now, from various subsequent calculations assuming no little probability, it may be important that you should not remain in further ignorance of.

"It is my solemn duty to warn you, sir, that there is architectural cause to conjecture that somewhere concealed in your chimney is a reserved space, hermetically closed, in short, a secret chamber, or rather closet. How long it has been there, it is for me impossible to say. What it contains is hid, with itself, in darkness. But probably a secret closet would not have been contrived except for some extraordinary object, whether for the concealment of treasure, or what other purpose, may be left to those better acquainted with the history of the house to guess.

"But enough: in making this disclosure, sir, my conscience is eased. Whatever step you choose to take upon it, is of course a matter of indifference to me; though, I confess, as respects the character of the closet, I cannot but share in a natural curiosity.

"Trusting that you may be guided aright, in determining whether it is Christian-like knowingly to reside in a house, hidden in which is a secret closet,

"I remain,
"With much respect,
"Yours very humbly,
"HIRAM SCRIBE."

My first thought upon reading this note was, not of the alleged mystery of manner to which, at the outset, it alluded

—for none such had I at all observed in the master mason during his surveys—but of my late kinsman, Captain Julian Dacres,* long a ship-master and merchant in the Indian trade, who, about thirty years ago, and at the ripe age of ninety, died a bachelor, and in this very house, which he had built. He was supposed to have retired into this country with a large fortune. But to the general surprise, after being at great cost in building himself this mansion, he settled down into a sedate, reserved, and inexpensive old age, which by the neighbors was thought all the better for his heirs: but lo! upon opening the will, his property was found to consist but of the house and grounds, and some ten thousand dollars in stocks; but the place, being found heavily mortgaged, was in consequence sold. Gossip had its day, and left the grass quietly to creep over the captain's grave, where he still slumbers in a privacy as unmolested as if the billows of the Indian Ocean, instead of the billows of inland verdure, rolled over him. Still, I remembered long ago, hearing strange solutions whispered by the country people for the mystery involving his will, and, by reflex, himself; and that, too, as well in conscience as purse. But people who could circulate the report (which they did), that Captain Julian Dacres had, in his day, been a Borneo pirate, surely were not worthy of credence in their collateral notions. It is queer what wild whimsies of rumors will, like toadstools, spring up about any eccentric stranger, who, settling down among a rustic population, keeps quietly to himself. With some, inoffensiveness would seem a prime cause of offense. But what chiefly had led me to scout at these rumors, particularly as referring to concealed treasure, was the circumstance, that the stranger (the same who razeed the roof and the chimney) into whose hands the estate had passed on my kinsman's death, was of that sort of character, that had there been the least ground for those reports, he would speedily have tested them, by tearing down and rummaging the walls.

Nevertheless, the note of Mr. Scribe, so strangely recalling the memory of my kinsman, very naturally chimed in with what had been mysterious, or at least unexplained, about him; vague flashings of ingots united in my mind with vague gleamings of skulls. But the first cool thought soon dismissed such chimeras; and, with a calm smile, I turned towards my wife, who, meantime, had been sitting near by, impatient enough, I dare say, to know who could have taken it into his head to write me a letter.

"Well, old man," said she, "who is it from, and what is it about?"

"Read it, wife," said I, handing it.

Read it she did, and then—such an explosion! I will not pretend to describe her emotions, or repeat her expressions. Enough that my daughters were quickly called in to share the excitement. Although they had never before dreamed of such a revelation as Mr. Scribe's; yet upon the first suggestion they instinctively saw the extreme likelihood of it. In corroboration, they cited first my kinsman, and second, my chimney; alleging that the profound mystery involving the former, and the equally profound masonry involving the latter, though both acknowledged facts, were alike preposterous on any other supposition than the secret closet.

But all this time I was quietly thinking to myself: Could it be hidden from me that my credulity in this instance would operate very favorably to a certain plan of theirs? How to get to the secret closet, or how to have any certainty about it at all, without making such fell work with the chimney as to render its set destruction superfluous? That my wife wished to get rid of the chimney, it needed no reflection to show; and that Mr. Scribe, for all his pretended disinterestedness, was not opposed to pocketing five hundred dollars by the operation, seemed equally evident. That my wife had, in secret, laid heads together with Mr. Scribe, I at present refrain from affirming. But when I consider her enmity against my chimney, and the steadiness with which at the last she is wont to carry out her schemes, if by hook or by crook she can, especially after having been once baffled, why, I scarcely knew at what step of hers to be surprised.

Of one thing only was I resolved, that I and my chimney should not budge.

In vain all protests. Next morning I went out into the road, where I had noticed a diabolical-looking old gander, that, for its doughty exploits in the way of scratching into forbidden inclosures, had been rewarded by its master with a portentous, four-pronged, wooden decoration, in the shape of a collar of the Order of the Garotte.* This gander I cornered, and rummaging out its stiffest quill, plucked it, took it home, and making a stiff pen, inscribed the following stiff note:

"CHIMNEY SIDE, April 2.

"Mr. SCRIBE.

"Sir:—For your conjecture, we return you our joint thanks and compliments, and beg leave to assure you, that

"We shall remain,

"Very faithfully,

"The same,

"I and my Chimney."

Of course, for this epistle we had to endure some pretty sharp raps. But having at last explicitly understood from me that Mr. Scribe's note had not altered my mind one jot, my wife, to move me, among other things said, that if she remembered aright, there was a statute placing the keeping in private houses of secret closets on the same unlawful footing with the keeping of gunpowder. But it had no effect.

A few days after, my spouse changed her key.

It was nearly midnight, and all were in bed but ourselves, who sat up, one in each chimney-corner; she, needles in hand, indefatigably knitting a sock; I, pipe in mouth, indolently weaving my vapors.

It was one of the first of the chill nights in autumn. There was a fire on the hearth, burning low. The air without was torpid and heavy; the wood, by an oversight, of the sort called soggy.

"Do look at the chimney," she began; "can't you see that something must be in it?"

"Yes, wife. Truly there is smoke in the chimney, as in Mr. Scribe's note."

"Smoke? Yes, indeed, and in my eyes, too. How you two wicked old sinners do smoke!—this wicked old chimney and you."

"Wife," said I, "I and my chimney like to have a quiet smoke together, it is true, but we don't like to be called names."

"Now, dear old man," said she, softening down, and a little shifting the subject, "when you think of that old kinsman of yours, you *know* there must be a secret closet in this chimney."

"Secret ash-hole, wife, why don't you have it? Yes, I dare say there is a secret ash-hole in the chimney; for where do all the ashes go to that we drop down the queer hole yonder?"

"I know where they go to; I've been there almost as many times as the cat."

"What devil, wife, prompted you to crawl into the ash-hole! Don't you know that St. Dunstan's devil* emerged from the ash-hole? You will get your death one of these days, exploring all about as you do. But supposing there be a secret closet, what then?"

"What, then? why what should be in a secret closet but——"

"Dry bones, wife," broke in I with a puff, while the sociable old chimney broke in with another.

"There again! Oh, how this wretched old chimney smokes," wiping her eyes with her handkerchief. "I've no doubt the reason it smokes so is, because that secret closet interferes with the flue. Do see, too, how the jams here keep settling; and it's down hill all the way from the door to this hearth. This horrid old chimney will fall on our heads yet; depend upon it, old man."

"Yes, wife, I do depend on it; yes, indeed, I place every dependence on my chimney. As for its settling, I like it. I, too, am settling, you know, in my gait. I and my chimney are settling together, and shall keep settling, too, till, as in a great feather-bed, we shall both have settled away clean out of sight. But this secret oven; I mean, secret closet of yours, wife; where exactly do you suppose that secret closet is?"

"That is for Mr. Scribe to say."

"But suppose he cannot say exactly; what, then?"

"Why then he can prove, I am sure, that it must be some-where or other in this horrid old chimney."

"And if he can't prove that; what, then?"

"Why then, old man," with a stately air, "I shall say little more about it."

"Agreed, wife," returned I, knocking my pipe-bowl against the jam, "and now, to-morrow, I will a third time send for Mr. Scribe. Wife, the sciatica takes me; be so good as to put this pipe on the mantel."

"If you get the step-ladder for me, I will. This shocking old chimney, this abominable old-fashioned old chimney's mantels are so high, I can't reach them."

No opportunity, however trivial, was overlooked for a sub-ordinate fling at the pile.

Here, by way of introduction, it should be mentioned, that besides the fire-places all round it, the chimney was, in the most hap-hazard way, excavated on each floor for certain curious out-of-the-way cupboards and closets, of all sorts and sizes, clinging here and there, like nests in the crotches of some old oak. On the second floor these closets were by far the most irregular and numerous. And yet this should hardly have been so, since the theory of the chim-ney was, that it pyramidically diminished as it ascended. The abridgment of its square on the roof was obvious enough; and it was supposed that the reduction must be methodically graduated from bottom to top.

"Mr. Scribe," said I when, the next day, with an eager aspect, that individual again came, "my object in sending for you this morning is, not to arrange for the demolition of my chimney, nor to have any particular conversation about it, but simply to allow you every reasonable facility for verifying, if you can, the conjecture communicated in your note."

Though in secret not a little crestfallen, it may be, by my phlegmatic reception, so different from what he had looked for; with much apparent alacrity he commenced the survey; throwing open the cupboards on the first floor, and peering into the closets on the second; measuring one within, and then comparing that measurement with the measurement without. Removing the fire-boards, he would gaze up the flues. But no sign of the hidden work yet.

Now, on the second floor the rooms were the most rambling conceivable. They, as it were, dovetailed into each other. They were of all shapes; not one mathematically square room among them all—a peculiarity which by the master-mason had not been unobserved. With a significant, not to say portentous expression, he took a circuit of the chimney, measuring the area of each room around it; then going down stairs, and out of doors, he measured the entire ground area; then compared the sum total of all the areas of all the rooms on the second floor with the ground area; then, returning to me in no small excitement, announced that there was a difference of no less than two hundred and odd square feet—room enough, in all conscience, for a secret closet.

"But, Mr. Scribe," said I stroking my chin, "have you allowed for the walls, both main and sectional? They take up some space, you know."

"Ah, I had forgotten that," tapping his forehead; "but," still ciphering on his paper, "that will not make up the deficiency."

"But, Mr. Scribe, have you allowed for the recesses of so many fire-places on a floor, and for the fire-walls, and the flues; in short, Mr. Scribe, have you allowed for the legitimate chimney itself—some one hundred and forty-four square feet or thereabouts, Mr. Scribe?"

"How unaccountable. That slipped my mind, too."

"Did it, indeed, Mr. Scribe?"

He faltered a little, and burst forth with, "But we must not allow one hundred and forty-four square feet for the legitimate chimney. My position is, that within those undue limits the secret closet is contained."

I eyed him in silence a moment; then spoke:

"Your survey is concluded, Mr. Scribe; be so good now as to lay your finger upon the exact part of the chimney wall where you believe this secret closet to be; or would a witch-hazel wand* assist you, Mr. Scribe?"

"No, sir, but a crow-bar would," he, with temper, rejoined.

Here, now, thought I to myself, the cat leaps out of the bag. I looked at him with a calm glance, under which he seemed somewhat uneasy. More than ever now I suspected a plot. I remembered what my wife had said about abiding by the decision of Mr. Scribe. In a bland way, I resolved to buy up the decision of Mr. Scribe.

"Sir," said I, "really, I am much obliged to you for this survey. It has quite set my mind at rest. And no doubt you, too, Mr. Scribe, must feel much relieved. Sir," I added, "you have made three visits to the chimney. With a business man, time is money. Here are fifty dollars, Mr. Scribe. Nay, take it. You have earned it. Your opinion is worth it. And by the way,"—as he modestly received the money—"have you any objections to give me a—a—little certificate—something, say, like a steam-boat certificate, certifying that you, a competent surveyor, have surveyed my chimney, and found no reason to believe any unsoundness;* in short, any—any secret closet in it. Would you be so kind, Mr. Scribe?"

"But, but, sir," stammered he with honest hesitation.

"Here, here are pen and paper," said I, with entire assurance.

Enough.

That evening I had the certificate framed and hung over the dining-room fire-place, trusting that the continual sight of it would forever put at rest at once the dreams and stratagems of my household.

But, no. Inveterately bent upon the extirpation of that noble old chimney, still to this day my wife goes about it, with my daughter Anna's geological hammer, tapping the wall all over, and then holding her ear against it, as I have seen the physicians of life insurance companies tap a man's chest, and then incline over for the echo. Sometimes of nights she almost frightens one, going about on this phantom errand, and still following the sepulchral response of the chimney, round and round, as if it were leading her to the threshold of the secret closet.

"How hollow it sounds," she will hollowly cry. "Yes, I declare," with an emphatic tap, "there is a secret closet here. Here, in this very spot. Hark! How hollow!"

"Psha! wife, of course it is hollow. Who ever heard of a solid chimney?"

But nothing avails. And my daughters take after, not me, but their mother.

Sometimes all three abandon the theory of the secret closet, and return to the genuine ground of attack—the unsightliness of so cumbrous a pile, with comments upon the great addition of room to be gained by its demolition, and the fine effect of the projected grand hall, and the convenience resulting from the collateral running in one direction and another of their various partitions. Not more ruthlessly did the Three Powers partition away poor Poland,* than my wife and daughters would fain partition away my chimney.

But seeing that, despite all, I and my chimney still smoke our pipes, my wife reoccupies the ground of the secret closet, enlarging upon what wonders are there, and what a shame it is, not to seek it out and explore it.

"Wife," said I, upon one of these occasions, "why speak more of that secret closet, when there before you hangs contrary testimony of a master mason, elected by yourself to decide. Besides, even if there were a secret closet, secret it should remain, and secret it shall. Yes, wife, here for once I must say my say. Infinite sad mischief has resulted from the profane bursting open of secret recesses. Though standing in the heart of this house, though hitherto we have all nestled about it, unsuspicious of aught hidden within, this chimney may or may not have a secret closet. But if it have, it is my kinsman's. To break into that wall, would be to break into his breast. And that wall-breaking wish of Momus* I account the wish of a church-robbing gossip and knave. Yes, wife, a vile eaves-dropping varlet was Momus."

"Moses?—Mumps? Stuff with your mumps and your Moses!"

The truth is, my wife, like all the rest of the world, cares not a fig for my philosophical jabber. In dearth of other philosophical companionship, I and my chimney have to smoke and philosophize together. And sitting up so late as we do at it, a mighty smoke it is that we two smoky old philosophers make.

But my spouse, who likes the smoke of my tobacco as little as she does that of the soot, carries on her war against both. I live in continual dread lest, like the golden bowl,* the pipes of me and my chimney shall yet be broken. To stay that mad project of my wife's, naught answers. Or, rather, she herself is incessantly answering, incessantly besetting me with her terrible alacrity for improvement, which is a softer name for destruction. Scarce a day I do not find her with her tape-measure, measuring for her grand hall, while Anna holds a yard-stick on one side, and Julia looks approvingly on from the other. Mysterious intimations appear in the nearest village paper, signed "Claude," to the effect that a certain structure, standing on a certain hill, is a sad blemish to an otherwise lovely landscape. Anonymous letters arrive, threatening me with I know not what, unless I remove my chimney. Is it my wife, too, or who, that sets up the neighbors to badgering me on the same subject, and hinting to me that my chimney, like a huge elm, absorbs all moisture from my garden? At night, also, my wife will start from sleep, professing to hear ghostly noises from the secret closet. Assailed on all sides, and in all ways, small peace have I and my chimney.

Were it not for the baggage, we would together pack up, and remove from the country.

What narrow escapes have been ours! Once I found in a drawer a whole portfolio of plans and estimates. Another time, upon returning after a day's absence, I discovered my wife standing before the chimney in earnest conversation with a person whom I at once recognized as a meddlesome architectural reformer, who, because he had no gift for putting up anything, was ever intent upon pulling down; in various parts of the country having prevailed upon half-witted old folks to destroy their old-fashioned houses, particularly the chimneys.

But worst of all was, that time I unexpectedly returned at early morning from a visit to the city, and upon approaching the house, narrowly escaped three brickbats which fell, from high aloft, at my feet. Glancing up, what was my horror to see three savages, in blue jean overalls, in the very act of

commencing the long-threatened attack. Aye, indeed, thinking of those three brickbats, I and my chimney have had
narrow escapes.

It is now some seven years since I have stirred from
home. My city friends all wonder why I don't come to see
them, as in former times. They think I am getting sour and
unsocial. Some say that I have become a sort of mossy old
misanthrope,* while all the time the fact is, I am simply
standing guard over my mossy old chimney; for it is resolved
between me and my chimney, that I and my chimney will
never surrender.

BILLY BUDD, SAILOR
(An Inside Narrative) *

Dedicated to JACK CHASE,* Englishman
Wherever that great heart may now be
Here on Earth or harbored in Paradise
Captain of the Maintop in the year 1843
in the U.S. Frigate *United States*

1

IN the time before steamships, or then more frequently than
now, a stroller along the docks of any considerable seaport
would occasionally have his attention arrested by a group
of bronzed mariners, man-of-war's men or merchant sailors
in holiday attire, ashore on liberty. In certain instances they
would flank, or like a bodyguard quite surround, some superior figure of their own class, moving along with them like
Aldebaran* among the lesser lights of his constellation. That
signal object was the "Handsome Sailor" of the less prosaic
time* alike of the military and merchant navies. With no perceptible trace of the vainglorious about him, rather with the
offhand unaffectedness of natural regality, he seemed to accept
the spontaneous homage of his shipmates.

A somewhat remarkable instance recurs to me. In Liverpool, now half a century ago, I saw under the shadow of
the great dingy street-wall of Prince's Dock (an obstruction
long since removed) a common sailor so intensely black that
he must needs have been a native African of the unadulterate blood of Ham*—a symmetric figure much above the
average height. The two ends of a gay silk handkerchief
thrown loose about the neck danced upon the displayed
ebony of his chest, in his ears were big hoops of gold, and
a Highland bonnet with a tartan band set off his shapely
head. It was a hot noon in July; and his face, lustrous with
perspiration, beamed with barbaric good humor. In jovial

sallies right and left, his white teeth flashing into view, he rollicked along, the center of a company of his shipmates. These were made up of such an assortment of tribes and complexions as would have well fitted them to be marched up by Anacharsis Cloots* before the bar of the first French Assembly as Representatives of the Human Race. At each spontaneous tribute rendered by the wayfarers to this black pagod of a fellow—the tribute of a pause and stare, and less frequently an exclamation—the motley retinue showed that they took that sort of pride in the evoker of it which the Assyrian priests doubtless showed for their grand sculptured Bull when the faithful prostrated themselves.

To return. If in some cases a bit of a nautical Murat in setting forth his person ashore, the Handsome Sailor of the period in question evinced nothing of the dandified Billy-be-Dam, an amusing character all but extinct now, but occasionally to be encountered, and in a form yet more amusing than the original, at the tiller of the boats on the tempestuous Erie Canal* or, more likely, vaporing in the groggeries along the towpath. Invariably a proficient in his perilous calling, he was also more or less of a mighty boxer or wrestler. It was strength and beauty. Tales of his prowess were recited. Ashore he was the champion; afloat the spokesman; on every suitable occasion always foremost. Close-reefing topsails in a gale, there he was, astride the weather yardarm-end, foot in the Flemish horse as stirrup, both hands tugging at the earing as at a bridle, in very much the attitude of young Alexander curbing the fiery Bucephalus.* A superb figure, tossed up as by the horns of Taurus against the thunderous sky, cheerily hallooing to the strenuous file along the spar.

The moral nature was seldom out of keeping with the physical make. Indeed, except as toned by the former, the comeliness and power, always attractive in masculine conjunction, hardly could have drawn the sort of honest homage the Handsome Sailor in some examples received from his less gifted associates.

Such a cynosure, at least in aspect, and something such too in nature, though with important variations made apparent as the story proceeds, was welkin-eyed* Billy Budd—or

Baby Budd, as more familiarly, under circumstances hereafter to be given, he at last came to be called—aged twenty-one, a foretopman of the British fleet toward the close of the last decade of the eighteenth century. It was not very long prior to the time of the narration that follows that he had entered the King's service, having been impressed on the Narrow Seas* from a homeward-bound English merchantman into a seventy-four outward bound, H.M.S. *Bellipotent*;* which ship, as was not unusual in those hurried days, having been obliged to put to sea short of her proper complement of men. Plump upon Billy at first sight in the gangway the boarding officer, Lieutenant Ratcliffe, pounced, even before the merchantman's crew was formally mustered on the quarter-deck for his deliberate inspection. And him only he elected. For whether it was because the other men when ranged before him showed to ill advantage after Billy, or whether he had some scruples in view of the merchantman's being rather short-handed, however it might be, the officer contented himself with his first spontaneous choice. To the surprise of the ship's company, though much to the lieutenant's satisfaction, Billy made no demur. But, indeed, any demur would have been as idle as the protest of a goldfinch popped into a cage.

Noting this uncomplaining acquiescence, all but cheerful, one might say, the shipmaster turned a surprised glance of silent reproach at the sailor. The shipmaster was one of those worthy mortals found in every vocation, even the humbler ones—the sort of person whom everybody agrees in calling "a respectable man." And—nor so strange to report as it may appear to be—though a ploughman of the troubled waters, lifelong contending with the intractable elements, there was nothing this honest soul at heart loved better than simple peace and quiet. For the rest, he was fifty or thereabouts, a little inclined to corpulence, a prepossessing face, unwhiskered, and of an agreeable color—a rather full face, humanely intelligent in expression. On a fair day with a fair wind and all going well, a certain musical chime in his voice seemed to be the veritable unobstructed outcome of the innermost man. He had much prudence, much conscientiousness,

and there were occasions when these virtues were the cause
of overmuch disquietude in him. On a passage, so long as
his craft was in any proximity to land, no sleep for Captain
Graveling. He took to heart those serious responsibilities not
so heavily borne by some shipmasters.

Now while Billy Budd was down in the forecastle getting his kit together, the *Bellipotent's* lieutenant, burly and
bluff, nowise disconcerted by Captain Graveling's omitting to
proffer the customary hospitalities on an occasion so unwelcome to him, an omission simply caused by preoccupation
of thought, unceremoniously invited himself into the cabin,
and also to a flask from the spirit locker, a receptacle which
his experienced eye instantly discovered. In fact he was one
of those sea dogs in whom all the hardship and peril of naval
life in the great prolonged wars of his time never impaired
the natural instinct for sensuous enjoyment. His duty he
always faithfully did; but duty is sometimes a dry obliga-
tion, and he was for irrigating its aridity, whensoever possible, with a fertilizing decoction of strong waters. For the
cabin's proprietor there was nothing left but to play the part
of the enforced host with whatever grace and alacrity were
practicable. As necessary adjuncts to the flask, he silently
placed tumbler and water jug before the irrepressible guest.
But excusing himself from partaking just then, he dismally
watched the unembarrassed officer deliberately diluting his
grog a little, then tossing it off in three swallows, pushing
the empty tumbler away, yet not so far as to be beyond
easy reach, at the same time settling himself in his seat and
smacking his lips with high satisfaction, looking straight at
the host.

These proceedings over, the master broke the silence;
and there lurked a rueful reproach in the tone of his voice:
"Lieutenant, you are going to take my best man from me,
the jewel of 'em."

"Yes, I know," rejoined the other, immediately drawing
back the tumbler preliminary to a replenishing. "Yes, I know.
Sorry."

"Beg pardon, but you don't understand, Lieutenant. See
here, now. Before I shipped that young fellow, my forecastle

was a rat-pit of quarrels. It was black times, I tell you,
aboard the *Rights* here. I was worried to that degree my pipe
had no comfort for me. But Billy came; and it was like a
Catholic priest striking peace in an Irish shindy. Not that
he preached to them or said or did anything in particular;
but a virtue went out of him, sugaring the sour ones. They
took to him like hornets to treacle; all but the buffer of the
gang, the big shaggy chap with the fire-red whiskers. He
indeed, out of envy, perhaps, of the newcomer, and thinking such a "sweet and pleasant fellow," as he mockingly designated him to the others, could hardly have the spirit of a
gamecock, must needs bestir himself in trying to get up an
ugly row with him. Billy forebore with him and reasoned
with him in a pleasant way—he is something like myself,
Lieutenant, to whom aught like a quarrel is hateful—but
nothing served. So, in the second dogwatch one day, the
Red Whiskers in presence of the others, under pretense of
showing Billy just whence a sirloin steak was cut—for the
fellow had once been a butcher—insultingly gave him a dig
under the ribs. Quick as lightning Billy let fly his arm. I
dare say he never meant to do quite as much as he did,
but anyhow he gave the burly fool a terrible drubbing. It
took about half a minute, I should think. And, lord bless
you, the lubber was astonished at the celerity. And will you
believe it, Lieutenant, the Red Whiskers now really loves
Billy—loves him, or is the biggest hypocrite that ever I heard
of. But they all love him. Some of 'em do his washing, darn
his old trousers for him; the carpenter is at odd times making a pretty little chest of drawers for him. Anybody will do
anything for Billy Budd; and it's the happy family here. But
now, Lieutenant, if that young fellow goes—I know how it
will be aboard the *Rights*. Not again very soon shall I, coming up from dinner, lean over the capstan smoking a quiet
pipe—no, not very soon again, I think. Ay, Lieutenant, you
are going to take away the jewel of 'em; you are going to
take away my peacemaker!" And with that the good soul
had really some ado in checking a rising sob.

"Well," said the lieutenant, who had listened with amused
interest to all this and now was waxing merry with his tipple;

"well, blessed are the peacemakers, especially the fighting peacemakers. And such are the seventy-four beauties some of which you see poking their noses out of the portholes of yonder warship lying to for me," pointing through the cabin window at the *Bellipotent*. "But courage! Don't look so downhearted, man. Why, I pledge you in advance the royal approbation. Rest assured that His Majesty will be delighted to know that in a time when his hardtack is not sought for by sailors with such avidity as should be, a time also when some shipmasters privily resent the borrowing from them a tar or two for the service; His Majesty, I say, will be delighted to learn that *one* shipmaster at least cheerfully surrenders to the King the flower of his flock, a sailor who with equal loyalty makes no dissent.—But where's my beauty? Ah," looking through the cabin's open door, "here he comes; and, by Jove, lugging along his chest—Apollo with his portmanteau!—My man," stepping out to him, "you can't take that big box aboard a warship. The boxes there are mostly shot boxes. Put your duds in a bag, lad. Boot and saddle for the cavalryman, bag and hammock for the man-of-war's man."

The transfer from chest to bag was made. And, after seeing his man into the cutter and then following him down, the lieutenant pushed off from the *Rights-of-Man*.* That was the merchant ship's name, though by her master and crew abbreviated in sailor fashion into the *Rights*. The hard-headed Dundee owner was a staunch admirer of Thomas Paine, whose book in rejoinder to Burke's arraignment of the French Revolution had then been published for some time and had gone everywhere. In christening his vessel after the title of Paine's volume the man of Dundee was something like his contemporary shipowner, Stephen Girard of Philadelphia, whose sympathies, alike with his native land and its liberal philosophers, he evinced by naming his ships after Voltaire, Diderot, and so forth.

But now, when the boat swept under the merchantman's stern, and officer and oarsmen were noting—some bitterly and others with a grin—the name emblazoned there; just then it was that the new recruit jumped up from the bow where the coxswain had directed him to sit, and waving hat to his silent shipmates sorrowfully looking over at him from the taffrail, bade the lads a genial good-bye. Then, making a salutation as to the ship herself, "And good-bye to you too, old *Rights-of-Man.*"

"Down, sir!" roared the lieutenant, instantly assuming all the rigor of his rank, though with difficulty repressing a smile.

To be sure, Billy's action was a terrible breach of naval decorum. But in that decorum he had never been instructed; in consideration of which the lieutenant would hardly have been so energetic in reproof but for the concluding farewell to the ship. This he rather took as meant to convey a covert sally on the new recruit's part, a sly slur at impressment in general, and that of himself in especial. And yet, more likely, if satire it was in effect, it was hardly so by intention, for Billy, though happily endowed with the gaiety of high health, youth, and a free heart, was yet by no means of a satirical turn. The will to it and the sinister dexterity were alike wanting. To deal in double meanings and insinuations of any sort was quite foreign to his nature.

As to his enforced enlistment, that he seemed to take pretty much as he was wont to take any vicissitude of weather. Like the animals, though no philosopher, he was, without knowing it, practically a fatalist. And it may be that he rather liked this adventurous turn in his affairs, which promised an opening into novel scenes and martial excitements.

Aboard the *Bellipotent* our merchant sailor was forthwith rated as an able seaman and assigned to the starboard watch of the foretop. He was soon at home in the service, not at all disliked for his unpretentious good looks and a sort of genial happy-go-lucky air. No merrier man in his mess: in marked contrast to certain other individuals included like himself among the impressed portion of the ship's company; for these when not actively employed were sometimes, and more particularly in the last dogwatch when the drawing near of twilight induced revery, apt to fall into a saddish mood which in some partook of sullenness. But they were not so young as our foretopman, and no few of them must have known a hearth of some sort, others may have had wives and children left, too probably, in uncertain circumstances, and hardly any but must have had acknowledged kith and kin, while for Billy, as will shortly be seen, his entire family was practically invested in himself.

2

THOUGH our new-made foretopman was well received in the top and on the gun decks, hardly here was he that cynosure he had previously been among those minor ship's companies of the merchant marine, with which companies only had he hitherto consorted.

He was young; and despite his all but fully developed frame, in aspect looked even younger than he really was, owing to a lingering adolescent expression in the as yet smooth face all but feminine in purity of natural complexion but where, thanks to his seagoing, the lily was quite suppressed and the rose had some ado visibly to flush through the tan.

To one essentially such a novice in the complexities of factitious life, the abrupt transition from his former and simpler sphere to the ampler and more knowing world of a great warship; this might well have abashed him had there been any conceit or vanity in his composition. Among her miscellaneous multitude, the *Bellipotent* mustered several individuals who however inferior in grade were of no common natural stamp, sailors more signally susceptive of that air which continuous martial discipline and repeated presence in battle can in some degree impart even to the average man. As the Handsome Sailor, Billy Budd's position aboard the seventy-four was something analogous to that of a rustic beauty transplanted from the provinces and brought into competition with the highborn dames of the court. But this change of circumstances he scarce noted. As little did he observe that something about him provoked an ambiguous smile in one or two harder faces among the bluejackets. Nor less unaware was he of the peculiar favorable effect his person and demeanor had upon the more intelligent gentlemen of the quarter-deck. Nor could this well have been otherwise. Cast in a mold peculiar to the finest physical examples of those Englishmen in whom the Saxon strain would seem not at all to partake of any Norman or other admixture, he showed in face that humane look of reposeful good nature which the Greek sculptor in some instances gave to his heroic strong man, Hercules. But this again was subtly modified by another and pervasive quality. The ear, small and shapely, the arch of the foot, the curve in mouth and nostril, even the indurated hand dyed to the orange-tawny of the toucan's bill, a hand telling alike of the halyards and tar bucket; but, above all, something in the mobile expression, and every chance attitude and movement, something suggestive of a mother eminently favored by Love and the Graces; all this strangely indicated a lineage in direct contradiction to his lot. The mysteriousness here became less mysterious through a matter of fact elicited when Billy at the capstan was being formally mustered into the service. Asked by the officer, a small, brisk little gentleman as it chanced, among other questions, his place of birth, he replied, "Please, sir, I don't know."

"Don't know where you were born? Who was your father?"

"God knows, sir."

Struck by the straightforward simplicity of these replies, the officer next asked, "Do you know anything about your beginning?"

"No, sir. But I have heard that I was found in a pretty silk-lined basket hanging one morning from the knocker of a good man's door in Bristol."

"*Found*, say you? Well," throwing back his head and looking up and down the new recruit; "well, it turns out to have been a pretty good find. Hope they'll find some more like you, my man; the fleet sadly needs them."

Yes, Billy Budd was a foundling, a presumable by-blow,* and, evidently, no ignoble one. Noble descent was as evident in him as in a blood horse.

For the rest, with little or no sharpness of faculty or any trace of the wisdom of the serpent, nor yet quite a dove, he possessed that kind and degree of intelligence going along with the unconventional rectitude of a sound human creature, one to whom not yet has been proffered the questionable apple of knowledge. He was illiterate; he could not read, but he could sing, and like the illiterate nightingale was sometimes the composer of his own song.

Of self-consciousness he seemed to have little or none, or about as much as we may reasonably impute to a dog of Saint Bernard's breed.

Habitually living with the elements and knowing little more of the land than as a beach, or, rather, that portion of the terraqueous globe providentially set apart for dance-houses, doxies, and tapsters, in short what sailors call a "fiddler's green," his simple nature remained unsophisticated by those moral obliquities which are not in every case incompatible with that manufacturable thing known as respectability. But are sailors, frequenters of fiddlers' greens, without vices? No; but less often than with landsmen do their vices, so called, partake of crookedness of heart, seeming less to proceed from viciousness than exuberance of vitality after long constraint: frank manifestations in accordance with natural law. By his original constitution aided by the co-operating influences of his lot, Billy in many respects was little more than a sort of upright barbarian, much such perhaps as Adam presumably might have been ere the urbane Serpent wriggled himself into his company.

And here be it submitted that apparently going to corroborate the doctrine of man's Fall, a doctrine now popularly ignored, it is observable that where certain virtues pristine and unadulterate peculiarly characterize anybody in the external uniform of civilization, they will upon scrutiny seem not to be derived from custom or convention, but rather to be out of keeping with these, as if indeed exceptionally transmitted from a period prior to Cain's city and citified man.* The character marked by such qualities has to an unvitiated taste an untampered-with flavor like that of berries, while the man thoroughly civilized, even in a fair specimen of the breed, has to the same moral palate a questionable smack as of a compounded wine. To any stray inheritor of these primitive qualities found, like Caspar Hauser,* wandering dazed in any Christian capital of our time, the good-natured poet's famous invocation, near two thousand years ago, of the good rustic out of his latitude in the Rome of the Caesars, still appropriately holds:

> Honest and poor, faithful in word and thought,
> What hath thee, Fabian, to the city brought?*

Though our Handsome Sailor had as much of masculine beauty as one can expect anywhere to see; nevertheless, like the beautiful woman in one of Hawthorne's minor tales,* there was just one thing amiss in him. No visible blemish indeed, as with the lady; no, but an occasional liability to a vocal defect. Though in the hour of elemental uproar or peril he was everything that a sailor should be, yet under sudden provocation of strong heart-feeling his voice, otherwise singularly musical, as if expressive of the harmony within, was apt to develop an organic hesitancy, in fact more or less of a stutter or even worse. In this particular Billy was a striking instance that the arch interferer, the envious marplot of Eden, still has more or less to do with every human consignment to this planet of Earth. In every case, one way or another he is sure to slip in his little card, as much as to remind us—I too have a hand here.

The avowal of such an imperfection in the Handsome Sailor should be evidence not alone that he is not presented as a conventional hero, but also that the story in which he is the main figure is no romance.

3

AT the time of Billy Budd's arbitrary enlistment into the *Bellipotent* that ship was on her way to join the Mediterranean fleet. No long time elapsed before the junction was effected. As one of that fleet the seventy-four participated in its movements, though at times on account of her superior sailing qualities, in the absence of frigates, dispatched on separate duty as a scout and at times on less temporary service. But with all this the story has little concernment, restricted as it is to the inner life of one particular ship and the career of an individual sailor.

It was the summer of 1797. In the April of that year had occurred the commotion at Spithead followed in May by a second and yet more serious outbreak in the fleet at the Nore.* The latter is known, and without exaggeration in the epithet, as "the Great Mutiny." It was indeed a demonstration more menacing to England than the contemporary manifestoes and conquering and proselyting armies of the French Directory. To the British Empire the Nore Mutiny was what a strike in the fire brigade would be to London threatened by general arson. In a crisis when the kingdom might well have anticipated the famous signal that some years later published along the naval line of battle what it was that upon occasion England expected of Englishmen; *that* was the time when at the mastheads of the three-deckers and seventy-fours moored in her own roadstead—a fleet the right arm of a Power then all but the sole free conservative one of the Old World—the bluejackets, to be numbered by thousands, ran up with huzzas the British colors with the union and cross wiped out; by that cancellation transmuting the flag of founded law and freedom defined, into the enemy's red meteor of unbridled and unbounded revolt. Reasonable discontent growing out of practical grievances in the fleet had been ignited into irrational combustion as by live cinders blown across the Channel from France in flames.

The event converted into irony for a time those spirited strains of Dibdin*—as a song-writer no mean auxiliary to the English government at that European conjuncture—strains celebrating, among other things, the patriotic devotion of the British tar: "And as for my life, 'tis the King's!"

Such an episode in the Island's grand naval story her naval historians naturally abridge, one of them (William James)* candidly acknowledging that fain would he pass it over did not "impartiality forbid fastidiousness." And yet his mention is less a narration than a reference, having to do hardly at all with details. Nor are these readily to be found in the libraries. Like some other events in every age befalling states everywhere, including America, the Great Mutiny was of such character that national pride along with views of policy would fain shade it off into the historical background. Such events cannot be ignored, but there is a considerate way of historically treating them. If a well-constituted individual refrains from blazoning aught amiss or calamitous in his family, a nation in the like circumstance may without reproach be equally discreet.

Though after parleyings between government and the ringleaders, and concessions by the former as to some glaring abuses, the first uprising—that at Spithead—with difficulty was put down, or matters for the time pacified; yet at the Nore the unforeseen renewal of insurrection on a yet larger scale, and emphasized in the conferences that ensued by demands deemed by the authorities not only inadmissible but aggressively insolent, indicated—if the Red Flag did not sufficiently do so—what was the spirit animating the men. Final suppression, however, there was; but only made possible perhaps by the unswerving loyalty of the marine corps and a voluntary resumption of loyalty among influential sections of the crews.

To some extent the Nore Mutiny may be regarded as analogous to the distempering irruption of contagious fever in a frame constitutionally sound, and which anon throws it off.

At all events, of these thousands of mutineers were some of the tars who not so very long afterwards—whether wholly prompted thereto by patriotism, or pugnacious instinct, or by both—helped to win a coronet for Nelson at the Nile, and the naval crown of crowns for him at Trafalgar.* To the mutineers, those battles and especially Trafalgar were a plenary absolution and a grand one. For all that goes to make up scenic naval display and heroic magnificence in arms, those battles, especially Trafalgar, stand unmatched in human annals.

4

IN this matter of writing, resolve as one may to keep to the main road, some bypaths have an enticement not readily to be withstood. I am going to err into such a bypath.* If the reader will keep me company I shall be glad. At the least, we can promise ourselves that pleasure which is wickedly said to be in sinning, for a literary sin the divergence will be.

Very likely it is no new remark that the inventions of our time have at last brought about a change in sea warfare in degree corresponding to the revolution in all warfare effected by the original introduction from China into Europe of gunpowder. The first European firearm, a clumsy contrivance, was, as is well known, scouted by no few of the knights as a base implement, good enough peradventure for weavers too craven to stand up crossing steel with steel in frank fight. But as ashore knightly valor, though shorn of its blazonry, did not cease with the knights, neither on the seas—though nowadays in encounters there a certain kind of displayed gallantry be fallen out of date as hardly applicable under changed circumstances—did the nobler qualities of such naval magnates as Don John of Austria, Doria, Van Tromp, Jean Bart, the long line of British admirals, and the American Decaturs of 1812 become obsolete with their wooden walls.

Nevertheless, to anybody who can hold the Present at its worth without being inappreciative of the Past, it may be forgiven, if to such an one the solitary old hulk at Portsmouth, Nelson's *Victory*, seems to float there, not alone as the decaying monument of a fame incorruptible, but also as a poetic reproach, softened by its picturesqueness, to the *Monitors* and yet mightier hulls of the European ironclads. And this not altogether because such craft are unsightly, unavoidably lacking the symmetry and grand lines of the old battleships, but equally for other reasons.

There are some, perhaps, who while not altogether inaccessible to that poetic reproach just alluded to, may yet on behalf of the new order be disposed to parry it; and this to the extent of iconoclasm, if need be. For example, prompted by the sight of the star inserted in the *Victory*'s quarter-deck designating the spot where the Great Sailor fell, these martial utilitarians may suggest considerations implying that Nelson's ornate publication of his person in battle was not only unnecessary, but not military, nay, savored of foolhardiness and vanity. They may add, too, that at Trafalgar it was in effect nothing less than a challenge to death; and death came; and that but for his bravado the victorious admiral might possibly have survived the battle, and so, instead of having his sagacious dying injunctions overruled by his immediate successor in command, he himself when the contest was decided might have brought his shattered fleet to anchor, a proceeding which might have averted the deplorable loss of life by shipwreck in the elemental tempest that followed the martial one.

Well, should we set aside the more than disputable point whether for various reasons it was possible to anchor the fleet, then plausibly enough the Benthamites of war* may urge the above. But the *might-have-been* is but boggy ground to build on. And, certainly, in foresight as to the larger issue of an encounter, and anxious preparations for it—buoying the deadly way and mapping it out, as at Copenhagen—few commanders have been so painstakingly circumspect as this same reckless declarer of his person in fight.

Personal prudence, even when dictated by quite other than selfish considerations, surely is no special virtue in a military man; while an excessive love of glory, impassioning a less burning impulse, the honest sense of duty, is the first. If the name *Wellington* is not so much of a trumpet to the blood as the simpler name *Nelson*, the reason for this may perhaps be inferred from the above. Alfred in his funeral ode* on the victor of Waterloo ventures not to call him the greatest soldier of all time, though in the same ode he invokes Nelson as "the greatest sailor since our world began."

At Trafalgar Nelson on the brink of opening the fight sat down and wrote his last brief will and testament. If under the presentiment of the most magnificent of all victories to be crowned by his own glorious death, a sort of priestly motive led him to dress his person in the jewelled vouchers of his own shining deeds; if thus to have adorned himself for the altar and the sacrifice were indeed vainglory, then affectation and fustian is each more heroic line in the great epics and dramas, since in such lines the poet but embodies in verse those exaltations of sentiment that a nature like Nelson, the opportunity being given, vitalizes into acts.

5

YES, the outbreak at the Nore was put down. But not every grievance was redressed. If the contractors, for example, were no longer permitted to ply some practices peculiar to their tribe everywhere, such as providing shoddy cloth, rations not sound, or false in the measure; not the less impressment, for one thing, went on. By custom sanctioned for centuries, and judicially maintained by a Lord Chancellor as late as Mansfield,* that mode of manning the fleet, a mode now fallen into a sort of abeyance but never formally renounced, it was not practicable to give up in those years. Its abrogation would have crippled the indispensable fleet, one wholly under canvas, no steam power, its innumerable sails and thousands of cannon, everything in short, worked by muscle alone; a fleet the more insatiate in demand for men, because then multiplying its ships of all grades against contingencies present and to come of the convulsed Continent.

Discontent foreran the Two Mutinies, and more or less it lurkingly survived them. Hence it was not unreasonable to apprehend some return of trouble sporadic or general. One instance of such apprehensions: In the same year with this story, Nelson, then Rear Admiral Sir Horatio, being with the fleet off the Spanish coast, was directed by the admiral in command to shift his pennant from the *Captain* to the *Theseus*; and for this reason: that the latter ship having newly arrived on the station from home, where it had taken part in the Great Mutiny, danger was apprehended from the temper of the men; and it was thought that an officer like Nelson was the one, not indeed to terrorize the crew into base subjection, but to win them, by force of his mere presence and heroic personality, back to an allegiance if not as enthusiastic as his own yet as true.*

So it was that for a time, on more than one quarter-deck, anxiety did exist. At sea, precautionary vigilance was strained against relapse. At short notice an engagement might come on. When it did, the lieutenants assigned to batteries felt it incumbent on them, in some instances, to stand with drawn swords behind the men working the guns.

6

BUT on board the seventy-four in which Billy now swung
his hammock, very little in the manner of the men and nothing obvious in the demeanor of the officers would have suggested to an ordinary observer that the Great Mutiny was
a recent event. In their general bearing and conduct the
commissioned officers of a warship naturally take their tone
from the commander, that is if he have that ascendancy of
character that ought to be his.

Captain the Honorable Edward Fairfax Vere,* to give his
full title, was a bachelor of forty or thereabouts, a sailor
of distinction even in a time prolific of renowned seamen.
Though allied to the higher nobility, his advancement had
not been altogether owing to influences connected with that
circumstance. He had seen much service, been in various
engagements, always acquitting himself as an officer mindful of the welfare of his men, but never tolerating an in-
fraction of discipline; thoroughly versed in the science of his
profession, and intrepid to the verge of temerity, though
never injudiciously so. For his gallantry in the West Indian
waters as flag lieutenant under Rodney in that admiral's
crowning victory over De Grasse,* he was made a post
captain.

Ashore, in the garb of a civilian, scarce anyone would
have taken him for a sailor, more especially that he never
garnished unprofessional talk with nautical terms, and grave
in his bearing, evinced little appreciation of mere humor. It
was not out of keeping with these traits that on a passage
when nothing demanded his paramount action, he was the
most undemonstrative of men. Any landsman observing this
gentleman not conspicuous by his stature and wearing no
pronounced insignia, emerging from his cabin to the open
deck, and noting the silent deference of the officers retiring
to leeward, might have taken him for the King's guest,
a civilian aboard the King's ship, some highly honorable
discreet envoy on his way to an important post. But in
fact this unobtrusiveness of demeanor may have proceeded
from a certain unaffected modesty of manhood sometimes

accompanying a resolute nature, a modesty evinced at all times not calling for pronounced action, which shown in any rank of life suggests a virtue aristocratic in kind. As with some others engaged in various departments of the world's more heroic activities, Captain Vere though practical enough upon occasion would at times betray a certain dreaminess of mood. Standing alone on the weather side of the quarter-deck, one hand holding by the rigging, he would absently gaze off at the blank sea.* At the presentation to him then of some minor matter interrupting the current of his thoughts, he would show more or less irascibility; but instantly he would control it.

In the navy he was popularly known by the appellation "Starry Vere." How such a designation happened to fall upon one who whatever his sterling qualities was without any brilliant ones, was in this wise: A favorite kinsman, Lord Denton, a freehearted fellow, had been the first to meet and congratulate him upon his return to England from his West Indian cruise; and but the day previous turning over a copy of Andrew Marvell's poems had lighted, not for the first time, however, upon the lines entitled "Appleton House," the name of one of the seats of their common ancestor, a hero in the German wars of the seventeenth century, in which poem occur the lines:

> This 'tis to have been from the first
> In a domestic heaven nursed,
> Under the discipline severe
> Of Fairfax and the starry Vere.*

And so, upon embracing his cousin fresh from Rodney's great victory wherein he had played so gallant a part, brimming over with just family pride in the sailor of their house, he exuberantly exclaimed, "Give ye joy, Ed; give ye joy, my starry Vere!" This got currency, and the novel prefix serving in familiar parlance readily to distinguish the *Bellipotent*'s captain from another Vere his senior, a distant relative, an officer of like rank in the navy, it remained permanently attached to the surname.

7

In view of the part that the commander of the *Bellipotent*
plays in scenes shortly to follow, it may be well to fill out
that sketch of him outlined in the previous chapter.

Aside from his qualities as a sea officer Captain Vere
was an exceptional character. Unlike no few of England's
renowned sailors, long and arduous service with signal devotion to it had not resulted in absorbing and *salting* the entire
man. He had a marked leaning toward everything intellectual. He loved books, never going to sea without a newly
replenished library, compact but of the best. The isolated
leisure, in some cases so wearisome, falling at intervals to
commanders even during a war cruise, never was tedious
to Captain Vere. With nothing of that literary taste which
less heeds the thing conveyed than the vehicle, his bias was
toward those books to which every serious mind of superior
order occupying any active post of authority in the world naturally inclines: books treating of actual men and events no
matter of what era—history, biography, and unconventional
writers like Montaigne,* who, free from cant and convention,
honestly and in the spirit of common sense philosophize
upon realities. In this line of reading he found confirmation
of his own more reserved thoughts—confirmation which he
had vainly sought in social converse, so that as touching
most fundamental topics, there had got to be established in
him some positive convictions which he forefelt would abide
in him essentially unmodified so long as his intelligent part
remained unimpaired. In view of the troubled period in
which his lot was cast, this was well for him. His settled
convictions were as a dike against those invading waters of
novel opinion social, political, and otherwise, which carried
away as in a torrent no few minds in those days, minds by
nature not inferior to his own. While other members of that
aristocracy to which by birth he belonged were incensed at
the innovators mainly because their theories were inimical
to the privileged classes, Captain Vere disinterestedly opposed
them not alone because they seemed to him insusceptible

of embodiment in lasting institutions, but at war with the peace of the world and the true welfare of mankind.

With minds less stored than his and less earnest, some officers of his rank, with whom at times he would necessarily consort, found him lacking in the companionable quality, a dry and bookish gentleman, as they deemed. Upon any chance withdrawal from their company one would be apt to say to another something like this: "Vere is a noble fellow, Starry Vere. 'Spite the gazettes, Sir Horatio" (meaning him who became Lord Nelson) "is at bottom scarce a better seaman or fighter. But between you and me now, don't you think there is a queer streak of the pedantic running through him? Yes, like the King's yarn in a coil of navy rope?"

Some apparent ground there was for this sort of confidential criticism; since not only did the captain's discourse never fall into the jocosely familiar, but in illustrating of any point touching the stirring personages and events of the time he would be as apt to cite some historic character or incident of antiquity as he would be to cite from the moderns. He seemed unmindful of the circumstance that to his bluff company such remote allusions, however pertinent they might really be, were altogether alien to men whose reading was mainly confined to the journals. But considerateness in such matters is not easy to natures constituted like Captain Vere's. Their honesty prescribes to them directness, sometimes far-reaching like that of a migratory fowl that in its flight never heeds when it crosses a frontier.

8

THE lieutenants and other commissioned gentlemen forming Captain Vere's staff it is not necessary here to particularize, nor needs it to make any mention of any of the warrant officers. But among the petty officers was one who, having much to do with the story, may as well be forthwith introduced. His portrait I essay, but shall never hit it. This was John Claggart, the master-at-arms. But that sea title may to landsmen seem somewhat equivocal. Originally, doubtless, that petty officer's function was the instruction of the men in the use of arms, sword or cutlass. But very long ago, owing to the advance in gunnery making hand-to-hand encounters less frequent and giving to niter and sulphur the pre-eminence over steel, that function ceased; the master-at-arms of a great warship becoming a sort of chief of police charged among other matters with the duty of preserving order on the populous lower gun decks.

Claggart was a man about five-and-thirty, somewhat spare and tall, yet of no ill figure upon the whole. His hand was too small and shapely to have been accustomed to hard toil. The face was a notable one, the features all except the chin cleanly cut as those on a Greek medallion; yet the chin, beardless as Tecumseh's,* had something of strange pro-tuberant broadness in its make that recalled the prints of the Reverend Dr. Titus Oates,* the historic deponent with the clerical drawl in the time of Charles II and the fraud of the alleged Popish Plot. It served Claggart in his office that his eye could cast a tutoring glance. His brow was of the sort phrenologically associated with more than average intellect; silken jet curls partly clustering over it, making a foil to the pallor below, a pallor tinged with a faint shade of amber akin to the hue of time-tinted marbles of old. This complexion, singularly contrasting with the red or deeply bronzed visages of the sailors, and in part the result of his official seclusion from the sunlight, though it was not exactly displeasing, nevertheless seemed to hint of something defect-ive or abnormal in the constitution and blood. But his gen-eral aspect and manner were so suggestive of an education and career incongruous with his naval function that when not actively engaged in it he looked like a man of high qual-ity, social and moral, who for reasons of his own was keep-ing incog. Nothing was known of his former life. It might be that he was an Englishman; and yet there lurked a bit of accent in his speech suggesting that possibly he was not such by birth, but through naturalization in early childhood. Among certain grizzled sea gossips of the gun decks and forecastle went a rumor perdue that the master-at-arms was a *chevalier** who had volunteered into the King's navy by

way of compounding for some mysterious swindle whereof
he had been arraigned at the King's Bench. The fact that
nobody could substantiate this report was, of course, nothing
against its secret currency. Such a rumor once started on
the gun decks in reference to almost anyone below the rank
of a commissioned officer would, during the period assigned
to this narrative, have seemed not altogether wanting in credibility to the tarry old wiseacres of a man-of-war crew. And
indeed a man of Claggart's accomplishments, without prior
nautical experience entering the navy at mature life, as he
did, and necessarily allotted at the start to the lowest grade
in it; a man too who never made allusion to his previous
life ashore; these were circumstances which in the dearth
of exact knowledge as to his true antecedents opened to the
invidious a vague field for unfavorable surmise.

But the sailors' dogwatch gossip concerning him derived
a vague plausibility from the fact that now for some period
the British navy could so little afford to be squeamish in the
matter of keeping up the muster rolls, that not only were
press gangs notoriously abroad both afloat and ashore, but
there was little or no secret about another matter, namely,
that the London police were at liberty to capture any able-
bodied suspect, any questionable fellow at large, and summarily ship him to the dockyard or fleet. Furthermore, even
among voluntary enlistments there were instances where the
motive thereto partook neither of patriotic impulse nor yet
of a random desire to experience a bit of sea life and martial adventure. Insolvent debtors of minor grade, together
with the promiscuous lame ducks of morality, found in the
navy a convenient and secure refuge, secure because, once
enlisted aboard a King's ship, they were as much in sanctu-
ary as the transgressor of the Middle Ages harboring himself
under the shadow of the altar. Such sanctioned irregular-
ities, which for obvious reasons the government would hardly
think to parade at the time and which consequently, and as
affecting the least influential class of mankind, have all but
dropped into oblivion, lend color to something for the truth
whereof I do not vouch, and hence have some scruple in
stating; something I remember having seen in print though

the book I cannot recall; but the same thing was personally communicated to me now more than forty years ago by an old pensioner in a cocked hat with whom I had a most interesting talk on the terrace at Greenwich, a Baltimore Negro, a Trafalgar man. It was to this effect: In the case of a warship short of hands whose speedy sailing was imperative, the deficient quota, in lack of any other way of making it good, would be eked out by drafts culled direct from the jails. For reasons previously suggested it would not perhaps be easy at the present day directly to prove or disprove the allegation. But allowed as a verity, how significant would it be of England's straits at the time confronted by those wars which like a flight of harpies rose shrieking from the din and dust of the fallen Bastille. That era appears measurably clear to us who look back at it, and but read of it. But to the grandfathers of us graybeards, the more thoughtful of them, the genius of it presented an aspect like that of Camoëns' Spirit of the Cape,* an eclipsing menace mysterious and prodigious. Not America was exempt from apprehension. At the height of Napoleon's unexampled conquests, there were Americans who had fought at Bunker Hill who looked forward to the possibility that the Atlantic might prove no barrier against the ultimate schemes of this French portentous upstart from the revolutionary chaos who seemed in act of fulfilling judgment prefigured in the Apocalypse.

But the less credence was to be given to the gun-deck talk touching Claggart, seeing that no man holding his office in a man-of-war can ever hope to be popular with the crew. Besides, in derogatory comments upon anyone against whom they have a grudge, or for any reason or no reason mislike, sailors are much like landsmen: they are apt to exaggerate or romance it.

About as much was really known to the *Bellipotent*'s tars of the master-at-arms' career before entering the service as an astronomer knows about a comet's travels prior to its first observable appearance in the sky. The verdict of the sea quidnuncs has been cited only by way of showing what sort of moral impression the man made upon rude uncultivated natures whose conceptions of human wickedness were necessarily of the narrowest, limited to ideas of vulgar rascality—a thief among the swinging hammocks during a night watch, or the man-brokers and land-sharks of the seaports.

It was no gossip, however, but fact that though, as before hinted, Claggart upon his entrance into the navy was, as a novice, assigned to the least honorable section of a man-of-war's crew, embracing the drudgery, he did not long remain there. The superior capacity he immediately evinced, his constitutional sobriety, an ingratiating deference to superiors, together with a peculiar ferreting genius manifested on a singular occasion; all this, capped by a certain austere patriotism, abruptly advanced him to the position of master-at-arms.

Of this maritime chief of police the ship's corporals, so called, were the immediate subordinates, and compliant ones; and this, as is to be noted in some business departments ashore, almost to a degree inconsistent with entire moral volition. His place put various converging wires of underground influence under the chief's control, capable when astutely worked through his understrappers of operating to the mysterious discomfort, if nothing worse, of any of the sea commonalty.

9

LIFE in the foretop well agreed with Billy Budd. There, when not actually engaged on the yards yet higher aloft, the topmen, who as such had been picked out for youth and activity, constituted an aerial club lounging at ease against the smaller stun'sails rolled up into cushions, spinning yarns like the lazy gods, and frequently amused with what was going on in the busy world of the decks below. No wonder then that a young fellow of Billy's disposition was well content in such society. Giving no cause of offense to anybody, he was always alert at a call. So in the merchant service it had been with him. But now such a punctiliousness in duty was shown that his topmates would sometimes good-naturedly laugh at him for it. This heightened alacrity had its cause, namely, the impression made upon him by the first formal gangway-punishment he had ever witnessed, which befell the day following his impressment. It had been incurred by a little fellow, young, a novice afterguardsman absent from his assigned post when the ship was being put about; a dereliction resulting in a rather serious hitch to that maneuver, one demanding instantaneous promptitude in letting go and making fast. When Billy saw the culprit's naked back under the scourge, gridironed with red welts and worse, when he marked the dire expression in the liberated man's face as with his woolen shirt flung over him by the executioner he rushed forward from the spot to bury himself in the crowd, Billy was horrified. He resolved that never through remissness would he make himself liable to such a visitation or do or omit aught that might merit even verbal reproof. What then was his surprise and concern when ultimately he found himself getting into petty trouble occasionally about such matters as the stowage of his bag or something amiss in his hammock, matters under the police oversight of the ship's corporals of the lower decks, and which brought down on him a vague threat from one of them.

So heedful in all things as he was, how could this be? He could not understand it, and it more than vexed him. When he spoke to his young topmates about it they were either lightly incredulous or found something comical in his unconcealed anxiety. "Is it your bag, Billy?" said one. "Well, sew yourself up in it, bully boy, and then you'll be sure to know if anybody meddles with it."

Now there was a veteran aboard who because his years began to disqualify him for more active work had been recently assigned duty as mainmastman in his watch, looking to the gear belayed at the rail roundabout that great spar near the deck. At off-times the foretopman had picked up some acquaintance with him, and now in his trouble it occurred to him that he might be the sort of person to go to for wise counsel. He was an old Dansker* long anglicized in the service, of few words, many wrinkles, and some honorable scars. His wizened face, time-tinted and weatherstained to the complexion of an antique parchment, was here and there peppered blue by the chance explosion of a gun cartridge in action.

He was an *Agamemnon* man, some two years prior to the time of this story having served under Nelson when still captain in that ship immortal in naval memory, which dismantled and in part broken up to her bare ribs is seen a grand skeleton in Haden's etching.* As one of a boarding party from the *Agamemnon* he had received a cut slantwise along one temple and cheek leaving a long pale scar like a streak of dawn's light falling athwart the dark visage. It was on account of that scar and the affair in which it was known that he had received it, as well as from his blue-peppered complexion, that the Dansker went among the *Bellipotent*'s crew by the name of "Board-Her-in-the-Smoke."

Now the first time that his small weasel eyes happened to light on Billy Budd, a certain grim internal merriment set all his ancient wrinkles into antic play. Was it that his eccentric unsentimental old sapience, primitive in its kind, saw or thought it saw something which in contrast with the warship's environment looked oddly incongruous in the Handsome Sailor? But after slyly studying him at intervals, the old Merlin's equivocal merriment was modified; for now when the twain would meet, it would start in his face a quizzing sort of look, but it would be but momentary and sometimes replaced by an expression of speculative query as to what might eventually befall a nature like that, dropped into a world not without some mantraps and against whose subtleties simple courage lacking experience and address, and without any touch of defensive ugliness, is of little avail; and where such innocence as man is capable of does yet in a moral emergency not always sharpen the faculties or enlighten the will.

However it was, the Dansker in his ascetic way rather took to Billy. Nor was this only because of a certain philosophic interest in such a character. There was another cause. While the old man's eccentricities, sometimes bordering on the ursine, repelled the juniors, Billy, undeterred thereby, revering him as a salt hero, would make advances, never passing the old *Agamemnon* man without a salutation marked by that respect which is seldom lost on the aged, however crabbed at times or whatever their station in life.

There was a vein of dry humor, or what not, in the mastman; and, whether in freak of patriarchal irony touching Billy's youth and athletic frame, or for some other and more recondite reason, from the first in addressing him he always substituted *Baby* for Billy, the Dansker in fact being the originator of the name by which the foretopman eventually became known aboard ship.

Well then, in his mysterious little difficulty going in quest of the wrinkled one, Billy found him off duty in a dogwatch ruminating by himself, seated on a shot box of the upper gun deck, now and then surveying with a somewhat cynical regard certain of the more swaggering promenaders there. Billy recounted his trouble, again wondering how it all happened. The salt seer attentively listened, accompanying the foretopman's recital with queer twitchings of his wrinkles and problematical little sparkles of his small ferret eyes. Making an end of his story, the foretopman asked, "And now, Dansker, do tell me what you think of it."

The old man, shoving up the front of his tarpaulin and deliberately rubbing the long slant scar at the point where it entered the thin hair, laconically said, "Baby Budd, *Jemmy Legs*"* (meaning the master-at-arms) "is down on you."

"*Jemmy Legs!*" ejaculated Billy, his welkin eyes expanding. "What for? Why, he calls me 'the sweet and pleasant young fellow,' they tell me."

"Does he so?" grinned the grizzled one; then said, "Ay, Baby lad, a sweet voice has Jemmy Legs."

"No, not always. But to me he has. I seldom pass him but there comes a pleasant word."

"And that's because he's down upon you, Baby Budd."

Such reiteration, along with the manner of it, incomprehensible to a novice, disturbed Billy almost as much as the mystery for which he had sought explanation. Something less unpleasingly oracular he tried to extract; but the old sea Chiron,* thinking perhaps that for the nonce he had

sufficiently instructed his young Achilles, pursed his lips, gathered all his wrinkles together, and would commit himself to
nothing further.

Years, and those experiences which befall certain shrewder
men subordinated lifelong to the will of superiors, all this
had developed in the Dansker the pithy guarded cynicism
that was his leading characteristic.

10

THE next day an incident served to confirm Billy Budd in
his incredulity as to the Dansker's strange summing up of
the case submitted. The ship at noon, going large before
the wind, was rolling on her course, and he below at dinner
and engaged in some sportful talk with the members of his
mess, chanced in a sudden lurch to spill the entire contents
of his soup pan upon the new-scrubbed deck. Claggart, the
master-at-arms, official rattan in hand, happened to be passing along the battery in a bay of which the mess was lodged,
and the greasy liquid streamed just across his path. Stepping
over it, he was proceeding on his way without comment,
since the matter was nothing to take notice of under the circumstances, when he happened to observe who it was that
had done the spilling. His countenance changed. Pausing,
he was about to ejaculate something hasty at the sailor, but
checked himself, and pointing down to the streaming soup,
playfully tapped him from behind with his rattan, saying in
a low musical voice peculiar to him at times, "Handsomely
done, my lad! And handsome is as handsome did it, too!"
And with that passed on. Not noted by Billy as not coming
within his view was the involuntary smile, or rather grimace,
that accompanied Claggart's equivocal words. Aridly it drew
down the thin corners of his shapely mouth. But everybody
taking his remark as meant for humorous, and at which
therefore as coming from a superior they were bound to
laugh "with counterfeited glee," acted accordingly; and Billy,
tickled, it may be, by the allusion to his being the Handsome

Sailor, merrily joined in; then addressing his messmates exclaimed, "There now, who says that Jemmy Legs is down on me!"

"And who said he was, Beauty?" demanded one Donald with some surprise. Whereat the foretopman looked a little foolish, recalling that it was only one person, Board-Her-in-the-Smoke, who had suggested what to him was the smoky idea that this master-at-arms was in any peculiar way hostile to him. Meantime that functionary, resuming his path, must have momentarily worn some expression less guarded than that of the bitter smile, usurping the face from the heart —some distorting expression perhaps, for a drummer-boy heedlessly frolicking along from the opposite direction and chancing to come into light collision with his person was strangely disconcerted by his aspect. Nor was the impression lessened when the official, impetuously giving him a sharp cut with the rattan, vehemently exclaimed, "Look where you go!"

11

WHAT was the matter with the master-at-arms? And, be the matter what it might, how could it have direct relation to Billy Budd, with whom prior to the affair of the spilled soup he had never come into any special contact official or otherwise? What indeed could the trouble have to do with one so little inclined to give offense as the merchant-ship's "peacemaker," even him who in Claggart's own phrase was "the sweet and pleasant young fellow"? Yes, why should Jemmy Legs, to borrow the Dansker's expression, be "down" on the Handsome Sailor? But, at heart and not for nothing, as the late chance encounter may indicate to the discerning, down on him, secretly down on him, he assuredly was.

Now to invent something touching the more private career of Claggart, something involving Billy Budd, of which something the latter should be wholly ignorant, some romantic incident implying that Claggart's knowledge of the young bluejacket began at some period anterior to catching sight of him on board the seventy-four—all this, not so difficult to do, might avail in a way more or less interesting to account for whatever of enigma may appear to lurk in the case. But in fact there was nothing of the sort. And yet the cause necessarily to be assumed as the sole one assignable is in its very realism as much charged with that prime element of Radcliffian romance,* the mysterious, as any that the ingenuity of the author of *The Mysteries of Udolpho* could devise. For what can more partake of the mysterious than an antipathy spontaneous and profound such as is evoked in certain exceptional mortals by the mere aspect of some other mortal, however harmless he may be, if not called forth by this very harmlessness itself?

Now there can exist no irritating juxtaposition of dissimilar personalities comparable to that which is possible aboard a great warship fully manned and at sea. There, every day among all ranks, almost every man comes into more or less of contact with almost every other man. Wholly there to avoid even the sight of an aggravating object one must needs give it Jonah's toss or jump overboard himself. Imagine how all this might eventually operate on some peculiar human creature the direct reverse of a saint!

But for the adequate comprehending of Claggart by a normal nature these hints are insufficient. To pass from a normal nature to him one must cross "the deadly space between." And this is best done by indirection.

Long ago an honest scholar,* my senior, said to me in reference to one who like himself is now no more, a man so unimpeachably respectable that against him nothing was ever openly said though among the few something was whispered, "Yes, X—— is a nut not to be cracked by the tap of a lady's fan. You are aware that I am the adherent of no organized religion, much less of any philosophy built into a system. Well, for all that, I think that to try and get into X——, enter his labyrinth and get out again, without a clue derived from some source other than what is known as 'knowledge of the world'—that were hardly possible, at least for me."

"Why," said I, "X——, however singular a study to some, is yet human, and knowledge of the world assuredly implies the knowledge of human nature, and in most of its varieties."

"Yes, but a superficial knowledge of it, serving ordinary purposes. But for anything deeper, I am not certain whether to know the world and to know human nature be not two distinct branches of knowledge, which while they may coexist in the same heart, yet either may exist with little or nothing of the other. Nay, in an average man of the world, his constant rubbing with it blunts that finer spiritual insight indispensable to the understanding of the essential in certain exceptional characters, whether evil ones or good. In a matter of some importance I have seen a girl wind an old lawyer about her little finger. Nor was it the dotage of senile love. Nothing of the sort. But he knew law better than he knew the girl's heart. Coke and Blackstone* hardly shed so much light into obscure spiritual places as the Hebrew prophets. And who were they? Mostly recluses."

At the time, my inexperience was such that I did not quite see the drift of all this. It may be that I see it now. And, indeed, if that lexicon which is based on Holy Writ were any longer popular, one might with less difficulty define and denominate certain phenomenal men. As it is, one must turn to some authority not liable to the charge of being tinctured with the biblical element.

In a list of definitions included in the authentic translation of Plato, a list attributed to him, occurs this: "Natural Depravity:* a depravity according to nature," a definition which, though savoring of Calvinism, by no means involves Calvin's dogma as to total mankind. Evidently its intent makes it applicable but to individuals. Not many are the examples of this depravity which the gallows and jail supply. At any rate, for notable instances, since these have no vulgar alloy of the brute in them, but invariably are dominated by intellectuality, one must go elsewhere. Civilization, especially if of the austerer sort, is auspicious to it. It folds itself in the mantle of respectability. It has its certain negative virtues serving as silent auxiliaries. It never allows wine

to get within its guard. It is not going too far to say that it
is without vices or small sins. There is a phenomenal pride
in it that excludes them. It is never mercenary or avaricious.
In short, the depravity here meant partakes nothing of the
sordid or sensual. It is serious, but free from acerbity. Though
no flatterer of mankind it never speaks ill of it.

But the thing which in eminent instances signalizes so
exceptional a nature is this: Though the man's even temper
and discreet bearing would seem to intimate a mind peculiarly subject to the law of reason, not the less in heart he
would seem to riot in complete exemption from that law,
having apparently little to do with reason further than to
employ it as an ambidexter implement for effecting the irrational. That is to say: Toward the accomplishment of an
aim which in wantonness of atrocity would seem to partake
of the insane, he will direct a cool judgment sagacious and
sound. These men are madmen, and of the most dangerous
sort, for their lunacy is not continuous, but occasional, evoked
by some special object; it is protectively secretive, which is as
much as to say it is self-contained, so that when, moreover,
most active it is to the average mind not distinguishable
from sanity, and for the reason above suggested: that whatever its aims may be—and the aim is never declared—the
method and the outward proceeding are always perfectly
rational.

Now something such an one was Claggart, in whom was
the mania of an evil nature, not engendered by vicious training or corrupting books or licentious living, but born with
him and innate, in short "a depravity according to nature."

Dark sayings are these, some will say. But why? Is it
because they somewhat savor of Holy Writ in its phrase
"mystery of iniquity"?* If they do, such savor was far enough
from being intended, for little will it commend these pages
to many a reader of today.

The point of the present story turning on the hidden
nature of the master-at-arms has necessitated this chapter.
With an added hint or two in connection with the incident
at the mess, the resumed narrative must be left to vindicate,
as it may, its own credibility.

12

THAT Claggart's figure was not amiss, and his face, save the chin, well molded, has already been said. Of these favorable points he seemed not insensible, for he was not only neat but careful in his dress. But the form of Billy Budd was heroic; and if his face was without the intellectual look of the pallid Claggart's, not the less was it lit, like his, from within, though from a different source. The bonfire in his heart made luminous the rose-tan in his cheek.

In view of the marked contrast between the persons of the twain, it is more than probable that when the master-at-arms in the scene last given applied to the sailor the proverb "Handsome is as handsome does," he there let escape an ironic inkling, not caught by the young sailors who heard it, as to what it was that had first moved him against Billy, namely, his significant personal beauty.

Now envy and antipathy,* passions irreconcilable in reason, nevertheless in fact may spring conjoined like Chang and Eng* in one birth. Is Envy then such a monster? Well, though many an arraigned mortal has in hopes of mitigated penalty pleaded guilty to horrible actions, did ever anybody seriously confess to envy? Something there is in it universally felt to be more shameful than even felonious crime. And not only does everybody disown it, but the better sort are inclined to incredulity when it is in earnest imputed to an intelligent man. But since its lodgment is in the heart not the brain, no degree of intellect supplies a guarantee against it. But Claggart's was no vulgar form of the passion. Nor, as directed toward Billy Budd, did it partake of that streak of apprehensive jealousy that marred Saul's visage perturbedly brooding on the comely young David.* Claggart's envy struck deeper. If askance he eyed the good looks, cheery health, and frank enjoyment of young life in Billy Budd, it was because these went along with a nature that, as Claggart magnetically felt, had in its simplicity never willed malice or experienced the reactionary bite of that serpent. To him, the spirit lodged within Billy, and looking out from his welkin eyes as from windows, that ineffability it was which made the dimple in his dyed cheek, suppled his joints, and dancing in his yellow curls made him pre-eminently the Handsome Sailor. One person excepted, the master-at-arms was perhaps the only man in the ship intellectually capable of adequately appreciating the moral phenomenon presented in Billy Budd. And the insight but intensified his passion, which assuming various secret forms within him, at times assumed that of cynic disdain, disdain of innocence—to be nothing more than innocent! Yet in an aesthetic way he saw the charm of it, the courageous free-and-easy temper of it, and fain would have shared it, but he despaired of it.

With no power to annul the elemental evil in him, though readily enough he could hide it; apprehending the good, but powerless to be it; a nature like Claggart's, surcharged with energy as such natures almost invariably are, what recourse is left to it but to recoil upon itself and, like the scorpion for which the Creator alone is responsible, act out to the end the part allotted it.

13

PASSION, and passion in its profoundest, is not a thing demanding a palatial stage whereon to play its part. Down among the groundlings, among the beggars and rakers of the garbage, profound passion is enacted. And the circumstances that provoke it, however trivial or mean, are no measure of its power. In the present instance the stage is a scrubbed gun deck, and one of the external provocations a man-of-war's man's spilled soup.

Now when the master-at-arms noticed whence came that greasy fluid streaming before his feet, he must have taken it—to some extent wilfully, perhaps—not for the mere accident it assuredly was, but for the sly escape of a spontaneous feeling on Billy's part more or less answering to the antipathy on his own. In effect a foolish demonstration, he must have thought, and very harmless, like the futile kick of a heifer, which yet were the heifer a shod stallion would not be so harmless. Even so was it that into the gall of Claggart's envy he infused the vitriol of his contempt. But the incident confirmed to him certain telltale reports purveyed to his ear by "Squeak," one of his more cunning corporals, a grizzled little man, so nicknamed by the sailors on account of his squeaky voice and sharp visage ferreting about the dark corners of the lower decks after interlopers, satirically suggesting to them the idea of a rat in a cellar.

From his chief's employing him as an implicit tool in laying little traps for the worriment of the foretopman—for it was from the master-at-arms that the petty persecutions heretofore adverted to had proceeded—the corporal, having naturally enough concluded that his master could have no love for the sailor, made it his business, faithful understrapper that he was, to foment the ill blood by perverting to his chief certain innocent frolics of the good-natured foretopman, besides inventing for his mouth sundry contumelious epithets he claimed to have overheard him let fall. The master-at-arms never suspected the veracity of these reports, more especially as to the epithets, for he well knew how secretly unpopular may become a master-at-arms, at least a master-at-arms of those days, zealous in his function, and how the bluejackets shoot at him in private their raillery and wit; the nickname by which he goes among them (Jemmy Legs) implying under the form of merriment their cherished disrespect and dislike. But in view of the greediness of hate for pabulum it hardly needed a purveyor to feed Claggart's passion.

An uncommon prudence is habitual with the subtler depravity, for it has everything to hide. And in case of an injury but suspected, its secretiveness voluntarily cuts it off from enlightenment or disillusion; and, not unreluctantly, action is taken upon surmise as upon certainty. And the retaliation is apt to be in monstrous disproportion to the supposed offense; for when in anybody was revenge in its exactions aught else but an inordinate usurer? But how with Claggart's conscience? For though consciences are unlike as foreheads, every intelligence, not excluding the scriptural devils* who "believe and tremble," has one. But Claggart's conscience

being but the lawyer to his will, made ogres of trifles, probably arguing that the motive imputed to Billy in spilling the
soup just when he did, together with the epithets alleged,
these, if nothing more, made a strong case against him; nay,
justified animosity into a sort of retributive righteousness.
The Pharisee is the Guy Fawkes prowling in the hid chambers underlying some natures like Claggart's. And they can
really form no conception of an unreciprocated malice. Probably the master-at-arms' clandestine persecution of Billy was
started to try the temper of the man; but it had not developed any quality in him that enmity could make official
use of or even pervert into plausible self-justification; so that
the occurrence at the mess, petty if it were, was a welcome
one to that peculiar conscience assigned to be the private
mentor of Claggart; and, for the rest, not improbably it put
him upon new experiments.

14

NOT many days after the last incident narrated, something
befell Billy Budd that more graveled him than aught that
had previously occurred.

It was a warm night for the latitude; and the foretopman,
whose watch at the time was properly below, was dozing on
the uppermost deck whither he had ascended from his hot
hammock, one of hundreds suspended so closely wedged
together over a lower gun deck that there was little or
no swing to them. He lay as in the shadow of a hillside,
stretched under the lee of the booms, a piled ridge of spare
spars amidships between foremast and mainmast among
which the ship's largest boat, the launch, was stowed. Alongside of three other slumberers from below, he lay near that
end of the booms which approaches the foremast; his station
aloft on duty as a foretopman being just over the deck-station
of the forecastlemen, entitling him according to usage to
make himself more or less at home in that neighborhood.

Presently he was stirred into semiconsciousness by somebody, who must have previously sounded the sleep of the

others, touching his shoulder, and then, as the foretopman
raised his head, breathing into his ear in a quick whisper,
"Slip into the lee forechains, Billy; there is something in
the wind. Don't speak. Quick, I will meet you there," and
disappearing.

Now Billy, like sundry other essentially good-natured ones,
had some of the weaknesses inseparable from essential good
nature; and among these was a reluctance, almost an incapa-
city of plumply saying *no* to an abrupt proposition not obviously absurd on the face of it, nor obviously unfriendly, nor
iniquitous. And being of warm blood, he had not the phlegm
tacitly to negative any proposition by unresponsive inaction.
Like his sense of fear, his apprehension as to aught outside
of the honest and natural was seldom very quick. Besides,
upon the present occasion, the drowse from his sleep still
hung upon him.

However it was, he mechanically rose and, sleepily wondering what could be in the wind, betook himself to the designated place, a narrow platform, one of six, outside of the
high bulwarks and screened by the great deadeyes and mul-
tiple columned lanyards of the shrouds and backstays; and,
in a great warship of that time, of dimensions commensurate
to the hull's magnitude; a tarry balcony in short, overhanging
the sea, and so secluded that one mariner of the *Bellipotent*,
a Nonconformist old tar of a serious turn, made it even in
daytime his private oratory.

In this retired nook the stranger soon joined Billy Budd.
There was no moon as yet; a haze obscured the starlight.
He could not distinctly see the stranger's face. Yet from
something in the outline and carriage, Billy took him, and
correctly, for one of the afterguard.

"Hist! Billy," said the man, in the same quick cautionary
whisper as before. "You were impressed, weren't you? Well,
so was I"; and he paused, as to mark the effect. But Billy,
not knowing exactly what to make of this, said nothing.
Then the other: "We are not the only impressed ones, Billy.
There's a gang of us.—Couldn't you—help—at a pinch?"

"What do you mean?" demanded Billy, here thoroughly
shaking off his drowse.

"Hist, hist!" the hurried whisper now growing husky. "See here," and the man help up two small objects faintly twinkling in the night-light; "see, they are yours, Billy, if you'll only——"

But Billy broke in, and in his resentful eagerness to deliver himself his vocal infirmity somewhat intruded. "D—d—damme, I don't know what you are d—d—driving at, or what you mean, but you had better g—g—go where you belong!" For the moment the fellow, as confounded, did not stir; and Billy, springing to his feet, said, "If you d—don't start, I'll t—t—toss you back over the r—rail!" There was no mistaking this, and the mysterious emissary decamped, disappearing in the direction of the mainmast in the shadow of the booms.

"Hallo, what's the matter?" here came growling from a forecastleman awakened from his deck-doze by Billy's raised voice. And as the foretopman reappeared and was recognized by him: "Ah, Beauty, is it you? Well, something must have been the matter, for you st—st—stuttered."

"Oh," rejoined Billy, now mastering the impediment, "I found an afterguardsman in our part of the ship here, and I bid him be off where he belongs."

"And is that all you did about it, Foretopman?" gruffly demanded another, an irascible old fellow of brick-colored visage and hair who was known to his associate forecastlemen as "Red Pepper." "Such sneaks I should like to marry to the gunner's daughter!"—by that expression meaning that he would like to subject them to disciplinary castigation over a gun.

However, Billy's rendering of the matter satisfactorily accounted to these inquirers for the brief commotion, since of all the sections of a ship's company the forecastlemen, veterans for the most part and bigoted in their sea prejudices, are the most jealous in resenting territorial encroachments, especially on the part of any of the afterguard, of whom they have but a sorry opinion—chiefly landsmen, never going aloft except to reef or furl the mainsail, and in no wise competent to handle a marlinspike or turn in a deadeye, say.

15

THIS incident sorely puzzled Billy Budd. It was an entirely new experience, the first time in his life that he had ever been personally approached in underhand intriguing fashion. Prior to this encounter he had known nothing of the afterguardsman, the two men being stationed wide apart, one forward and aloft during his watch, the other on deck and aft.

What could it mean? And could they really be guineas, those two glittering objects the interloper had held up to his (Billy's) eyes? Where could the fellow get guineas? Why, even spare buttons are not so plentiful at sea. The more he turned the matter over, the more he was nonplussed, and made uneasy and discomfited. In his disgustful recoil from an overture which, though he but ill comprehended, he instinctively knew must involve evil of some sort, Billy Budd was like a young horse fresh from the pasture suddenly inhaling a vile whiff from some chemical factory, and by repeated snortings trying to get it out of his nostrils and lungs. This frame of mind barred all desire of holding further parley with the fellow, even were it but for the purpose of gaining some enlightenment as to his design in approaching him. And yet he was not without natural curiosity to see how such a visitor in the dark would look in broad day.

He espied him the following afternoon in his first dogwatch below, one of the smokers on that forward part of the upper gun deck allotted to the pipe. He recognized him by his general cut and build more than by his round freckled face and glassy eyes of pale blue, veiled with lashes all but white. And yet Billy was a bit uncertain whether indeed it were he—yonder chap about his own age chatting and laughing in freehearted way, leaning against a gun; a genial young fellow enough to look at, and something of a rattlebrain, to all appearance. Rather chubby too for a sailor, even an afterguardsman. In short, the last man in the world, one would think, to be overburdened with thoughts, especially those perilous thoughts that must needs belong to a conspirator in any serious project, or even to the underling of such a conspirator.

Although Billy was not aware of it, the fellow, with a sidelong watchful glance, had perceived Billy first, and then noting that Billy was looking at him, thereupon nodded a familiar sort of friendly recognition as to an old acquaintance, without interrupting the talk he was engaged in with the group of smokers. A day or two afterwards, chancing in the evening promenade on a gun deck to pass Billy, he offered a flying word of good-fellowship, as it were, which by its unexpectedness, and equivocalness under the circumstances, so embarrassed Billy that he knew not how to respond to it, and let it go unnoticed.

Billy was now left more at a loss than before. The ineffectual speculations into which he was led were so disturbingly alien to him that he did his best to smother them. It never entered his mind that here was a matter which, from its extreme questionableness, it was his duty as a loyal bluejacket to report in the proper quarter. And, probably, had such a step been suggested to him, he would have been deterred from taking it by the thought, one of novice magnanimity, that it would savor overmuch of the dirty work of a telltale. He kept the thing to himself. Yet upon one occasion he could not forbear a little disburdening himself to the old Dansker, tempted thereto perhaps by the influence of a balmy night when the ship lay becalmed; the twain, silent for the most part, sitting together on deck, their heads propped against the bulwarks. But it was only a partial and anonymous account that Billy gave, the unfounded scruples above referred to preventing full disclosure to anybody. Upon hearing Billy's version, the sage Dansker seemed to divine more than he was told; and after a little meditation, during which his wrinkles were pursed as into a point, quite effacing for the time that quizzing expression his face sometimes wore: "Didn't I say so, Baby Budd?"

"Say what?" demanded Billy.

"Why, *Jemmy Legs* is *down* on you."

"And what," rejoined Billy in amazement, "has *Jemmy Legs* to do with that cracked afterguardsman?"

"Ho, it was an afterguardsman, then. A cat's-paw, a cat's-paw!" And with that exclamation, whether it had reference to a light puff of air just then coming over the calm sea, or a subtler relation to the afterguardsman, there is no telling, the old Merlin gave a twisting wrench with his black teeth at his plug of tobacco, vouchsafing no reply to Billy's impetuous question, though now repeated, for it was his wont to relapse into grim silence when interrogated in skeptical sort as to any of his sententious oracles, not always very clear ones, rather partaking of that obscurity which invests most Delphic deliverances from any quarter.

Long experience had very likely brought this old man to that bitter prudence which never interferes in aught and never gives advice.

16

YES, despite the Dansker's pithy insistence as to the master-at-arms being at the bottom of these strange experiences of Billy on board the *Bellipotent*, the young sailor was ready to ascribe them to almost anybody but the man who, to use Billy's own expression, "always had a pleasant word for him." This is to be wondered at. Yet not so much to be wondered at. In certain matters, some sailors even in mature life remain unsophisticated enough. But a young seafarer of the disposition of our athletic foretopman is much of a child-man. And yet a child's utter innocence is but its blank ignorance, and the innocence more or less wanes as intelligence waxes. But in Billy Budd intelligence, such as it was, had advanced while yet his simple-mindedness remained for the most part unaffected. Experience is a teacher indeed; yet did Billy's years make his experience small. Besides, he had none of that intuitive knowledge of the bad which in natures not good or incompletely so foreruns experience, and therefore may pertain, as in some instances it too clearly does pertain, even to youth.

And what could Billy know of man except of man as a mere sailor? And the old-fashioned sailor, the veritable man before the mast, the sailor from boyhood up, he, though indeed of the same species as a landsman, is in some respects singularly distinct from him. The sailor is frankness, the landsman is finesse. Life is not a game with the sailor, demanding the long head—no intricate game of chess where few moves are made in straightforwardness and ends are attained by indirection, an oblique, tedious, barren game hardly worth that poor candle burnt out in playing it.

Yes, as a class, sailors are in character a juvenile race. Even their deviations are marked by juvenility, this more especially holding true with the sailors of Billy's time. Then too, certain things which apply to all sailors do more pointedly operate here and there upon the junior one. Every sailor, too, is accustomed to obey orders without debating them; his life afloat is externally ruled for him; he is not brought into that promiscuous commerce with mankind where unobstructed free agency on equal terms—equal superficially, at least—soon teaches one that unless upon occasion he exercise a distrust keen in proportion to the fairness of the appearance, some foul turn may be served him. A ruled undemonstrative distrustfulness is so habitual, not with businessmen so much as with men who know their kind in less shallow relations than business, namely, certain men of the world, that they come at last to employ it all but unconsciously; and some of them would very likely feel real surprise at being charged with it as one of their general characteristics.

17

BUT after the little matter at the mess Billy Budd no more found himself in strange trouble at times about his hammock or his clothes bag or what not. As to that smile that occasionally sunned him, and the pleasant passing word, these were, if not more frequent, yet if anything more pronounced than before.

But for all that, there were certain other demonstrations now. When Claggart's unobserved glance happened to light on belted Billy rolling along the upper gun deck in the leisure of the second dogwatch, exchanging passing broadsides of fun with other young promenaders in the crowd, that glance would follow the cheerful sea Hyperion with a settled meditative and melancholy expression, his eyes strangely suffused with incipient feverish tears. Then would Claggart look like the man of sorrows.* Yes, and sometimes the melancholy expression would have in it a touch of soft yearning, as if Claggart could even have loved Billy but for fate and ban. But this was an evanescence, and quickly repented of, as it were, by an immitigable look, pinching and shriveling the visage into the momentary semblance of a wrinkled walnut. But sometimes catching sight in advance of the foretopman coming in his direction, he would, upon their nearing, step aside a little to let him pass, dwelling upon Billy for the moment with the glittering dental satire of a Guise.* But upon any abrupt unforeseen encounter a red light would flash forth from his eye like a spark from an anvil in a dusk smithy. That quick, fierce light was a strange one, darted from orbs which in repose were of a color nearest approaching a deeper violet, the softest of shades.

Though some of these caprices of the pit could not but be observed by their object, yet were they beyond the construing of such a nature. And the thews of Billy were hardly compatible with that sort of sensitive spiritual organization which in some cases instinctively conveys to ignorant innocence an admonition of the proximity of the malign. He thought the master-at-arms acted in a manner rather queer at times. That was all. But the occasional frank air and pleasant word went for what they purported to be, the young sailor never having heard as yet of the "too fair-spoken man."

Had the foretopman been conscious of having done or said anything to provoke the ill will of the official, it would have been different with him, and his sight might have been purged if not sharpened. As it was, innocence was his blinder.

So was it with him in yet another matter. Two minor officers, the armorer and captain of the hold, with whom he had never exchanged a word, his position in the ship not bringing him into contact with them, these men now for the first began to cast upon Billy, when they chanced to encounter him, that peculiar glance which evidences that the man from whom it comes has been some way tampered with, and to the prejudice of him upon whom the glance lights. Never did it occur to Billy as a thing to be noted or a thing suspicious, though he well knew the fact, that the armorer and captain of the hold, with the ship's yeoman, apothecary, and others of that grade, were by naval usage messmates of the master-at-arms, men with ears convenient to his confidential tongue.

But the general popularity that came from our Handsome Sailor's manly forwardness upon occasion and irresistible good nature, indicating no mental superiority tending to excite an invidious feeling, this good will on the part of most of his shipmates made him the less to concern himself about such mute aspects toward him as those whereto allusion has just been made, aspects he could not so fathom as to infer their whole import.

As to the afterguardsman, though Billy for reasons already given necessarily saw little of him, yet when the two did happen to meet, invariably came the fellow's offhand cheerful recognition, sometimes accompanied by a passing pleasant word or two. Whatever that equivocal young person's original design may really have been, or the design of which he might have been the deputy, certain it was from his manner upon these occasions that he had wholly dropped it.

It was as if his precocity of crookedness (and every vulgar villain is precocious) had for once deceived him, and the man he had sought to entrap as a simpleton had through his very simplicity ignominiously baffled him.

But shrewd ones may opine that it was hardly possible for Billy to refrain from going up to the afterguardsman and bluntly demanding to know his purpose in the initial interview so abruptly closed in the forechains. Shrewd ones may also think it but natural in Billy to set about sounding some of the other impressed men of the ship in order to discover what basis, if any, there was for the emissary's obscure suggestions as to plotting disaffection aboard. Yes, shrewd ones may so think. But something more, or rather something else than mere shrewdness is perhaps needful for the due understanding of such a character as Billy Budd's.

As to Claggart, the monomania in the man—if that indeed it were—as involuntarily disclosed by starts in the manifestations detailed, yet in general covered over by his self-contained and rational demeanor; this, like a subterranean fire, was eating its way deeper and deeper in him. Something decisive must come of it.

18

AFTER the mysterious interview in the forechains, the one so abruptly ended there by Billy, nothing especially germane to the story occurred until the events now about to be narrated.

Elsewhere it has been said that in the lack of frigates (of course better sailers than line-of-battle ships) in the English squadron up the Straits* at that period, the *Bellipotent 74* was occasionally employed not only as an available substitute for a scout, but at times on detached service of more important kind. This was not alone because of her sailing qualities, not common in a ship of her rate, but quite as much, probably, that the character of her commander, it was thought, specially adapted him for any duty where under unforeseen difficulties a prompt initiative might have to be taken in some matter demanding knowledge and ability in addition to those qualities implied in good seamanship. It was on an expedition of the latter sort, a somewhat distant one, and when the *Bellipotent* was almost at her furthest remove from the fleet, that in the latter part of an afternoon watch she unexpectedly came in sight of a ship of the enemy. It proved to be a frigate. The latter, perceiving through the glass that the weight of men and metal would be heavily against her, invoking her light heels crowded sail to get away. After a chase urged almost against hope and lasting until about the middle of the first dogwatch, she signally succeeded in effecting her escape.

Not long after the pursuit had been given up, and ere the excitement incident thereto had altogether waned away, the master-at-arms, ascending from his cavernous sphere, made his appearance cap in hand by the mainmast respectfully waiting the notice of Captain Vere, then solitary walking the weather side of the quarter-deck, doubtless somewhat chafed at the failure of the pursuit. The spot where Claggart stood was the place allotted to men of lesser grades seeking some more particular interview either with the officer of the deck or the captain himself. But from the latter it was not often that a sailor or petty officer of those days would seek a hearing; only some exceptional cause would, according to established custom, have warranted that.

Presently, just as the commander, absorbed in his reflections, was on the point of turning aft in his promenade, he became sensible of Claggart's presence, and saw the doffed cap held in deferential expectancy. Here be it said that Captain Vere's personal knowledge of this petty officer had only begun at the time of the ship's last sailing from home, Claggart then for the first, in transfer from a ship detained for repairs, supplying on board the *Bellipotent* the place of a previous master-at-arms disabled and ashore.

No sooner did the commander observe who it was that now deferentially stood awaiting his notice than a peculiar expression came over him. It was not unlike that which uncontrollably will flit across the countenance of one at unawares encountering a person who, though known to him indeed, has hardly been long enough known for thorough knowledge, but something in whose aspect nevertheless now for the first provokes a vaguely repellent distaste. But coming to a stand and resuming much of his wonted official manner, save that a sort of impatience lurked in the intonation of the opening word, he said "Well? What is it, Master-at-arms?"

With the air of a subordinate grieved at the necessity of being a messenger of ill tidings, and while conscientiously determind to be frank yet equally resolved upon shunning overstatement, Claggart at this invitation, or rather summons to disburden, spoke up. What he said, conveyed in the language of no uneducated man, was to the effect following, if not altogether in these words, namely, that during the chase and preparations for the possible encounter he had seen enough to convince him that at least one sailor aboard was a dangerous character in a ship mustering some who not only had taken a guilty part in the late serious troubles, but others also who, like the man in question, had entered His Majesty's service under another form than enlistment.

At this point Captain Vere with some impatience interrupted him: "Be direct, man; say *impressed men.*"

Claggart made a gesture of subservience, and proceeded. Quite lately he (Claggart) had begun to suspect that on the gun decks some sort of movement prompted by the sailor in question was covertly going on, but he had not thought himself warranted in reporting the suspicion so long as it remained indistinct. But from what he had that afternoon observed in the man referred to, the suspicion of something clandestine going on had advanced to a point less removed from certainty. He deeply felt, he added, the serious responsibility assumed in making a report involving such possible consequences to the individual mainly concerned, besides tending to augment those natural anxieties which every naval commander must feel in view of extraordinary outbreaks so recent as those which, he sorrowfully said it, it needed not to name.

Now at the first broaching of the matter Captain Vere, taken by surprise, could not wholly dissemble his disquietude. But as Claggart went on, the former's aspect changed into restiveness under something in the testifier's manner in giving his testimony. However, he refrained from interrupting him. And Claggart, continuing, concluded with this: "God forbid, your honor, that the *Bellipotent*'s should be the experience of the ——"

"Never mind that!" here peremptorily broke in the superior, his face altering with anger, instinctively divining the ship that the other was about to name, one in which the Nore Mutiny had assumed a singularly tragical character that for a time jeopardized the life of its commander. Under the circumstances he was indignant at the purposed allusion. When the commissioned officers themselves were on all occasions very heedful how they referred to the recent events in the fleet, for a petty officer unnecessarily to allude to them in the presence of his captain, this struck him as a most immodest presumption. Besides, to his quick sense of self-respect it even looked under the circumstances something like an attempt to alarm him. Nor at first was he without some surprise that one who so far as he had hitherto come under his notice had shown considerable tact in his function should in this particular evince such lack of it.

But these thoughts and kindred dubious ones flitting across his mind were suddenly replaced by an intuitional surmise which, though as yet obscure in form, served practically to affect his reception of the ill tidings. Certain it is that, long versed in everything pertaining to the complicated gun-deck life, which like every other form of life has its secret mines and dubious side, the side popularly disclaimed, Captain Vere did not permit himself to be unduly disturbed by the general tenor of his subordinate's report.

Furthermore, if in view of recent events prompt action should be taken at the first palpable sign of recurring insubordination, for all that, not judicious would it be, he thought, to keep the idea of lingering disaffection alive by undue forwardness in crediting an informer, even if his own subordinate and charged among other things with police surveillance of the crew. This feeling would not perhaps have so prevailed with him were it not that upon a prior occasion the patriotic zeal officially evinced by Claggart had somewhat irritated him as appearing rather supersensible and strained. Furthermore, something even in the official's self-possessed and somewhat ostentatious manner in making his specifications strangely reminded him of a bandsman, a perjurous witness in a capital case before a court-martial ashore of which when a lieutenant he (Captain Vere) had been a member.

Now the peremptory check given to Claggart in the matter of the arrested allusion was quickly followed up by this: "You say that there is at least one dangerous man aboard. Name him."

"William Budd, a foretopman, your honor."

"William Budd!" repeated Captain Vere with unfeigned astonishment. "And mean you the man that Lieutenant

Ratcliffe took from the merchantman not very long ago, the young fellow who seems to be so popular with the men—Billy, the Handsome Sailor, as they call him?"

"The same, your honor; but for all his youth and good looks, a deep one. Not for nothing does he insinuate himself into the good will of his shipmates, since at the least they will at a pinch say—all hands will—a good word for him, and at all hazards. Did Lieutenant Ratcliffe happen to tell your honor of that adroit fling of Budd's, jumping up in the cutter's bow under the merchantman's stern when he was being taken off? It is even masked by that sort of good-humored air that at heart he resents his impressment. You have but noted his fair cheek. A mantrap may be under the ruddy-tipped daisies."

Now the Handsome Sailor as a signal figure among the crew had naturally enough attracted the captain's attention from the first. Though in general not very demonstrative to his officers, he had congratulated Lieutenant Ratcliffe upon his good fortune in lighting on such a fine specimen of the *genus homo*, who in the nude might have posed for a statue of young Adam before the Fall. As to Billy's adieu to the ship *Rights-of-Man*, which the boarding lieutenant had indeed reported to him, but, in a deferential way, more as a good story than aught else, Captain Vere, though mistakenly understanding it as a satiric sally, had but thought so much the better of the impressed man for it; as a military sailor, admiring the spirit that could take an arbitrary enlistment so merrily and sensibly. The foretopman's conduct, too, so far as it had fallen under the captain's notice, had confirmed the first happy augury, while the new recruit's qualities as a "sailor-man" seemed to be such that he had thought of recommending him to the executive officer for promotion to a place that would more frequently bring him under his own observation, namely, the captaincy of the mizzentop, replacing there in the starboard watch a man not so young whom partly for that reason he deemed less fitted for the post. Be it parenthesized here that since the mizzen-topmen have not to handle such breadths of heavy canvas as the lower sails on the mainmast and foremast, a young

man if of the right stuff not only seems best adapted to duty
there, but in fact is generally selected for the captaincy of
that top, and the company under him are light hands and
often but striplings. In sum, Captain Vere had from the
beginning deemed Billy Budd to be what in the naval parlance of the time was called a "King's bargain": that is to
say, for His Britannic Majesty's navy a capital investment
at small outlay or none at all.

After a brief pause, during which the reminiscences above
mentioned passed vividly through his mind and he weighed
the import of Claggart's last suggestion conveyed in the phrase
"mantrap under the daisies," and the more he weighed it
the less reliance he felt in the informer's good faith, suddenly he turned upon him and in a low voice demanded:
"Do you come to me, Master-at-arms, with so foggy a tale?
As to Budd, cite me an act or spoken word* of his confirm-
atory of what you in general charge against him. Stay,"
drawing nearer to him; "heed what you speak. Just now,
and in a case like this, there is a yardarm-end for the false
witness."

"Ah, your honor!" sighed Claggart, mildly shaking his
shapely head as in sad deprecation of such unmerited sever-
ity of tone. Then, bridling—erecting himself as in virtuous
self-assertion—he circumstantially alleged certain words and
acts which collectively, if credited, led to presumptions mor-
tally inculpating Budd. And for some of these averments,
he added, substantiating proof was not far.

With gray eyes impatient and distrustful essaying to fathom
to the bottom Claggart's calm violet ones, Captain Vere
again heard him out; then for the moment stood ruminating. The mood he evinced, Claggart—himself for the time
liberated from the other's scrutiny—steadily regarded with
a look difficult to render: a look curious of the operation of
his tactics, a look such as might have been that of the
spokesman of the envious children of Jacob deceptively
imposing upon the troubled patriarch the blood-dyed coat
of young Joseph.*

Though something exceptional in the moral quality of
Captain Vere made him, in earnest encounter with a fellow

man, a veritable touchstone of that man's essential nature, yet now as to Claggart and what was really going on in him his feeling partook less of intuitional conviction than of strong suspicion clogged by strange dubieties. The perplexity he evinced proceeded less from aught touching the man informed against—as Claggart doubtless opined—than from considerations how best to act in regard to the informer. At first, indeed, he was naturally for summoning that substantiation of his allegations which Claggart said was at hand. But such a proceeding would result in the matter at once getting abroad, which in the present stage of it, he thought, might undesirably affect the ship's company. If Claggart was a false witness—that closed the affair. And therefore, before trying the accusation, he would first practically test the accuser; and he thought this could be done in a quiet, undemonstrative way.

The measure he determined upon involved a shifting of the scene, a transfer to a place less exposed to observation than the broad quarter-deck. For although the few gun-room officers there at the time had, in due observance of naval etiquette, withdrawn to leeward the moment Captain Vere had begun his promenade on the deck's weather side; and though during the colloquy with Claggart they of course ventured not to diminish the distance; and though throughout the interview Captain Vere's voice was far from high, and Claggart's silvery and low; and the wind in the cordage and the wash of the sea helped the more to put them beyond earshot; nevertheless, the interview's continuance already had attracted observation from some topmen aloft and other sailors in the waist or further forward.

Having determined upon his measures, Captain Vere forthwith took action. Abruptly turning to Claggart, he asked, "Master-at-arms, is it now Budd's watch aloft?"

"No, your honor."

Whereupon, "Mr. Wilkes!" summoning the nearest midshipman. "Tell Albert to come to me." Albert was the captain's hammock-boy, a sort of sea valet in whose discretion and fidelity his master had much confidence. The lad appeared.

"You know Budd, the foretopman?"

"I do, sir."

"Go find him. It is his watch off. Manage to tell him out of earshot that he is wanted aft. Contrive it that he speaks to nobody. Keep him in talk yourself. And not till you get well aft here, not till then let him know that the place where he is wanted is my cabin. You understand. Go.—Master-at-arms, show yourself on the decks below, and when you think it time for Albert to be coming with his man, stand by quietly to follow the sailor in."

19

NOW when the foretopman found himself in the cabin, closeted there, as it were, with the captain and Claggart, he was surprised enough. But it was a surprise unaccompanied by apprehension or distrust. To an immature nature essentially honest and humane, forewarning intimations of subtler danger from one's kind come tardily if at all. The only thing that took shape in the young sailor's mind was this: Yes, the captain, I have always thought, looks kindly upon me. Wonder if he's going to make me his coxswain. I should like that. And may be now he is going to ask the master-at-arms about me.

"Shut the door there, sentry," said the commander; "stand without, and let nobody come in.—Now, Master-at-arms, tell this man to his face what you told of him to me," and stood prepared to scrutinize the mutually confronting visages.

With the measured step and calm collected air of an asylum physician approaching in the public hall some patient beginning to show indications of a coming paroxysm, Claggart deliberately advanced within short range of Billy and, mesmerically looking him in the eye, briefly recapitulated the accusation.

Not at first did Billy take it in. When he did, the rose-tan of his cheek looked struck as by white leprosy. He stood like one impaled and gagged. Meanwhile the accuser's eyes, removing not as yet from the blue dilated ones, underwent a phenomenal change, their wonted rich violet color blurring into a muddy purple. Those lights of human intelligence, losing human expression, were gelidly protruding like the alien eyes of certain uncatalogued creatures of the deep. The first mesmeristic glance was one of serpent fascination; the last was as the paralyzing lurch of the torpedo fish.*

"Speak, man!" said Captain Vere to the transfixed one, struck by his aspect even more than by Claggart's. "Speak! Defend yourself!" Which appeal caused but a strange dumb gesturing and gurgling in Billy; amazement at such an accusation so suddenly sprung on inexperienced nonage; this, and, it may be, horror of the accuser's eyes, serving to bring out his lurking defect and in this instance for the time intensifying it into a convulsed tongue-tie; while the intent head and entire form straining forward in an agony of ineffectual eagerness to obey the injunction to speak and defend himself, gave an expression to the face like that of a condemned vestal priestess in the moment of being buried alive, and in the first struggle against suffocation.

Though at the time Captain Vere was quite ignorant of Billy's liability to vocal impediment, he now immediately divined it, since vividly Billy's aspect recalled to him that of a bright young schoolmate of his whom he had once seen struck by much the same startling impotence in the act of eagerly rising in the class to be foremost in response to a testing question put to it by the master. Going close up to the young sailor, and laying a soothing hand on his shoulder, he said, "There is no hurry, my boy. Take your time, take your time." Contrary to the effect intended, these words so fatherly in tone, doubtless touching Billy's heart to the quick, prompted yet more violent efforts at utterance—efforts soon ending for the time in confirming the paralysis, and bringing to his face an expression which was as a crucifixion to behold. The next instant, quick as the flame from a discharged cannon at night, his right arm shot out, and Claggart dropped to the deck. Whether intentionally or but owing to the young athlete's superior height, the blow had taken effect full upon the forehead, so shapely and intellectual-looking a feature in the master-at-arms; so that the body fell over lengthwise, like a heavy plank tilted from erectness. A gasp or two, and he lay motionless.

"Fated boy," breathed Captain Vere in tone so low as to be almost a whisper, "what have you done! But here, help me."

The twain raised the felled one from the loins up into a sitting position. The spare form flexibly acquiesced, but inertly. It was like handling a dead snake. They lowered it back. Regaining erectness, Captain Vere with one hand covering his face stood to all appearance as impassive as the object at his feet. Was he absorbed in taking in all the bearings of the event and what was best not only now at once to be done, but also in the sequel? Slowly he uncovered his face; and the effect was as if the moon emerging from eclipse should reappear with quite another aspect than that which had gone into hiding. The father in him, manifested towards Billy thus far in the scene, was replaced by the military disciplinarian. In his official tone he bade the foretopman retire to a stateroom aft (pointing it out), and there remain till thence summoned. This order Billy in silence mechanically obeyed. Then going to the cabin door where it opened on the quarter-deck, Captain Vere said to the sentry without, "Tell somebody to send Albert here." When the lad appeared, his master so contrived it that he should not catch sight of the prone one. "Albert," he said to him, "tell the surgeon I wish to see him. You need not come back till called."

When the surgeon entered—a self-poised character of that grave sense and experience that hardly anything could take him aback—Captain Vere advanced to meet him, thus unconsciously intercepting his view of Claggart, and, interrupting the other's wonted ceremonious salutation, said, "Nay. Tell me how it is with yonder man," directing his attention to the prostrate one.

The surgeon looked, and for all his self-command somewhat started at the abrupt revelation. On Claggart's always pallid complexion, thick black blood was now oozing from nostril and ear. To the gazer's professional eye it was unmistakably no living man that he saw.

"Is it so, then?" said Captain Vere, intently watching him. "I thought it. But verify it." Whereupon the customary tests

confirmed the surgeon's first glance, who now, looking up
in unfeigned concern, cast a look of intense inquisitiveness
upon his superior. But Captain Vere, with one hand to his
brow, was standing motionless. Suddenly, catching the surgeon's arm convulsively, he exclaimed, pointing down to the
body, "It is the divine judgment on Ananias!* Look!"

Disturbed by the excited manner he had never before
observed in the *Bellipotent*'s captain, and as yet wholly ignorant of the affair, the prudent surgeon nevertheless held his
peace, only again looking an earnest interrogatory as to what
it was that had resulted in such a tragedy.

But Captain Vere was now again motionless, standing absorbed in thought. Again starting, he vehemently exclaimed,
"Struck dead by an angel of God! Yet the angel must
hang!"*

At these passionate interjections, mere incoherences to the
listener as yet unapprised of the antecedents, the surgeon
was profoundly discomposed. But now, as recollecting himself, Captain Vere in less passionate tone briefly related the
circumstances leading up to the event. "But come; we must
dispatch," he added. "Help me to remove him" (meaning
the body) "to yonder compartment," designating one opposite that where the foretopman remained immured. Anew disturbed by a request that, as implying a desire for secrecy,
seemed unaccountably strange to him, there was nothing for
the subordinate to do but comply.

"Go now," said Captain Vere with something of his
wonted manner. "Go now. I presently shall call a drumhead
court. Tell the lieutenants what has happened, and tell Mr.
Mordant" (meaning the captain of marines), "and charge
them to keep the matter to themselves."

20

FULL of disquietude and misgiving, the surgeon left the
cabin. Was Captain Vere suddenly affected in his mind,
or was it but a transient excitement, brought about by so
strange and extraordinary a tragedy? As to the drumhead

court, it struck the surgeon as impolitic, if nothing more. The thing to do, he thought, was to place Billy Budd in confinement, and in a way dictated by usage, and post-pone further action in so extraordinary a case to such time as they should rejoin the squadron, and then refer it to the admiral. He recalled the unwonted agitation of Captain Vere and his excited exclamations, so at variance with his normal manner. Was he unhinged?*

But assuming that he is, it is not so susceptible of proof. What then can the surgeon do? No more trying situation is conceivable than that of an officer subordinate under a cap-tain whom he suspects to be not mad, indeed, but yet not quite unaffected in his intellects. To argue his order to him would be insolence. To resist him would be mutiny.

In obedience to Captain Vere, he communicated what had happened to the lieutenants and captain of marines, saying nothing as to the captain's state. They fully shared his own surprise and concern. Like him too, they seemed to think that such a matter should be referred to the admiral.

21

WHO in the rainbow can draw the line where the violet tint ends and the orange tint begins? Distinctly we see the dif-ference of the colors, but where exactly does the one first blendingly enter into the other? So with sanity and insanity. In pronounced cases there is no question about them. But in some supposed cases, in various degrees supposedly less pronounced, to draw the exact line of demarcation few will undertake, though for a fee becoming considerate some professional experts will. There is nothing namable but that some men will, or undertake to, do it for pay.

Whether Captain Vere, as the surgeon professionally and privately surmised, was really the sudden victim of any degree of aberration, every one must determine for himself by such light as this narrative may afford.

That the unhappy event which has been narrated could not have happened at a worse juncture was but too true.

For it was close on the heel of the suppressed insurrections, an aftertime very critical to naval authority, demanding from every English sea commander two qualities not readily interfusable—prudence and rigor. Moreover, there was something crucial in the case.

In the jugglery of circumstances preceding and attending the event on board the *Bellipotent*, and in the light of that martial code whereby it was formally to be judged, innocence and guilt personified in Claggart and Budd in effect changed places. In a legal view the apparent victim of the tragedy was he who had sought to victimize a man blameless; and the indisputable deed of the latter, navally regarded, constituted the most heinous of military crimes. Yet more. The essential right and wrong involved in the matter, the clearer that might be, so much the worse for the responsibility of a loyal sea commander, inasmuch as he was not authorized to determine the matter on that primitive basis.

Small wonder then that the *Bellipotent*'s captain, though in general a man of rapid decision, felt that circumspectness not less than promptitude was necessary. Until he could decide upon his course, and in each detail; and not only so, but until the concluding measure was upon the point of being enacted, he deemed it advisable, in view of all the circumstances, to guard as much as possible against publicity. Here he may or may not have erred. Certain it is, however, that subsequently in the confidential talk of more than one or two gun rooms and cabins he was not a little criticized by some officers, a fact imputed by his friends and vehemently by his cousin Jack Denton to professional jealousy of Starry Vere. Some imaginative ground for invidious comment there was. The maintenance of secrecy in the matter, the confining all knowledge of it for a time to the place where the homicide occurred, the quarter-deck cabin; in these particulars lurked some resemblance to the policy adopted in those tragedies of the palace which have occurred more than once in the capital founded by Peter the Barbarian.*

The case indeed was such that fain would the *Bellipotent*'s captain have deferred taking any action whatever respecting it further than to keep the foretopman a close prisoner till the ship rejoined the squadron and then submitting the matter to the judgment of his admiral.

But a true military officer is in one particular like a true monk. Not with more of self-abnegation will the latter keep his vows of monastic obedience than the former his vows of allegiance to martial duty.

Feeling that unless quick action was taken on it, the deed of the foretopman, so soon as it should be known on the gun decks, would tend to awaken any slumbering embers of the Nore among the crew, a sense of the urgency of the case overruled in Captain Vere every other consideration. But though a conscientious disciplinarian, he was no lover of authority for mere authority's sake. Very far was he from embracing opportunities for monopolizing to himself the perils of moral responsibility, none at least that could properly be referred to an official superior or shared with him by his official equals or even subordinates. So thinking, he was glad it would not be at variance with usage to turn the matter over to a summary court of his own officers, reserving to himself, as the one on whom the ultimate accountability would rest, the right of maintaining a supervision of it, or formally or informally interposing at need. Accordingly a drumhead court* was summarily convened, he electing the individuals composing it: the first lieutenant, the captain of marines, and the sailing master.

In associating an officer of marines with the sea lieutenant and the sailing master in a case having to do with a sailor, the commander perhaps deviated from general custom. He was prompted thereto by the circumstance that he took that soldier to be a judicious person, thoughtful, and not altogether incapable of grappling with a difficult case unprecedented in his prior experience. Yet even as to him he was not without some latent misgiving, for withal he was an extremely good-natured man, an enjoyer of his dinner, a sound sleeper, and inclined to obesity—a man who though he would always maintain his manhood in battle might not prove altogether reliable in a moral dilemma involving aught of the tragic. As to the first lieutenant and the sailing master, Captain Vere could not but be aware that though honest natures, of approved gallantry upon occasion, their intelligence was mostly confined to the matter of active seamanship and the fighting demands of their profession.

The court was held in the same cabin where the unfortunate affair had taken place. This cabin, the commander's, embraced the entire area under the poop deck. Aft, and on either side, was a small stateroom, the one now temporarily a jail and the other a dead-house, and a yet smaller compartment, leaving a space between expanding forward into a goodly oblong of length coinciding with the ship's beam. A skylight of moderate dimension was overhead, and at each end of the oblong space were two sashed porthole windows easily convertible back into embrasures for short carronades.*

All being quickly in readiness, Billy Budd was arraigned, Captain Vere necessarily appearing as the sole witness in the case, and as such temporarily sinking his rank, though singularly maintaining it in a matter apparently trivial, namely, that he testified from the ship's weather side, with that object having caused the court to sit on the lee side. Concisely he narrated all that had led up to the catastrophe, omitting nothing in Claggart's accusation and deposing as to the manner in which the prisoner had received it. At this testimony the three officers glanced with no little surprise at Billy Budd, the last man they would have suspected either of the mutinous design alleged by Claggart or the undeniable deed he himself had done. The first lieutenant, taking judicial primacy and turning toward the prisoner, said, "Captain Vere has spoken. Is it or is it not as Captain Vere says?"

In response came syllables not so much impeded in the utterance as might have been anticipated. They were these: "Captain Vere tells the truth. It is just as Captain Vere says, but it is not as the master-at-arms said. I have eaten the King's bread and I am true to the King."

"I believe you, my man," said the witness, his voice indicating a suppressed emotion not otherwise betrayed.

"God will bless you for that, your honor!" not without stammering said Billy, and all but broke down. But immediately he was recalled to self-control by another question, to which with the same emotional difficulty of utterance he said, "No, there was no malice between us. I never bore malice against the master-at-arms. I am sorry that he is dead. I did not mean to kill him. Could I have used my tongue I would not have struck him. But he foully lied to my face and in presence of my captain, and I had to say something, and I could only say it with a blow, God help me!"

In the impulsive aboveboard manner of the frank one the court saw confirmed all that was implied in words that just previously had perplexed them, coming as they did from the testifier to the tragedy and promptly following Billy's impassioned disclaimer of mutinous intent—Captain Vere's words, "I believe you, my man."

Next it was asked of him whether he knew of or suspected aught savoring of incipient trouble (meaning mutiny, though the explicit term was avoided) going on in any section of the ship's company.

The reply lingered. This was naturally imputed by the court to the same vocal embarrassment which had retarded or obstructed previous answers. But in main it was otherwise here, the question immediately recalling to Billy's mind the interview with the afterguardsman in the forechains. But an innate repugnance to playing a part at all approaching that of an informer against one's own shipmates—the same erring sense of uninstructed honor which had stood in the way of his reporting the matter at the time, though as a loyal man-of-war's man it was incumbent on him, and failure so to do, if charged against him and proven, would have subjected him to the heaviest of penalties; this, with the blind feeling now his that nothing really was being hatched, prevailed with him. When the answer came it was a negative.

"One question more," said the officer of marines, now first speaking and with a troubled earnestness. "You tell us that what the master-at-arms said against you was a lie. Now why should he have so lied, so maliciously lied, since you declare there was no malice between you?"

At that question, unintentionally touching on a spiritual sphere wholly obscure to Billy's thoughts, he was nonplussed, evincing a confusion indeed that some observers, such as can readily be imagined, would have construed into involuntary evidence of hidden guilt. Nevertheless, he strove some way to answer, but all at once relinquished the vain endeavor, at the same time turning an appealing glance towards Captain Vere as deeming him his best helper and friend. Captain Vere, who had been seated for a time, rose to his feet, addressing the interrogator. "The question you put to him comes naturally enough. But how can he rightly answer it?—or anybody else, unless indeed it be he who lies within there," designating the compartment where lay the corpse. "But the prone one there will not rise to our summons. In effect, though, as it seems to me, the point you make is hardly material. Quite aside from any conceivable motive actuating the master-at-arms, and irrespective of the provocation to the blow, a martial court must needs in the present case confine its attention to the blow's consequence, which consequence justly is to be deemed not otherwise than as the striker's deed."

This utterance, the full significance of which it was not at all likely that Billy took in, nevertheless caused him to turn a wistful interrogative look toward the speaker, a look in its dumb expressiveness not unlike that which a dog of generous breed might turn upon his master, seeking in his face some elucidation of a previous gesture ambiguous to the canine intelligence. Nor was the same utterance without marked effect upon the three officers, more especially the soldier. Couched in it seemed to them a meaning unanticipated, involving a prejudgment on the speaker's part. It served to augment a mental disturbance previously evident enough.

The soldier once more spoke, in a tone of suggestive dubiety addressing at once his associates and Captain Vere: "Nobody is present—none of the ship's company, I mean—who might shed lateral light, if any is to be had, upon what remains mysterious in this matter."

"That is thoughtfully put," said Captain Vere; "I see your drift. Ay, there is a mystery; but, to use a scriptural phrase, it is a 'mystery of iniquity,' a matter for psychologic

theologians to discuss. But what has a military court to do
with it? Not to add that for us any possible investigation of
it is cut off by the lasting tongue-tie of—him—in yonder,"
again designating the mortuary stateroom. "The prisoner's
deed—with that alone we have to do."

To this, and particularly the closing reiteration, the marine
soldier, knowing not how aptly to reply, sadly abstained from
saying aught. The first lieutenant, who at the outset had not
unnaturally assumed primacy in the court, now overrulingly
instructed by a glance from Captain Vere, a glance more
effective than words, resumed that primacy. Turning to
the prisoner, "Budd," he said, and scarce in equable tones,
"Budd, if you have aught further to say for yourself, say
it now."

Upon this the young sailor turned another quick glance
toward Captain Vere; then, as taking a hint from that aspect,
a hint confirming his own instinct that silence was now best,
replied to the lieutenant, "I have said all, sir."

The marine—the same who had been the sentinel without the cabin door at the time that the foretopman, followed
by the master-at-arms, entered it—he, standing by the sailor
throughout these judicial proceedings, was now directed to
take him back to the after compartment originally assigned
to the prisoner and his custodian. As the twain disappeared
from view, the three officers, as partially liberated from some
inward constraint associated with Billy's mere presence, simultaneously stirred in their seats. They exchanged looks of
troubled indecision, yet feeling that decide they must and
without long delay. For Captain Vere, he for the time stood
—unconsciously with his back toward them, apparently in
one of his absent fits—gazing out from a sashed porthole to
windward upon the monotonous blank of the twilight sea.
But the court's silence continuing, broken only at moments
by brief consultations, in low earnest tones, this served to
arouse him and energize him. Turning, he to-and-fro paced
the cabin athwart; in the returning ascent to windward climbing the slant deck in the ship's lee roll, without knowing it
symbolizing thus in his action a mind resolute to surmount
difficulties even if against primitive instincts strong as the

wind and the sea. Presently he came to a stand before the three. After scanning their faces he stood less as mustering his thoughts for expression than as one inly deliberating how best to put them to well-meaning men not intellectually mature, men with whom it was necessary to demonstrate certain principles that were axioms to himself. Similar impatience as to talking is perhaps one reason that deters some minds from addressing any popular assemblies.

When speak he did, something, both in the substance of what he said and his manner of saying it, showed the influence of unshared studies modifying and tempering the practical training of an active career. This, along with his phraseology, now and then was suggestive of the grounds whereon rested that imputation of a certain pedantry socially alleged against him by certain naval men of wholly practical cast, captains who nevertheless would frankly concede that His Majesty's navy mustered no more efficient officer of their grade than Starry Vere.

What he said was to this effect: "Hitherto I have been but the witness, little more; and I should hardly think now to take another tone, that of your coadjutor for the time, did I not perceive in you—at the crisis too—a troubled hesitancy, proceeding, I doubt not, from the clash of military duty with moral scruple—scruple vitalized by compassion. For the compassion, how can I otherwise than share it? But, mindful of paramount obligations, I strive against scruples that may tend to enervate decision. Not, gentlemen, that I hide from myself that the case is an exceptional one. Speculatively regarded, it well might be referred to a jury of casuists. But for us here, acting not as casuists or moralists, it is a case practical, and under martial law practically to be dealt with.

"But your scruples: do they move as in a dusk? Challenge them. Make them advance and declare themselves. Come now; do they import something like this: If, mindless of palliating circumstances, we are bound to regard the death of the master-at-arms as the prisoner's deed, then does that deed constitute a capital crime whereof the penalty is a mortal one. But in natural justice is nothing but the prisoner's

overt act to be considered? How can we adjudge to summary
and shameful death a fellow creature innocent before God,
and whom we feel to be so?—Does that state it aright? You
sign sad assent. Well, I too feel that, the full force of that.
It is Nature. But do these buttons that we wear attest that
our allegiance is to Nature? No, to the King. Though the
ocean, which is inviolate Nature primeval, though this be
the element where we move and have our being as sailors,
yet as the King's officers lies our duty in a sphere corres-
pondingly natural? So little is that true, that in receiving our
commissions we in the most important regards ceased to be
natural free agents. When war is declared are we the commissioned fighters previously consulted? We fight at command.
If our judgments approve the war, that is but coincidence.
So in other particulars. So now. For suppose condemnation
to follow these present proceedings. Would it be so much we
ourselves that would condemn as it would be martial law
operating through us? For that law and the rigor of it, we
are not responsible. Our vowed responsibility is in this: That
however pitilessly that law may operate in any instances, we
nevertheless adhere to it and administer it.

"But the exceptional in the matter moves the hearts within
you. Even so too is mine moved. But let not warm hearts
betray heads that should be cool. Ashore in a criminal case,
will an upright judge allow himself off the bench to be waylaid by some tender kinswoman of the accused seeking to
touch him with her tearful plea? Well, the heart here, sometimes the feminine in man, is as that piteous woman, and
hard though it be, she must here be ruled out."

He paused, earnestly studying them for a moment; then
resumed.

"But something in your aspect seems to urge that it is
not solely the heart that moves in you, but also the conscience, the private conscience. But tell me whether or not,
occupying the position we do, private conscience should
not yield to that imperial one formulated in the code under
which alone we officially proceed?"

Here the three men moved in their seats, less convinced
than agitated by the course of an argument troubling but
the more the spontaneous conflict within.

Perceiving which, the speaker paused for a moment; then abruptly changing his tone, went on.

"To steady us a bit, let us recur to the facts.—In wartime at sea a man-of-war's man strikes his superior in grade, and the blow kills. Apart from its effect the blow itself is, according to the Articles of War,* a capital crime. Furthermore——"

"Ay, sir," emotionally broke in the officer of marines, "in one sense it was. But surely Budd purposed neither mutiny nor homicide."

"Surely not, my good man. And before a court less arbitrary and more merciful than a martial one, that plea would largely extenuate. At the Last Assizes* it shall acquit. But how here? We proceed under the law of the Mutiny Act.* In feature no child can resemble his father more than that Act resembles in spirit the thing from which it derives— War. In His Majesty's service—in this ship, indeed—there are Englishmen forced to fight for the King against their will. Against their conscience, for aught we know. Though as their fellow creatures some of us may appreciate their position, yet as navy officers what reck we of it? Still less recks the enemy. Our impressed men he would fain cut down in the same swath with our volunteers. As regards the enemy's naval conscripts, some of whom may even share our own abhorrence of the regicidal French Directory, it is the same on our side. War looks but to the frontage, the appearance. And the Mutiny Act, War's child, takes after the father. Budd's intent or non-intent is nothing to the purpose.

"But while, put to it by those anxieties in you which I cannot but respect, I only repeat myself—while thus strangely we prolong proceedings that should be summary—the enemy may be sighted and an engagement result. We must do; and one of two things must we do—condemn or let go."

"Can we not convict and yet mitigate the penalty?" asked the sailing master, here speaking, and falteringly, for the first.

"Gentlemen, were that clearly lawful for us under the circumstances, consider the consequences of such clemency. The people" (meaning the ship's company) "have native sense; most of them are familiar with our naval usage and tradition; and how would they take it? Even could you explain to them—which our official position forbids—they,

long molded by arbitrary discipline, have not that kind of
intelligent responsiveness that might qualify them to comprehend and discriminate. No, to the people the foretopman's deed, however it be worded in the announcement,
will be plain homicide committed in a flagrant act of mutiny.
What penalty for that should follow, they know. But it does
not follow. *Why?* they will ruminate. You know what sailors
are. Will they not revert to the recent outbreak at the Nore?
Ay. They know the well-founded alarm—the panic it struck
throughout England. Your clement sentence they would
account pusillanimous. They would think that we flinch,
that we are afraid of them—afraid of practicing a lawful rigor
singularly demanded at this juncture, lest it should provoke
new troubles. What shame to us such a conjecture on their
part, and how deadly to discipline. You see then, whither,
prompted by duty and the law, I steadfastly drive. But I
beseech you, my friends, do not take me amiss. I feel as
you do for this unfortunate boy. But did he know our hearts,
I take him to be of that generous nature that he would feel
even for us on whom in this military necessity so heavy a
compulsion is laid."

With that, crossing the deck he resumed his place by
the sashed porthole, tacitly leaving the three to come to a
decision. On the cabin's opposite side the troubled court sat
silent. Loyal lieges, plain and practical, though at bottom
they dissented from some points Captain Vere had put to
them, they were without the faculty, hardly had the inclination, to gainsay one whom they felt to be an earnest man,
one too not less their superior in mind than in naval rank.
But it is not improbable that even such of his words as were
not without influence over them, less came home to them
than his closing appeal to their instinct as sea officers: in the
forethought he threw out as to the practical consequences
to discipline, considering the unconfirmed tone of the fleet at
the time, should a man-of-war's man's violent killing at sea
of a superior in grade be allowed to pass for aught else than
a capital crime demanding prompt infliction of the penalty.

Not unlikely they were brought to something more or less
akin to that harassed frame of mind which in the year 1842

actuated the commander of the U.S. brig-of-war *Somers* to resolve, under the so-called Articles of War, Articles modeled upon the English Mutiny Act, to resolve upon the execution at sea of a midshipman and two sailors as mutineers designing the seizure of the brig.* Which resolution was carried out though in a time of peace and within not many days' sail of home. An act vindicated by a naval court of inquiry subsequently convened ashore. History, and here cited without comment. True, the circumstances on board the *Somers* were different from those on board the *Bellipotent*. But the urgency felt, well-warranted or otherwise, was much the same.

Says a writer whom few know,* "Forty years after a battle it is easy for a noncombatant to reason about how it ought to have been fought. It is another thing personally and under fire to have to direct the fighting while involved in the obscuring smoke of it. Much so with respect to other emergencies involving considerations both practical and moral, and when it is imperative promptly to act. The greater the fog the more it imperils the steamer, and speed is put on though at the hazard of running somebody down. Little ween the snug card players in the cabin of the responsibilities of the sleepless man on the bridge."

In brief, Billy Budd was formally convicted and sentenced to be hung at the yardarm in the early morning watch, it being now night. Otherwise, as is customary in such cases, the sentence would forthwith have been carried out. In wartime on the field or in the fleet, a mortal punishment decreed by a drumhead court—on the field sometimes decreed by but a nod from the general—follows without delay on the heel of conviction, without appeal.

22

IT was Captain Vere himself who of his own motion communicated the finding of the court to the prisoner, for that purpose going to the compartment where he was in custody and bidding the marine there to withdraw for the time.

Beyond the communication of the sentence, what took place at this interview was never known. But in view of the character of the twain briefly closeted in that stateroom, each radically sharing in the rarer qualities of our nature—so rare indeed as to be all but incredible to average minds however much cultivated—some conjectures may be ventured.

It would have been in consonance with the spirit of Captain Vere should he on this occasion have concealed nothing from the condemned one—should he indeed have frankly disclosed to him the part he himself had played in bringing about the decision, at the same time revealing his actuating motives. On Billy's side it is not improbable that such a confession would have been received in much the same spirit that prompted it. Not without a sort of joy, indeed, he might have appreciated the brave opinion of him implied in his captain's making such a confidant of him. Nor, as to the sentence itself, could he have been insensible that it was imparted to him as to one not afraid to die. Even more may have been. Captain Vere in end may have developed the passion sometimes latent under an exterior stoical or indifferent. He was old enough to have been Billy's father. The austere devotee of military duty, letting himself melt back into what remains primeval in our formalized humanity, may in end have caught Billy to his heart, even as Abraham may have caught young Isaac on the brink of resolutely offering him up in obedience to the exacting behest.* But there is no telling the sacrament, seldom if in any case revealed to the gadding world, wherever under circumstances at all akin to those here attempted to be set forth two of great Nature's nobler order embrace. There is privacy at the time, inviolable to the survivor; and holy oblivion, the sequel to each diviner magnanimity, providentially covers all at last.

The first to encounter Captain Vere in act of leaving the compartment was the senior lieutenant. The face he beheld, for the moment one expressive of the agony of the strong, was to that officer, though a man of fifty, a startling revelation. That the condemned one suffered less than he who mainly had effected the condemnation was apparently

indicated by the former's exclamation in the scene soon per-
force to be touched upon.

23

OF a series of incidents within a brief term rapidly following
each other, the adequate narration may take up a term less
brief, especially if explanation or comment here and there
seem requisite to the better understanding of such incidents.
Between the entrance into the cabin of him who never left
it alive, and him who when he did leave it left it as one condemned to die; between this and the closeted interview
just given, less than an hour and a half had elapsed. It was
an interval long enough, however, to awaken speculations
among no few of the ship's company as to what it was that
could be detaining in the cabin the master-at-arms and the
sailor; for a rumor that both of them had been seen to enter
it and neither of them had been seen to emerge, this rumor
had got abroad upon the gun decks and in the tops, the
people of a great warship being in one respect like villagers,
taking microscopic note of every outward movement or non-
movement going on. When therefore, in weather not at all
tempestuous, all hands were called in the second dogwatch,
a summons under such circumstances not usual in those hours,
the crew were not wholly unprepared for some announcement extraordinary, one having connection too with the continued absence of the two men from their wonted haunts.

   There was a moderate sea at the time; and the moon,
newly risen and near to being at its full, silvered the white
spar deck wherever not blotted by the clear-cut shadows hori-
zontally thrown of fixtures and moving men. On either side
the quarter-deck the marine guard under arms was drawn
up; and Captain Vere, standing in his place surrounded by
all the wardroom officers, addressed his men. In so doing,
his manner showed neither more nor less than that properly
pertaining to his supreme position aboard his own ship. In
clear terms and concise he told them what had taken place
in the cabin: that the master-at-arms was dead, that he who
had killed him had been already tried by a summary court

and condemned to death, and that the execution would take place in the early morning watch. The word *mutiny* was not named in what he said. He refrained too from making the occasion an opportunity for any preachment as to the maintenance of discipline, thinking perhaps that under existing circumstances in the navy the consequence of violating discipline should be made to speak for itself.

Their captain's announcement was listened to by the throng of standing sailors in a dumbness like that of a seated congregation of believers in hell listening to the clergyman's announcement of his Calvinistic text.

At the close, however, a confused murmur went up. It began to wax. All but instantly, then, at a sign, it was pierced and suppressed by shrill whistles of the boatswain and his mates. The word was given to about ship.

To be prepared for burial Claggart's body was delivered to certain petty officers of his mess. And here, not to clog the sequel with lateral matters, it may be added that at a suitable hour, the master-at-arms was committed to the sea with every funeral honor properly belonging to his naval grade.

In this proceeding as in every public one growing out of the tragedy strict adherence to usage was observed. Nor in any point could it have been at all deviated from, either with respect to Claggart or Billy Budd, without begetting undesirable speculations in the ship's company, sailors, and more particularly men-of-war's men, being of all men the greatest sticklers for usage. For similar cause, all communication between Captain Vere and the condemned one ended with the closeted interview already given, the latter being now surrendered to the ordinary routine preliminary to the end. His transfer under guard from the captain's quarters was effected without unusual precautions—at least no visible ones. If possible, not to let the men so much as surmise that their officers anticipate aught amiss from them is the tacit rule in a military ship. And the more that some sort of trouble should really be apprehended, the more do the officers keep that apprehension to themselves, though not the less unostentatious vigilance may be augmented. In the present instance, the sentry placed over the prisoner had strict orders to let no one have communication with him but the chaplain. And certain unobtrusive measures were taken absolutely to insure this point.

24

IN a seventy-four of the old order the deck known as the upper gun deck was the one covered over by the spar deck, which last, though not without its armament, was for the most part exposed to the weather. In general it was at all hours free from hammocks; those of the crew swinging on the lower gun deck and berth deck, the latter being not only a dormitory but also the place for the stowing of the sailors' bags, and on both sides lined with the large chests or movable pantries of the many messes of the men.

On the starboard side of the *Bellipotent*'s upper gun deck, behold Billy Budd under sentry lying prone in irons in one of the bays formed by the regular spacing of the guns comprising the batteries on either side. All these pieces were of the heavier caliber of that period. Mounted on lumbering wooden carriages, they were hampered with cumbersome harness of breeching and strong side-tackles for running them out. Guns and carriages, together with the long rammers and shorter linstocks lodged in loops overhead—all these, as customary, were painted black; and the heavy hempen breechings, tarred to the same tint, wore the like livery of the undertakers. In contrast with the funereal hue of these surroundings, the prone sailor's exterior apparel, white jumper and white duck trousers, each more or less soiled, dimly glimmered in the obscure light of the bay like a patch of discolored snow in early April lingering at some upland cave's black mouth. In effect he is already in his shroud, or the garments that shall serve him in lieu of one. Over him but scarce illuminating him, two battle lanterns swing from two massive beams of the deck above. Fed with the oil supplied by the war contractors (whose gains, honest or otherwise, are in every land an anticipated portion of the harvest of death), with flickering splashes of dirty yellow light they pollute the pale moonshine all but ineffectually struggling in obstructed flecks through the open ports from which the tampioned cannon protrude. Other lanterns at intervals serve but to bring out somewhat the obscurer bays which, like small confessionals or side-chapels in a cathedral, branch from the long dim-vistaed broad aisle between the two batteries of that covered tier.

Such was the deck where now lay the Handsome Sailor. Through the rose-tan of his complexion no pallor could have shown. It would have taken days of sequestration from the winds and the sun to have brought about the effacement of that. But the skeleton in the cheekbone at the point of its angle was just beginning delicately to be defined under the warm-tinted skin. In fervid hearts self-contained, some brief experiences devour our human tissue as secret fire in a ship's hold consumes cotton in the bale.

But now lying between the two guns, as nipped in the vice of fate, Billy's agony, mainly proceeding from a gener-ous young heart's virgin experience of the diabolical incarn-ate and effective in some men—the tension of that agony was over now. It survived not the something healing in the closeted interview with Captain Vere. Without movement, he lay as in a trance, that adolescent expression previously noted as his taking on something akin to the look of a slum-bering child in the cradle when the warm hearth-glow of the still chamber at night plays on the dimples that at whiles mysteriously form in the cheek, silently coming and going there. For now and then in the gyved one's trance a serene happy light born of some wandering reminiscence or dream would diffuse itself over his face, and then wane away only anew to return.

The chaplain, coming to see him and finding him thus, and perceiving no sign that he was conscious of his presence, attentively regarded him for a space, then slipping aside, with-drew for the time, peradventure feeling that even he, the minister of Christ though receiving his stipend from Mars,* had no consolation to proffer which could result in a peace transcending that which he beheld. But in the small hours he came again. And the prisoner, now awake to his sur-roundings, noticed his approach, and civilly, all but cheer-fully, welcomed him. But it was to little purpose that in the interview following, the good man sought to bring Billy Budd to some godly understanding that he must die, and at dawn. True, Billy himself freely referred to his death as a thing close at hand; but it was something in the way that children will refer to death in general, who yet among their other sports will play a funeral with hearse and mourners.

Not that like children Billy was incapable of conceiving what death really is. No, but he was wholly without irrational fear of it, a fear more prevalent in highly civilized communities than those so-called barbarous ones which in all respects stand nearer to unadulterate Nature. And, as elsewhere said, a barbarian Billy radically was—as much so, for all the costume, as his countrymen the British captives, living trophies, made to march in the Roman triumph of Germanicus. Quite as much so as those later barbarians, young men probably, and picked specimens among the earlier British converts to Christianity, at least nominally such, taken to Rome (as today converts from lesser isles of the sea may be taken to London), of whom the Pope of that time, admiring the strangeness of their personal beauty so unlike the Italian stamp, their clear ruddy complexion and curled flaxen locks, exclaimed, "Angles" (meaning *English*, the modern derivative), "Angles, do you call them? And is it because they look so like angels?" Had it been later in time, one would think that the Pope had in mind Fra Angelico's seraphs, some of whom, plucking apples in gardens of the Hesperides, have the faint rosebud complexion of the more beautiful English girls.

If in vain the good chaplain sought to impress the young barbarian with ideas of death akin to those conveyed in the skull, dial, and crossbones on old tombstones, equally futile to all appearance were his efforts to bring home to him the thought of salvation and a Savior. Billy listened, but less out of awe or reverence, perhaps, than from a certain natural politeness, doubtless at bottom regarding all that in much the same way that most mariners of his class take any discourse abstract or out of the common tone of the workaday world. And this sailor way of taking clerical discourse is not wholly unlike the way in which the primer of Christianity, full of transcendent miracles, was received long ago on tropic isles by any superior *savage*, so called—a Tahitian, say, of Captain Cook's time or shortly after that time. Out of natural courtesy he received, but did not appropriate. It was like a gift placed in the palm of an outreached hand upon which the fingers do not close.

But the *Bellipotent*'s chaplain was a discreet man possessing the good sense of a good heart. So he insisted not in his vocation here. At the instance of Captain Vere, a lieutenant had apprised him of pretty much everything as to Billy; and since he felt that innocence was even a better thing than religion wherewith to go to Judgment, he reluctantly withdrew; but in his emotion not without first performing an act strange enough in an Englishman, and under the circumstances yet more so in any regular priest. Stooping over, he kissed on the fair cheek his fellow man, a felon in martial law, one whom though on the confines of death he felt he could never convert to a dogma; nor for all that did he fear for his future.

Marvel not that having been made acquainted with the young sailor's essential innocence the worthy man lifted not a finger to avert the doom of such a martyr to martial discipline. So to do would not only have been as idle as invoking the desert, but would also have been an audacious transgression of the bounds of his function, one as exactly prescribed to him by military law as that of the boatswain or any other naval officer. Bluntly put, a chaplain is the minister of the Prince of Peace serving in the host of the God of War—Mars. As such, he is as incongruous as a musket would be on the altar at Christmas. Why, then, is he there? Because he indirectly subserves the purpose attested by the cannon; because too he lends the sanction of the religion of the meek to that which practically is the abrogation of everything but brute Force.

25

THE night so luminous on the spar deck, but otherwise on the cavernous ones below, levels so like the tiered galleries in a coal mine—the luminous night passed away. But like the prophet in the chariot disappearing in heaven and dropping his mantle to Elisha,* the withdrawing night transferred its pale robe to the breaking day. A meek, shy light appeared in the East, where stretched a diaphanous fleece of white furrowed vapor. That light slowly waxed. Suddenly *eight bells* was struck aft, responded to by one louder metallic stroke from forward. It was four o'clock in the morning. Instantly the silver whistles were heard summoning all hands to witness punishment. Up through the great hatchways rimmed with racks of heavy shot the watch below came pouring, overspreading with the watch already on deck the space between the mainmast and foremast including that occupied by the capacious launch and the black booms tiered on either side of it, boat and booms making a summit of observation for the powder-boys and younger tars. A different group comprising one watch of topmen leaned over the rail of that sea balcony, no small one in a seventy-four, looking down on the crowd below. Man or boy, none spake but in whisper, and few spake at all. Captain Vere—as before, the central figure among the assembled commissioned officers—stood nigh the break of the poop deck facing forward. Just below him on the quarter-deck the marines in full equipment were drawn up much as at the scene of the promulgated sentence.

At sea in the old time, the execution by halter of a military sailor was generally from the foreyard. In the present instance, for special reasons the mainyard was assigned. Under an arm of that yard the prisoner was presently brought up, the chaplain attending him. It was noted at the time, and remarked upon afterwards, that in this final scene the good man evinced little or nothing of the perfunctory. Brief speech indeed he had with the condemned one, but the genuine Gospel was less on his tongue than in his aspect and manner towards him. The final preparations personal to the latter being speedily brought to an end by two boatswain's mates, the consummation impended. Billy stood facing aft. At the penultimate moment, his words, his only ones, words wholly unobstructed in the utterance, were these: "God bless Captain Vere!" Syllables so unanticipated coming from one with the ignominious hemp about his neck—a conventional felon's benediction directed aft towards the quarters of honor; syllables too delivered in the clear melody of a singing bird on the point of launching from the twig—had a phenomenal effect, not unenhanced by the rare personal beauty of the young sailor, spiritualized now through late experiences so poignantly profound.

Without volition, as it were, as if indeed the ship's populace were but the vehicles of some vocal current electric, with one voice from alow and aloft came a resonant sympathetic echo: "God bless Captain Vere!" And yet at that instant Billy alone must have been in their hearts, even as in their eyes.

At the pronounced words and the spontaneous echo that voluminously rebounded them, Captain Vere, either through stoic self-control or a sort of momentary paralysis induced by emotional shock, stood erectly rigid as a musket in the ship-armorer's rack.

The hull, deliberately recovering from the periodic roll to leeward, was just regaining an even keel when the last signal, a preconcerted dumb one, was given. At the same moment it chanced that the vapory fleece hanging low in the East was shot through with a soft glory as of the fleece of the Lamb of God seen in mystical vision, and simultaneously therewith, watched by the wedged mass of upturned faces, Billy ascended; and, ascending, took the full rose of the dawn.*

In the pinioned figure arrived at the yard-end, to the wonder of all no motion was apparent, none save that created by the slow roll of the hull in moderate weather, so majestic in a great ship ponderously cannoned.

26

WHEN some days afterwards, in reference to the singularity just mentioned, the purser, a rather ruddy, rotund person more accurate as an accountant than profound as a philosopher, said at mess to the surgeon, "What testimony to the force lodged in will power," the latter, saturnine, spare, and tall, one in whom a discreet causticity went along with a manner less genial than polite, replied, "Your pardon, Mr. Purser. In a hanging scientifically conducted—and under special orders I myself directed how Budd's was to be effected —any movement following the completed suspension and originating in the body suspended, such movement indicates mechanical spasm in the muscular system. Hence the absence of that is no more attributable to will power, as you call it, than to horsepower—begging your pardon."

"But this muscular spasm you speak of, is not that in a degree more or less invariable in these cases?"

"Assuredly so, Mr. Purser."

"How then, my good sir, do you account for its absence in this instance?"

"Mr. Purser, it is clear that your sense of the singularity in this matter equals not mine. You account for it by what you call will power—a term not yet included in the lexicon of science. For me, I do not, with my present knowledge, pretend to account for it at all. Even should we assume the hypothesis that at the first touch of the halyards the action of Budd's heart, intensified by extraordinary emotion at its climax, abruptly stopped—much like a watch when in carelessly winding it up you strain at the finish, thus snapping the chain—even under that hypothesis how account for the phenomenon that followed?"

"You admit, then, that the absence of spasmodic movement was phenomenal."

"It was phenomenal, Mr. Purser, in the sense that it was an appearance the cause of which is not immediately to be assigned."

"But tell me, my dear sir," pertinaciously continued the other, "was the man's death effected by the halter, or was it a species of euthanasia?"*

"*Euthanasia*, Mr. Purser, is something like your *will power*: I doubt its authenticity as a scientific term—begging your pardon again. It is at once imaginative and metaphysical— in short, Greek.—But," abruptly changing his tone, "there is a case in the sick bay that I do not care to leave to my assistants. Beg your pardon, but excuse me." And rising from the mess he formally withdrew.

27

THE silence at the moment of execution and for a moment or two continuing thereafter, a silence but emphasized by the regular wash of the sea against the hull or the flutter of a sail caused by the helmsman's eyes being tempted astray, this emphasized silence was gradually disturbed by a sound not easily to be verbally rendered. Whoever has heard the freshet-wave of a torrent suddenly swelled by pouring showers in tropical mountains, showers not shared by the plain; whoever has heard the first muffled murmur of its sloping advance through precipitous woods may form some conception of the sound now heard. The seeming remoteness of its source was because of its murmurous indistinctness, since it came from close by, even from the men massed on the ship's open deck. Being inarticulate, it was dubious in significance further than it seemed to indicate some capricious revulsion of thought or feeling such as mobs ashore are liable to, in the present instance possibly implying a sullen revocation on the men's part of their involuntary echoing of Billy's benediction. But ere the murmur had time to wax into clamor it was met by a strategic command, the more telling that it came with abrupt unexpectedness: "Pipe down the starboard watch, Boatswain, and see that they go."

Shrill as the shriek of the sea hawk, the silver whistles of the boatswain and his mates pierced that ominous low sound, dissipating it; and yielding to the mechanism of discipline the throng was thinned by one-half. For the remainder, most of them were set to temporary employments connected with trimming the yards and so forth, business readily to be got up to serve occasion by any officer of the deck.

Now each proceeding that follows a mortal sentence pronounced at sea by a drumhead court is characterized by promptitude not perceptibly merging into hurry, though bordering that. The hammock, the one which had been Billy's bed when alive, having already been ballasted with shot and otherwise prepared to serve for his canvas coffin, the last offices of the sea undertakers, the sailmaker's mates, were now speedily completed. When everything was in readiness a second call for all hands, made necessary by the strategic movement before mentioned, was sounded, now to witness burial.

The details of this closing formality it needs not to give. But when the tilted plank let slide its freight into the sea, a second strange human murmur was heard, blended now with another inarticulate sound proceeding from certain larger seafowl who, their attention having been attracted by the peculiar commotion in the water resulting from the heavy sloped dive of the shotted hammock into the sea, flew screaming to the spot. So near the hull did they come, that the stridor or bony creak of their gaunt double-jointed pinions was audible. As the ship under light airs passed on, leaving the burial spot astern, they still kept circling it low down with the moving shadow of their outstretched wings and the croaked requiem of their cries.

Upon sailors as superstitious as those of the age preceding ours, men-of-war's men too who had just beheld the prodigy of repose in the form suspended in air, and now foundering in the deeps; to such mariners the action of the seafowl, though dictated by mere animal greed for prey, was big with no prosaic significance. An uncertain movement began among them, in which some encroachment was made. It was tolerated but for a moment. For suddenly the drum beat to quarters, which familiar sound happening at least twice every day, had upon the present occasion a signal peremptoriness in it. True martial discipline long continued superinduces in average man a sort of impulse whose operation at the official word of command much resembles in its promptitude the effect of an instinct.

The drumbeat dissolved the multitude, distributing most of them along the batteries of the two covered gun decks. There, as wonted, the guns' crews stood by their respective cannon erect and silent. In due course the first officer, sword under arm and standing in his place on the quarter-deck, formally received the successive reports of the sworded lieutenants commanding the sections of batteries below; the last of which reports being made, the summed report he delivered with the customary salute to the commander. All this occupied time, which in the present case was the object in beating to quarters at an hour prior to the customary one. That such variance from usage was authorized by an officer like Captain Vere, a martinet as some deemed him, was evidence of the necessity for unusual action implied in what he deemed to be temporarily the mood of his men. "With mankind," he would say, "forms, measured forms, are everything; and that is the import couched in the story of Orpheus with his lyre spellbinding the wild denizens of the wood." And this he once applied to the disruption of forms going on across the Channel and the consequences thereof.

At this unwonted muster at quarters, all proceeded as at the regular hour. The band on the quarter-deck played a sacred air, after which the chaplain went through the customary morning service. That done, the drum beat the retreat; and toned by music and religious rites subserving the discipline and purposes of war, the men in their wonted orderly manner dispersed to the places allotted them when not at the guns.

And now it was full day. The fleece of low-hanging vapor had vanished, licked up by the sun that late had so glorified it. And the circumambient air in the clearness of its serenity was like smooth white marble in the polished block not yet removed from the marble-dealer's yard.

28

THE symmetry of form attainable in pure fiction cannot so readily be achieved in a narration essentially having less to do with fable than with fact. Truth uncompromisingly told will always have its ragged edges; hence the conclusion of such a narration is apt to be less finished than an architectural finial.

How it fared with the Handsome Sailor during the year of the Great Mutiny has been faithfully given. But though properly the story ends with his life, something in way of sequel will not be amiss. Three brief chapters will suffice.

In the general rechristening under the Directory of the craft originally forming the navy of the French monarchy, the *St. Louis* line-of-battle ship was named the *Athée* (the *Atheist*). Such a name, like some other substituted ones in the Revolutionary fleet, while proclaiming the infidel audacity of the ruling power, was yet, though not so intended to be, the aptest name, if one consider it, ever given to a warship; far more so indeed than the *Devastation*, the *Erebus* (the *Hell*), and similar names bestowed upon fighting ships.

On the return passage to the English fleet from the detached cruise during which occurred the events already recorded, the *Bellipotent* fell in with the *Athée*. An engagement ensued, during which Captain Vere, in the act of putting his ship alongside the enemy with a view of throwing his boarders across her bulwarks, was hit by a musket ball from a porthole of the enemy's main cabin. More than disabled, he dropped to the deck and was carried below to the same cockpit where some of his men already lay. The senior lieutenant took command. Under him the enemy was finally captured, and though much crippled was by rare good fortune successfully taken into Gibraltar, an English port not very distant from the scene of the fight. There, Captain Vere with the rest of the wounded was put ashore. He lingered for some days, but the end came. Unhappily he was cut off too early for the Nile and Trafalgar. The spirit that 'spite its philosophic austerity may yet have indulged in the most secret of all passions, ambition, never attained to the fulness of fame.

Not long before death, while lying under the influence of that magical drug which, soothing the physical frame, mysteriously operates on the subtler element in man, he was heard to murmur words inexplicable to his attendant: "Billy Budd, Billy Budd." That these were not the accents of remorse would seem clear from what the attendant said to the *Bellipotent*'s senior officer of marines, who, as the most reluctant to condemn of the members of the drumhead court, too well knew, though here he kept the knowledge to himself, who Billy Budd was.

29

SOME few weeks after the execution, among other matters under the head of "News from the Mediterranean," there appeared in a naval chronicle of the time, an authorized weekly publication, an account of the affair. It was doubtless for the most part written in good faith, though the medium, partly rumor, through which the facts must have reached the writer served to deflect and in part falsify them. The account was as follows:

"On the tenth of the last month a deplorable occurrence took place on board H.M.S. *Bellipotent*. John Claggart, the ship's master-at-arms, discovering that some sort of plot was incipient among an inferior section of the ship's company, and that the ringleader was one William Budd; he, Claggart, in the act of arraigning the man before the captain, was vindictively stabbed to the heart by the suddenly drawn sheath knife of Budd.

"The deed and the implement employed sufficiently suggest that though mustered into the service under an English name the assassin was no Englishman, but one of those aliens adopting English cognomens whom the present extraordinary necessities of the service have caused to be admitted into it in considerable numbers.

"The enormity of the crime and the extreme depravity of the criminal appear the greater in view of the character of the victim, a middle-aged man respectable and discreet, belonging to that minor official grade, the petty officers, upon whom, as none know better than the commissioned gentlemen, the efficiency of His Majesty's navy so largely depends. His function was a responsible one, at once onerous and thankless; and his fidelity in it the greater because of his strong patriotic impulse. In this instance as in so many other instances in these days, the character of this unfortunate man signally refutes, if refutation were needed, that peevish saying attributed to the late Dr. Johnson, that patriotism is the last refuge of a scoundrel.

"The criminal paid the penalty of his crime. The promptitude of the punishment has proved salutary. Nothing amiss is now apprehended aboard H.M.S. *Bellipotent*."

The above, appearing in a publication now long ago super-annuated and forgotten, is all that hitherto has stood in human record to attest what manner of men respectively were John Claggart and Billy Budd.

30

EVERYTHING is for a term venerated in navies. Any tangible object associated with some striking incident of the service is converted into a monument. The spar from which the foretopman was suspended was for some few years kept trace of by the bluejackets. Their knowledges followed it from ship to dockyard and again from dockyard to ship, still pursuing it even when at last reduced to a mere dockyard boom. To them a chip of it was as a piece of the Cross. Ignorant though they were of the secret facts of the tragedy, and not thinking but that the penalty was somehow unavoidably inflicted from the naval point of view, for all that, they instinctively felt that Billy was a sort of man as incapable of mutiny as of wilful murder. They recalled the fresh young image of the Handsome Sailor, that face never deformed by a sneer or subtler vile freak of the heart within. This impression of him was doubtless deepened by the fact that he was gone, and in a measure mysteriously gone. On the gun decks of the *Bellipotent* the general estimate of his nature and its unconscious simplicity eventually found rude utterance from another foretopman, one of his own watch, gifted, as some sailors are, with an artless *poetic* temperament. The tarry hand made some lines which, after circulating among the shipboard crews for a while, finally got rudely printed at Portsmouth as a ballad. The title given to it was the sailor's.

BILLY IN THE DARBIES*

Good of the chaplain to enter Lone Bay
And down on his marrowbones here and pray
For the likes just o' me, Billy Budd.—But, look:
Through the port comes the moonshine astray!
It tips the guard's cutlass and silvers this nook;
But 'twill die in the dawning of Billy's last day.

A jewel-block they'll make of me tomorrow,
Pendant pearl from the yardarm-end
Like the eardrop I gave to Bristol Molly—
O, 'tis me, not the sentence they'll suspend.
Ay, ay, all is up; and I must up too,
Early in the morning, aloft from alow.
On an empty stomach now never it would do.
They'll give me a nibble—bit o' biscuit ere I go.
Sure, a messmate will reach me the last parting cup;
But, turning heads away from the hoist and the belay,
Heaven knows who will have the running of me up!
No pipe to those halyards.—But aren't it all sham?
A blur's in my eyes; it is dreaming that I am.
A hatchet to my hawser? All adrift to go?
The drum roll to grog, and Billy never know?
But Donald he has promised to stand by the plank;
So I'll shake a friendly hand ere I sink.
But—no! It is dead then I'll be, come to think.
I remember Taff the Welshman when he sank.
And his cheek it was like the budding pink.
But me they'll lash in hammock, drop me deep.
Fathoms down, fathoms down, how I'll dream fast asleep.
I feel it stealing now. Sentry, are you there?
Just ease these darbies at the wrist,
And roll me over fair!
I am sleepy, and the oozy weeds about me twist.

APPENDIX

Extract from Amasa Delano, *Narrative of Voyages and Travels, in the Northern and Southern Hemispheres* (1817), the chief source for 'Benito Cereno'

CHAPTER XVIII

Particulars of the Capture of the Spanish Ship Tryal, at the island of St. Maria; with the Documents relating to that affair.

IN introducing the account of the capture of the Spanish ship Tryal, I shall first give an extract from the journal of the ship Perseverance, taken on board that ship at the time, by the officer who had the care of the log book.

"Wednesday, February 20th, commenced with light airs from the north east, and thick foggy weather. At six A. M. observed a sail opening round the south head of St. Maria, coming into the bay. It proved to be a ship. The captain took the whale boat and crew, and went on board her. As the wind was very light, so that a vessel would not have much more than steerage way at the time; observed that the ship acted very awkwardly. At ten A. M. the boat returned. Mr. Luther informed that Captain Delano had remained on board her, and that she was a Spaniard from Buenos Ayres, four months and twenty six days out of port, with slaves on board; and that the ship was in great want of water, had buried many white men and slaves on her passage, and that captain Delano had sent for a large boat load of water, some fresh fish, sugar, bread, pumpkins, and bottled cider, all of which articles were immediately sent. At twelve o'clock (Meridian) calm. At two P. M. the large boat returned from the Spaniards, had left our water casks on board her. At four P. M. a breeze sprung up from the southern quarter, which brought the Spanish ship into the roads. She anchored about two cables length to the south east of our ship. Immediately after she anchored, our captain with his boat was shoving off from along side the Spanish ship; when to his great surprise the Spanish captain leaped into the boat, and called out in Spanish, that the slaves on board had risen and murdered many of the people; and that he did not then command her; on which manœuvre, several of the Spaniards who remained on board jumped overboard, and swam for our boat, and were picked up by our people. The Spaniards, who remained on board, hurried up the rigging, as high aloft as they could possibly get, and called out repeatedly for help—that they should be murdered by the slaves. Our captain came immediately on board, and brought the Spanish captain and the men who were picked up in the water; but before the boat arrived, we observed that the slaves had cut the Spanish ship adrift. On learning this, our captain hailed, and ordered the ports to be got up, and the guns cleared; but unfortunately, we could not bring but one of our guns to bear on the ship. We fired five or six shot with it, but could not bring her too. We soon observed her making sail, and standing directly out of the bay. We dispatched two boats well manned, and well armed after her, who, after much trouble, boarded the ship and retook her. But unfortunately in the business, Mr. Rufus Low, our chief officer, who commanded the party, was desperately wounded in the breast, by being stabbed with a pike, by one of the slaves. We likewise had one man badly wounded and two or three slightly. To continue the misfortune, the chief officer of the Spanish ship, who was compelled by the slaves to steer her out of the bay, received two very bad wounds, one in the side, and one through the thigh, both from musket balls. One Spaniard, a gentleman passenger on board, was likewise killed by a musket ball. We have not rightly ascertained what number of slaves were killed; but we believe seven, and a great number wounded. Our people brought the ship in, and came to nearly where she first anchored, at about two o'clock in the morning of the 21st. At six A. M. the two captains went on board the Spanish ship; took with them irons from our ship, and doubled ironed all the remaining men of the slaves who were living. Left Mr. Brown, our second officer, in charge of the ship, the gunner with him as mate, and eight other hands; together with the survivors of the Spanish crew. The captain, and chief officer, were removed to our ship, the latter for the benefit of having his wounds better attended to with us, than he could have had them on board his own ship. At nine A. M. the two captains returned, having put every thing aright, as they supposed, on board the Spanish ship.

The Spanish captain then informed us that he was compelled by the slaves to say, that he was from Buenos Ayres, bound to Lima; that he was not from Buenos Ayres, but sailed on the 20th of December last from Valparaiso for Lima, with upwards of seventy slaves on board; that on the 26th of December, the slaves rose upon the ship, and took possession of her, and put to death eighteen white men, and threw overboard at different periods after, seven more; that the slaves had commanded him to go to Senegal; that he had kept to sea until his water was expended, and had made this port to get it; and also with a view to save his own and the remainder of his people's lives if possible, by runing [sic] away from his ship with his boat."

I shall here add some remarks of my own, to what is stated above from the ship's journal, with a view of giving the reader a correct understanding of the peculiar situation under which we were placed at the time this affair happened. We were in a worse situation to effect any important enterprize than I had been in during the voyage. We had been from home a year and a half, and had not made enough to amount to twenty dollars for each of my people, who were all on shares, and our future prospects were not very flattering. To make our situation worse, I had found after leaving New Holland, on mustering my people, that I had seventeen men, most of whom had been convicts at Botany bay. They had secreted themselves on board without my knowledge. This was a larger number than had been inveigled away from me at the same place, by people who had been convicts, and were then employed at places that we visited. The men whom we lost were all of them extraordinarily good men. This exchange materially altered the quality of the crew. Three of the Botany-bay-men were outlawed convicts; they had been shot at many times, and several times wounded. After making this bad exchange, my crew were refractory; the convicts were ever unfaithful, and took all the advantage that opportunity gave them. But sometimes exercising very strict discipline, and giving them good wholesome floggings; and at other times treating them with the best I had, or could get, according as their deeds deserved, I managed them without much difficulty during the passage across the South Pacific Ocean; and all the time I had been on the coast of Chili. I had lately been at the islands of St. Ambrose and St. Felix, and left there fifteen of my best men, with the view of procuring seals; and left that place in company with my consort the Pilgrim. We appointed Massa Fuero as our place of rendezvous, and if we did not meet there, again to rendezvous at St. Maria. I proceeded to the first place appointed; the Pilgrim had not arrived. I then determined to take a look at Juan Fernandez, and see if we could find any seals, as some persons had informed me they were to be found on some part of the island. I accordingly visited that place, as has been stated; from thence I proceeded to St. Maria; and arrived the 13th of February at that place, where we commonly find visitors. We found the ship Mars of Nantucket, commanded by captain Jonathan Barney. The day we arrived, three of my Botany bay men run from the boat when on shore. The next day, (the 14th) I was informed by Captain Barney, that some of my convict men had planned to run away with one of my boats, and go over to the main. This information he obtained through the medium of his people. I examined into the affair, and was satisfied as to the truth of it; set five more of the above description of men on shore, making eight in all I had gotten clear of in two days. Captain Barney sailed about the 17th, and left me quite alone. I continued in that unpleasant situation till the 20th, never at any time after my arrival at this place, daring to let my whale boat be in the water fifteen minutes unless I was in her myself, from a fear that some of my people would run away with her. I always hoisted her in on deck the moment I came along side, by which means I had the advantage of them; for should they run away with any other boat belonging to the ship, I could overtake them with the whale boat, which they very well knew. They were also well satisfied of the reasons why that boat was always kept on board, except when in my immediate use. During this time, I had no fear from them, except of their running away. Under these disadvantages the Spanish ship Tryal made her appearance on the morning of the 20th, as has been stated; and I had in the course of the day the satisfaction of seeing the great utility of good discipline. In every part of the business of the Tryal, not one disaffected word was spoken by the men, but all flew to obey the commands they received; and to their credit it should be recorded, that no men ever behaved better than they, under such circumstances. When it is considered that we had but two boats, one a whale boat, and the other built by ourselves, while on the coast of New Holland, which was very little larger than the whale boat; both of them were clinker built, one of cedar, and the other not much stouter; with only twenty men to board and carry a ship, containing so many slaves, made desperate by their situation; for they were certain, if taken, to suffer death; and when arriving along side of the ship, they might have staved the bottom of the boats, by heaving into them a ballast stone or log of wood of twenty pounds: when all these things are taken into view, the reader may conceive of the hazardous nature of the enterprise, and the skill and the intrepidity which were requisite to carry it into execution.

On the afternoon of the 19th, before night, I sent the boatswain with the large boat and seine to try if he could catch some fish; he returned at night with but few, observing that the morning would be better, if he went early. I then wished him to go as early as he thought proper, and he accordingly went at four o'clock. At sunrise, or about that time, the officer who commanded the deck, came down to me while I was in my cot, with information that a sail was just opening round the south point, or head of the island. I immediately rose, went on deck, and observed that she was too near the land, on account of a reef that lay off the head; and at the same time remarked to my people, that she must be a stranger, and I did not well understand what she was about. Some of them observed that they did not know who she was, or what she was doing; but that they were accustomed to see vessels shew their colours, when coming into a port. I ordered the whale boat to be hoisted out and manned, which was accordingly done. Presuming the vessel was from sea, and had been many days out, without perhaps fresh provisions, we put the fish which had been caught the night before into the boat, to be presented if necessary. Every thing being soon ready, as I thought the strange ship was in danger, we made all the haste in our power to get on board, that we might prevent her getting on the reefs; but before we came near her, the wind headed her off, and she was doing well. I went along side, and saw the decks were filled with slaves. As soon as I got on deck, the captain, mate, people and slaves, crowded around me to relate their stories, and to make known their grievances; which could not but impress me with feelings of pity for their sufferings. They told me they had no water, as is related in their different accounts and depositions. After promising to relieve all the wants they had mentioned, I ordered the fish to be put on board, and sent the whale boat to our ship, with orders that the large boat, as soon as she returned from fishing, should take a set of gang casks to the watering place, fill them, and bring it for their relief as soon as possible. I also ordered the small boat to take what fish the large one had caught, and what soft bread they had baked, some pumpkins, some sugar, and bottled cider, and return to me without delay. The boat left me on board the Spanish ship, went to our own, and executed the orders; and returned to me again about eleven o'clock. At noon the large boat came with the water, which I was obliged to serve out to them myself, to keep them from drinking so much as to do themselves injury. I gave them at first one gill each, an hour after, half a pint, and the third hour, a pint. Afterward, I permited [sic] them to drink as they pleased. They all looked up to me as a benefactor; and as I was deceived in them, I did them every possible kindness. Had it been otherwise there is no doubt I should have fallen a victim to their power. It was to my great advantage, that, on this occasion, the temperament of my mind was unusually pleasant. The apparent sufferings of those about me had softened my feelings into sympathy; or, doubtless my interference with some of their transactions would have cost me my life. The Spanish captain had evidently lost much of his authority over the slaves, whom he appeared to fear, and whom he was unwilling in any case to oppose. An instance of this occurred in the conduct of the four cabin boys, spoken of by the captain. They were eating with the slave boys on the main deck, when, (as I was afterwards informed) the Spanish boys, feeling some hopes of release, and not having prudence sufficient to keep silent, some words dropped respecting their expectations, which were understood by the slave boys. One of them gave a stroke with a knife on the head of one of the Spanish boys, which penetrated to the bone, in a cut four inches in length. I saw this and inquired what it meant. The captain replied, that it was merely the sport of the boys, who had fallen out. I told him it appeared to me to be rather serious sport, as the wound had caused the boy to lose about a quart of blood. Several similar instances of unruly conduct, which, agreeably to my manner of thinking, demanded immediate resistance and punishment, were thus easily winked at, and passed over. I felt willing however to make some allowance even for conduct so gross, when I considered them to have been broken down with fatigue and long suffering.

The act of the negro, who kept constantly at the elbows of Don Bonito and myself, I should, at any other time, have immediately resented; and although it excited my wonder, that his commander should allow this extraordinary liberty, I did not remonstrate against it, until it became troublesome to myself. I wished to have some private conversation with the captain alone, and the negro as usual following us into the cabin, I requested the captain to send him on deck, as the business about which we were to talk could not be conveniently communicated in presence of a third person. I spoke in Spanish, and the negro understood me. The captain assured me, that his remaining with us would be of no disservice; that he had made him his confidant and companion since he had lost so many of his officers and men. He had introduced him to me before, as captain of the slaves, and told me he kept them in good order. I was alone with them, or rather on board by myself, for three or four hours, during the absence of my boat, at which time the ship drifted out with the current three leagues from my own, when the breeze sprung up from the south east. It was nearly four o'clock in the afternoon. We ran the ship as near to the Perseverance as we could without either ship's swinging afoul the other. After the Spanish ship was anchored, I invited the captain to go on board my ship and take tea or coffee with me. His answer was short and seemingly reserved; and his air very different from that with which he had received my assistance. As I was at a loss to account for this change in his demeanour, and knew he had seen nothing in my conduct to justify it, and as I felt certain that he treated me with intentional neglect; in return I became less sociable, and said little to him. After I had ordered my boat to be hauled up and manned, and as I was going to the side of the vessel, in order to get into her, Don Bonito came to me, gave my hand a hearty squeeze, and, as I thought, seemed to feel the weight of the cool treatment with which I had retaliated. I had committed a mistake in attributing his apparent coldness to neglect; and as soon as the discovery was made, I was happy to rectify it, by a prompt renewal of friendly intercourse. He continued to hold my hand fast till I stepped off the gunwale down the side, when he let it go, and stood making me compliments. When I had seated myself in the boat, and ordered her to be shoved off, the people having their oars up on end, she fell off at a sufficient distance to leave room for the oars to drop. After they were down, the Spanish captain, to my great astonishment, leaped from the gunwale of the ship into the middle of our boat. As soon as he had recovered a little, he called out in so alarming a manner, that I could not understand him; and the Spanish sailors were then seen jumping overboard and making for our boat. These proceedings excited the wonder of us all. The officer whom I had with me anxiously inquired into their meaning. I smiled and told him, that I neither knew, nor cared; but it seemed the captain was trying to impress his people with a belief that we intended to run away with him. At this moment one of my Portuguese sailors in the boat, spoke to me, and gave me to understand what Don Bonito said. I desired the captain to come aft and sit down by my side, and in a calm deliberate manner relate the whole affair. In the mean time the boat was employed in picking up the men who had jumped from the ship. They had picked up three, (leaving one in the water till after the boat had put the Spanish captain and myself on board my ship,) when my officer observed the cable was cut, and the ship was swinging. I hailed the Perseverance, ordering the ports got up, and the guns run out as soon as possible. We pulled as fast as we could on board; and then despatched the boat for the man who was left in the water, whom we succeeded to save alive.

We soon had our guns ready; but the Spanish ship had dropped so far astern of the Perseverance, that we could bring but one gun to bear on her, which was the after one. This was fired six times, without any other effect than cutting away the fore top-mast stay, and some other small ropes which were no hindrance to her going away. She was soon out of reach of our shot, steering out of the bay. We then had some other calculations to make. Our ship was moored with two bower anchors, which were all the cables or anchors of that description we had. To slip and leave them would be to break our policy of insurance by a deviation, against which I would here caution the masters of all vessels. It should always be borne in mind, that to do any thing which will destroy the guaranty of their policies, how great soever may be the inducement, and how generous soever the motive, is not justifiable; for should any accident subsequently occur, whereby a loss might accrue to the underwriters, they will be found ready enough, and sometimes too ready, to avail themselves of the opportunity to be released from responsibility; and the damage must necessarily be sustained by the owners. This is perfectly right. The law has wisely restrained the powers of the insured, that the insurer should not be subject to imposition, or abuse. All bad consequences may be avoided by one who has a knowledge of his duty, and is disposed faithfully to obey its dictates.

At length, without much loss of time, I came to a determination to pursue, and take the ship with my two boats. On inquiring of the captain what fire arms they had on board the Tryal, he answered, they had none which they could use; that he had put the few they had out of order, so that they could make no defence with them; and furthermore, that they did not understand their use, if they were in order. He observed at the same time, that if I attempted to take her with boats we should all be killed; for the negros were such bravos and so desperate, that there would be no such thing as conquering them. I saw the man in the situation that I have seen others, frightened at his own shadow. This was probably owing to his having been effectually conquered and his spirits broken.

After the boats were armed, I ordered the men to get into them; and they obeyed with cheerfulness. I was going myself, but Don Bonito took hold of my hand and forbade me, saying, you have saved my life, and now you are going to throw away your own. Some of my confidential officers asked me if it would be prudent for me to go, and leave the Perseverance in such an unguarded state; and also, if any thing should happen to me, what would be the consequence to the voyage. Every man on board, they observed, would willingly go, if it were my pleasure. I gave their remonstrances a moment's consideration, and felt their weight. I

then ordered into the boats my chief officer, Mr. Low, who commanded the party; and under him, Mr. Brown, my second officer;
my brother William, Mr. George Russell, son to major Benjamin
Russell of Boston, and Mr. Nathaniel Luther, midshipmen; William
Clark, boatswain; Charles Spence, gunner; and thirteen seamen.
By way of encouragement, I told them that Don Bonito considered
the ship and what was in her as lost; that the value was more than
one hundred thousand dollars; that if we would take her, it should
be all our own; and that if we should afterwards be disposed to
give him up one half, it would be considered as a present. I likewise reminded them of the suffering condition of the poor Spaniards
remaining on board, whom I then saw with my spy-glass as high
aloft as they could get on the top-gallant-masts, and knowing that
death must be their fate if they came down. I told them, never to
see my face again, if they did not take her; and these were all of
them pretty powerful stimulants. I wished God to prosper them in
the discharge of their arduous duty, and they shoved off. They
pulled after and came up with the Tryal, took their station upon
each quarter, and commenced a brisk fire of musketry, directing it
as much at the man at the helm as they could, as that was likewise a place of resort for the negroes. At length they drove the
chief mate from it, who had been compelled to steer the ship. He
ran up the mizen rigging as high as the cross jack yard, and called
out in Spanish, "Don't board." This induced our people to believe
that he favoured the cause of the negroes; they fired at him, and
two balls took effect; one of them went through his side, but did
not go deep enough to be mortal; and the other went through one
of his thighs. This brought him down on deck again. They found
the ship made such head way, that the boats could hardly keep
up with her, as the breeze was growing stronger. They then called
to the Spaniards, who were still as high aloft as they could get, to
come down on the yards, and cut away the robings and earings of
the topsails, and let them fall from the yards, so that they might
not hold any wind. They accordingly did so. About the same time,
the Spaniard who was steering the ship, was killed; (he is sometimes called *passenger*, and sometimes *clerk*, in the different depositions,) so that both these circumstances combined, rendered her
unmanageable by such people as were left on board. She came
round to the wind, and both boats boarded, one on each bow,
when she was carried by hard fighting. The negroes defended themselves with desperate courage; and after our people had boarded
them, they found they had barricadoed the deck by making a breast
work of the water casks which we had left on board, and sacks of

matta, abreast the mainmast, from one side of the ship to the other, to the height of six feet; behind which they defended themselves with all the means in their power to the last; and our people had to force their way over this breast work before they could compel them to surrender. The other parts of the transaction have some of them been, and the remainder will be hereafter stated.

On going on board the next morning with hand-cuffs, leg-irons, and shackled bolts, to secure the hands and feet of the negroes, the sight which presented itself to our view was truly horrid. They had got all the men who were living made fast, hands and feet, to the ring bolts in the deck; some of them had part of their bowels hanging out, and some with half their backs and thighs shaved off. This was done with our boarding lances, which were always kept exceedingly sharp, and as bright as a gentleman's sword. Whilst putting them in irons, I had to exercise as much authority over the Spanish captain and his crew, as I had to use over my own men on any other occasion, to prevent them from cutting to pieces and killing these poor unfortunate beings. I observed one of the Spanish sailors had found a razor in the pocket of an old jacket of his, which one of the slaves had on; he opened it, and made a cut upon the negro's head. He seemed to aim at his throat, and it bled shockingly. Seeing several more about to engage in the same kind of barbarity, I commanded them not to hurt another one of them, on pain of being brought to the gang-way and flogged. The captain also, I noticed, had a dirk, which he had secreted at the time the negroes were massacreing the Spaniards. I did not observe, however, that he intended to use it, until one of my people gave me a twitch by the elbow, to draw my attention to what was passing, when I saw him in the act of stabbing one of the slaves. I immediately caught hold of him, took away his dirk, and threatened him with the consequences of my displeasure, if he attempted to hurt one of them. Thus I was obliged to be continually vigilant, to prevent them from using violence towards these wretched creatures.

After we had put every thing in order on board the Spanish ship, and swept for and obtained her anchors, which the negroes had cut her from, we sailed on the 23d, both ships in company, for Conception, where we anchored on the 26th. After the common forms were passed, we delivered the ship, and all that was on board her, to the captain, whom we had befriended. We delivered him also a bag of doubloons, containing, I presume, nearly a thousand; several bags of dollars, containing a like number; and several baskets of watches, some gold, and some silver: all of which had been brought on board the Perseverance for safe keeping. We detained no part of this treasure to reward us for the services we had rendered:—all that we received was faithfully returned.

After our arrival at Conception, I was mortified and very much hurt at the treatment which I received from Don Bonito Sereno; but had this been the only time that I ever was treated with ingratitude, injustice, or want of compassion, I would not complain. I will only name one act of his towards me at this place. He went to the prison and took the depositions of five of my Botany bay convicts, who had left us at St. Maria, and were now in prison here. This was done by him with a view to injure my character, so that he might not be obliged to make us any compensation for what we had done for him. I never made any demand of, nor claimed in any way whatever, more than that they should give me justice; and did not ask to be my own judge, but to refer it to government. Amongst those who swore against me were the three outlawed convicts, who have been before mentioned. I had been the means, undoubtedly, of saving every one of their lives, and had supplied them with clothes. They swore every thing against me they could to effect my ruin. Amongst other atrocities, they swore I was a pirate, and made several statements that would operate equally to my disadvantage had they been believed; all of which were brought before the viceroy of Lima against me. When we met at that place, the viceroy was too great and too good a man to be misled by these false representations. He told Don Bonito, that my conduct towards him proved the injustice of these depositions, taking his own official declaration at Conception for the proof of it; that he had been informed by Don Jose Calminaries, who was commandant of the marine, and was at that time, and after the affair of the Tryal, on the coast of Chili; that Calminaries had informed him how both Don Bonito and myself had conducted, and he was satisfied that no man had behaved better, under all circumstances, than the American captain had done to Don Bonito, and that he never had seen or heard of any man treating another with so much dishonesty and ingratitude as he had treated the American. The viceroy had previously issued an order, on his own authority, to Don Bonito, to deliver to me eight thousand dollars as part payment for services rendered him. This order was not given till his Excellency had consulted all the tribunals holding jurisdiction over similar cases, except the twelve royal judges. These judges exercise a supreme authority over all the courts in Peru, and reserve to themselves the right of giving a final decision in all questions of law. Whenever either party is dissatisfied with the decision of the inferior courts in this kingdom, they have a right of appeal to the twelve judges. Don Bonito had attempted an appeal from the viceroy's order to the royal judges. The viceroy sent for me, and acquainted me of Don Bonito's attempt; at the same time recommending to me to accede to it, as the royal judges well understood the nature of the business, and would do much better for me than his order would. He observed at the same time, that they were men of too great characters to be biassed or swayed from doing justice by any party; they holding their appointments immediately from his majesty. He said, if I requested it, Don Bonito should be holden to his order. I then represented, that I had been in Lima nearly two months, waiting for different tribunals, to satisfy his Excellency what was safe for him, and best to be done for me, short of a course of law, which I was neither able nor willing to enter into; that I had then nearly thirty men on different islands, and on board my tender, which was then somewhere amongst the islands on the coast of Chili; that they had no method that I knew of to help themselves, or receive succour, except from me; and that if I was to defer the time any longer it amounted to a certainty, that they must suffer. I therefore must pray that his Excellency's order might be put in force.

Don Bonito, who was owner of the ship and part of the cargo, had been quibbling and using all his endeavours to delay the time of payment, provided the appeal was not allowed, when his Excellency told him to get out of his sight, that he would pay the money himself, and put him (Don Bonito) into a dungeon, where he should not see sun, moon, or stars; and was about giving the order, when a very respectable company of merchants waited on him and pleaded for Don Bonito; praying that his Excellency would favour him on account of his family, who were very rich and respectable. The viceroy remarked that Don Bonito's character had been such as to disgrace any family, that had any pretensions to respectability; but that he should grant their prayer, provided there was no more reason for complaint. The last transaction brought me the money in two hours; by which time I was extremely distressed, enough, I believe, to have punished me for a great many of my bad deeds.

When I take a retrospective view of my life, I cannot find in my soul, that I ever have done any thing to deserve such misery and ingratitude as I have suffered at different periods, and in general, from the very persons to whom I have rendered the greatest services.

EXPLANATORY NOTES

Bartleby, the Scrivener

3 *Wall-Street*: the major street in the financial district of New York City in lower Manhattan. Melville's subtitle—omitted from the *Piazza Tales* version of 1856 but restored by the editors of the Northwestern–Newberry text—suggests the relevance of the story to *laissez-faire* capitalism. It also introduces the motif of 'walls' that functions on several interpretative levels —social, economic, psychological, and metaphysical.

4 *John Jacob Astor*: German-born American merchant and philanthropist (1763–1848) who made a legendary fortune from fur trading and Manhattan real estate and who died the richest man in the nation.

Master in Chancery: Courts of Chancery, established in the colonies on the English model and preserved after the American Revolution, were abolished in New York in the 1840s as an obstruction and a nuisance. The narrator is objecting to the loss of a lucrative sinecure.

5 *Turkey . . . Nippers . . . Ginger Nut*: the nicknames of these three Dickensian figures all refer to food ('nippers' are lobster or crab claws) and belong to the story's running motif of nourishment, literal and symbolic.

7 *Tombs*: a prison in New York City built in the 1830s and stylistically part of the Egyptian revival in American architecture during the first half of the nineteenth century. Images of Egyptian tombs, mummies, sphinxes, and hieroglyphics are prominent in Melville's fiction even before he visited Egypt in 1856 and nearly always connote the sinister or vexingly unknowable. The hero of *Pierre* commits suicide in the Tombs, where he has been incarcerated for murder.

8 *red ink*: a euphemism for wine.

9 *Spitzenbergs*: an American variety of apple.

10 *Bartleby*: interpretations of the character Bartleby are almost as numerous as interpretations of Moby Dick. He has been read (among other things) as Melville the discontented marketplace writer, as Marx's oppressed or alienated labourer, as a proto-existentialist, a nihilist, a schizophrenic, or an anorexic,

as a Hindu or Buddhist ascetic, as a Christ figure, and as a precursor of Kafka's 'hunger artist'. The conjectured sources for Bartleby, literary and historical, are also quite various. Lea Newman helpfully surveys the backgrounds and symbolism of Bartleby in *A Reader's Guide to the Short Stories of Herman Melville* (Boston, 1986), 19–78.

11 *sanguine temperaments*: here, as often in his stories, Melville rests his characterization on a comic use of the old medieval–Renaissance notion of the four humours, in which an excess or deficiency of one or another bodily fluid was seen as producing an exaggeration of character. A sanguine, or cheerful, temperament was caused by a surplus of blood and marked by high colour, in contrast to the settled dejection of the 'pallid' Bartleby. Influenced largely by Robert Burton's seventeenth-century *Anatomy of Melancholy*, Melville's use of the humours psychology should be understood as a symbolic shorthand rather than a deterministic theory of personality.

  Byron: George Gordon Byron, sixth baron (1788–1824), English Romantic poet whose tumultuous life and writings made him a symbol for iconoclastic rebellion.

12 *Cicero*: Marcus Tullius Cicero (106–43 BCE), illustrious Roman orator and statesman and, for the narrator, a model of reason and moderation.

13 *a pillar of salt*: Lot's wife was transformed into a pillar of salt for disobeying God by looking back at the wicked cities of Sodom and Gomorrah during their destruction (Genesis 19: 26).

19 *Trinity Church*: an Episcopal church constructed in 1847 in Gothic Revival style and located at the corner of Wall Street and Broadway.

20 *Petra*: an ancient and remote fortress-city in present-day Jordan whose discovery in 1812 was a major archaeological event.

  Marius . . . Carthage: Gaius Marius (*c*.157–86 BCE), plebeian Roman general and consul who, after victorious campaigns in Africa and Gaul, lost a power struggle to patricians at home and fled back to Africa. His message to his prospective African host, Sextilius, is reported in Plutarch's *Lives*: 'Go tell him that you have seen Gaius Marius sitting in exile among the ruins of Carthage.' Melville may also have known American artist John Vanderlyn's painting 'Gaius Marius Amidst the Ruins of Carthage' (1807).

26 *a millstone to me*: an echo of Matthew 18: 6: 'But whoso shall offend . . . it were better for him that a millstone were hanged about his neck, and that he were drowned in the depth of the sea.'

30 *Adams . . . Colt*: an allusion to a lurid and widely reported New York crime of 1841 in which John C. Colt murdered his creditor Samuel Adams with a hatchet in Adams's printing office. Convicted, imprisoned in the Tombs, and sentenced to be hanged, Colt stabbed himself to death just before his scheduled execution.

"*A new commandment . . . another*": Jesus's words to his disciples (John 13: 34).

31 "*Edwards on the Will," and "Priestley on Necessity*": New England theologian Jonathan Edwards's magisterial neo-Calvinist *A Careful and Strict Inquiry into the Prevailing Notions of the Freedom of the Will* (1754) and English theologian and scientist Joseph Priestley's *The Doctrine of Philosophical Necessity Illustrated* (1777) both deny the existence and meaningfulness of free will.

34 *the man you allude to is nothing to me*: an echo of Peter's denial of Christ (Mark 14: 68, 70–1).

37 *rockaway*: a four-wheeled carriage, open at the sides, with two or three seats and a standing top, used in the United States in the mid-nineteenth century (*OED*).

Jersey City and Hoboken . . . Manhattanville and Astoria: suburban towns located across the Hudson River in New Jersey (Jersey City and Hoboken), far north in sparsely settled Manhattan (Manhattanville), and across the East River on Long Island (Astoria, which was renamed for John Jacob Astor).

39 *Monroe Edwards*: a notorious genteel American forger (1803?–47) whose swindles rocked the banking community in 1841. Tried and convicted the following year, he was held in the Tombs before being transferred to Sing Sing Prison in Ossining, New York, where he died.

40 *With kings and counsellors*: an allusion to Job 3: 13–14.

41 *the Dead Letter Office at Washington*: a section of the General Post Office in the nation's capital where the gloomy business of destroying undeliverable letters was carried out. Newspaper

articles about dead letters were popular in the 1850s and may have served Melville as a source.

Cock-A-Doodle-Doo!

42 *high-spirited revolts from rascally despotisms*: an allusion to the revolutions of 1848 that had recently swept through Europe.

hypoes: an abbreviation for hypochondria, or morbid depression without real cause (*OED*). In *Moby-Dick* Ishmael describes himself as periodically afflicted with the hypoes. His remedy is to take to sea; the narrator of 'Cock-A-Doodle-Doo!' goes for a country walk.

43 *What a horrid accident . . . flue*: there is no single identifiable source for this reference, but during the spring and summer of 1853, as Melville composed the story, a number of fatal train and steamboat accidents were reported, some the result of negligence or incompetence.

Charon: in Greek mythology, the ferryman who carried the dead across the River Styx to Hades.

Don't the heavens themselves ordain these things: a diminished echo of Ahab's complaint against the gods in *Moby-Dick*. The ultimate responsibility of an omnipotent Providence for suffering and evil—or at least its acquiescence in these things—is a central theme in Melville's work from *Mardi* (1849) through to *Billy Budd*.

44 *Tartarus*: the mythological abyss below Hades where the Titans were confined and punished; generally, hell.

Great improvements of the age!: in the 1840s and early 1850s the railroad became a focus for literary attacks on runaway technology and its deformation of human life. See, for example, Hawthorne's *The Celestial Rail-road* (1843), the chapter 'Sounds' in Thoreau's *Walden* (1854), and the Revd Frederick W. Shelton's popular 'Letters from Up the River', which appeared in New York's *Knickerbocker Magazine* in 1852 and 1853. Leo Marx discusses American writers' response to the railroad in *The Machine in the Garden* (1964).

Moloch: a Canaanite idol to whom children were sacrificed as burnt offerings (Leviticus 18: 21).

dunning fiend: a debt-collector. Melville himself was in debt during these years and is voicing his exasperations, if not quite any actual persecutions.

45 *"Glory be to God in the highest!"*: from Luke 2: 14.

46 *without discourse of reason*: an allusion to *Hamlet*, I. ii. 150–1.

a Shanghai: Shanghai roosters were quite fashionable in the American North-East in the 1850s. Shelton's letters in the *Knickerbocker* described and contributed to this craze and were probably a suggestive source for Melville. The *Knickerbocker* was widely available, and one of Shelton's accounts of the Shanghais was reprinted in Melville's local newspaper, the Pittsfield *Culturalist and Gazette*, in February 1853. See Allan Moore Emery, 'The Cocks of Melville's "Cock-A-Doodle-Doo!" ', *ESQ: A Journal of the American Renaissance*, 28 (1982), 89–111.

"Of fine mornings . . . madness": a parodic revision of Words-worth's lines from 'Resolution and Independence': 'We Poets in our youth begin in gladness; | But thereof comes in the end, despondency and madness'. Melville is visibly playing his story off against Wordsworth's poem, though critics differ about the degree of irony he assumes toward the 'redemptive' figure of Merrymusk, his analogue to Wordsworth's leech-gatherer.

St. Paul's: London cathedral built in 1675–1710 by Sir Christopher Wren on the site of a thirteenth-century church destroyed by the Great Fire of London in 1666.

from Mile-End . . . to Primrose Hill: geographical extremities of London; Mile-End is in the eastern part of the city, Primrose Hill in the north-western part, just north of Regent's Park.

47 *Tristram Shandy*: Laurence Sterne's eighteenth-century novel, which Melville first read in 1849 and whose bawdiness and comic eccentricity he thoroughly enjoyed. The phallic humour of 'Cock-A-Doodle-Doo!' owes much to Sterne. The passage the narrator mentions to his creditor is most likely the one in which Uncle Toby, a war veteran and confirmed bachelor, and the Widow Wadman, who pursues him tirelessly but with concern about his possible emasculation, have a comic mis-understanding about the 'place' where he was wounded (geo-graphical place, bodily place).

49 *the Catacombs*: subterranean vaults and galleries that served as burial places and refuges from persecution for the early Chris-tians; the most famous catacombs are those just outside Rome.

50 *the invincible Socrates*: according to Plato's *Phaedo*, Socrates' last words were: 'Crito, we owe a cock to Aesculapius [the god of medicine]; pay it, therefore, and do not neglect it.'

51 *chanticleer*: a generic name for roosters dating back to medieval
verse narratives, including Chaucer's 'Nun's Priest's Tale'.
Melville drew upon a variety of secular and religious sources
for his story. He was familiar with the traditional Christian conception of the cock as a symbol of resurrection and eternal
life and, in St Peter, as a call to repentance; he also knew
Chaucer's tale and had probably read or heard stories about
cocks in American folklore. In *Moby-Dick* he had used the
cock as a symbol of the proud defiance of death. He was also
thoroughly aware of—and delighted to exploit—the long tradition of phallic punning on the word 'cock', as in Rabelais,
Shakespeare, and Sterne.

56 *Burton's Anatomy of Melancholy*: an exhaustive, quirky, serio-
comic work by Robert Burton (1577–1640), first published in
1621, that explores the roots and branches of melancholy with
a philosophical and psychological adventurousness that fas-
cinated Melville, who purchased a copy of the book in 1848.
Melville's characterization in 'Cock-A-Doodle-Doo!' and other
stories owes much to Burton's emphasis upon temperament
and the four humours. William B. Dillingham dicsusses the
influence of Burton on 'Cock-A-Doodle-Doo!' in *Melville's
Short Fiction 1853–1856* (Athens, Ga., 1977).

57 *Solomon*: son of David and king of the Hebrews (*c.*972–*c.*932
BCE), noted for his wisdom. For Melville, Solomon was also
the author of Ecclesiastes and therefore the symbol of a dark
but not unbalanced view of life. 'I read Solomon more and
more', Melville told Hawthorne in 1851, 'and every time see
deeper and deeper and more unspeakable meanings in him.
. . . It seems to me now that Solomon was the truest man who
ever spoke, and yet that he *managed* the truth with a view to
popular conservatism.' There was, that is, a darkness that even
Solomon dared not announce. In this respect, Merrymusk the
philosophical optimist ('All well') is anything but Solomonic.

Batavia: the old Dutch capital of the East Indies.

58 *October Mountain*: the name Melville used to refer to the
mountain south-east of his native Pittsfield.

59 *A cock, more like a golden eagle . . . than a cock*: Melville's allusions to British Admiral Horatio Nelson (1758–1805), a hero
of the Napoleonic Wars, and the French emperor Charlemagne
(742–814), draw upon the traditional image of the cock as a
noble, martial bird, though it is hard to decide whether the
tone of the passage is heroic, mock-heroic, or both at once.

Signor Beneventano: the contemporary Italian opera star Ferdinando Beneventano, whom Melville saw perform in Donizetti's *Lucia di Lammermoor* at the New Astor Place Opera House on Christmas Eve, 1847. It is interesting to note the etymology of the tenor's name, which combines *bene* (good or well) and *ventare* (to blow hard) with hints of *ventrola* (a weathervane or weathercock).

62 *the triumph ... Ajalon*: an allusion to Joshua 10: 12.

65 *I saw angels where they lay*: cf. 1 Corinthians 15: 52: 'In a moment, in the twinkling of an eye, at the last trump: for the trumpet shall sound, and the dead shall be raised incorruptible, and we shall be changed.' The name Trumpet given the rooster by Merrymusk's children suggests the Pauline text with its prospect of immortality.

66 *"Oh! death ... victory?"*: 1 Corinthians 15: 55. The question raised by the ending of 'Cock-A-Doodle-Doo!' is whether Melville is endorsing or grotesquely parodying the Christian hope that suffering and mortality will be redressed in an afterlife—in Merrymusk's terms, that 'all' is indeed 'well'.

The Fiddler

68 *Cleothemes the Argive*: an invented historical figure whose name and situation give some sense of the stilted, bombastic poem Helmstone has written.

69 *its bright side nor its dark side*: Melville had used the opposition of bright and dark in his earlier work but to nowhere near the extent he would in his stories and in *The Confidence-Man*. His language here would seem to establish Hautboy as a golden mean, but the passage is filled with ambiguities that leave his status unclear. Has Hautboy solved the problem of how to live or has he simply reached a comfortable but unaspiring accommodation?

70 *Genius, like Cassius, is lank*: Shakespeare's Cassius is described as having a 'lean and hungry look' (*Julius Caesar*, I. ii. 193).

spleen: generally, ill-will or bad temper, but within the humours psychology of Robert Burton and others the word denoted a form of irritable melancholy that was temperamental and ultimately physiological in origin.

Master Betty: William Henry Best Betty (1791–1874), an English child actor who retired from the stage before he was 33.

Melville may also have been thinking of the child-prodigy violinist Joseph Burke (1815–1902), who had a successful career in England and Ireland before settling down in Albany, New York, near where the Melvill family was living. It has been suggested that Melville heard Burke play on 10 February 1834 at Duffy's Theatre in Albany.

70 *ousted the Siddons and the Kembles from Drury Lane*: John Philip Kemble (1757–1823) and Mrs Sarah Siddons (1775–1831) were leading figures of the early nineteenth-century English stage. Drury Lane, the present-day Covent Garden area of London, was the home of the Theatre Royal.

72 *Orpheus*: in Greek mythology, the legendary Thracian poet whose lyre could charm even rocks, trees, and animals. See Ovid's *Metamorphoses*, Book X.

the charmed Bruin: an animal entranced by Orpheus; also a reference to one of the principal characters in the *Roman de Renart*, a series of popular satirical fables written in early medieval France. Melville would have read about Bruin the Bear in his copy of *Reynard the Fox*.

But to-day he walks Broadway and no man knows him: a projection of Melville's own situation during this period, as he may have felt it, and a curious foreshadowing of his last years in New York City. When Melville died in 1891 most of his writings had long been out of print, and the chief surprise to readers who remembered him at all was that he had died so recently.

The Paradise of Bachelors and the Tartarus of Maids

74 *Temple-Bar*: an old gateway to London built by Christopher Wren *c*.1672 and situated close to the entrance of the Inner and Middle Temples, Inns of Court where lawyers were admitted to the Bar and where many traditionally resided.

Fleet Street: London thoroughfare running from Ludgate Circus to the Strand, formerly noted for its bookshops and later as a centre of journalism.

Benedick: a sworn bachelor caught in the snares of matrimony, from Benedick in Shakespeare's *Much Ado About Nothing*.

Templar: founded in the early twelfth century to protect pilgrims to the Holy Land, the Knights Templars were a military-religious order with quarters near the site of Solomon's Temple in Jerusalem. The order was renowned for its martial courage and, by the end of the thirteenth century, for its wealth and power. More for their economic influence than for signs of internal corruption, the Knights Templars were opposed by Philip IV of France, who accused them of various crimes and abuses including sexual laxity and sodomy. With the aid of the Pope, the order was dissolved by the Council of Vienna in 1312 and its last grand master, Jacques de Molay, was burned two years later.

Brian de Bois Guilbert: a character in Sir Walter Scott's medieval romance *Ivanhoe*; a monk-knight, he tries to rape a Jewish girl, Rebecca, then concocts a charge of witchcraft against her when she repulses him.

75 *the Strand*: London avenue running parallel to the Thames from Trafalgar Square to the Temple.

pard: an archaic name for a panther or leopard.

Anacreon: Greek lyric poet (sixth century BCE) who wrote chiefly in praise of love and wine.

Holy Sepulchre: the tomb in Jerusalem in which Christ was placed.

76 *the knight-combatant of the Saracen*: 'Saracen' was the Medieval Christians' term for Arabs and for Muslims in general. Acre is a Palestinian seaport held by the Crusaders through most of the twelfth and thirteenth centuries until it was lost to the Saracens in 1291, a turning-point in the history of the Crusades. With the suppression of the Knights Templars in the early fourteenth century, the property of the English branch of the order was confiscated and its quarters in London (save for the consecrated parts) were let to lawyers, who occupied the buildings in Melville's time and after.

77 *R. F. C. and his imperial brother*: Robert Francis Cooke, a partner of publisher John Murray, and Melville's host at Temple Bar; and William Henry Cooke, Robert's brother, who also lived in Elm Court, Temple—'a barrister with a quizzical eye', Melville called him in the journal of his 1849–50 visit to England and the Continent. Melville enjoyed three dinners with the Cookes, one in Elm Court itself and two at the Erechtheum Club in St James's Square. 'Up in the 5th story we dined. The Paradise of Batchelors', Melville wrote of the first occasion; 'an exceedingly agreeable company', he remarked of the second. Melville delighted in good food, good wine,

and good talk, but the carefree life of the bachelor looked quite different when set against the social and metaphysical evils his bachelors characteristically deny.

77 *Dr. Johnson*: Samuel Johnson (1709–84), foremost English man of letters of the eighteenth century, who resided at the Inner Temple from 1760 to 1765.

Charles Lamb: English Romantic critic and essayist (1775–1834) who lived at the Inner Temple from 1809 to 1817, and whose sketch 'The Old Benchers of the Inner Temple' (from *Essays of Elia*, 1823) was one of Melville's sources. Lamb, too, discussed the Knights Templars and described the Inner Temple as a 'Paradise'.

"Carry me back to old Virginny!": a reference not to James A. Bland's ballad, the state song of Virginia, but to a similarly titled song by Edwin P. Christy published in 1847.

78 *Lincoln's Inn, Furnival's Inn . . . Gray's Inn*: along with the Inner and Middle Temples, Lincoln's Inn and Gray's Inn were Inns of Court dating from before the fourteenth century and possessing exclusive right to admit lawyers to the Bar. Furnival's Inn became attached to Gray's Inn in 1422. Lord Verulam— Sir Francis Bacon (1561–1626), lawyer, statesman, essayist, and philosopher of science—was admitted to Gray's Inn in 1576.

South Down: mutton of high quality from the South Down breed of sheep, originally reared on the South Downs of Sussex and Hampshire (*OED*).

79 *like Blucher's army . . . Waterloo*: a reference to the Battle of Waterloo (18 June 1815) in which the Prussian army of Gebhard Leberecht von Blücher, arriving late on the scene, was instrumental in helping the Duke of Wellington defeat Napoleon.

80 *Old Granada*: capital of Granada province, Andalusia, in southern Spain, founded by the Moors in the eighth century.

the Iron Duke: Arthur Wellesley, 1st Duke of Wellington (1769– 1852), so named because of his force of will.

a comic poem of Pulci's: Luigi Pulci (1432–84), a Florentine poet patronized by the Medicis.

81 *Epsom Heath*: an English racetrack.

a regular Jericho horn: in Joshua 6: 1–21 the Israelites are described as capturing Jericho after destroying its walls by a blast from a ram's horn. Like so many of the biblical, historical, literary, and mythological allusions in the story, this one seems to function mock-heroically.

82 *the Decameron*: the masterful collection of tales, many of them ribald, by Giovanni Boccaccio (1313–75)—a telling detail to close the sketch of quasi-monastic, sybaritic bachelors and anticipate one about exploited maids.

83 *Woedolor Mountain*: judging from geographical details, Melville's model is Mt. Greylock in the Berkshires, which he looked out upon from the piazza of his farm, but he also seems to have incorporated elements of the wilder scenery of the rugged and remote White Mountains in New Hampshire, famous for their winding passes, or 'notches'. 'Dolor' (grief) may perhaps be a pun on 'dollar', pointing up the theme of capitalist exploitation.

Dantean gateway: an entrance into hell, as in Dante's *Inferno*.

a great, purple, hopper-shaped hollow: the first of many details that associate the landscape with the female anatomy. As Marvin Fisher remarks, 'the approach to the mill . . . is described in terms so frankly physiological and so nearly scatological that their appearance in a mid-nineteenth-century issue of the highly respectable *Harper's Magazine* documents not only Melville's audacity but also the unsuspecting innocence and complacency of editor and audience' (Fisher, *Going Under: Melville's Short Fiction and the American 1850s* (Baton Rouge, La., 1977), 74).

84 *like some great whited sepulchre*: see Jesus's words in Matthew 23: 27: 'Woe unto you, scribes and Pharisees, hypocrites! for ye are like unto whited sepulchres, which indeed appear beautiful outward, but are within full of dead men's bones, and of all uncleanness.' Melville seems to be making an analogous comment about America's vaunted industrialism and the marvels of technology.

the seedsman's business: a continuation of the story's sexual imagery. Though only a visitor to the mill—and a tender-hearted one at that—the male narrator is implicated in the processes of copulation and generation that bind women to the reproductive machinery of nature. Melville's model for the factory was probably Carson's 'Old Red Mill' in nearby Dalton, Massachusetts, which he apparently visited on a paper-buying trip late in January 1851.

84 *pung*: a sleigh with a boxlike body drawn by a single horse, used in New England (*OED*).

86 *ancient arch of Wren*: see above, n. to p. 74; one of several details intended to link the two sections of the story together.

87 *dread-naught*: a thick outer garment worn in extreme cold.

89 *Actæon*: in Greek mythology, a huntsman who, having surprised the goddess Diana while she was bathing, was changed into a stag and torn to pieces by his own hounds. So far as he, too, is a voyeur of female intimacies, the narrator can be called an Actaeon.

90 *bachelor's buttons*: European flowers often cultivated in America; also called cornflowers. The allusion is largely an occasion for an extended play on the notion of 'bachelors' and their carefree, exploitative relationship to the factory's maids. Melville's pointed reference to 'the dormitories of the Paradise of Bachelors' associates even the distant transatlantic bachelors of the Temple with a gender and class domination characteristic of Western society at large, not simply of a New England paper-mill.

94 *John Locke . . . blank paper*: reacting against notions of innate ideas, British empirical philosopher John Locke (1632–1704) compared the mind at birth to a blank sheet of paper (*tabula rasa*) upon which experience writes.

Behemoth: a large, monstrous animal (probably a hippopotamus) described in Job 40: 15–24, a land analogue to the sea-beast Leviathan. Both represent the oppressive powers of the natural world, but in Melville's time such figures were also used to represent the tyrannizing menace of machines.

95 *the handkerchief of Saint Veronica*: a reference to the woman of Jerusalem who gave her head-cloth to Christ on his way to Calvary. According to legend, the imprint of his face remained on the cloth.

The Lightning-Rod Man

97 *the Acroceraunian hills*: literally, 'the high-thundering hills'. Acroceraunia was a section of ancient Greece on the Adriatic Sea famous for its frequent and violent thunderstorms and not far from the legendary seat of Jupiter. Melville may also have been thinking of chapter III of the Sixth Book of Puritan

theologian Cotton Mather's *Magnalia Christi Americana* (1702)
—'Ceraunius. Relating remarkables done by thunder'.

Jupiter Tonans: god of thunder; one of the Roman names for
the Greek Zeus, the epithet 'Tonans' emphasizing the wrath-
ful side of his divinity. In Calvinist divinity, too, the absolute
sovereignty of God (particularly the doctrine of predestina-
tion) is often physically imaged in the thunderstorm, as in
Jonathan Edwards's 'Personal Narrative'.

99 *a dealer in lightning-rods*: in the autumn of 1853 the Berkshires were subject to an intense sales campaign by pedlars of
lightning-rods.

Was it not at Criggan . . . struck?: Melville is drawing on local
history here; a large elm tree in Pittsfield was hit twice by
lightning, and in 1835 the assembly room of the First Church
of Pittsfield was also dramatically struck.

"Of what use is your rod then?": Allan Moore Emery has argued
that Melville is satirizing the proud claims of Franklinian science with its confidence in demystifying the awful powers of
nature. See Emery, 'Melville on Science: "The Lightning-Rod
Man"', *New England Quarterly*, 56 (1983), 555–68.

100 *Mine is the only true rod*: the lightning-rod man has also been
read as a preacher of evangelical religion who preys on human
fears of divine wrath and is intolerant of all faiths other than
his own. In Melville's time the Congregationalist First Church
of Pittsfield, under Revd John Todd, conducted several successful revivals.

103 *the granite Taconics and Hoosics*: mountain ranges in eastern New
York State and western New England; Melville's Berkshires
are part of the Taconic chain.

strike a bit of green light from the Leyden jar: Benjamin Franklin
was the first scientist to perform detailed experiments with the
Leyden jar and to explain its workings in terms of equal and
opposite charges. In his novel *Israel Potter*, serialized in 1854–5
in *Putnam's*, Melville sketched a shrewdly comic portrait of
Franklin, whom he saw as part genius and part confidence-
man.

you Tetzel: the notorious Johann Tetzel (*c.*1460–1519), German
Dominican preacher whose peddling of indulgences (insurance
against divine wrath) infuriated Luther and became a symbol
for the Protestant revolt against the corrupt Church.

104 *See, the scroll of the storm is rolled back*: an echo perhaps of the covenant between God and Noah in Genesis 9: 13–15.

The Encantadas

107 *Salvator R. Tarnmoor*: Melville's pseudonym in the *Putnam's* version of 'The Encantadas', although, as with several of the stories, his authorship was mentioned in a contemporary newspaper account and was publicly known. The pseudonym was omitted in the 1856 *Piazza Tales*, which bore Melville's name, but it was restored by the Northwestern–Newberry editors on the ground that it belonged to his original intention and has critical implications for the story. Melville seems to have been thinking of the seventeenth-century Italian landscape painter Salvator Rosa, whose scenes of wild and blasted nature have a figurative appropriateness to 'The Encantadas'.

"That may not be . . . howl": from Edmund Spenser's *The Faerie Queene*, II. XII. xi. 1–18. The epigraphs to the ten sketches lend them an allegorical dimension and help elevate 'The Encantadas' from travelogue to philosophical meditation. Melville's text of *The Faerie Queene* is based on John Upton's 1758 edition and may have been the one used in an anthology compiled by Robert Anderson. The Northwestern–Newberry editors use the Upton text to correct errors made during the original transcribing, but they preserve changes they judge Melville to have made intentionally. Readers wishing to gauge Melville's purposes in the epigraphs should check his wording against Spenser's, with reference to the Editorial Appendix in the Northwestern–Newberry edition of *The Piazza Tales* (600–17).

108 *Idumea*: the desolate, mountainous land of Edom stretching from the Dead Sea to the Red Sea; the land where the Israelites wandered.

send Lazarus . . . flame: an allusion to the biblical story of Lazarus and Dives (Luke 16: 19–24), in which Dives had to endure eternal fire.

that the jackal should den . . . Babylon: see Jeremiah 51: 37.

Atacama: arid desert in northern Chile.

110 *Apples of Sodom*: the Dead Sea apples described by Josephus, which, though beautiful, were full of ashes.

111 *I have indeed slept upon evilly enchanted ground*: Melville visited the Galapagos Islands three times: as a sailor aboard the whale-

ship *Acushnet*, which anchored near Chatham's Isle on 19–25 November 1841 and was in view of Hood's and Charles's Isles on 6 January 1842; in the winter of 1842/3 as a crewman on the whaler *Charles and Henry*; and on 19–20 November 1843, while *en route* home as an ordinary seaman on the frigate *United States*.

112 *"Memento ****"*: a reminder of death; literally, 'remember you must die'. The Northwestern–Newberry edition uses four asterisks in place of the five that appear in both the *Putnam's* text and *The Piazza Tales*—assuming that Melville, a shaky Latinist, intended the familiar graveyard words 'Memento mori'.

"Most ugly shapes . . . lye": *Faerie Queene*, II. XII. xxiii. 1–5; xxv. 6–9; xxvi. 1–3, 6, 8–9. In stanza xxiii, l. 6, Melville substituted 'do a man' for 'did the knight'; in l. 7, 'at home' for 'on earth'; and in l. 9, 'these isles' for 'the seas'. He made other minor substitutions, a few of them corrected in the Northwestern–Newberry text as probable accidents. Tethys (referred to in the last line) was the wife of Ocean.

113 *Enjoy the bright . . . don't deny the black*: an epigrammatic statement of the theme that runs through Melville's writings of the mid-1850s. Interestingly, as Darwin reported, the giant tortoises will not bear to have their bright sides exposed for long but struggle to regain their upright position.

114 *whereon the Hindoo plants this total sphere*: a reference to the Hindu tortoise as an avatar of Vishnu and the bearer of the world upon his back.

115 *their drudging impulse to straightforwardness in a belittered world*: Darwin was also astonished by the tortoises' tendency to travel 'so methodically along the well-chosen tracks'. Darwin, of course, writes as a naturalist noting scientific fact, Melville as a symbolist hinting at analogies to the moral world.

tortoise steaks and tortoise stews: tortoises were considered a rare delicacy, especially by sailors accustomed to poor rations.

Rock Rodondo: a rock foundation located just north-west of Albemarle Island; the correct Spanish would be 'Redonda'.

116 *"Forthy this hight . . . flocked were"*: *Faerie Queene*, II. XII. viiii. 1–6; xxxiii. 1–4, 8–9; xxxv. 6–9; xxxvi. 1–2. Here, too, Melville made a number of minor changes from the original.

St. Mark: St Mark's Cathedral in Venice.

118 *study the Natural History of strange sea-fowl*: Melville may have
     been thinking here of Darwin, who visited the Galapagos as
     a naturalist aboard HMS *Beagle* in 1835 during a voyage that
     would prove decisive for his later career. Darwin was espe-
     cially struck by the varieties of finches he observed in the
     Galapagos. Melville purchased a copy of Darwin's *Voyage of
     the 'Beagle'* in 1847 and may have read portions of it even
     earlier as a sailor aboard the *United States*.

120 *A Pisgah View From the Rock*: 'And Moses went up from the
     plains of Moab unto the mountain of Nebo, to the top of
     Pisgah, that is over against Jericho. And the LORD shewed him
     all the land of Gilead . . .' (Deuteronomy 34: 1).

     "That done . . . did show": *Faerie Queene*, I. x. lii. 1; lv. 1. In
     these lines the old hermit Heavenly Contemplation shows the
     Red Cross Knight a vision of the New Jerusalem—a promised
     land like Moses' and utterly different from the Tartarean land-
     scape visible from Rock Rodondo.

     Peak of Teneriffe: a mountainous, volcanic island in the Canary
     Islands.

121 *Quito*: capital of Ecuador.

     *the isles St. Felix and St. Ambrose, the isles Juan Fernandes and
     Massafuero*: Pacific islands Melville himself sailed among while
     on board the *United States* in 1843. Alexander Selkirk—the his-
     torical prototype for Robinson Crusoe—lived on one of the
     Juan Fernandez group for four years.

124 *kelsons*: lengthwise timber or metal structures running inter-
     nally along the bottom of a ship, parallel with and bolted to
     the keel, fastening the floor timbers or plating to the keel
     (*OED*).

126 *the luckless Stuart, Duke of York*: James II of England (1633–
     1701), who was forced to abdicate in 1688 after converting to
     Catholicism and siring a male heir.

     that excellent Buccaneer himself: William Ambrose Cowley, cap-
     tain of the *Bachelor's Delight* whose name Melville borrowed
     for Captain Delano's ship in 'Benito Cereno'. The quotation
     that follows is from Cowley's *Voyage Round the World*, a work
     anthologized in William Hacke's *A Collection of Original Voyages*
     (1699).

     the mildly thoughtful, and self-upbraiding poet Cowley: Abraham
     Cowley (1618–67), one of the later Metaphysical poets.

127 *"Looking far forth . . . flight"*: the wording here follows Anderson's text of Spenser's 'Visions of the World's vanity', ix. 1–4.

Captain David Porter: American naval officer (1780–1843), explorer of the Pacific, and author of *Journal of a Cruise Made to the Pacific Ocean* (1815, 1822), which Melville drew upon in 'The Encantadas', as he earlier had in *Typee*. The account that follows here is closely adapted from Porter.

128 *Valparaiso*: the main port of Chile and a commercial centre.

but three eye-witness authorities worth mentioning: in addition to the narratives of Cowley and Porter, Melville consulted Captain James Colnett's *A Voyage to the South Atlantic and Round Cape Horn into the Pacific Ocean* (1798) (Melville's 1793 date is incorrect). Melville also used, but does not mention, other accounts, among them Captain Amasa Delano's *A Narrative of Voyages and Travels, in the Northern and Southern Hemispheres* (1817), his chief source for 'Benito Cereno'.

129 *"Let us all servile base subjection scorn . . . hand"*: Spenser, 'Prosopopoia: or Mother Hubberds Tale', ll. 134–9.

"Lords of the world . . . uncontroll'd of any": ibid., ll. 168–9. Melville changes 'earth' to 'world' in l. 169.

"How bravely now we live . . . little troubles!": from Beaumont and Fletcher's play *Wit Without Money*, I. i.

long Toledos: swords with finely tempered blades, especially those made in Toledo, Spain (*OED*).

130 *a sentimental voyager*: in the paragraphs that follow Melville adapts a passage from Colnett, adding romantic flourishes and recasting the rough buccaneers as meditative philosophers and poets. However distanced by its ascription to 'a sentimental voyager', the tableau is a Melvillean daydream combining the adventurous and contemplative lives—the impossible (and, Melville knows, ultimately undesirable) fantasy of a man in middle life who feels himself besieged by family and creditors and who indulges a vision of picaresque freedom.

the poet Gray . . . Crebillon: Thomas Gray (1716–71), English poet, best known for his 'Elegy Written in a Country Church-Yard' (1751). The French romancer Claude Crébillon (1707–77) was a favourite of Gray's, as Melville might have read in Gray's letters.

a Dampier, a Wafer, and a Cowley: William Dampier (1652–1715), buccaneer, circumnavigator, captain in the navy, and hydrographer; Lionel Wafer (1660?–1705?), surgeon and buccaneer, an associate of Dampier's; and William Ambrose Cowley, mentioned above.

131 *So with outragious cry . . . warmd*: Faerie Queene, II. IX. xiii. 1–7.

132 *We will not be of any occupation . . . toyle*: 'Prosopopoia', ll. 155–8.

  Callao: port and capital of Callao Department, western Peru.

  Selkirk: Alexander Selkirk (1676–1721), Scottish sailor whose story furnished the basis of Defoe's *Robinson Crusoe*.

135 *Alsatia*: the Whitefriars district of London, situated between the Thames and Fleet Street and a haven for debtors and criminals.

136 *"At last they in an island did espy . . . evermore"*: Faerie Queene, II. XII. xxvii. 5–9.

  "Black his eye as the midnight sky . . . cactus tree": from eighteenth-century poet Thomas Chatterton's *Aella: A Tragycal Enterlude* ('The Mynstreelles Songe'), l. 82–3. The lines contain several substitutions and mistranscriptions.

137 *"Each lonely scene shall thee restore . . . dead"*: the last stanza (vi) of eighteenth-century poet William Collins's 'A Song from Shakespear's Cymbeline'; added to the epigraph in the 1856 *Piazza Tales* text.

  Charles' Isle: possibly Porters Isle, renamed.

  Peruvian pisco: a white brandy made in Peru from muscat grapes (*OED*).

138 *Chola widow*: sources for the sketch of Hunilla are discussed by Robert Sattelmeyer and James Barbour in 'The Sources and Genesis of Melville's Norfolk Isle and the Chola Widow', *American Literature*, 50 (1978), 398–417.

141 *Ah, Heaven . . . faithful one?*: an echo of Ahab's complaint against the heavens in chapter 70 of *Moby-Dick* ('The Sphynx').

150 *"That darkesome glen . . . wrapt abouts"*: Faerie Queene, I. IX. xxxv. 1–9; xxxvi. 1–3.

  Oberlus: based on Patrick Watkins, a red-haired Irishman whose portrait Melville derived, as he acknowledges, largely from Porter's *Journal*. Other sources are Dr John Coulter's *Adventures in the Pacific* (1854) and Amasa Delano's *Narrative of Voyages and Travels . . .* (1817). Watkins may also have been a figure in sailor tradition.

151 *Circe's cup*: the poisonous cup the sorceress Circe offered Ulysses and his men during a feast she held for them (Homer,

Odyssey, Bk. 10). The potion transformed Ulysses' companions into pigs, but he himself, forewarned of Circe's powers, avoided this fate.

152 *"This island's mine . . . mother"*: Caliban's words in Shakespeare's *Tempest* (I. ii. 332).

158 *Guayaquil*: major Ecuadorian seaport and commercial city.

159 *"And all about . . . hanged been"*: *Faerie Queene*, I. IX. xxxiv. 1–4.

162 *Potter's Field*: a name given (after Matthew 27: 7) to a plot of ground used as a burial place for the poor and for strangers (*OED*).

163 *"Oh Brother Jack . . . clinkers!"*: Melville comically modified the traditional bit of graveyard verse in Porter's *Journal*, which Porter claimed to have seen on Charles (not Chatham) Isle: 'Gentle reader, as you pass by, | As you are now, so wonce was I; | As now my body is in the dust, | I hope in heaven my soul to rest.'

Benito Cereno

164 *In the year 1799, Captain Amasa Delano . . . water*: 'Benito Cereno' is based upon chapter 18 of Amasa Delano's *A Narrative of Voyages and Travels, in the Northern and Southern Hemispheres . . .* (1817); the narrative portion of the source is reprinted as an Appendix to the present edition. Among Melville's most notable alterations were changing the names of Delano's ship (from the *Perseverance* to the *Bachelor's Delight*) and Cereno's ship (from the *Tryal* to the *San Dominick*) and redating events from 1805 to 1799. He also added numerous scenes and details, altered the behaviour of Cereno after the recapture of his ship, and elaborated the portrait of Delano he found suggested in the *Narrative*. Melville's use of Delano was discovered by Horace Scudder in 1928 and has since become an important resource for criticism.

Shadows present, foreshadowing deeper shadows to come: the opening paragraphs establish a sense of ominous foreboding and moral uncertainty that work against any simplistic black-and-white interpretation of the tale. Delano holds to a bright view of life, Cereno to a dark one, but reality itself (like Melville's commitment in the story) is hazy, uncertain, and, as the third paragraph emphasizes, 'gray'.

164 *of a singularly undistrustful good nature*: though an experienced
sailor with a broad knowledge of the human and natural worlds,
Captain Delano is temperamentally another of Melville's
'bachelors' uninitiated into, or impervious to, the darker side
of life.

165 *saya-y-manta*: a woman's robe that conceals her almost entirely
except for parts of her face.

166 *like a white-washed monastery*: images of monks and monasteries
figure prominently in the tale and have often been remarked
upon. See Newman, *A Reader's Guide*, for a discussion of the
criticism of 'Benito Cereno'.

Black Friars: Dominican monks were called Black Friars in
England because of the black capes they wore.

Ezekiel's Valley of Dry Bones: Ezekiel 37: 1–14. Carolyn L.
Karcher comments on the significance of this allusion within
the slavery theme in *Shadow Over the Promised Land* (Baton
Rouge, La., 1980).

white noddy: a seabird similar to a gull.

167 *SAN DOMINICK*: in renaming Cereno's ship the *San Dominick*,
Melville seems to have been alluding to the Caribbean island
of Santo Domingo, on which Toussaint L'Ouverture (*c*.1744–
1803) successfully led a slave rebellion in the 1790s. The name
also suggests the order of Dominicans, sinister in the Anglo-
Saxon imagination because of their prominence in the Spanish
Inquisition.

168 *Lascars*: East Indian sailors.

171 *Babo*: in the deposition Delano appends to his narrative of
events, Cereno's servant is identified as Muri; Babo is Muri's
father. Melville dramatically enlarged the figure of Babo and
made him the mastermind of the revolt.

172 *Charles V*: (1500–58), Holy Roman Emperor (1519–58), King
of Spain (1516–56), and Archduke of Austria; the greatest of
the Hapsburg emperors. In 1554 he abdicated all his titles and
two years later retired to the monastery of Yuste. Among his
other acts, Charles agreed to the importation of slaves into
the New World with a large shipment to Santo Domingo in
1517, partly on the advice of Dominican priest Bartholomew
de Las Casas, who argued that Africans were needed to replace
the declining number of native workers on the island.

174 *mate*: Paraguay tea, or maté.

178   *hawse-hole*: the hole in the bow of the ship through which the anchor cable passes (*OED*).

      Conception: capital of Concepción province, central Chile.

181   *Ashantee*: a West African people who inhabited what is now Ghana and were known for their ferocity in resisting the British.

      Alexandro Aranda: the original Aranda allowed his slaves to roam the decks without chains, convinced of their tractability. He was murdered and his body was thrown overboard; the treatment of Aranda's body in 'Benito Cereno' is Melville's invention.

186   *a sort of Castilian Rothschild*: a reference to the wealthy German-Jewish banking family that negotiated many of the great government loans of the nineteenth century and had noble relatives in several European countries.

194   *a Caffre guard of honor*: Kaffir, a Bantu people of southern Africa.

196   *Mungo Park*: Scottish surgeon and explorer (1771–1806) who made a journey along the Nile in 1795–6 later recounted in his popular book *Travels in the Interior of Africa* (1799). Melville is probably alluding to a description of African women in chapter 20.

197   *a chance phantom cats-paw*: a light breeze that ripples the surface in places (*OED*).

198   *marlingspike*: a pointed iron tool used to lift the strands of rope in splicing (*OED*).

199   *the shrewder race*: readers see events through the eyes of Delano, a kindly man but one who shares the racial stereotypes of his—and of Melville's—age. Discussions of race were heated in the 1850s, as both pro- and anti-slavery forces sought justification for their views in theories of the Negro character. In *Types of Mankind* (1854), American ethnologist Josiah C. Nott and his British collaborator, the renowned Egyptologist George R. Gliddon, argued that the human races were distinct species. Melville would have known of their work through a sympathetic review published in the July 1854 issue of *Putnam's*, which also included a serialized section of Melville's *Israel Potter*.

      making gordian knots for the temple of Ammon: a knot tied by Gordius, king of Phrygia, and held to be insoluble except by the man who would come to rule Asia; Alexander the Great cut the knot with his sword. In general usage, an intricate or irresolvable problem.

200 *congé*: a ceremonious bow.

203 *Guy-Fawkish*: Guy Fawkes (1570–1606) was the most famous figure in the Gunpowder Plot of November 1605 that aimed to blow up the Parliament building while James I and his chief ministers were in attendance, in reprisal for James's persecution of Roman Catholics and as a prelude to a nation-wide Catholic rebellion. Fawkes was arrested the day of the planned explosion (5 November) and executed two months later.

gurried: slimy from whale or fish offal.

206 *cuddy*: a room or cabin in a ship.

209 *Johnson and Byron*: eighteenth-century man of letters Samuel Johnson (1709–84) and the Romantic poet Byron (1788–1824). Francis Barber was Johnson's trusted black servant, whom Johnson treated kindly and to whom he left a handsome legacy in his will. William Fletcher, Byron's long-time valet, was a white Englishman whom Melville may have confused with the black servant of Byron's travelling companion Edward Trelawny.

211 *James the First of England*: (1566–1625), first Stuart king of England (1603–25) who ascended the throne in a time of religious and political turmoil and was extremely sensitive to hints of opposition.

213 *Nubian*: from Nubia, an ancient black kingdom in what is now Sudan and a seat of high civilization in Africa.

214 *Chesterfieldian*: worldly, sophisticated, elegant; from the manners and writings of Philip Stanhope, fourth Earl of Chesterfield (1694–1773).

215 *Canary*: sweet wine from the Canary Islands.

216 *but the hand of his servant*: cf. Luke 22: 21: 'But, behold, the hand of him that betrayeth me is with me on the table.'

217 *the hand of his servant, mute as that on the wall*: an allusion to the appearance of a mysterious hand at King Belshazzar's feast (Daniel 5: 5): 'In the same hour came forth fingers of a man's hand, and wrote over against the candlestick upon the plais-ter of the wall of the king's palace.' The prophet Daniel takes these words to mean that Belshazzar's kingdom is doomed.

223 *less hardened than the Jew*: Judas Iscariot at the Last Supper (Matthew 26: 20–5).

226 *while his right foot . . . ground the prostrate negro*: the tableau recalls the description of the masked satyr on the ship's stern-piece as well as iconographic paintings like Renaissance artist Guido Reni's of the Archangel Michael standing triumphantly upon the defeated Satan after the War in Heaven.

231 *Preston Pans*: the scene of a battle during the Jacobite Rebellion of 1745 in which 2,500 Highland Scots under the Pretender, Charles Edward Stuart, and Lord George Murray routed a similar number of British troops.

233 *the deposition goes on*: while following the official documents of the case in most respects, Melville's deposition includes many thematically significant changes (see the Northwestern–Newberry edition of *The Piazza Tales*, 826–36).

234 *Senegal*: a region in West Africa.

236 *the image of Christopher Colon*: the Columbus figurehead was Melville's invention and adds a representative dimension to the events of the tale.

243 *a votive offering . . . Spain*: another of Melville's inventions; an irony intended, it would seem, to comment on the watchfulness of Providence.

was aiming it at the negro's throat: in Delano's narrative it is Benito Cereno himself who tries to stab the shackled black.

244 *betake himself to the monastery on Mount Agonia*: Melville's addition, recalling the abdication and monastic retirement of Charles V. The historical Cereno ungratefully opposed Delano's efforts to share in the rewards of recapturing his ship.

I and My Chimney

248 *Cardinal Wolsey*: Thomas Wolsey (1473?–1530), ambitious and powerful English ecclesiastic who served as Henry VIII's lord chancellor (1515–29) and was greatly responsible for England's domestic and foreign policy. The allusion has a certain irony to it, for in the end Wolsey's allegiance to Rome surpassed that to his king, and he was arrested and charged with treason but died of natural causes before he could be tried.

a huge, corpulent old Harry VIII. of a chimney: late portraits of Henry VIII (reigned 1509–47) show him massive and corpulent.

248 *Lord Rosse's monster telescope*: astronomer William Parsons, third Earl of Rosse (1800–67), erected a huge telescope at Parsonstown in King's County, Ireland, in the 1840s.

249 *In those houses . . . quarrelsome family*: the language of this paragraph has prompted critical speculation that Melville is writing about the contemporary American political situation, specifically about the federal Union divided acrimoniously along regional lines over the issue of slavery. See, for example, Fisher, *Going Under*, and Emery, 'The Political Significance of Melville's Chimney', *New England Quarterly*, 55 (1982), 201–18.

251 *Kossuth's rising*: Louis Kossuth (1802–94) was a leader of the Hungarian revolution of 1848 and, with its suppression the following year, a lifelong exile thereafter. His visit to America in 1851 was widely reported in newspapers and magazines.

Champs de Mars: the 'Field of Mars' in Paris served as a parade ground for the Military Academy (constructed 1769–72) and was the site of two great rallies during the French Revolution.

That in which I and my chimney dwell: the narrator's house seems patterned after Melville's Pittsfield farmhouse, Arrowhead, which also contained a large chimney, though not nearly so dominating as the one in the story. A neighbouring house, Broadhall—familiar to Melville for many years and formerly the home of a paternal uncle—may also have been a model.

252 *the pyramid of Cheops*: the Great Pyramid at Giza on the west bank of the Nile built by Khufu (Cheops), second king of the fourth dynasty (c.2575–c.2464 BCE) of Egypt; the largest single structure in the world in its time and a masterpiece of engineering and construction.

a regicidal act: a reference to the execution of King Charles I (1600–49) by Parliamentary forces under Oliver Cromwell during the English Civil War. The narrator's sympathy with Charles and his deprecation of Cromwell belong to the comically exaggerated traditionalism of his character and ought not to be taken for Melville's opinions at the time. For complicated reasons Melville the story-writer seems to have enjoyed projecting himself into crusty, humorously conservative narrators, perhaps as a way of venting his indignation at the shallowness and pretence of his times.

253 *elephant-and-castle*: a well-known English tavern (built c.1674, rebuilt 1824) located about a mile beyond London Bridge at

the Southwark intersection of the main roads south and east.
Though the tavern was destroyed during World War II, the
name of the intersection remains.

Kenilworth: a town in Warwickshire, in central England, with
a castle of that name; also the title of a historical romance by
Sir Walter Scott (1821).

254 *Atlas*: in Greek mythology, a Titan condemned by Zeus for
his part in the war of the Titans to uphold the heavens on his
shoulders.

those stones at Gilgal: see Joshua 4: 19–24.

257 *this enterprising wife of mine*: according to Melville's wife, Lizzie,
the wife in 'I and My Chimney' with her endless plans for
improvement is based not upon herself but upon Melville's
mother, Maria, who lived with the family at Arrowhead. Biographically, this may be true, but Melville casts the wife as
a root-and-branch reformer given to newfangledness and as
hostile to tradition as the narrator himself is fond of it.

258 *sciatica*: a condition characterized by pain in the lower back
or the back of the hips or thighs. Melville himself suffered
from sciatica at this time, probably as a result of prolonged
labour at his writing-desk.

my old wife . . . herself: an allusion to Genesis 18: 12–15 in which
Abraham's wife, Sarah, long past the age of childbearing,
laughs when Abraham tells her she is to bear a son.

259 *old Montaigne*: French essayist and sceptic Michel de Montaigne
(1533–92), a favourite author of Melville's.

daughter of Nebuchadnezzar . . . spinages: Nebuchadnezzar was
the King of Babylon from 605 to 562 BCE who destroyed
Jerusalem and carried its people into captivity (2 Kings 24–5).
Daniel's interpretation of Nebuchadnezzar's dream was ful-
filled when the latter 'was driven from men, and did eat grass
as oxen' (Daniel 4: 33).

Swedenborgianism, and the Spirit Rapping philosophy: Swedenborgianism was the religious system incorporated in the
Church of the New Jerusalem, based on the philosophy of
Swedish theologian Emanuel Swedenborg (1688–1772). It had
branches in London and in north-eastern American cities in
the late eighteenth and early nineteenth centuries and was an
important influence on Emerson, among others. 'Spiritualism',
or the 'spirit-rapping philosophy', was initiated in 1848 by

the Fox sisters of Hydesville (near Rochester), New York, who claimed to receive messages from the spiritual world in the form of tappings. The two women enjoyed a tremendous vogue through most of the nineteenth century, though late in life Katherine Fox revealed that the noises were a hoax. Melville's story 'The Apple-Tree Table', published in *Putnam's* in 1856, was a satire on this phenomenon.

260 *the Ladies' Magazine*: the highly popular *Godey's Lady's Book* or its imitator *Graham's*, illustrated magazines published in Philadelphia and devoted chiefly to matters of fashion and taste, though they sometimes also included the work of important writers like Emerson and Thoreau.

Charles V.: see above, note to p. 172. Benito Cereno is also likened—more seriously—to Charles V.

261 *Belzoni*: Giovanni Battista Belzoni (1778–1823), Italian traveller and explorer who made important discoveries in Egypt in the early nineteenth century.

263 *a Bunker Hill monument*: completed in 1843, the Bunker Hill Monument commemorating a Revolutionary War battle near Boston was a prominent symbol of American nationalism. At the ground-breaking ceremony in 1825, Daniel Webster gave a famous speech praising the sanctity of American institutions and the dignity of the sons' Revolutionary inheritance. In a complex gesture of irony, Melville dedicated his historical novel *Israel Potter* (1855) to 'His Highness, the Bunker Hill Monument'.

264 *one Mr Scribe*: Merton M. Sealts, Jr., has suggested that Scribe (his name denoting 'writer') is based on Melville's Pittsfield neighbour Oliver Wendell Holmes—doctor, author, and noted wit—who may have examined Melville in the early 1850s for signs of mental illness at the request of Melville's family (see Sealts, 'Herman Melville's "I and My Chimney"', reprinted in Sealts, *Pursuing Melville 1940–1980* (Madison, Wisc., 1982), 11–22). Like the lightning-rod man, Scribe the hack architect seems another of Melville's confidence-men, in this case a venal, literal-minded utilitarian without depth or reverence. The name 'Scribe' may take its origin from Matthew 5: 20 ('except your righteousness shall exceed the righteousness of the scribes and Pharisees, ye shall in no case enter into the kingdom of heaven').

267 *Holofernes*: as related in the Apocrypha, Judith, a Jewish widow, seduced the Assyrian general Holofernes and beheaded him in

the night; traditionally, an image of righteous female revenge against male tyranny.

Caligula: Roman Emperor (reigned AD 37–41) infamous for his voluptuousness and cruelty. Like the allusion to Holofernes, this one is comically hyperbolic, but it may also reflect tensions within the Melvilles' marriage that would come to a head in the mid-1860s, when Lizzie doubted her husband's sanity and considered leaving him. The death of their son Malcolm in 1867 seems to have brought husband and wife together. Melville wrote his last collection of verse, *Weeds and Wildings*, specifically for Lizzie, and after his death she was the devoted guardian of his reputation. Charges like Elizabeth Renker's that Melville beat his wife have very little evidence to support them (see Renker, 'Herman Melville, Wife Beating, and the Written Page', *American Literature*, 66 (1994), 123–51).

269 *Captain Julian Dacres*: as Sealts pointed out, Dacres is an anagram of sacred—in Sealts's reading, a symbol of the blasphemy attending the violation of the inmost recesses of a self as represented by the secret compartment in the chimney (see Sealts, 'Herman Melville's "I and My Chimney" ').

271 *a collar of the Order of the Garotte*: a reference to the Spanish method of execution by strangulation in which a wire or iron collar is tightened around the neck.

272 *St. Dunstan's devil*: St Dunstan, tenth-century prelate, Archbishop of Canterbury, and patron saint of goldsmiths, having been an accomplished goldsmith himself. He is often represented in clerical robes carrying a pair of pincers in his right hand in reference to the legend that on one occasion he seized the devil with a pair of red-hot tongs and refused to release him until the devil promised never to tempt him again.

274 *a witch-hazel wand*: a wand cut from a North American shrub of the genus *Hamamelis* reputed to have magical powers as a divining rod.

275 *no reason to believe any unsoundness*: if Melville's story originated in a mental examination performed by Holmes or another doctor, this line may suggest that Melville was given a clean bill of health.

276 *poor Poland*: during the eighteenth and early nineteenth centuries Poland was repeatedly partitioned by its powerful neighbours, Austria, Russia, and Prussia.

276 *that wall-breaking wish of Momus*: Momus, the Greek god of ridicule, complained that humans should have been constructed with doors in their chests so that they could contain no secrets.

277 *the golden bowl*: see Ecclesiastes 12: 6: 'Or ever the silver cord be loosed, or the golden bowl be broken', a reminder of human fragility and mortality.

278 *a sort of mossy old misanthrope*: a comic projection, perhaps, of how Melville was beginning to feel about himself as he was in the middle 1850s or as he might become. The chimney he clings to in his isolation is a symbol of his core self, identified with the literary career his family would have him abandon.

Billy Budd, Sailor

279 *Billy Budd, Sailor (An Inside Narrative)*: Hayford and Sealts take this title to be Melville's final choice, replacing the earlier '*Billy Budd | Foretopman | What befell him | in the year of the | Great Mutiny | &c*', a title chosen by previous editors Raymond Weaver and F. Barron Freeman. By 'inside narrative' Melville seems to mean, among other things, a story giving the inward truth of the case in all its manifold complications.

Jack Chase: a much-admired shipmate of Melville's on the frigate *United States* and a prominent figure in *White-Jacket* (1850), based on Melville's naval experience. As much as any character in Melville's fiction, Jack Chase is a 'natural aristocrat'—that is, a commoner and fervent democrat whose ascendancy among his peers is owing to his personal qualities of intelligence, geniality, and magnanimity.

Aldebaran: a star of exceptional brightness that forms the eye in the constellation Taurus.

the less prosaic time: Melville's nostalgia for the colour and romance of sailing-ship days is a major theme in the sea monologues in *John Marr* (1888) and, earlier, in several of the poems in *Battle-Pieces and Aspects of the War* (1866).

the unadulterate blood of Ham: Noah placed a curse on the descendants of his son Ham, the father of Canaan, who had looked upon him drunken and naked in his tent. Noah's words —'Cursed be Canaan; a servant of servants shall he be unto his brethen' (Genesis 9: 25)—were later interpreted as referring to the black race and were commonly cited by Europeans and Americans as justifications for Negro slavery. By contrast, the African in *Billy Budd* is another of nature's aristocrats.

280 *Anacharsis Cloots*: Prussian-born revolutionary Jean-Baptiste du Val de Grâce, Baron de Cloots (1755–94), whom Thomas Carlyle in *The French Revolution* described as introducing a representative assortment of humanity before the French National Assembly in token of the widespread support for the French Revolution. Figuratively, a microcosm of the human race. The *Pequod* in *Moby-Dick* is called an 'Anacharsis Clootz deputation', the Mississippi steamboat *Fidèle* in *The Confidence-Man* 'an Anacharsis Cloots congress'.

the tempestuous Erie Canal: an ironic allusion to the placid commercial waterway through central New York State.

Alexander curbing the fiery Bucephalus: an allusion to Alexander the Great taming the steed Bucephalus, recounted in Plutarch's *Lives*.

welkin-eyed: blue-eyed, as the heavens are blue.

281 *impressed on the Narrow Seas*: impressment, or the forced recruitment of sailors from merchant ships or from ashore, was a common practice in the English Navy during the Napoleonic Wars; the Narrow Seas are the English and Irish Channels.

Bellipotent: in early drafts of *Billy Budd* the *Bellipotent*, a formidable 74-gun warship, was called the *Indomitable*, a name chosen by editors prior to Hayford and Sealts, who judged *Bellipotent* to be Melville's later preference.

284 *the Rights-of-Man*: an allusion to Thomas Paine's 1791 *The Rights of Man*, written in answer to Edmund Burke's conservative *Reflections on the Revolution in France* (1790). In moving from a merchant ship to a man-of-war, Billy leaves behind whatever abstract natural rights human beings may be said to possess and enters the fallen world of history, authoritarianism, martial law, and repression.

287 *by-blow*: an illegitimate child. Allegorical readings of Billy as an Adam place significance on his answer to the officer's question about his parentage, ' "God knows, sir" '.

288 *Cain's city and citified man*: after slaying his brother Abel, Cain was banished from pastoral innocence and the face of God and founded a city in the land of Nod (Genesis 4: 13–16).

288 *Caspar Hauser*: a foundling (1812?–1833), possibly amnesiac, who appeared on the streets of Nuremberg in 1828; a figure of uncertain orgins and without a remembered history.

289 *Honest and poor . . . brought?*: from the *Epigrams* of the Roman satirist Martial (*c.*40–*c.*104) as translated by Cowley in the Bohn edition (1865).

   the beautiful woman in one of Hawthorne's minor tales: a reference to Georgiana in 'The Birth-mark', whose sole blemish and sign of human earthliness and imperfection is a small hand-shaped birthmark on her left cheek.

290 *at Spithead . . . at the Nore*: two insurrections within the British fleet that were a symptom of the political turmoil of the times and form an important context for understanding Vere's precipitous behaviour in the story.

   Dibdin: Charles Dibdin (1745–1814), English playwright and song-writer whose celebrations of sailor life Melville admired for their 'sea-chivalry and romance' (his own words) even as he understood them to be rose-coloured in tone and chauvinistic in posture.

   William James: British historian, from whose *Naval History of Great Britain* (6 vols.; 1860) Melville quotes.

291 *a coronet for Nelson . . . Trafalgar*: as recounted in Robert Southey's *Life of Nelson*, which Melville owned and used as a source, Admiral Horatio Nelson received a baron's coronet for his victory in the Battle of the Nile (1798). Nelson died heroically in the decisive Battle of Trafalgar (1805), where the British fleet under his direction destroyed twenty French and Spanish ships while losing none of their own. To Melville, Nelson was not only a great military hero but a symbol of romantic magnanimity, in contrast to the able but constitutionally prudent Vere.

   such a bypath: Melville wrote this chapter, deleted it from the 1888 manuscript, then apparently decided to reinsert it during a later stage of composition. Hershel Parker argues that Melville 'may have felt' the chapter 'was simply too good to throw away' (*Reading 'Billy Budd'* (Evanston, Ill., 1990), 112), but Melville would have been obtuse indeed if he failed to understand how Nelson's largeness of spirit casts a questioning light on Vere's by-the-book prudence. It seems a greater act of faith to claim that Melville meant nothing pertinent by the chapter, as Parker does, than to imagine that he reinserted it with an awareness of its implications. See, for example,

Ralph W. Willett, 'Nelson and Vere: Hero and Victim in *Billy Budd, Sailor*', *PMLA* 82 (1967), 370–6.

293 *Benthamites of war*: a reference to English Utilitarian philosopher Jeremy Bentham (1748–1832), whose calculating ethics of pleasure and pain, advantage and disadvantage, struck Melville as the epitome of small-mindedness. In his poem 'A Utilitarian View of the Monitor's Fight', from the 1866 *Battle-Pieces and Aspects of the War*, Melville contrasts grimy modern warfare with its impersonal technology to the glory of 'pomp' and 'glory' of 'lace and feather' days.

Alfred in his funeral ode: an allusion to Alfred, Lord Tennyson's 'Ode on the Death of the Duke of Wellington' (1852).

294 *Mansfield*: William Murray, Earl of Mansfield (1705–93), became Lord Chief Justice of Britain in 1756.

an officer like Nelson . . . true: here again, Nelson's imagination and force of character become an implicit standard (though hardly the only one) for measuring the captain with 'sterling qualities' but 'without any brilliant ones' whom Melville is about to introduce.

295 *Vere*: Vere's name has sometimes been read as a play upon the Latin *vir* (man) or *verus* (true) as well as on the word 'severe'.

Rodney . . . De Grasse: at a battle off Dominica in 1782, British admiral George Brydges, Baron Rodney (1719–92), defeated the French commander de Grasse with important help from Sir William George Fairfax.

296 *the blank sea*: at a crucial point in the trial scene (Ch. 21), Vere will gaze out 'upon the monotonous blank of the twilight sea', a reminder perhaps of the indifference of nature against which human institutions are a necessary but flawed bulwark.

starry Vere: Anne Fairfax Vere, whose daughter Mary had been tutored by Marvell. Denton was another estate of the Fairfaxes, also mentioned in Marvell's poem.

297 *Montaigne*: see note to p. 259. Sceptic and man of the world, Montaigne was an important philosopher for Melville as well as for Vere, though his secular point of view was never definitive for Melville. Along with his dreaminess, Vere's taste in reading—so atypical of his class and vocation—suggests that he is not a representative member of the upper class or the military establishment but a special individual whose assimilation of reigning conventions has been modified by his temperament

and habits of mind and forged into a deeper, more reflective conservatism closer to Edmund Burke's than to the Realpolitik of contemporary statesmen.

299 *Tecumseh*: Shawnee Indian chief (1768?–1813) who sided with the British in the war of 1812.

Titus Oates: a clergyman who in 1678 invented the story of a Catholic plot to assassinate Charles II, burn London, and massacre English Protestants. As a result of Oates's charges, many Catholics were persecuted and killed before the story was exposed as a fabrication.

chevalier: as used here, a confidence-man or rogue.

310 *Camoëns' Spirit of the Cape*: an allusion to Adamastor, the monster in the *Lusiad* of Portuguese poet Luis Vaz de Camoens (1525–80) who tries to annihilate Vasco Da Gama and his crew.

303 *Dansker*: a Dane.

304 *Haden's etching*: 'The Breaking Up of the *Agamemnon*', a famous 1874 etching by Sir Francis Seymour Haden.

305 *Jemmy Legs*: sailor slang for the master-at-arms.

Chiron: in Greek mythology, the wise centaur (part man, part horse) who taught Achilles and others.

308 *Radcliffian romance*: Ann Radcliffe (1764–1823) was a popular British Gothic novelist best known for *The Mysteries of Udolpho*.

an honest scholar: another of Melville's invented personae intended to suggest but not definitively authorize a perspective on events.

309 *Coke and Blackstone*: Sir Edward Coke (1552–1634) and Sir William Blackstone (1723–80), important figures in the development of English law.

Natural Depravity: a phrase Melville borrowed from the Bohn edition of Plato's works (6 vols.; 1848–54), as Hayford and Sealts note, and suggestive of a wickedness inexplicable through any appeal to environmental influences.

310 *"mystery of iniquity"*: 2 Thessalonians 2: 7: 'For the mystery of iniquity doth already work: only he who now letteth will let, until he be taken out of the way.'

311 *envy and antipathy*: Hayford and Sealts observe that Melville entitled this chapter 'Pale ire, envy, and despair', an allusion

to Satan's feelings in Bk. IV of Milton's *Paradise Lost* (ll. 114–17). Echoes of *Paradise Lost* abound in the early sections of *Billy Budd*, which reflect the theological emphasis of the 1888 manuscript. The seemingly motiveless malice of Claggart also owes much in conception to Shakespeare's portrait of Iago in *Othello*.

Chang and Eng: Siamese twins who were exhibited as a freak show; Melville is likely to have seen them during their visit to Pittsfield in August 1853.

that streak of apprehensive jealousy . . . David: see 1 Samuel 16: 18, 18: 8–9.

313   *scriptural devils*: see James 2: 19.

321   *man of sorrows*: see Isaiah 53: 3; a phrase often applied to Christ.

the glittering dental satire of a Guise: a French ducal family known for its anti-Protestant activities. The most notorious of the Guises in Protestant eyes was Henri de Guise (1550–88), who played an active role in the St Bartholomew's Day massacre of Huguenots in 1572.

323   *up the Straits*: the English Mediterranean squadron was then patrolling off Cadiz in the Strait of Gibraltar.

328   *cite me an act or spoken word*: Hayford and Sealts find a resemblance here to Othello's demand from Iago for 'ocular proof' of Desdemona's infidelity.

the spokesman . . . Joseph: jealous of Joseph because he was their father's favourite, Joseph's brothers sold him into slavery, then dipped his coat into the blood of a kid to convince Jacob that his son had been killed by a wild beast (Genesis 37: 1–36).

331   *torpedo fish*: the electric ray, the shock from whose tail can paralyse its victim.

333   *the divine judgment on Ananias*: hearing Peter's charge that he has lied 'unto God', Ananias 'fell down, and gave up the ghost' (Acts 5: 1–5).

Yet the angel must hang!: even before he assembles three of his officers to hear evidence, render a verdict, and recommend a sentence, Vere is convinced that Billy must be executed.

334   *Was he unhinged?*: by having the surgeon ask this question, Melville sows a measure of doubt on the judiciousness and tragic necessity of Vere's conduct.

335 *Peter the Barbarian*: Peter the Great of Russia (1672–1725), who founded St Petersburg in 1703 and made it the new Russian capital.

336 *a drumhead court*: a court martial convened in the field in time of emergency to judge serious offences. As Hayford and Sealts observe, 'British naval regulations in effect at this period made no provision for a drumhead court. . . . According to statute, moreover, regular naval courts-martial consisted of commanders and captains' (178), not of subordinate officers. Procedure required 'a captain on foreign station' such as Vere to refer all grave infractions 'to his "Chief Commander" as the convening authority' for a court martial (176). It may be, as Hayford and Sealts suggest, that 'Melville simply had not familiarized himself with statutes of the period concerning administration of British naval justice' (176), or it may be that for fictive purposes he chose to create a legal world of his own. The point, in either case, is not whether Vere's behaviour is at variance with the actual law and procedure of the 1790s but whether Melville gives the reader sufficient cause to believe that it is. The surgeon wonders about Vere's sanity, and he and other officers believe that the case of Billy 'should be referred to the admiral'. But none of these men are portrayed as having special expertise or being in any way personally exceptional, and it is hard to weigh the force of their opinion against Vere's conviction that the statutes are clear-cut. The situation is ambiguous, and as Melville enlarged the role of the surgeon during the late revisions it became even more so.

337 *embrasures for short carronades*: openings in parapets that widen toward the outside, through which the carronades, or short large-calibred guns, are fired (*OED*).

343 *the Articles of War*: Hayford and Sealts (180) cite Article XXII, as quoted in McArthur, *Principles and Practice of Naval and Military Courts Martial* (4th edn., 2 vols., 1813), i. 333: 'If any officer, mariner, soldier, or other person in the fleet, shall strike any of his superior officers, or draw, or offer to draw, or lift any weapon against him, being in the execution of his office, *on any pretence whatsoever*, every such person being convicted of such offense, by the sentence of a court martial, shall suffer death.' The explicitness of the statute, however, does not imply that Vere is empowered to convene a court martial and enforce it.

the Last Assizes: the Day of Judgement.

the Mutiny Act: the British Navy did not operate under the Mutiny Act of 1689 (subsequently amended), which applied only to land forces, but under a distinct act of 1749 that built upon earlier naval laws and practices (Hayford and Sealts, 181). Intentionally or not, Melville departs from fact here, but he provides his readers with no basis for knowing this.

345 *the U.S. brig-of-war Somers . . . brig*: on a training cruise during peacetime in 1842, three crewmen on the *Somers*—one of them an acting midshipman, Philip Spencer, son of the American Secretary of War—were hanged for conspiracy to mutiny by Captain Alexander Slidell Mackenzie. As Hayford and Sealts report, 'the prisoners were not arraigned, not formally tried, not allowed to confront witnesses or offer a defense' (29). The verdict was reached by Mackenzie himself in consultation with his officers, prominent among them First Lieutenant Guert Gansevoort, Melville's cousin. Although Mackenzie was later formally vindicated, the incident remained controversial and its effects haunted Gansevoort professionally and personally for years. The *Somers* incident was not the inciting 'source' for *Billy Budd*, but once the lines of the story began to take shape it could not have been far from Melville's mind, especially after June 1888 when the *American Magazine* published an article on the *Somers*; the following year a three-part article, 'The Murder of Philip Spencer', would appear in *Cosmopolitan*. Guert Gansevoort is fondly recalled in Melville's poem 'Bridegroom Dick', from *John Marr* (1888).

a writer whom few know: Melville himself.

346 *even as Abraham . . . behest*: Genesis 22: 1–18. See Warner Berthoff's sensitive reading of this scene and others in *The Example of Melville* (Princeton, 1962), 183–203.

350 *the minister of Christ though receiving his stipend from Mars*: Melville had commented at length on this contradiction in chapter 38 of *White-Jacket*. In a deeper sense it belongs to his lifelong outrage at the disparity between the Sermon on the Mount and the ways of the so-called Christian world. 'Mars', or the warring spirit generally, was only one aspect of humanity's betrayal of Christian ethics, but it was a major one. See Joyce Sparer Adler, *War in Melville's Imagination* (New York, 1981), esp. 160–85.

353 *dropping his mantle to Elisha*: see 2 Kings 2: 11–13.

354 *took the full rose of the dawn*: a parallel to Christ's ascension in the early morning as reported in the gospels.

355 *euthanasia*: it has been suggested that Melville may be using the word in the Greek sense of 'wilful sacrifice of one's self for one's country' or in the sense described by Schopenhauer, whom Melville read toward the end of his life, as 'an easy death, not ushered in by disease, and free from all pain and struggle'.

361 *BILLY IN THE DARBIES*: a revised version of the poem with which, along with an accompanying prose headnote, Melville seems to have begun *Billy Budd* in or around 1886. *Darbies* is an archaic term for chains or handcuffs.

The Oxford World's Classics Website

www.worldsclassics.co.uk

- Browse the full range of Oxford World's Classics online

- Sign up for our monthly e-alert to receive information on new titles

- Read extracts from the Introductions

- Listen to our editors and translators talk about the world's greatest literature with our Oxford World's Classics audio guides

- Join the conversation, follow us on Twitter at OWC_Oxford

- Teachers and lecturers can order inspection copies quickly and simply via our website

www.worldsclassics.co.uk

American Literature

British and Irish Literature

Children's Literature

Classics and Ancient Literature

Colonial Literature

Eastern Literature

European Literature

Gothic Literature

History

Medieval Literature

Oxford English Drama

Poetry

Philosophy

Politics

Religion

The Oxford Shakespeare

A complete list of Oxford World's Classics, including Authors in Context, Oxford English Drama, and the Oxford Shakespeare, is available in the UK from the Marketing Services Department, Oxford University Press, Great Clarendon Street, Oxford OX2 6DP, or visit the website at www.oup.com/uk/worldsclassics.

In the USA, visit www.oup.com/us/owc for a complete title list.

Oxford World's Classics are available from all good bookshops. In case of difficulty, customers in the UK should contact Oxford University Press Bookshop, 116 High Street, Oxford OX1 4BR.

WASHINGTON IRVING	The Sketch-Book of Geoffrey Crayon, Gent.
HENRY JAMES	The Ambassadors
	The American
	The Aspern Papers and Other Stories
	The Awkward Age
	The Bostonians
	Daisy Miller and Other Stories
	The Europeans
	The Golden Bowl
	The Portrait of a Lady
	The Spoils of Poynton
	The Turn of the Screw and Other Stories
	Washington Square
	What Maisie Knew
	The Wings of the Dove
JACK LONDON	The Call of the Wild
	White Fang and Other Stories
	John Barleycorn
	The Sea-Wolf
	The Son of the Wolf
HERMAN MELVILLE	Billy Budd, Sailor and Selected Tales
	The Confidence-Man
	Moby-Dick
	White-Jacket
FRANK NORRIS	McTeague
FRANCIS PARKMAN	The Oregon Trail
EDGAR ALLAN POE	The Narrative of Arthur Gordon Pym of Nantucket and Related Tales
	Selected Tales
HARRIET BEECHER STOWE	Uncle Tom's Cabin
HENRY DAVID THOREAU	Walden